Totally Bound Publishing books by Maren Jenner

Sweet Nothings
The Cupcake Standard
The Jellybean Dilemma
The Red-Hot Stakes

Wrighting the Wrongs
The Wrong Brother

I0563851

Wrighting the Wrongs

THE WRONG BROTHER

MAREN JENNER

The Wrong Brother
ISBN # 978-1-80250-755-3
©Copyright Maren Jenner 2024
Cover Art by Kelly Martin ©Copyright October 2024
Interior text design by Claire Siemaszkiewicz
Totally Bound Publishing

THE WRONG BROTHER

Dedication

Here's to my amazing critique partner, Christine Layne. I couldn't do this without you. Thanks for always being there for me, whether it's to bounce around ideas or talk through complicated scenes or point out plot holes. I know Shawn is one of your favorites, so this one's for you!

Acknowledgements

First of all, I'd like to thank Totally Bound for helping this story reach its full potential and allowing me to continue my dream of becoming a published author. I'd also like to thank Rebecca for her editing help.

I couldn't have done this without my beta readers, specifically Lindsay, and my friend Damian who is always there to cheer me on. But the biggest thank-you goes to my CP Christine who is always available to hear my ideas or read another revision.

To all my friends and family who supported me on this journey, who believed in me, who never let me give up—thank you and I love you.

Lastly, a big thanks to you, my readers, because this wouldn't be possible without you.

A full list of trigger warnings for this and all my books is available on my website at marenjennerbooks.com.

Chapter One

Leah

People are always asking how to get a guy, but I already know the secret.

Garlic.

I started sautéing my green beans with freshly minced garlic minutes ago, and now it sounds like a herd of elephants above my head. I listen as the four Wrighting brothers thunder down the stairs then spill into the kitchen. It's a good-sized room until we all try to cram in it. They are not little.

All of them are at least three inches taller than my five-foot-nine frame, and have varying degrees of muscle. Steven, the oldest, beats me to the microwave. I set my plate of chicken and mashed potatoes back on the counter then call out that I'm next.

While I'm waiting, I walk over to nudge Sebastian, my boyfriend. "Hey."

He doesn't even look up from his book.

"Sebastian!" I poke my head between him and the pages.

His hazel eyes widen as he registers my face. "Leah! Hi."

I grin back, and the microwave beeps. Steven removes his food, leaving the door wide open. Of course, his chili exploded everywhere, leaving a horrendous mess. Grumbling, I grab a paper towel and scoop out most of it, then pop in my chicken.

When I turn around again, Sebastian has pickles, cheese and mayonnaise on the counter. His eyes are glued to his book, though he holds a mayo-slathered knife in his other hand, about to spread it all over a piece of still-wrapped cheese.

Without a single slice of bread nearby.

I sigh at the familiar sight. "Trying to make a sandwich?"

"Hmm?" He follows my pointed stare and frowns. "Oh."

Silas, the youngest and closest to my twenty-two years, passes me the bread as we exchange exasperated looks. The microwave beeps, and I bring my plate to the stove only to find half my green beans are missing.

I know exactly what happened. After living in this house with all of them for almost four years, I only have one complaint, and I can sum it up with a single word.

Shawn.

I whirl around to find the bane of my existence with a bowl in his hands. And he's chewing. I storm up to him, snatching away the bowl.

"Those are mine!" I growl when I see only five beans left.

He shrugs, giving me his most infuriating smirk. "Sorry, thought they were fair game. If it helps, they were delicious."

Fury sears through me, a constant whenever he's around. "How many times do I have to tell you to ask before you just start eating?" I don't bother waiting for a response before I stomp back to scrape what's left of my beans onto my plate. Then I hurry to the table before anything else can go wrong.

I grew up with the Wrightings. Our parents are close and I had no siblings, so they became my family. Even Shawn. We haven't always hated each other — that came later — but our rivalry has always been there.

As the brothers file in to sit around the table, I marvel at their differences. Sure they all have brown hair, but the shade varies. Their noses are all the same, regal and straight, and there is a resemblance in their smiles.

Steven scrolls through his phone as he eats his chili. His hair and eyes are the darkest but his skin is the palest. Sebastian is the tallest of them, with close-cropped hair, hazel eyes and glasses. Even he is tanner than Steven, since his love of plants often takes him outside. He absently sets his plate next to me then almost misses his chair because he's so focused on his book.

Silas keeps his dark brown curls on the longer side. His amber eyes and easy smile lend to the Golden Retriever air he exudes. His normal exuberance is missing today as he slumps in his seat, his blank stare focused on the two cold slices of pizza on his plate. A sure sign he was out too late last night.

If I had to choose one brother to call the most attractive, I'd have to pick Shawn. *Reluctantly*. And I'd refuse to tell him because his ego doesn't need any more fuel. His green eyes, sandy brown hair and sculpted physique all combine into one delicious package that even I can't deny.

But looks definitely aren't everything. I glance over at my boyfriend — steady, dependable Sebastian. My heart may not flutter when he enters the room and my stomach may not flip, but the safe routine of our relationship is exactly what I need right now.

Shawn takes the chair to my right, setting his heaping plate of casserole on the table. Comfortable silence fills the air as we all dig in, only to be broken when Sebastian bites into his sandwich.

Or tries to.

He pulls back, confused, and I hold back a snort at the still-wrapped piece of cheese with teeth marks impressed upon it. He sighs as everyone starts laughing, then he peels back the layers to actually unwrap the cheese.

Shawn shakes his head. "Sebastian, man, how many times do we have to tell you? You gotta pay attention when you're making food."

"Look who's talking," I say with a glare. "Paying attention is important, especially to key details like whose food it actually is!"

"I said I was sorry," he huffs. "Yeesh."

"It doesn't change the fact that I no longer have a good chunk of my dinner." I stab at the last green beans on my plate, shoving them in my mouth. One thing Shawn and I agree on, the beans were delicious. Too bad I don't have more of them.

"It's not like you don't have other food."

I keep chewing as I try to resist retorting, but my tongue refuses to listen. "You know, if this was the first time, it'd be one thing. You do this all the time! Yester — "

"Seriously, guys," Steven grunts, setting down his phone. "I'm trying to eat."

Silas nods, and even Sebastian arches an eyebrow in agreement.

I sigh in resignation, not wanting to ruin everyone's dinner. "Sorry."

Shawn, however, says nothing, and it makes me feel better when Sebastian leans forward to address him. "You are in the wrong here, Shawn."

Shawn's lips press tighter together, then he bites out, "I said I'm sorry."

I bristle again, but Sebastian simply says, "Sometimes actions speak louder than words."

And Shawn deflates, all the fight whooshing out of him. "I'll do the dishes tonight, Lee."

My lips part at the offering, and I study him, making sure it's not some trick. But he is all sincerity, so I nod. "Thanks, Shawn. That'd be nice."

"So, am I forgiven?"

It's more of an olive branch than I want to give, but all the brothers are watching my reaction. I concentrate on cutting my next bite of chicken, dragging out the silence.

Except Shawn isn't done. "C'mon, Lee. Please?" And he juts his lower lip, tilts his head slightly, then turns on the puppy dog eyes.

I hate that expression with every fiber of my being because I can't resist it. Oh, how I've tried. Today is no different, and I finally huff out, "Fine. You're forgiven."

His triumphant grin makes me want to take it back, so I turn to Sebastian. "What's tomorrow like for you? We could have lunch." His blank stare sends exasperation zipping through me. "You know, to make up for Friday? I had to finish my English paper?"

I'm in my senior year at Southern Michigan University—Smoo, to us students. This is the last semester before I graduate with my bachelor's degree in history. Not that I know what I'm going to do with it.

Understanding dawns on Sebastian's face, and he pushes his glasses higher up on his nose. "I believe that would work."

"Meet at one? Then I can be done in time for my shift at the library."

He nods, and we have a plan. Conversation starts to pick up as Silas regains his usual energy. Soon he regales us with tales from his date the night before, and we're all chuckling. My gaze lands on the empty seat at the table, and I wish Meg were here. She's my best friend, our other housemate, and as much of a serial-dater as Silas.

If anyone could one-up his story, it'd be her, I think as Silas wraps up. I always thought he and Meg might end up together, but that ship has sailed. They hate each other even more than Shawn and I do.

Sebastian's chair screeches as he pushes back from the table, hurrying to take care of his plate before retreating to the living room with his book. I fondly watch him go. I'm in the middle of a steamy romance about a count and his lady that I can't wait to get back to. I can't think of a better way to spend a Sunday night than reading, curled up on the couch next to Sebastian. Especially in snowy February.

One of the many reasons he and I get along so well.

I tune back into the conversation as Steven begins complaining about someone stealing his food at work. Again. The only one of us not still in college, he graduated two years ago with some technical degree, and now works nine to five. I've heard about the food thief every day for the last week. And it's getting old.

"So do something about it," I interrupt. He frowns, and I feel bad for my harsh tone. "I mean...there's got to be some way to catch them."

Shawn leans forward. "Yeah, make your food like normal then chop up a ghost pepper to put it in."

"That would be awesome!" Silas reaches over to high-five Shawn.

A pensive look crosses Steven's face. "That could actually work."

The three of them start plotting, and I push away from the table. I'm sure I'll hear all the details when it goes down. I make sure to rinse my plate before I put my sauté pan in the sink. Just because Shawn said he'd do the dishes, doesn't mean I can't do my part.

More than ready for my book, I hurry through the living room where Sebastian is already engrossed in his reading, then I pop into the mini suite I share with Meg. We have our own little sitting room with a cute couch and end tables. My bedroom is on the right and Meg's is on the far left, with a bathroom in between.

This house is perfect for all of us. Bought as an investment by the guys' parents as a hedge against paying for four kids rooming at college, the nearness to campus is an added bonus. The brothers all have separate rooms upstairs along with another bathroom. The rest of the downstairs we share, and it's nice to have my own space when they get to be too much. Tonight, though, I'm ready for some company.

I grab my book, trotting back into the living room where Silas and Steven already have on a basketball game. I don't mind, though, knowing I'll be able to tune it out. But I stop in my tracks when I see the book Sebastian has in hand.

The title contains wombats—his latest obsession. He only has so much capacity to learn about plants, then he has to switch to "fluff," as he calls it. His photographic memory imprints all the facts on his brain, making him a walking encyclopedia.

A walking, *talking* encyclopedia.

So far this week I've heard a variety of wonderful facts. Yesterday he asked if I knew that wombat feces are in the shape of a cube. No, nor did I need to know that.

Two days ago, he told me that a group of wombats is called a wisdom, and I still don't know what I'm supposed to do with that information.

I nibble on my lip, not ready for another wombat fact. I decide to grab a bottle of water, if only to prolong the inevitable, but my movement catches Sebastian's attention. An eager smile lights his face as I bite back my sigh, though I try to keep my expression kind.

"Leah! Did you know that the main defense of a wombat is its rear-end?" He turns the page as he finishes with, "If a predator is around, the wombat will dive into its burrow, using its rear to block the hole. It's mainly made of cartilage and very resilient."

So much weird-ass knowledge I don't need. I laugh to myself just thinking about my dumb pun. Aloud, I say, "Neat."

But he only hums, back to devouring his book once more. I shake my head, sauntering into the kitchen amidst the clink and thunk of Shawn doing the dishes. He glances my way, but I ignore him, going right to the fridge.

My fingers close around a bottle of water when he exclaims, "Oh, shit," followed by the sound of glass shattering.

"You okay?" I hurry over as he mutters to himself.

"I'm fine," he bites out, reaching into the clear water of the rinsing side of the sink to adjust the plug. The gurgle of water draining fills the air then he yelps, jerking his hand away.

I grab a napkin and hand it to him as I glimpse the blood on his finger. He takes it from me, his lips tight, annoyance all over his face. Without another word, I set my book down then go to the end cupboard where we keep a mini first-aid kit for situations like this.

"Everyone all right?" Steven calls.

I peek my head around the corner and nod. "Shawn broke a glass."

Relief crosses his face before he returns to watching his game.

Armed with antibiotic ointment and a Band-Aid, I cross back to Shawn. "Let me see."

"It's just a scratch, Lee. I can put a Band-Aid on myself."

I grab his wrist firmly, saying in my best no-nonsense tone, "You might have glass in it. Besides, it's easier with two hands."

He huffs but extends his hand over the sink. I tug away the bloody napkin, turning his wrist one way then the other to be sure the wound is clean.

"All clear." I dry off his finger as best I can then open the Band-Aid and smear ointment on it. It takes no time to wrap it around Shawn's finger, and I make sure the adhesive ends overlap just right. "There you go."

When I look up, Shawn's emerald eyes are so intense, they take my breath away. I back up on instinct, swallowing at my suddenly dry mouth. My gaze lands on the dishes. "Um, I can finish these. So you don't get that wet."

But he blinks and the hardness returns. "I've got this." Without another word, he faces the sink, a silent dismissal.

I sigh at his stubbornness. "You really shouldn't get a wound wet."

He glares my way, his gaze catching on my book. "Why don't you go bother one of your fictional boyfriends?"

My teeth grind together at the derogatory way he says the words. "What's that supposed to mean?"

"C'mon, Lee," he scoffs, ripping the trash can from beneath the sink before he starts tossing glass into it. "You and Sebastian are the least romantic couple I know. Don't you think you might be compensating for something?"

The accusation pierces me to the core. "What Sebastian and I do isn't your business, especially in our romantic life," I say coldly. I snatch up my book, whirling on my heel, but I pause before I stomp away. "That was crossing a line, Shawn. I thought even you could understand why we're taking it slow."

His head whips up, but his stricken expression does little to mollify me. "Shit, Lee, I didn't mean —"

"I don't want to hear it." I storm toward the door to find Sebastian hovering. The glower on his face tells me he at least heard some of it, and I'm grateful when he glares at Shawn, cutting off any further words from his brother.

Sebastian steps into the living room with me, concern furrowing his forehead. "Are you okay?"

I fight against the memories struggling to surface, and my throat is tight as I answer, "I will be." Gratitude surges through me when he pulls me into one of his rare hugs, and I rest in his embrace for several moments. Then I clear my throat and move away. Holding up my book, I say, "I'm gonna hole up for the night."

He nods, and movement behind him catches my attention. Shawn turns away, guilt and remorse all over his face as he returns to the kitchen.

Good. Maybe he'll think about what he says before he opens his mouth.

I wave goodnight to the others before retreating to the safety of my mini suite. I shove the door closed behind me, but it doesn't latch. The finicky doorknob is unreliable at the best of times, and I'm used to babying it. I glare at it for a long moment, wishing I was one of those people who lost their temper. I could rage and scream and slam the door until I beat it into submission.

But that's not me.

Instead, I turn the handle just so, then shut the door gently. The latch clicks into place, the quiet sound taunting my need for self-control. But I ignore it, trudging to my room while trying to tell myself I'm not compensating.

Even if my gut isn't quite convinced.

Chapter Two

Shawn

I lean against the sink, staring at the window, but all I see are Lee's blue eyes filled with pain and her brown hair swishing in its ponytail as she stalked away. It's for the best, I remind myself. It's better if she hates me.

Sebastian steps into the kitchen. "I hope you know what you're doing, Shawn."

"Leave it, Seb," I growl, tightening my grip on the sink.

"I—"

"I said leave it." I glare at him with all the fury I'm feeling, even though none of it is directed at my brother.

It's all on me. For breaking the glass, for allowing my walls to drop for that split second her hands were on me, for the hurt on her face when I didn't think before I spoke.

Sebastian studies me for a moment. "I'll wash. You dry." He crosses the room then nudges me out of the way.

The sink is sterile once more, clear of glass and blood. I run hot water into it, gratitude washing over me that he's allowing me to avoid the subject.

For now.

Sebastian is the smartest of us. He may not have the best social skills, and he can get so preoccupied that he forgets to eat—dangerous, since he also has Type 1 diabetes. But book smarts? He is the most brilliant person I know.

While I took a year off between graduating high school and starting college, he finished high school a year early. While I waffled over my career choices and what I wanted to do with my life, he jumped right into pursuing his bachelor's degree. Now, I'm twenty-five and almost halfway through my last semester of senior year for my own bachelor's degree while he, at twenty-three, is one year into his master's for botany.

I envy him in many ways—his drive, his laser focus on his career, his intelligence. Those are also qualities that make him perfect for Leah. She deserves someone as smart as her, who knows what he wants out of life.

Especially after that incident with Vance.

I shove aside images of that night along with the anger that always pops up at the memory. I bump my bandaged finger as I dry off a plate and grit my teeth when it stings. It distracts me enough that I can focus once more on the task at hand, keeping an iron grip on my mind so it doesn't wander. At all.

Once the dishes are done, my anger is gone, fully replaced by guilt. Sebastian's continued silence only amplifies it, and I feel like I owe him an explanation. I grab a bag of chips from the cupboard, tossing a handful into my mouth then offering him the bag. He shakes his head as he finishes drying his hands.

I sigh, forcing myself to say, "I wasn't trying—"

"I know, Shawn." He leans against the counter. "You never mean to. You press all her buttons, tease her constantly, and let her think you hate her. But you never hurt her on purpose."

The stark way he lays out my relationship with Lee startles me. Sebastian has his nose in a book more often than not, and I always forget how much he sees.

I shift my weight, unsure what to do next. "So should I apologize or what?"

"No, let her be for tonight."

The crunch of the chips helps drown out my restless thoughts but my mouth tastes like garbage from the guilt saturating me. Frustrated, I roll the top of the bag down then swipe my greasy fingers on my jeans.

"We have napkins."

Shooting Sebastian a glare, I stalk toward the cupboard to return the chips. "I'm going for a run."

"Would you like to talk first? We could go upstairs where it's more private. Figure out what actually made you tease Leah about our lack of a sex life."

And there it is, the crux of it all. I set my jaw, not willing to unbox that insinuation with a ten-foot pole. "It was a harmless comment. I don't need to talk, I need to move."

Sebastian pushes his glasses further up his nose. "Because that's worked so well for you so far."

Grinding my teeth, I shove the chips into the cupboard and stomp upstairs to change into my warmest running gear. Yanking on my reflective vest, I thunder down the stairs where I stuff my feet in my shoes and pull the laces tight.

Outside it's freezing, but the sidewalk is mostly clear of snow. I blow on my hands, knowing I'll be fine once I get moving. Then I force my feet down the steps and into my warm-up pace. I try to avoid running Sunday night because of how quiet it is. The lack of activity makes my run more boring than usual and allows my thoughts to turn inward.

Which I don't want, especially tonight.

I love my brothers. And living with them can be tough, but it's free housing. My parents bought the place cheap years ago, knowing it was perfect for college kids with its nearness to campus. They rented it out until we enrolled. They don't even charge us, provided we're attending school and our grades are decent.

I couldn't ask for better roommates but it doesn't come without its drawbacks. There's always someone to butt in when they think you're wrong. This time though, Sebastian was completely right to call me out about commenting about his and Leah's sex life.

Or lack thereof.

It's none of my business. Hasn't ever been my business. I lost that chance the summer before she moved in. Our parents were out of town, so Silas organized one last bash before he and Leah joined us at college. A joint no-more-high-school and Leah's nineteenth birthday party. I was twenty-three at the time.

I showed up late. I'd worked a ton that summer, needing some extra credit for my education major, so I'd coached and tutored during my break.

When I got to the party, I nodded, greeting friends, neighbors, my brothers. I hadn't seen much of Leah in the last couple years. Even though I'd attended her graduation, we hadn't caught up afterwards. And she'd worn the mandatory baggy gown, so I had no idea of the transformation she'd gone through.

When a feminine voice called my name from the pool, I headed that way. A beautiful woman swam toward me, her hot pink bikini hugging her curves, her long brown hair hanging over her shoulders. My mouth went dry just watching her.

She climbed the ladder, and I instinctively offered my hand. Those smooth fingers slid into mine without hesitation. I hauled her up onto the concrete, mesmerized.

"I'm nineteen now, and I think I deserve a birthday present." Then she grabbed the front of my shirt and kissed me.

I was stunned. I automatically closed my eyes, kissing her back. Until my brain at last connected the dots. I pulled away to look at her.

And I saw Lee.

The little pigtailed girl who had followed me and my brothers around since she started walking. The one who had begged me for piggyback rides or to take her and Meg to the mall. The awkward gangly teen whose grin sported braces.

The girl I'd always thought of as family.

My hands raised on their own, and she'd stepped back on instinct, the pool right behind her. The confusion on her face turned to panic, her eyes widening, her arms flailing as she lost her balance. I tried to grab her, but her slick arm slipped right through my fingers.

The splash drew everyone's attention, but all I cared about was making sure she was okay. I held my breath as I waited for her to surface, exhaling in a whoosh when she emerged.

Until I saw her expression.

The utter humiliation and hurt dripping from her burned into my mind. In the commotion of her friends checking on her, I slipped away, unable to make myself stay and try to explain.

Even if I could find the words.

A dog barking jolts me back to the present, and I survey the area, trying to regain my bearings. I've run further than I thought, so I make a quick about-face to head back.

Things with Lee have been messed up since then. We'd always had a tenuous relationship, mostly based on rivalry. It had been easier to let her think I hated her than to admit how amazing that kiss had been. How it had taken hours before my half staff had deflated. How I never had been able to rid myself of the feeling of her soft lips touching mine, her hand fisted in my shirt.

My attraction to her had blindsided me, and I couldn't reconcile the Leah I'd grown up with to the Leah that had kissed me. It didn't help when she moved in weeks later and flaunted a parade of guys in front of me, but now everything had changed. She had changed.

All because of that asshole Vance.

Where once she'd been the life of the party, carefree, dating whomever, wherever, whenever, now she barely left the house. She'd become a shell of herself. It didn't help when she couldn't go anywhere without it being shoved into her face. She had been the talk of campus, and it had left her gun-shy about people.

My brothers and Meg were the only ones she sought out. She already thought I hated her, and I was desperate to see some spark back in her, so I'd started pushing. Started teasing.

Like the green beans. I knew she'd be pissed, but that was the point. And I hadn't eaten them all.

Something about when she gets mad—eyes flashing, that no-nonsense edge to her voice, all confidence. It reminds me of before, and I want that.

For her.

Chapter Three

Leah

In my room, I toss my finished book on my bed, flopping onto my back. Stretching my arms overhead, I huff out a breath, still frustrated over Shawn's words. I always know where I stand with Steven and Silas. They treat me like a sister, and I love them like brothers.

But Shawn? His playful side, I can handle. Usually I don't mind the teasing, but sometimes it holds a truth I haven't even recognized yet. That I'm not ready to face.

Which is why it bothers me that his comment won't leave me alone.

Was it just a flippant remark? Or did he actually mean more by it?

I think back to my last relationship, before Sebastian. Vance was tall and built, similar in stature to Shawn but everything about him was darker. His hair, his eyes…his soul. I flinch at the phantom feeling of his knuckles cracking against my cheekbone, at the sound of his harsh words echoing in my ears.

Slut.

I quickly banish the memory. Is it any wonder I'd waited a year and a half to dip my toes back into the murky waters of dating? Any surprise I chose a safe bet like Sebastian?

Shawn's comment flits through my mind once more, needling at me. I curl onto my side. Before Vance, I'd dated plenty of guys for the thrill of romance. I loved the high of stomach flips and electric jolts, the first brush of our lips and every first that followed.

But I haven't felt ready since that night.

I'm lucky Sebastian understands. He isn't very physical anyway, so it hasn't been an issue. We've barely even kissed, not more than a few quick pecks. I try to picture making out with him and fight to keep from wrinkling my nose.

Not exactly the reaction one *should* have when thinking of kissing their boyfriend.

I nibble on my lip. It's probably nothing, just that I'm not ready for that step, but a heaviness weighs on me like I'm lying to myself. I search for a distraction, my thoughts circling once more to Shawn. Annoyance flares again, and I wonder why he had to go there.

He had his chance.

Lingering humiliation drips from the memory, and I push it away, mopping up all signs of it as I shove it back into the pool where it belongs. The door to our sitting room opens and I pop upright, delighted to see Meg stepping in. I barrel over, catching her by surprise when she flicks on the light.

She shrieks. "Holy shit, Leah!" I laugh as she clutches her chest and glares. "What the hell were you doing in the dark?"

"I lost track of time." Shawn's comments play through my mind again, and my annoyance grows that I've wasted so much of the evening on his words.

"That must have been some serious thinking. You okay?" She studies me as I lift my shoulders in a little shrug, and her lips press together. "Let's talk in my room. My feet are killing me."

Meg, shorter than me by a couple of inches, never fails to wear heels. I loathe how they make my feet feel, one of the many ways we are opposites. She hurries to her room, sinks onto her bed and yanks off the offending boots.

I trail after her. "How was your date?"

"Meh." She groans in relief as she flops back, and I perch beside her. "So spill."

I run my finger over the seam of her comforter. "Is my relationship with Sebastian weird?"

Her forehead crinkles, and she sits up. "Okay, what did Shawn say this time?"

"How'd you know it was Shawn?"

"It's always Shawn when you get in these obsessive moods. I don't know why his words crawl under your skin, but they do." She raises her eyebrows, daring me to argue.

I wrinkle my nose but reluctantly admit, "He said my romance books are compensation for what I'm *not* doing with Sebastian."

"Whoa." She blinks several times. "That's a lot, even for him."

"I know. Except I can't quit thinking about it. I love Sebastian, but I've never felt butterflies or tingles for him. He's my best friend." I let out a shaky breath as I crisscross my legs. "We don't even kiss." My gaze flicks to Meg's assessing one. "Is that wrong? Is there something wrong with me because I haven't been missing it, or wanting more?"

"Lee-bug."

My childhood nickname makes me smile. Meg used to think it was my real name, and when she came around, the guys picked it up. They all still use it occasionally.

Meg scoots closer to wrap her arm around my shoulders. "I think when that asshole hurt you, you went into protective mode, and you haven't come out yet." She pauses, squeezing my arm. "Don't hate me for this, but are you dating Sebastian because you want to date him? Or because he was the safe choice?"

Her words stab me right in the chest, and I tense.

"I'm only asking because you're my best friend, and I would hate to see you settle for less than you deserve. I know you love him. But maybe it's in the same way you love me—not in the all-consuming, no holds barred, true love forever way."

My chin sinks to my chest. I can't form a definitive answer...although me not defiantly shouting "Yes, I love him!" might be answer enough.

She holds me for several seconds until I shift away to stand up.

"I'm sorry if I overstepped, Lee."

I shake my head. "No, Meg. I needed that. I'm not ready to do anything about it, but I needed to hear it. Love you."

She reaches out to squeeze my hand. "Love you, too."

I let her fingers slide from mine as I shuffle toward my room. Meg's words swim in my head, but her questions go unanswered. It's a long time before my mind lets me go to sleep, and I'm still unsettled the next afternoon as I rush out of English to meet Sebastian for lunch.

My thoughts circle back to last night's conversation with Meg. Again. I keep wrestling with the idea that the only reason I'm with Sebastian is because I needed a boyfriend, and he was an easy pick.

Am I really that selfish? I hope not. I do love him, and I don't want to hurt him. Not only has he been my best friend forever, he's also a much needed calm, steady presence in my life.

Which did make him really accessible…

"Hey, Leah," Sebastian calls from the bench outside and tucks his ever-present book into his backpack.

Thankful for a distraction from my endless loop of doubt, I hurry over to greet him. I link my arm through his as we make our way off campus. "How was your day?"

I love walking, especially on these rare February days when the sun is actually shining. We automatically head for our favorite restaurant, Eat at Joe's. The little diner has something for everyone, and the whole gang eats there often.

Sebastian chatters about Professor Harrison's review of his latest paper. I envy his drive, how despite having a TA position, he's made time to write research papers. They've even been published, and he's already making a name for himself in the botany community.

"I hope he'll let me present it soon," he adds wistfully.

He lights up whenever he talks about botany, although I probably glaze over. But it makes him happy, so I listen as best I can. We take our usual route and a couple of blocks into town, a grand opening sign catches my attention. It's a new restaurant, done up like an old-fashioned fifties diner.

The place is adorable, so I tug on Sebastian's sleeve. "Let's try them out."

The corners of his mouth turn down. He hates deviating from established plans as much as he hates trying new things.

"Please, Sebastian? A chocolate malt sounds amazing." When his forehead crinkles, I get a visual of our time in the restaurant — him sullen and sulking over the change, me trying to coax him back to his normal self.

It isn't worth it, and my shoulders sag. "Forget it."

A relieved smile brightens his face. "Thanks, Leah. I'm looking forward to my number three."

The turkey burger combo he always gets. "*Side salad, please — hold the fries.*" Because they wouldn't have that at the new place. I nearly roll my eyes but catch myself in time.

I let him carry the conversation, trying not to feel resentful. This is why I'm with him, I remind myself, because he's safe and predictable. Another part of my brain adds *and boring,* but I tell it to shut up as guilt pricks me for thinking badly of him.

That tension remains as we reach Joe's, where he orders the same thing, in the same manner. We eat and chat, but I can't shake the feeling that our dynamic has shifted. We've always been so in sync.

Until lately.

Our date nights have been less frequent, both of us needing to reschedule more often. Professor Harrison has been demanding more of his time while I've been needing to focus on my studies with graduation looming.

Then I remember how he stood up to Shawn for me twice yesterday, and I push the worry away. I'm over-tired from tossing and turning last night. Every couple goes through rough patches. This is just one of ours.

After lunch, I hurry to my second home — the on-campus library. I've been lucky enough to score a work-study position to offset my partial scholarship, and my parents are generous in covering the rest provided I keep up my grades. The library job is perfect, letting me study in my down time with any book I need a fingertip away.

"Hello, Leah," the head librarian, Kay, greets me.

"Hi, Kay! What's on the docket for today?" I'm anxious to get through my tasks and start my paper for my anthropology class. Hopefully that'll be enough to keep my mind occupied. I'm beginning to get a headache from all the spinning my thoughts are doing.

Chapter Four

Shawn

Friday night, I storm up the front steps, stopping before I slam the door behind me. Normally I can work out all my frustration at my job at the student rec center. Demonstrating machines for the newbies, helping them establish a routine, it all gives me a chance to slip in my extra reps, more than enough to burn off my extra energy.

But no matter how hard I pushed today, that stupid Spanish test grade still hung over my head. Lee's going to kill me. After all the tutoring, all the quizzing, I got a fucking C. My teeth grind together as I register Silas sulking on the couch, but I ignore him, unable to deal with his problems on top of mine.

Striding into the kitchen, I rack my brain for how I'm going to break this to Lee. Foreign language has been holding me back since the beginning. I've never been a stellar student, and I thought the five-year program would give me more time, let me go at my own pace once I'd finally decided what I wanted to do.

I loved sports, though I'd never excelled at one enough to make a career out of it. And I loved kids. When my dad made a comment about being a gym teacher or coach, the pieces I'd been struggling to assemble had clicked into place.

I'd barely passed Spanish in high school, so I'd put it off until now. If I don't graduate this year because of this...

After three tutors didn't work out at the beginning of the semester, I resigned myself to my last resort. Spanish is one of Lee's strengths, and I swallowed my pride to ask her to help me. She's been great though, and she doesn't just give in if I flash her my trademark grin. She pushes me to do my best, and I find myself not wanting to let her down.

I smack my hand against the table, but I quickly collect myself when the front door opens and Lee's voice echoes to me as she greets Silas. My anger fades at her cajoling tone.

Unable to help myself, I lean against the doorway, watching her attempt to pull Silas out of his funk.

"No hot date?" she teases.

He only grunts, "She bailed on me."

His pout is even more exaggerated, and I resist the urge to groan. For Silas, it's the end of the world to be home on Friday night. What a douche.

But she gives him a cocky smirk. "Well, a girl in my English class is just your type—long dark hair, curves I wish I had." When Silas leans forward in his seat, Lee pulls out her phone. "I got her number after showing her your pic. She's expecting your call."

"Really?" At her nod, he leaps off the couch and kisses her cheek with an exuberant smack. "You're the best, Lee!" Then he takes the stairs two at a time, phone in hand.

One corner of my mouth tips up, and I can't help the wave of gratitude for Lee. No matter what state she's in, she takes care of us.

Even me.

When she turns toward her suite without noticing me, I can't help saying, "Saving the world, one brother at a time?"

But a bitter edge underlines my words, and I fight the urge to kick myself when she stops in her tracks. Why didn't I keep my mouth shut?

A knowing gleam in her eye has me swallowing hard as she studies me. "Yep, and you're on deck. What do you need?"

I cross my arms and lean against the doorway, scowling at the floor. She knows I was supposed to get my test grade today. She's smart enough to figure it out.

"*Solamente en Español,*" she says, lifting her chin. *Only in Spanish.*

My scowl deepens.

"*¿Cómo estuvo tu examen?*" *How was your test?*

I shove off the frame, striding into the kitchen. I can't bring myself to answer. Can't handle the disappointment I know I'll see. I listen to her footsteps draw nearer as I stare out the window.

"Shawn, *respóndeme.*" *Answer me.*

With a resigned sigh, I mutter, "C."

"*Sí,* what?"

I'm too frustrated to humor her teasing and turn to face her, throwing my hands in the air. "I got a fucking C after all that studying and practicing and…"

"Hey."

Her gentleness makes me feel even worse, and I drop my chin. But she doesn't let me hide. She touches my shoulder, nudging me until I meet her empathetic smile.

"It's one test," she says, not a hint of disappointment in sight. "And you're doing better each time. Your papers are improving, and so is your vocab. We can do more."

I arch one eyebrow. "Now you're a pep talk expert, too?"

"That's me—jack of all trades."

Her undying optimism makes me relax, and I allow her encouragement to fuel me. My tension drains away until her fingers flex on my shoulder. I'm immediately aware of every fingertip, the short filed nails, the light touch of her palm with only my shirt between us. I look from her hand to her pretty blue eyes as I swallow at my suddenly dry mouth.

Her lips part, making my gaze drop. All I can think about is the day she kissed me. How her hand fisted in my shirt. How soft her lips were. The hum she made when—

The floor creaks as Steven saunters into the kitchen, and I hurry to step away from Lee. Disappointment washes over me, my shoulder now cold as the ghost of her touch lingers. I ignore the feeling, annoyed I let my guard down again, and I turn my attention to my brother, knowing he's up to something.

"Can you make me mac and cheese?" he begs. "Please, Leah, I'm starving."

I frown. Not only is Steven a grown-ass man who should know how to make a simple box of mac and cheese, Friday night is date night for her and Sebastian. She should be getting ready.

Leah crosses her arms, jutting her chin, and I can't help one corner of my mouth tipping up. I'm glad she watches out for us, but we shouldn't be walking over her either.

"It's from a box," she says dryly. "You can do that, I promise."

I like seeing her standing up to someone besides me for a change, and I decide to help. "Besides, Sebastian should be home soon. Shouldn't you be getting ready?"

Worry crinkles her brow, a sure sign she hasn't heard from him yet. Sebastian gets caught up in his work, tending to forget plans, and radio silence is never a good sign. Steven doesn't relent though, pulling out his most pathetic expression—one that always guarantees his way.

Lee sighs, giving in before I can protest. "I'll supervise, okay? It's not like my date will be anywhere fancy."

Steven wrinkles his nose but nods. The front door bangs open, and the three of us poke our heads out to investigate.

"Guys, guess what?" Sebastian talks faster than I've ever heard. "Professor Harrison asked me to present my paper at a conference in a couple of weeks! He wants to go over it tonight to tighten it up." He beams.

Disappointment crosses Lee's face, but it disappears in an instant. "That's great, Sebastian! I'm so proud of you!"

Always the martyr.

I clear my throat, intending to point out just how much of an ass Sebastian is being. But she shoves me into the kitchen, clamping her hand over my mouth until we're out of sight and earshot. One hand splays over my chest as she pushes me back. A tremor shoots through me at the close proximity and her heady floral scent underlined with raspberries.

Maybe she won't notice.

She quickly drops her hands, shooting me a glare. "If the next words out of your mouth aren't congratulations or something similar, don't bother speaking," she hisses. "Got it?"

This is the Leah I like to see. No room for argument, all defiance. Between the wave of longing that crashes into me and the lingering feel of her touch, I simply nod, not trusting my voice. She plasters on a smile, leading us back to the entryway where Sebastian is still talking about how great it is working with Professor Harrison.

I wait for a break in the conversation then say a pointed, "Congratulations." It earns me an admonishing look from Lee, but I really think Sebastian should be made aware he's ditching his girlfriend.

When Silas returns downstairs, Lee fills him in, and his forehead crinkles in concern, but she shakes her head. His lips press together before he also congratulates Sebastian. At least Silas is on my side. As Sebastian trots upstairs, we both swivel to her.

She walks back into the kitchen, stopping when she sees the boxed dinner on the counter. "Maybe we should go out for that mac and cheese…"

Understanding crosses Steven's face and I fight the urge to slap him upside the head. But he is the first to go to her and wrap an arm around her shoulders. "I'm sorry, Lee-bug."

Silas pipes up, "Well, I struck out, so I'm coming too. At least I'll have someone fun to hang out with." When her face contorts in confusion, he chuckles. "Don't worry—she didn't turn me down. We're going out tomorrow."

I shift to my other foot, weighing my options. If they're all going, I want to go but I don't want to make Lee's night any worse. "I need to eat, too." It comes out decidedly pathetic, but I fight a smile when she glares at me, pleased to see her attitude returning.

"What are you waiting for, an engraved invitation?" I can't hide my smirk, and her glare intensifies. She steps away from Steven, coming toe to toe with me. "You know what?" She folds her arms over her chest, raising her chin. "You can come—if you ask in Spanish."

My smirk falls, but I'll be damned if I fail her challenge. "*¿Por favor, puedo cenar con una mujer hermosa y mis hermanos?*" *Please, can I eat dinner with a beautiful woman and my brothers?* My grin returns at my smooth delivery. I even managed to sneak in a compliment—a surefire way to throw her off her game.

She gapes before snapping her mouth shut. "Since you put it like that."

Footsteps thunder downstairs. Sebastian calls her name, and she hurries to the living room. I follow to the edge of the kitchen to hear her response.

"What? What do you need?"

It's always about him. Always about us. I can't help wondering, who takes care of her?

"Our date. I—"

"Don't even worry about it."

I peek my head out, glimpsing her pressing her fingers to his lips and shining like he gave her the sun. That idiot brother of mine should be groveling at her feet, eating up every minute she gives him. Not blowing her off.

"This is your shot, and you need to take it."

But he simply takes her at her word, smiling wide and squeezing her tight. Jealousy digs its claws into me. What would it be like to be friendly enough to hug Lee whenever I want? She touched me more tonight than she has, well, in weeks, and I stare at my shoulder as if her hand still lingers.

After a quiet thank you, Sebastian steps back, and Lee asks, "Did you eat today?"

For once he doesn't even think. "Professor Harrison took me to lunch."

"And you have everything you need now? Wallet? Phone?" When he nods, she says cheerily, "Okay. Good luck!"

I watch him disappear, trying to rein in my jealousy. Sebastian holds Lee's heart in the palm of his hand and doesn't even know what he has. I frown at Leah now standing with her chin drooped and one arm crossed over her middle. The last thing she needs is to wallow, so I walk over to bump her arm with mine.

"Ready to go?" I say gruffly, wanting to turn her anger on me. "I'm hungry."

She reacts just like I hoped. She juts her jaw to one side, then pulls herself together, straightening her shoulders and raising her chin. At her sharp nod, we all move to put on our coats and shoes.

An unspoken goal of turning Leah's night around solidifies between me and my brothers. As we walk toward Joe's, Lee pauses in front of a newly opened diner and I notice the longing on her face. I nudge Silas who elbows Steven. We all share a look, then I clear my throat.

"I haven't been here yet. Wanna try it out?"

"Really?" Lee lights up, like the first star popping up in the night sky.

I can't answer in the brightness of her expression, nodding like an idiot as my brothers rush to agree. They head inside, but I hang back, shooting a text to Meg. She needs to know what happened, and I mention having a game night. She responds right away that she'll be there.

When I go in, Lee is settled next to Silas. He slings his arm behind her in the booth, and I know that's why she chose to sit with him. He lives for hugs and physical touch — probably why he can't keep a girlfriend. He's way too clingy.

But right now, that's what she needs. Another spark of anger ignites in me. Not only did Sebastian ditch her, he's not giving her enough of himself.

I shove it aside though, because tonight is about cheering Lee up. We all dive headfirst toward that goal. Between ordering, Steven hams up how he caught the lunch thief at his job. Our plan worked perfectly. Then Silas launches into his litany of ridiculous dating stories.

The food is decent and the mood is better as we walk home. She's more relaxed now, her smiles coming easier, and she doesn't stay within touching range of Silas.

The conversation flows the entire way to our house. I'm so busy staring at her mouth that I don't see the curb drop off before our driveway, and I misstep, stumbling before I can catch myself. I land next to her canvas tennis shoes.

"Are you okay?" she gasps.

As soon as I nod, her shoulders begin shaking. She presses her lips together, but she can't hold in the laughter. It tumbles from her, dancing on the air as I scramble upright again. My brothers join in, but all I can hear is her uninhibited delight. I'd do it again just for that delicious sound.

"All right, all right," I grumble when they don't stop.

She bumps me with her shoulder. "Hey, you can't blame me. It's not every day a guy falls at my feet."

When she winks, I almost stumble again. But I grin like an idiot, knowing that I helped bring her back. Meg hops out of her car parked on the street, and I groan when I see her smirk. She definitely saw me make an ass out of myself.

"Walk much, Shawn?" she teases, but the attention shifts off me when Leah squeals and launches herself at her best friend.

"What are you doing home?" she shrieks.

Meg hugs her back, glancing at me. "I heard there was going to be a rousing game of trains, and I wasn't about to miss out."

I subtly shake my head, not wanting Lee to know I was the one who told her. Meg's gaze takes on a knowing edge but she nods. When Lee frowns, pulling away to study each of us in turn, I keep my face carefully neutral.

Finally she gives up and links arms with Meg. "Thanks." We all head into the house.

Silas brings out Ticket to Ride, one of Lee's favorite games, and starts setting up. The object is to complete routes based on what cards you draw. Access points to some cities are limited, and Lee nabs a coveted one for her first play. Steven and Silas groan, but I fight to keep the amusement off my face.

There's the competitive Lee I grew up with.

By the end, she's ticked us all off more than once. My annoyance is outweighed by her triumph though, and I would do it all again. Meg hugs her before pretending to stomp off to bed. Then Lee suggests a movie.

Normally Steven and Silas would be all over that, so I frown when they both make excuses. Her face falls again, and I hear myself asking what she had in mind. I hate how shocked she looks.

"Um, I don't know." She lifts her right foot, rubbing the top of it on her calf, and I feel even more like shit. She only does that when she's really nervous.

I hold up my hands. "I'm not quite ready for bed, so if you want company…" She stays quiet, and I shift my weight. "I know you and I aren't as friendly as you and Steven or Silas, but I'm just as good as them." I don't know if I'm justifying myself to her or me, I only hope I don't sound pathetic. When she doesn't answer, I cut my losses and nod. "Okay, good night, then."

"Shawn, wait." She sighs. "You surprised me, that's all. Are you sure?"

Lifting a shoulder, I say, "Yeah, why not?"

She smiles tightly and echoes me. "Okay, why not?"

We sit on opposite ends of the couch, the silence between us beyond awkward. I shift the remote from hand to hand. "Any suggestions?"

She stares up and off to the side, thinking hard. "Have you seen *Plane* yet?"

Shaking my head, I search for it to read the description. It's right up my alley, so I push play. The movie is good—lots of tension to set the scene, more action as the plot progresses. Almost halfway through, Lee slumps in her seat. Her feet are propped up on the coffee table and her head lolls slightly to one side.

I pause the movie. "Want to stop here?"

"Are you going to bed?"

My answer is immediate. "Nah, I want to finish it." I can guess the ending, but I'd like to see it.

Her back straightens as she rights herself and folds her arms over her chest. "Me, too."

I resist the urge to sigh, knowing if it were any of my brothers, she'd simply say good night and head to bed. But it's me. And everything has to be a competition. "It's just a movie, Lee."

"I said I'm fine." Her lips clamp together as she raises her eyebrows, waiting for me to push play.

So I do. Not long later, she shifts to the middle of the couch, bringing her legs up as she curls into a ball. Another couple scenes pass, and she faces forward, her knees still up to her chest. Not even a minute goes by before her chin dips once, then she slides toward me. Her eyes are closed when she leans her head on my arm, her breathing even.

I frown at the awkward angle of her neck. It would be wrong to let her sleep like that. Only half an hour is left of the movie. Maybe if I...

Lifting my arm in a slow, easy motion, I guide her to snuggle against my side. Her cheek rests on my chest, and I keep my arm up on the back of the couch, careful not to touch her more than that. I try to focus on the screen, but I'm hyper aware of every breath she takes. Of her warmth seeping into my side. Of her sweet scent coating every one of my inhales.

Five minutes later, I punch the off button on the TV. It's obvious how the movie will end, so why torture myself? Especially when I can't concentrate on anything but Lee.

I glance down, sucking in a gasp at the way her V-neck shirt gapes. The supple curve of her creamy breasts greets me, and I yank my gaze away. My heart pounds as I try to erase the image by blinking rapidly, but it's seared into my brain, appearing every time I close my eyes.

Swallowing hard, I shift away. She hums and rolls back. I risk another glance, thankful the gap is gone and she's covered once more.

It's hard not to stare at her beautiful profile. I don't often get the chance since she's either glaring at me, yelling at me, or someone is watching. But here, in this moment, I trace the curve of her cheek with my eyes. Down her pert nose. Over those supple lips.

What would I do if she were mine?

The question blindsides me, and I barely keep myself from jerking at the startling thought. Sure, she's attractive, but she's my brother's girlfriend, for fuck's sake. What kind of man am I?

The thought makes her touch sear into me like fire, burning the guilt into my side and chest where she leans against me. I ease away and she flops onto the couch, not even stirring.

With her neck at a ridiculous angle again.

I sigh, wishing I could leave her like this, but she deserves better. Not to mention Sebastian would have my hide. I frown at her bedroom, the very idea of scooping her into my arms and carrying her to bed way more intimate than I can handle right now. Especially after that treacherous path my mind just wandered down.

Hurrying into her room, I feel even guiltier as I step over the threshold. She's very particular about who she lets into her sanctuary. I don't think Vance was even allowed in here, ever. I hope she'll forgive me since I'm doing it for her.

I grab the first pillow and blanket I can reach then march from the room, feigning a confidence I don't feel. Guilt and anger at myself war within me as I tuck her in, clashing with the warmth that spreads through my chest when she sighs and burrows into the blanket.

Like she misses my body heat.

I clench my teeth, yanking my mind back to safe spaces. I smack the light switch off, waiting until I can see in the dimness of the nightlight on the stairway before I trudge to my room.

Sebastian was right to question me and my motives. I never should have offered to watch a movie with her. I obviously can't trust myself around her and need to keep my distance, like I have been since the day I made her fall into the pool. It's better this way.

Not only because she deserves someone smart like Sebastian, but because every time I let my walls down, something happens to her. Being pushed into pools, getting hit by an ex, sleeping on the couch... I'm obviously no good for her.

She can never be mine, and I can live with that because it means she will be safe.

Chapter Five

Leah

Sunlight wakes me, streaming into my face as I blink in the harsh glare. I'm still on the couch. A pillow is tucked under my head and a blanket is draped over me.

I must have fallen asleep during the movie, and I rack my mind, trying to figure out the last scene I remember. I sit up to stretch, groaning at my stiffness. Why didn't Shawn just wake me so I could go to bed?

I stumble into the kitchen and there he is, hunched over a cup of coffee, scrolling on his phone. I fill a steaming mug, more than ready for the caffeine to hit my veins. The fact that he took the time to tuck me in with my own pillow and blanket lingers as I take my first sip. I glance at him again, wondering if maybe we can form a truce.

Maybe things can change after last night. Maybe he doesn't hate me quite so much. His actions have to mean something, right?

So I tentatively say, "Morning." When he only grunts, I try again, "I guess I fell asleep last night."

No response, then his gaze flicks to mine and he bites out, "Yeah, on my shoulder."

Surprise courses through me, followed by confusion. The words are harsh, but the gesture is sweet—he let me sleep on him.

He continues in the hostile tone, almost barking the words. "What did you want, Lee, for me to carry you to bed? To tuck you in?"

So much for sweet.

I can't believe he hates me that much, and a fresh wave of hurt slashes through my midsection. I can't handle his whiplash responses. I start to stalk past him then I pause, allowing my frustration to bubble over. "Maybe your shoulder is as good as your brothers' but that's about it."

"Lee," he says, then groans. "Wait."

But I ignore him and stomp to my room to take a shower.

I spend the weekend focusing on my schoolwork. I have a couple of study groups to break up the monotony of Sebastian being occupied. Any time my mind wanders, I focus solely on my issues with him. And they are *plenty*. Meg's words play on repeat in my mind, and I toy with the idea of breaking up.

But I'm not ready to act on it yet.

I feel like a child on the cusp of sleeping without their favorite blanket for the first time. Is that what our relationship is? Nothing more than a security blanket?

The questions swirl in the back of my mind as I slog through my Monday classes then grab a quick cafeteria dinner before heading to the library. Today is my late shift. I love working Monday nights because we're never busy, and I plan to tackle my anthropology paper. My research topic is glass Coca Cola bottles.

Once I've checked in and shelved all the books in the bin, I log into my account to work on my paper. I've enjoyed seeing how the logos and the sizes changed over time, and I'm quickly engrossed.

When a throat clears, I glance up, taking an extra second to register Shawn before me. I watch him warily, wondering which Shawn I'll get this time. Nothing has been normal since our movie night, and I find myself missing our usual fights. Somehow his cold shoulder has worn on me more than his constant teasing.

"I brought you coffee." He hands me a to-go mug from my favorite local shop, Not Your Average Joe. When I hesitate, he sets it on the counter with a sigh, swiping a hand over his face. "I was out of line Saturday, Lee. I'm not sure what happened, if I was grumpy or still half-asleep or what. Either way, there was no excuse to treat you like that." His next words are quiet but heartfelt. "I'm sorry."

"Thanks, Shawn." As I reach for the coffee, a weight lifts off my chest, but I don't examine the feeling too closely.

Relief crosses his face. "What are you working on?" When I tell him about my paper, he seems intrigued. "Can I see?"

Shocked by his interest, I give him a stunned nod. We're the only two in the library, so I let him pull a chair behind the counter. Then I flip through the document, showing off my work with pride. I especially love the illustrations.

When we're finished, he studies me. "You're really enjoying this."

"Yeah, I am." I took it to meet a gen. ed. requirement, but I've been surprised at how fast it turned into one of my favorite classes.

"Maybe you should think about becoming an anthropologist."

"Maybe I will." I file the words away for later and take another sip of my coffee. "So, did you just come down here to apologize, or did you want to get some studying in?" All this buttering up can only mean one thing.

He sighs. "*¿Por favor ayúdame con mi Español?*" *Will you help me with my Spanish?*

I can't help smiling. "*Claro que sí.*" *But of course.*

We move to a table near the desk, in case anyone comes in. Shawn plops next to me, and I catch a whiff of his scent—sandalwood and balsam. The heady aroma is refreshing, making me picture sunny hikes and pine trees. I'm so ready to get out of Michigan over Spring Break and bask in the sun for a little while.

His elbow brushes mine as he pulls his folder from his bag, and I try not to jerk at the electricity that shoots up my arm. What was that? But he hands me a pile of flash cards, and I focus on quizzing him on his vocabulary.

Shawn is not one for sitting still and he shifts often. More than once our knees bump, and tingles dance through me at every casual touch. It makes me uneasy, the way I'm reacting, but I refuse to move away. It's probably another game to see how much he can rattle me.

We make it through the stack of cards and he only missed two. I organize the pile, grinning as I hand it back to him. "Nice job."

His dazzling smile appears at my praise, and the air is sucked out of me. Then his fingers graze mine as he takes the cards, a shock startling me enough that I almost drop the entire stack. I yank my hand back, trying to mask my reaction by tucking my hair behind my ear.

This is ridiculous. I'm supposed to be tutoring the guy, not fawning over him. Sure he's attractive, but he's *Shawn*. He needs me to graduate, so I need to get a grip.

Properly scolded with my studying mindset restored, I take a deep, bracing breath and force myself to ignore my stomach flip at the noseful of his scent. "What's next?"

We move on to conjugating irregular verbs. After a solid hour of Spanish, he pushes away from the table. "That's it. My brain can't take any more."

As he stands up to stretch, his shirt lifts, giving me a glimpse of his flat stomach. I'm mesmerized by the appearance of his washboard abs. His body has always caught my attention, but since it's attached to *him*, I ignore it. *Usually*.

He says something I don't quite catch, and I have to tear my eyes away. Only to find him smirking. My cheeks heat at being caught checking him out, but I raise my chin anyway as he repeats his question.

"How're you getting home tonight?"

"Sebastian stayed to work with Professor Harrison, but he promised to give me a ride." Shawn's scoff is full of doubt, and I glare. "He *promised*."

Shawn raises an eyebrow, the unspoken *"we'll see"* landing like a gauntlet between us. But he changes the subject. "I've got a history paper due next week. I don't suppose you know any history majors who can recommend a decent Civil War era writer, something that I might enjoy?"

I reluctantly take the olive branch. "That's a pretty broad topic. Nothing more specific?" He shakes his head, and I drum my fingers on the counter. "Stephen Ambrose is one of my favorites. Good history with interesting tidbits but reads more like a story." I search the computer to give him the right section.

He waves his thanks, disappearing into the stacks. I'm left with only the company of the ticking clock counting down the minutes until closing time. My gut twists as the big hand approaches the twelve. With five minutes left, I pack up my things then try calling Sebastian.

It goes straight to voicemail.

Shawn checks out two books, staring at me the entire time.

Finally, I growl, "No, I haven't heard from him." I expect him to gloat, but the empathy emanating from him is even more unsettling.

As he puts his books in his bag, I mull over my options. I could ask Shawn for a ride, but with the way I've been reacting to him all day, I don't think that's the best idea. Besides, who's to say the nice guy bringing me coffee and smiling while we study won't suddenly disappear and it'll be grumpy Shawn once more?

Home isn't far. I don't love walking in the dark, but I can do it—*have done* it plenty of times. What's one more?

My mind made up, I start shutting down the system and begin practicing what I'm going to say to Sebastian.

Shawn hasn't left the counter. "Let me give you a ride," he demands. "I'll text Sebastian."

I bristle at the high-handed treatment, especially from him. "I'll walk."

Anger flashes across his face. "I wasn't asking."

"Neither was I." I glare back.

"This isn't about you losing or some stupid, competitive thing. Just let me give you a ride home."

The fact that he brought that up only makes me more determined to stick to my decision and I shake my head. A tiny voice tells me I'm being stupid, but I don't care. Hell will freeze over before I back down.

"Leah —"

"Look, Shawn," I say. I know how stubborn Shawn can be. I know just how far to push him to get him to leave. "I don't know what game you think you're playing, but you don't own me. I'm not your responsibility, so leave me alone." My strong words resonate through the empty building. Hurt crosses his face, making me want to take them all back. But I don't.

"Fine." He clamps his mouth shut and storms out of the door.

Guilt and annoyance twist in my gut, but I shove them aside as I lock up. I allow myself to seethe. I wouldn't be in this situation if Sebastian had followed through with his promise. I shoot him an annoyed text.

Don't bother coming to get me. I'll find my own way home.

I stomp across the well-lit parking lot, hiking my bag up on my shoulder as I fume. A car engine starts, and I know it's Shawn. I stride ahead with my jaw clenched, my chin high. The car revs, gaining on me.

Relief hits me when I reach the uneven sidewalk. I wouldn't put it past him to drag me into the car if he caught me in the wide-open parking lot. Now at least I'll have a barrier.

I'm too busy stewing to notice the guy loitering under the lamp post until he grabs my backpack. Luckily, I have my hand on the strap, and I cling to it, yelling, "Hey!"

He jerks to a stop when I don't let go, turning around with a menacing glare as I tug. He glares and demands in a raspy voice, "Let go, whore, or you'll be sorry."

The insult slices across my heart like the lash of a whip, making me freeze. I can't obey the command, can't do anything more than gape as the guy growls. The crack of his knuckles as he backhands me echoes as the layers of past and present entwine. My head jerks sideways from the blow, but I don't let go of my bag.

Headlights bathe me in their welcome glow, and Shawn jumps from his car. "Leah!"

The attacker curses as Shawn rushes him. Shawn gets in one punch before the guy scrambles away, and I lurch backward as he releases my backpack. I tumble to the ground, landing hard on my butt with an "Oof!"

Shawn immediately crouches by my side. "Lee, are you okay?"

The memory of Vance's knuckles on my cheek tangles with the guy hitting me moments ago, and it's too much. I flinch as Shawn's hand stretches toward me. He goes still, pain crossing his face. My brain reconnects, dismissing any threat.

Shawn is safe. He'd never hurt me.

I whisper his name, and he reaches out again, his movements slow as he watches my reaction. When I don't flinch, he touches my chin, studying my face. "Are you okay?" he repeats.

My cheek stings and my ass throbs, but that's all. At least on the physical side of things. I nod, and he grasps both my hands to haul me to my feet. Then he crushes me in his embrace. The trembling starts as I rest my good cheek on his shoulder, but it passes in a matter of moments as I ground myself in his arms.

I remember another embrace like this. Just as fervid. Just as tight.

Following the incident with Vance.

When at last I relax enough to quit shaking, Shawn pulls away, takes my bag and helps me to the car. I push the buckle into place with stiff, wooden motions then tuck my hands in my lap. We make the short drive home in silence, my brain muted as I stare blankly ahead.

Then the very air changes, and I register Sebastian's car in our driveway before I whip my head toward Shawn. His jaw is clenched, his lips tight and his knuckles are almost white on the steering wheel. He slams on the brakes so hard I lurch against the seatbelt. He leaps out of the car before his name leaves my lips.

Oh shit. Sebastian!

* * * *

Shawn

My vision tunnels as a reddish haze blurs the edges. I leap from the car, barely registering Lee call my name as I race toward the house with only one thing on my mind.

This time Sebastian has gone too far.

I slam the front door open. Silas and Steven sit up on the couch as we blaze by.

Steven jumps to his feet. "What's wrong?"

I just grunt, not able to take the time to explain. Leah is on my heels as I storm upstairs. Our bathroom sits at the top of the staircase with two bedrooms to the right and two to the left. Sebastian's is on the right, his door open.

I march in then grab Sebastian's collar with both hands, yanking him toward me. "Why didn't you pick her up?" Each word is clipped as I hover nose to nose with my brother.

Lee tries to pull me off, but I turn my glare on her and she blanches, backing away.

I refocus on Sebastian and repeat, "Why didn't you pick her up?"

He is paler than usual. "I forgot. I came right home to go over my notes from Professor Harrison." His gaze darts to her. "Why didn't you call?"

"I did, Sebastian." Exasperation coats her words.

Steven and Silas crowd the doorway, Silas asking, "What's going on?"

"Tell them, Leah," I bite out through gritted teeth, wanting them to hear it from her.

She stares at the floor, her answer barely audible. "Sebastian promised to give me a ride home tonight, but he didn't."

Her voice trembles, and I take in the way she retreats into herself. Her fingers are clenched, and she won't look at anyone. I realize the last thing she needs is to relive the event, and a fresh wave of anger plows through me as I readjust my grip. I take over. Sebastian flinches when I tell him the guy hit her, but I'm not finished.

"That's two promises you've broken to her this week. This one could have cost her something even more precious, maybe her life. If you're not going to take care of her, then you don't deserve her."

I've never been closer to hitting Sebastian than now, and it takes all my effort to keep from smashing my fist into his guilty face. I shove him backward then storm out of the room before I lose control completely. I stop in my doorway when I hear his voice, wanting to know what Leah will say. Will she roll over like usual? Put his needs before hers?

For once, she doesn't back down. "I should be a priority, Sebastian. I deserve more than this."

She pivots on her heel, striding down the hallway, and admiration ripples through me as she races downstairs. I take a step toward her, knowing how affected she is, knowing she needs someone. But Silas and Steven hurry after her, and I halt in my doorway. It's better this way.

I catch a glimpse of Sebastian whipping off his glasses and dropping his face into his hands. A fresh wave of rage encompasses me, and I slam my door, even though I know my rage isn't *all* directed at Sebastian. If I could, I'd hunt that cowardly asshole down, make him pay for what he'd done. I wish I could've taken him out right then, but checking on Leah had been more important.

I cross over to the window, where I lean against the frame and stare unseeingly into the night. My mind is filled with incomplete, ragged bits that tangle together with another night, so very similar. Both times a man struck her. Both times she'd let me help her right after.

And both times she'd let me hold her for a few brief seconds.

Her lithe figure walks across the yard, bulkier than usual in her winter coat as she hurries to her tree house.

Her refuge. The rage seeps from me like air leaking out of a tire, and guilt replaces it. I'd let her walk home when I knew it wasn't safe. Now that's twice she's been hit on my watch.

Never again, I vow, even as a voice in the depths of my mind reminds me that she's not mine to protect.

A quiet knock sounds on my door, and I sigh, making sure I'm calm enough for conversation. My jaw tightens when I see Sebastian in the hallway with his hands in his pockets. "What?" I bite out.

"We need to talk." Not waiting for an invitation, he strides in, and I shut the door behind him. "I'm sorry, Shawn. I had alarms set. I had my phone on me. I did everything I know how to do, and it still wasn't good enough."

His frustration has me feeling bad for my immediate harshness.

"I'm trying, but it's not working." He rakes his fingers through his hair. "I don't want to hurt her. She's my best friend."

I frown at his choice of words. Not the love of his life. Not his first real girlfriend. His best friend.

Ignoring that, I say, "You've got to make her a priority, Sebastian. That's what she needs."

"Which brings me to my next point of business." A crinkle appears in his forehead, and I shift under his scrutiny as he says, "I thought you were going to hit me tonight."

I feel like I'm straddling a fault line and the first tremor is ripping through. "I almost did." The admission tears through me as I remember how close I came.

"What's going on, Shawn?" His lips press together as he studies me. "I'm trying to assemble the pieces.

First the comment about our lack of sex life, then nearly punching me because Leah was in trouble. Not to mention the chokehold."

He rubs his neck, and another prick of guilt stabs me. Several moments tick by, the tension growing between us as my tangled emotions hover under the surface, threatening to boil over.

"You let her think you hate her, yet you protect her at every turn. You can't stand it when she's upset." He gives me a knowing look. "I know you were the one who told Meg she needed to come home on Friday. Then you stayed up and watched a movie with Leah, even tucked her in on the couch."

I don't want to hear any more. I want to shove my fingers in my ears and run right through the door, leaving all the carefully buried pieces of me where they lay.

But I don't, because Sebastian deserves the chance to talk.

He tilts his head. "Why?"

"I don't hate her," I say, sagging onto my bed. It's a non-answer, but all that I can admit right now.

"I know," he says simply, the bed bouncing as he sits next to me. He stares at the ceiling, and I know he's reassessing a million moments, myriad actions, of mine and hers. "The pool party?"

I sigh, leaning forward on my elbows. "I didn't know it was her until she kissed me. I stepped back, and she fell before I could catch her."

"Your trip out west?"

I have to swallow before I speak. "The parade of guys she brought in that first year... I couldn't handle it. I couldn't wrap my mind around her being all grown up. Being in the same house with her. I had to get away."

Sebastian takes my answers in stride, jumping right to the next question. "The night of the incident?"

Another wave of fury washes over me, but I push it aside, trying to stay the course. "She ran to me. I held her as she explained what happened and I gave her to you. Where I knew she'd be safe."

I glance at him then, afraid of what I might see. She's his girlfriend after all. But his expression is thoughtful, free from judgment. As if I'm a puzzle he must figure out.

He nods like he's affirming my choice. "Especially since you and Steven needed to chase after Vance." His lips press together for another long moment.

Long enough that I start to squirm. "What?"

"Why do you let her think you hate her?"

That's all the heart baring I can take, and I pop to my feet, stalking over to the window once more. I raise an arm above my head, leaning against the frame as I stare out at the treehouse, picturing her huddled inside. "It doesn't matter. She's not mine to want."

"Shawn..." Sebastian crosses the room, his hands in pockets as he stands near me. "I'm a stepping stone."

I frown, turning toward him in confusion.

"Lee chose me for the same reason you trusted me with her the night of the incident, because I'm safe. But I always knew she'd outgrow me." He shifts his weight as I try to process what he's saying. "She's my best friend, always taking care of me, and I wanted to do that for her. To take care of her for a change." A wry grin twists his lips. "I'm failing miserably as of late, but I hope the thought at least counts."

"You…you're not in love with her?" I ask, my heart beating harder in my chest.

He shakes his head as he smiles knowingly. "But I think you might be."

Chapter Six

Leah

Memories pummel me as I climb the ladder to my tree house in the corner of our fenced-in backyard. Silas and Steven finally got the memo that I want to be alone, and some of the tension in my chest loosens as I crawl into the familiar space. Some might think it silly and childish, but I love my refuge.

The wooden floor creaks on my entry, but I know it's safe. The guys helped make sure of that. A short half-wall runs around three sides, with a full wall at my back. I take a deep breath as I study the sprawling branches through the partially open view. Moonlight filters between the leaves until the neighbors' yard lamp flicks on and swallows it.

Vance creeps into my mind, and I don't fight him like I usually do. I know if I suppress him now, he'll just haunt my dreams.

He and I had an astronomy class together my sophomore year. I'd taken it to fulfill my science requirement because who doesn't like looking at stars? I wish I could see them now. I study the silhouetted trees lining the sidewalk as the memories flood me.

I noticed him walk into class that first day. He was cute and I melted for his smile when he sat at my table. He spoke first, asking if I'd dated Zach Sanders and I'd said yes.

"I thought so. I saw you at one of his parties and was intrigued." His dark gaze trailed over me. "I'm glad to get to know you better."

Two weeks later, he invited me to dinner. His treat, he'd said. Free food was always a yes from me, and he picked me up that Friday. When I asked where we were going, he raved about a hybrid Mexican-Chinese restaurant that has since closed. I wrinkled my nose. I'd gone once with Meg, and neither of us were impressed.

I gently asked, "Is there any way we could go somewhere else? I've been there and—"

He waved his hand, talking over me. "You have to try their shrimp egg rolls. They're delicious."

First red flag.

We had a decent time, and the food wasn't terrible. It wasn't good either, but I let it slide. He kissed my hand after he drove me home, saying he had a lovely time. My heart fluttered.

Class was full of flirting, then we had our second date. Maria's—a much better choice in my opinion. He asked to kiss me on my doorstep, and I nodded. The kiss stole my breath, until his hand grazed my breast. I jerked away, not ready for that.

"I'm sorry, Leah," he said—so sincerely. "I got carried away."

Red flag number two.

In the week that followed, we had more dinner followed by more kisses, but he never overstepped.

The following weekend, we went to a house party where we both drank and danced. Then he led me to a dark room to make out. When he tried to go farther, I was hesitant. He oozed charm as he told me how my beauty enchanted him and drove him wild. I fell under his spell, coerced into thinking the least I could do was give him a blow job.

Red flag number three.

Again, we hung out several times that week, making out after each date. Though he asked me for more, he respected the lines I drew. I blamed the previous pushiness on too much alcohol and let myself forget. Until I visited his dorm and found him in bed with a different girl from our class. I ended things then, figuring that would be the last I'd see of him.

The Wrightings threw a house party the next weekend, and I attended, thankful to be rid of Vance. But he wasn't done with me. He showed up on our doorstep, already tipsy, searching for me. Shawn wasn't going to let him in, but I said I could talk for a minute.

We stayed on the step with the door open as Vance pleaded his case, trying to convince me for another shot.

I shook my head. "All you want is to get in my pants. I've let you get away with enough, and I won't make that mistake again." I started to turn, but he grabbed my arm, holding me in place. "Let go of me."

His expression turned colder than a glacier as he glared. "You're all high and mighty, thinking you're so much better than the rest of us," he sneered. "You won't come out of this on top. I'm going to tell everyone what a little whore you are."

I wrenched out of his grasp. "Fuck off. If you think I'm going to come crawling back to you because of some half-assed threat, you don't know me at all."

Rage contorted his face, and his hand flew, so fast I couldn't react. His knuckles cracked against my cheek, my head whipping sideways from the perfect backhand. I yelped.

And Shawn heard.

He appeared in the doorway, calling my name. When he saw me clutching my cheek, pure fury engulfed him. He looked like a mythological god, and I half-expected lightning to shoot out of his eyes. Even so, I ran to him, knowing he was safe. He wrapped me in his arms, in the tightest hug ever, and he didn't let go until I stopped trembling.

Then he summoned Sebastian, passing me to him as he ran after Vance, whose car wouldn't start. Steven tore after them both, the brothers to my rescue. Sebastian brought me to my room, cuddled me in a blanket and held me until they got back.

Not one of Shawn's knuckles remained unmarred, and not all the blood was his own when he came back. He knelt before me and touched my good cheek. "You're all right?"

I nodded. He'd gotten there in time.

His gaze intensified and he leaned in slightly. For a brief moment, I thought he might kiss me. But instead he shot to his feet, gave a sharp nod and left.

Vance was smart enough to claim he was in a bike accident. Everyone knew the Wrightings' dad was best friends with Judge Carter. Unfortunately, not even that could deter Vance from living up to his promise of dragging my reputation through the dirt.

Whispers followed me everywhere, and I stopped going places other than class. Quit hanging out with people I didn't know well. For a while, one of the brothers or Meg came with me to my shifts at the library.

I even quit dating after receiving all sorts of propositions because of my undeserved reputation. I couldn't trust guys, but more than that, Vance had manipulated me so easily, I couldn't trust my own judgment.

At least I had my parents, the Wrightings and Meg to get me through. Meg had even rallied the guys to get tested with me, a perfect show of solidarity in the aftermath. Their unwavering support kept me together.

* * * *

Shawn

In love with Leah. I hesitantly roll the silent words on my tongue, and while they taste sweet, they also feel wrong. "I can't be," I blurt out. "I'm not good for her."

"What?" Sebastian asks, incredulous.

Fear spirals within me at the idea. It's a concrete thought now, instead of an invisible nuance in my mind. I stare at the plank floor, at the knot shaped like a face. A person trapped behind the varnish, staring up in a silent plea for help that will never be answered. "Every time we're together, something happens."

"Explain."

I've never voiced this to anyone. Saying it aloud would make it real, and it feels like a fragile thing that needs protection. But I never could say no to Sebastian. I sigh and drop my arm, then lean my shoulder against the window frame.

"I'm *not* good for her," I repeat, reminding myself and him why I can't possibly be in love with Leah. I tick the reasons off—the pool, me allowing Vance anywhere near her, her sleeping on the couch after our movie. "Then tonight...I couldn't even get her to ride home with me."

Sebastian's frown deepens.

I hesitate as another memory pours in. "I was the one who dared her to climb the swing set." I was old enough to know better, and Lee was a pesky kid I'd wanted to get rid of. "She broke her arm that day, because I dared her to do something stupid."

Frustration and guilt ratchet up inside me. I drop my forehead to touch the window pane, relishing the cool glass against my skin. "Besides, she deserves someone smarter, like you. Someone who doesn't have to struggle to get a C. Who only dreams of a B average." My self-deprecating thoughts have me clenching my fist.

Sebastian shoves me, hard enough that I have to take a step back. His glare has me all confused as he marches up to me. I take another step, wondering what the hell is going on as he shoves his finger in my chest, punctuating his next words.

"You're a damn fool, Shawn."

Sebastian rarely swears, and I stare at him, wide-eyed.

"First of all, you're plenty smart, but you've also got other things going for you. Like loyalty, motivation, ingenuity, drive. You know exactly how to nudge people out of their comfort zones and inspire them to do better, to be better. One of the many reasons you'll make an amazing teacher." He shoves his glasses up on his nose, staring down in frustration. "And you are just what Leah needs."

I can only gape.

"Those incidents? Not a single one was your fault." He pauses. "Okay, you could have reacted better at the pool. But the others? You were a kid when she broke her arm. And it's Leah. If you hadn't suggested it, she would've thought of it on her own."

My mouth twitches since Leah has always been spunky. She'd had to be, holding her own with us guys.

"And the thing with Vance, that was her decision. You stayed close. You were there when things got rough." He holds my gaze, as if wanting to be sure I hear him. "Same thing tonight. She made her decision, but you were there to help with the aftermath." His lips press together, a challenge rising in his eyes. "I think you're making excuses because you're too scared to admit how you really feel."

I stumble to the bed as his words hit me like a dump truck full of bricks. They have shoved aside the curtain, revealing what's always been right in front of me. What I've fought so hard to avoid.

"Fuck," I whisper. "I'm in love with Leah."

He shakes his head, exasperation all over his face. "Ding, ding, ding, we have a winner. Took you long enough."

"Wait. How long have you known?"

"I've suspected for a while, but that sex comment really tipped the scales. Then there was the whole almost choking me tonight because you were so furious you couldn't see straight."

I rub the back of my neck. "Sorry about that, by the way. I was pissed at myself, and that asshole, of course."

He sinks onto the bed next to me and sits quietly for a moment. "I should have been there."

"Yeah, you should have." I rest a hand on his shoulder, then drop my arm so I can lean onto my knees. "Leah thinks I hate her. Where the hell do I go from here?"

"I've been considering that, and I have an idea."

I turn to him, all ears.

"I want to stay here for Spring Break."

Our parents rented a condo in Myrtle Beach, but Dad has to leave early for a big company merger. The condo would sit empty, so they offered it to us, and since Leah is one of the family, she's coming too.

My eyebrows shoot up. "What?"

He mimics my position, leaning forward and lacing his fingers together. "Professor Harrison asked me to be a bigger part of his lectures. He invited me to speak at a conference over Spring Break, and I'd like to go." He sighs, cocking his jaw to one side before talking again. "We both know I'll have a much more enjoyable time at a presentation than I would at the beach."

I nod—it's definitely true.

"But Leah will be out of her element and she needs someone to commit to being there for her. You know Silas will be distracted by every girl that comes along. Especially if they have curves and black hair." We share a chuckle before he continues, "Steven is a gamble. He hasn't dated much since Bianca, but it's Spring Break."

Which leaves…

"She needs you, Shawn."

My mind races to all the time I could spend with her. The car ride, the small condo, the beach. My mouth goes dry at the thought of her in a swimsuit.

"This could be your chance to fix things between you."

I frown, reining in my thoughts. "But you're still together."

A fleeting hint of sadness crosses his face. "It won't be long, Shawn. I feel her pulling away more each day, and..." He sucks in a deep breath. "I think she's ready."

"For what?"

"You."

I lean back on my palms, reeling from this turn of events. "This is going to take some work."

"Yes, it is." He shifts toward me, more serious than I've ever seen. "I'm not going to abandon her for Spring Break if I don't see some improvement between you two. You've got to get beyond this ridiculous enemy farce and at least try being friends."

I swallow at the lump of nerves in my throat and nod. "Yeah. I can do that." I just have to figure out how.

He glances at the window and sighs. "I should probably go talk to her."

"She's at the treehouse so bring a blanket." A slow grin spreads over his face, and I defensively ask, "What?"

"You'll be fine, Shawn. Just fine." And he claps me on the shoulder before striding out of my door.

As soon as he's gone, I flop back onto my bed with a groan as the full weight of what I just agreed to crashes down. What the fuck am I going to do? How do you make someone who thinks you hate them realize you want to be friends? Or more?

I'm an idiot.

I swipe my hand over my face as my frustration grows. I better grab my shovel, 'cause this is one hell of a hole I need to dig myself out of.

And what if something else happens on my watch? What then?

I pound my fist against the bed, even more annoyed with myself for committing to this plan. What the fuck was I thinking?

Chapter Seven

Leah

A creaking floorboard jerks me back to the present as Sebastian crawls into the treehouse and says, "I knew I'd find you here." At my glare, he sighs, then tosses me a fuzzy blanket.

I don't move for a long moment, until his voice breaks the silence.

"I'm so sorry, Leah. I checked my phone, but it was dead." His expression is pleading as he continues, "I had it in my pocket in case you called. I had an alarm set and everything."

"Oh, Sebastian." My anger begins to fade, and I take the blanket, flinging it around my shoulders. I jerk my chin, allowing him to come in. As he settles next to me, wrapping his own blanket around him, I give him a small smile. "That makes me feel better. You had precautions in place, and I appreciate it."

I snuggle into the cozy fabric and lean against him, needing the contact. It is still February after all, not an ideal time to hang out in an open tree house.

He rests his cheek on my head. "You okay, Lee-bug?"

Sebastian never uses nicknames, and it takes me a moment to answer, needing to swallow down the tightness in my throat. "It was a lot like another night."

He laces his fingers through mine. "The guy backhanded you?"

"And called me a whore." My voice cracks on the word, but I keep it together as I grip Sebastian's hand.

"I'm glad you weren't hurt worse, but I wish you hadn't been hurt at all." His glasses frame his hazel eyes, a portrait of pain and regret.

"I should have rode home with Shawn, but...nothing is ever easy with him." I grit my teeth, remembering how he'd ordered me, but guilt squeezes my chest, since he also saved me. I anxiously peer at Sebastian's neck, picturing Shawn's tight hold on his collar. "Are you okay? He didn't hurt you, did he?"

Sebastian shakes his head. "We're okay now. We talked."

"I'm glad."

Sebastian studies me. "How about us, Leah? Are we okay? I mean, really okay?"

I freeze. I'm not prepared to do this tonight, not on the heels of everything else. "I don't know, Sebastian. Meg asked me some hard questions a few days ago, ones I haven't been able to answer yet. But it's more than that." I hesitate, feeling the sharp assessment of his stare. "We've both been really busy, which is totally understandable, but I...I don't know if I still fit in the picture with you."

Silence hangs between us until he finally says, "I've noticed things have felt off lately." He presses his lips together, scanning the tree house. "I don't know what to say."

"I don't know if there is anything more to say right now." I pat his thigh. "Let's give it some more time, okay? See what happens after your presentation."

He nods. "Night, Leah." He hesitates then opens his arms, offering me a hug.

I take it, inhaling his familiar coffee and mint scent and wishing for a stomach flip or a tingle or *something*. But all I feel is the steadfast comfort of the presence of my best friend.

"Good night," I whisper before I let him go then watch him disappear down the ladder.

My mind flits back to the study session with Shawn, to my reactions to him. Why can't I feel that with Sebastian? Why isn't this working?

I remember Shawn storming from the room, slamming his door after I'd raced down the stairs. Guilt pricks me. He saved me from that guy, comforted me, stood up for me, and what have I done? Hidden away in my tree house without even saying thank you. He at least deserves that.

Resigned, I clamber down the ladder. I practice what I'm going to say then force myself to go inside, climb the stairs and tap on Shawn's door.

He flings it open, bare-chested and tense, as if ready for a fight. His anger startles me, and I automatically lean back. Shawn glances down, making me realize I'm doing my biggest tell—rubbing the top of my foot against the back of my calf. I hurry to put my foot flat on the floor.

When I look up again, his eyes are closed. He opens them and the intense Shawn is gone, replaced by a much calmer version. An underlying tension still vibrates through him, but he asks, "What's up?"

His bare torso is way too distracting, and I yank my focus up to his face. "I never thanked you. So…thank you."

His sigh is huge, and he rakes long fingers through his sandy brown hair. The silky strands are unruly, one flopping down to brush his forehead. A sharp pain lingers in his emerald eyes that wasn't there before.

"Are you okay?"

His gaze latches onto me like a lifeline. An eternal moment stretches as he shifts ever so slightly toward me. Then he blinks and pulls back. "All right, you thanked me. Anything else?"

Every word is short and sharp, and I feel like I lost something important. I swallow back the unexpected hurt then force a smile. "No. Good night, Shawn."

"Night." He searches my face for the briefest of seconds, a muscle ticking in his jaw before he shuts the door in my confused face.

* * * *

Thankfully, the rest of the week goes without further incident. Sebastian is more attentive. Silas and Steven even pitch in more than usual, taking on my night for chores or ordering pizza when it's my turn to cook. Each of them caring for me in their own way. The only one who remains distant is Shawn, and his quiet unsettles me.

Friday night, I rush home for my weekly dinner with Sebastian. Tonight is extra special—we're celebrating

Sebastian's successful presentation. I throw on some cute jeans, a nice shirt and my favorite jacket, then pop into the living room.

When he's nowhere to be seen, I deflate slightly. He's been so careful about keeping our plans this week that I want to give him the benefit of the doubt though. Shawn and Silas sprawl on the couch, watching a basketball game, and I ask if they know where Sebastian is.

Shawn jerks his chin in the direction of the stairs, so I gather my resolve, hoping I'll find him ready. As I trudge upstairs, every step weighs on me more than the last.

Sebastian hunches over an open textbook at his desk, and I lean against the door frame. His desk is piled high with books and another stack as tall as the chair rests on the floor. A large bookshelf takes up one wall, its shelves crammed full. But the room is neat, the bed made, the floor clean. I walk in and sit on the edge of the desk.

He startles, glancing at his watch. "Oh, crap, Leah. I didn't realize the time." He shuts the book, peering up at me hopefully. "But I'm ready otherwise."

And I realize it's true. He wears a button-down shirt instead of a polo—which he only does for dates. "Great," I say, relieved. "I'm all ready, too. Let's go celebrate."

But he doesn't move. I know there's more he wants to say, so I wait.

"Professor Harrison said I did so well that he wants me to do more. I'm able to present my paper on dominant traits at another conference coming up."

"Is that the one where you studied the different roses and did all those experiments?" I try to keep up with his projects, but I'm so far out of my depth that most of the time I feel like I'm drowning.

His nod is eager, passion flaring as he answers, "Yes, that's the one."

"When's the conference?"

"Well, I wanted to talk to you about that." He runs a finger along the spine of his textbook.

My stomach sinks. "Spring Break." His head bobs, and I sigh, disappointment coursing through me. "Sebastian, I'm really looking forward to that trip."

It's only two weeks away and getting out of Michigan in mid-March is something I've been dreaming of. Away from the dreary gray skies, away from the back and forth of the freezing then thawing of almost spring.

"You should still go! Don't stay home because of me."

I frown. Tagging along with Sebastian is one thing, but me, alone with the other brothers? Unease gnaws at me when I think of Shawn since things haven't been normal since the night at the library. He hasn't even asked me for help with his Spanish once.

Downstairs, the slam of the front door echoes. Steven's home. He always makes the loudest entrance.

"Come on." Sebastian stands up. "Let's ask them."

I close my eyes, counting to five before I follow. Sebastian doesn't always understand what's going on in my head, and this is definitely one of those times. It's not as simple as, "Are your brothers comfortable with this?"

Steven sprawls on the recliner as we enter the living room.

Sebastian grabs the remote, muting the TV over his brothers' groans. "I'm not going on Spring Break. I've been invited to speak at a conference, an opportunity I can't pass up. Do you guys care if Leah still goes?"

Silas rolls his eyes. "Of course not."

"Fine by me." Steven shrugs.

Shawn's answer surprises me. "I don't mind." He shoots me a tentative half-smile, but I don't return it.

All four of them stare at me.

"Great." I throw my hands up, beyond frustrated. "I guess I'm still going to Myrtle Beach." I push past Sebastian to my room, ignoring his shocked expression.

I text Meg when I get inside and, despite being on her fourth date this week, she calls me right away. "Lee, what are you going to do?"

A toilet flushes in the background. "Are you in the bathroom?" I wrinkle my nose.

"Yeah, I told Penn I had to pee."

"I thought you were going out with Kyle."

She laughs. "That was last night. He was good, too."

"Nice." I sink onto my bed with a sigh. "I was really excited to spend time with Sebastian. Reconnecting, you know? He's been so busy lately." Meg isn't coming on the trip—she already had plans with her family, so I won't even have her for support.

She stays quiet for a moment, then says, "Maybe this is a sign."

Tears threaten and my throat tightens, rendering me unable to talk. I lean forward to rest my head in my hand and sniff.

"Oh, Lee-bug, I'm sorry." She pauses. "Everyone goes through rough patches. Maybe things will be better soon."

I hum, hoping it sounds positive enough for her. Silence hangs between us, punctuated by another flushing toilet.

"I think you should still go, especially if the guys are fine with it. You deserve a break, and it's a free place to stay. Get out of Michigan! Enjoy some warmth and sunshine."

Her words conjure up images of the beach and all the stuff I wanted to do. I try to reimagine it, picturing myself without Sebastian. Would it still be fun? Sebastian doesn't love lounging on the beach. He's not one for parties or dancing, two things I very much enjoy. And he doesn't drink much, if at all.

Going without him might not be so bad.

"Thanks, Meg. Maybe I will." We hang up, and someone taps on my door. "Come in."

Sebastian enters with his hands stuffed in his pockets. "Do you still want to get something to eat?"

I am hungry, and we definitely need to talk, so I nod. We decide on walking to our favorite Chinese restaurant, which we do in relative silence. Most people find Sebastian's quiet demeanor off-putting, but I don't usually mind it.

Today is an exception.

This distance between us is only growing, and I don't know how to stop it. Maybe Meg is right. Maybe this is a sign. Maybe it's time to let go of my security blanket and be on my own.

When Sebastian opens the door for me, I take an extra second to study him before I walk in. The Pad Thai is calling my name. I love it, but it's not a Chinese dish, which annoys Sebastian because he thinks it shouldn't be on the menu. The last thing I want to hear is a rant right now, so I settle for a chicken veggie stir fry.

The meal progresses in halting awkward stops and starts as I keep getting tangled in my internal tug of war. Finally, the waitress brings the bill. I scoop my leftovers in to-go containers, knowing they won't last long in our house.

When I set the box down, I can't take it anymore. "I don't want to break up…"

His lips press together, his brow furrows and he sets his drink down.

"But I don't see any other way around this. You're at a new point in your life, and you don't have time for me."

He doesn't hesitate, quietly saying, "I always have time for my best friend."

Those two words settle into my heart, resonating. That's what we are, that's what we have been and that's what we'll always be. Meg was right, Shawn was right…I was just too scared to admit it. I swallow at the lump in my throat, guilt rising up for the pain I'm about to cause Sebastian.

Except he speaks before I can. "I know I'm more distracted than usual lately, and I haven't been a good boyfriend—or even friend. But I love you, Leah." His pause holds a weight I don't want to face. "I know you love me too, but you and I were never going to last. You picked me because I'm safe, and you needed that after what happened last year."

The truth hits me hard. Relief unwinds the tension in my gut because I'm not devastating him. Then another wave of guilt has me ducking my head.

I used him.

"Don't you dare feel guilty." He grabs my hand. "It's been a privilege dating you. I can't believe you put up with me for as long as you have."

I stare at our joined hands, a wave of affection surging through me. "Thank you, Sebastian." I mean it with every fiber of my being.

"Promise me something?" One side of his mouth ticks up. "Go on Spring Break." His fingers tighten on mine. "It's not my scene, and you'll have more fun without me. Promise you'll go?"

How can I say no after everything he has done? A trickle of excitement flutters through me, pushing away the lingering guilt. "Okay, I promise."

We finish our night with more ease between us, and the rest of the weekend flies by. We read side by side on the couch, play games, eat together. I expect things to be awkward at some point, but everything feels normal.

Another sign that breaking up was the right move.

The following Wednesday, I sink onto the couch in our sitting room, wincing when my scraped side hits the cushion. Meg greets me, but I barely manage a wave. The library was a zoo today with everyone prepping for midterms, and I'm exhausted. I watch Meg check her reflection in the full-length mirror hooked to the closed bathroom door.

She is stunning in a dark red halter top. A black mini skirt combined with heels make her curvy legs look a mile long, despite her being several inches shorter than me.

"Hot date?" I ask.

"Yep, Chad from my English class finally asked me out. We're going to Club 42." She shimmies in front of me. Club 42 is swanky, the place to be. "What are you up to?"

"Sebastian and I are going to dinner, then we'll hit the bookstore." I sigh.

"You okay?"

"Yeah. It's just…I thought breaking up with Sebastian would be awkward, but here I am going to dinner with him. Like we always do." I wrinkle my nose. "I'm ready for a change."

"Maybe you'll meet someone on Spring Break."

The idea of meeting and falling for a total stranger makes me shiver. I'm not ready for a leap like that. Before Vance? Sure, it's something I could have done without thinking twice about.

But I'm not that person anymore.

Meg dabs at the bow of her mouth with her lip gloss, then spins around. "How do I look?"

I take my time, knowing she wants my honest opinion. "Gorgeous, as always."

She grins then comes over to pat my shoulder. "I know it seems weird that it isn't weird, but that just shows you made the right choice."

The words bolster me, reminding me of what I already know. I place my hand on hers. "Thanks."

"Meg, your latest boy's here!" Silas shouts from the other room.

She waves then crosses her fingers. I wave back, waiting till she shuts our door to shuck off my top and see the extent of injury. Frowning, I stand in front of the mirror. A big pink scratch stretches from my hip to below my left breast. That's what I get for only half-paying attention when shelving books. *Stupid, sharp-cornered book cart.*

Chapter Eight

Shawn

Meg and Silas glare at each other on her way out of the door. Those two are always sniping at one another. I'm not sure what happened because they got along fine while we were growing up. More than once I thought maybe they'd get together. But things changed between them after Lee's incident with Vance.

Of course, we all changed. A person can't get through that without something becoming different.

After Meg leaves, I glance at the door to Lee's sitting room. My big Spanish paper is due Monday, and I really want Lee to check it over first. I haven't asked her for help since the library catastrophe. It's not that I don't need it, I just haven't figured out how to change things between us.

Then she and Sebastian officially broke up, and I *really* didn't know what to do.

But Spring Break is barely a week away, and I need to start bridging this gap. Spanish has always been a neutral place for us, so I figure on killing two birds with one stone.

Squaring my shoulders, I walk up to the door to her suite which is open a crack, tapping on it while I push inside. "Hey, Lee, do you—?"

She yelps as she turns to face me, her torso bare except for her lacy blue bra. A large pink scratch spans her abdomen, but I can't tear my gaze away from her breasts. The lace barely hides her perfect nipples, which peak as I stare.

And I can't help wondering if it's because the air is cool or because of my attention.

I swallow at the dryness in my throat as she jumps to action, grabbing her top and clutching it to her chest. I should move. I should go back to the living room and give her privacy, but I'm frozen. The creamy glimpse of her mostly bare shoulders won't let me go.

Her glare spurs me out of my stupor, and I reach for my cocky confidence. Maybe if I act like nothing's wrong, it'll put her more at ease? So I lean casually against the frame. "What? It's nothing I haven't seen before."

"Out!" she shouts, pointing a finger as her gorgeous blue eyes flash.

I can't help one last peek before I smirk then step back into the living room. I shut the door behind me. Firmly. I rest my shoulder against the wooden barrier, wondering just how rattled she is.

Because I still need help with that paper.

"I know this may not be the best time to ask, but will you run through Spanish with me tomorrow?"

She doesn't respond right away. I picture her still clutching that shirt to her chest as she thinks. I shove the image away, needing to think about other things so my pants aren't straining.

At last, she answers, "Fine, but I want breakfast out of the deal."

I relax at her agreement. It's been a while since we've done that, and it aligns perfectly with my goals. "Deal," I call back, and I can't resist adding one parting comment. "Never pictured you as the lacy type. Looks good on you."

Her stomping footsteps make their way to her bedroom, and her frustrated growl makes me chuckle. For the first time since the night at the library, I feel like I can do this. That the canyon between us isn't too far to cross.

Silas tilts his head curiously. As I plop beside him, he asks, "Wanna fill us in?"

Steven arches an eyebrow, but I shake my head. "Nothing for you to worry about."

The basketball game snags their attention once more, taking the pressure off me. When Leah emerges half an hour later, I clench my jaw so it doesn't drop open. Her outfit isn't much different than usual, but her long-sleeved blouse is unbuttoned enough to get a glimpse of her perfect cleavage. And my mind quickly fills in the blanks about what's underneath.

Her jeans hug her hips, accentuating her curves and her hair rests in flowy waves on her shoulders. Her eyes pop even more than normal, and her lashes seem longer. But she doesn't even spare us a glance as she sashays upstairs.

Hopefully my absent-minded brother is ready. I might give Leah a heart attack if I swoop in and take his place as her date. But if she comes down alone, I'm sure as hell not letting her pout in her room the rest of the night.

Please, Sebastian, be ready.

Two sets of voices carry downstairs, Leah asking if Sebastian even had lunch today followed by his resigned negative response.

"Then we'll eat first." Halfway down the stairs, she pauses to ask, "Do you have your phone?"

He pats his pockets, coming up empty and she sighs before he hurries back upstairs.

I have a sudden, desperate need for a drink, so I hop off the couch, pausing near the landing as I check her out once more. "Still wearing the same thing?"

She frowns, and I can practically read her thoughts, that she obviously changed her outfit. Except I'm not talking about her outer clothes. I smirk when understanding dawns, and her cheeks tinge with pink.

I don't want her embarrassed though. Pissed off is always better than being unsure of herself, so I rack my mind for something more to say. Anything to tick her off that won't make me look like a complete asshole.

But she reaches that point on her own. Her flush heightens as her eyes flash and she raises her chin. Her hands clench as her nostrils flare. "It's none of your business, Shawn."

My mouth goes dry, seeing her almost crackling with anger. I can't even respond, just stand there staring like an idiot as I drink her in. Sebastian appears on the landing, and I jerk back to reality as he grins at me.

"You ready?" Lee asks him. At his nod, she tosses her hair then stalks away, bumping her shoulder into me as she passes.

I swipe a hand over my face as she flounces outside, the latching door allowing me to breathe again.

Sebastian chuckles as he walks over to pull on his shoes. "I have a conference this weekend. You guys will have to make sure Leah's not secluding herself the entire time." His words are addressed to all of us, but his attention lingers on me.

Right. I have a bargain to live up to. "We're doing Spanish and breakfast tomorrow."

A pleased grin crosses his face, and I know he understands that I'm trying.

After he leaves, I grab a bottle of water then attempt to watch the game, but thoughts of how to win Leah over keep circling in my head. One game finishes and another starts before she and Sebastian return. She comes in first, holding the door for Sebastian who has an armload of books.

He chatters happily about his latest obsession — kangaroos. "Did you know they can have three babies at once? One in the womb, one in the pouch, and one joey. They can even produce two kinds of milk simultaneously."

I think I hear Lee sigh as she shuts the door behind him. He barely says goodnight before hurrying to his room — to hole up with his new books, no doubt.

Lee takes the empty end of the couch that I'm on, and Steven turns down the volume before asking, "Did you even get a word in?"

She nods, immediately putting on a bright face. "We had fun. He's excited about the conference this weekend, and now I know all about kangaroos." Her expression softens as she adds, "Although we did talk in depth about anthropology."

She smiles right at me, sending a tingle up my abdomen to spread through my chest. She took my words to heart, and I can't help smiling back.

A bag still hangs from her wrist. I nod to it. "Did you find anything at the bookstore?"

She lights up, hurrying to pull out her books. She gushes over a fantasy book she's been wanting for weeks. Then there's *The Catcher in the Rye*, in great condition, which she can't wait to add to her classics shelf. Beneath both of those are two romance books, half-naked people on the covers.

Which gives me an idea, and I snap my fingers. "Hey, you're just the person to ask."

"What?" she says warily.

I make up a story on the spot. "So, we're doing this thing for English where we pick a…" I can't remember the word. It's not topic. It's not scenario. I frown as I think. "What's the gimmick of the book called? Like when two people pretend to date then fall in love because of it?"

"Fake dating?"

Frustration bubbles in me. "Yeah, but fake dating is one example."

"Oh! You mean trope!"

"Yes!" I beam and she leans back as if my exuberance startled her. I try to take it down a notch. "So we have to pick a trope and read a couple books on it, then write a report about it."

"That sounds fun. What trope did you pick?"

I say confidently, "Enemies to lovers." *I hope that's what it's called.*

"Ooh, that's a good one." She jumps up off the couch as my brothers stare at me like I've grown a second head.

But I ignore them, trailing after her into her sitting room. A few moments later, she emerges with her arms full of books with brawny, bare-chested men on the covers, each holding a precariously dressed lady.

If I read these in public, I'll be teased for the rest of my life. I clear my throat. "Do you have anything, um, a little more...subtle?"

She tips her head back and laughs before she lines the books up on the sofa. "This is what I've got. Take it or leave it."

I reach for one, reading the back and blinking at the tension in those few short paragraphs. "Damn, sounds intense." I replace it, staring at my choices and feeling completely lost. "What do you recommend?"

Another laugh echoes between us before she picks up two books. One has a pink cover, but only the title and the author's name decorate it otherwise. The other has a man in a kilt on the front, his torso and leg bare, dipping the lady back in his arms as his blond hair blows in a non-existent wind. The lady's dress is opened to show off the side of her breast, and an image of Lee in her lacy blue bra rises unbidden in my mind.

I yank my gaze away as she chatters about the books. Saying this is for English is absolute bull shit, but my interest in the subject matter is one hundred percent real. If these characters can become lovers after being enemies, then perhaps Lee can actually become my friend. Maybe more.

Though the more is yet to be determined.

"I'll take them." I manage a smile, stacking the one without pictures on top of the other.

"Um..." She stifles a giggle with her hand. "Don't forget they have a back."

I frown then flip the kilt one over to see an equally risqué picture on the back cover. I resist a groan, tucking it more into the crook of my arm. Hopefully I can get upstairs before my brothers see them.

As she gathers the rest of the books, I find myself reluctant to leave. "So...you guys talked about anthropology?"

Her face brightens as she nods, walking toward her room. I follow to hover in the doorway as she answers. "Yep. It felt good saying it out loud, you know?"

I make a noncommittal hum as she bends over to put the books on the shelf. I don't trust my voice not to crack at the delicious view of her pert ass.

"He said I'd probably need a master's degree, but it's a wide field. I could work in museums, labs, universities or even go do hands-on discoveries of my own." She stands, turning around with pink cheeks. "He thinks it'd be a good fit for me. Said I excel at writing papers and reports and do well with analyzing data."

"I bet that felt good." Sebastian doesn't give compliments lightly.

She studies me before she nods. "It did."

The silence between us turns awkward, and I rub the back of my neck. "Well, I know Sebastian ditched you, but you're welcome to watch the rest of the game with us."

"Nah." She rests one hand on the door handle. "I've got some homework to catch up on."

"Maybe..." I don't want her to hole up in her room all night, and we need to work on being friends. So I throw out the one thing I know can entice her away from anything, even studying. "After the game, we should play some cards."

Her whole face lights up. "Just let me know when."

"I will." I thank her again, then awkwardly walk into the living room. Silas and Steven are engrossed in the game, so I hurry to the stairs before I holler, "Lee's up for euchre after the game."

I get two acknowledging grunts as I rush to my room to stuff the books in my nightstand drawer. When I get back downstairs, I reclaim my spot. But my focus keeps straying to the closed door of the sitting room and the beautiful woman inside.

Chapter Nine

Leah

An hour into studying, a knock sounds on the sitting room door, and I holler, "Come in."

Shawn pokes his head in. "Damn, you're dressed."

I sit upright on the sofa, giving him a dirty look as I close my book. "What's up?"

"Card time." He shoves the door all the way open as he saunters off.

I hurry after him, excitement rippling through me.

When we say cards, we mean euchre, a very Michigan card game needing four players. We all learned when we were little, but Sebastian abhors it. Silas and I, being the youngest, learned together, challenging Steven and Shawn any chance we got. We had our asses handed to us more times than I can count before we finally got the hang of it.

Now, it's a long-standing rivalry—me and Silas against Steven and Shawn.

"There she is! My partner's in the house," Silas cheers, fist bumping me as I enter the kitchen. "You guys are going down tonight." He shoves his finger in Shawn's chest as he walks by.

"Sit down," Steven says. "You won the deal."

We all settle into our seats, me across from Silas with Shawn on my right and Steven on my left. Our team starts off slow, my crap cards making it impossible to call trump. They're ahead by five points when I'm dealt an amazing hand, one I can play alone.

If I get to call trump.

I hold my breath, waiting for each guy to pass. Shawn turns the card over, and I call spades alone. I lay them down—one after another—managing to collect all the tricks. I score us four points and Silas and I high-five across the table. The rest of the game goes fast, and we pull ahead to win by two.

I scoot back from the table after the last hand. "Popcorn?" Everyone agrees, and I hurry to the pantry.

As I pull out two bags of microwave popcorn, Shawn turns on the Bluetooth speaker we keep in the kitchen for party purposes. "I got a song for you, Lee."

I half-listen as I put the popcorn in the microwave and pull out bowls. Britney's *Lace and Leather* blares. I turn to scowl at him then go back to making our snack.

"No?" He smirks. "How about this one?" And *Chantilly Lace* by the Big Bopper plays.

"How about you knock it off, or you don't get any popcorn?"

He chuckles as the chorus comes to a close then switches to a more normal playlist—one not geared toward my underthings. While the second bag pops away, I decide I want a beer. Of course, the guys all want one too. An idea blooms, and I grin at the wickedness of it.

I sneakily shake the crap out of Shawn's beer. When I dole out the cans, I hand the special one to Shawn then hurry out of range. Foam sprays him right in the face, exploding all over his chest and arms.

He hollers in shock, scooting back from the table. I bat my eyes, the picture of innocence as he glares at me, dripping. Silas springs up to toss him a towel.

I set the bowls of popcorn down then grab his phone. "I've got a song for you."

Elvis' *All Shook Up* blasts through the kitchen over the laughter of Silas and Steven. I get high-fives from both of them, then I turn toward Shawn again as he stands.

His white shirt is now see-through.

It plasters to his body, clinging to each dent and defined muscle. My mouth goes dry at the unexpected sight of him, and I can't look away. His glare is replaced with the same intensity from earlier, when he caught me shirtless.

His eyes smolder as he murmurs, "Now you know how I felt." His shoulder knocks gently into mine as he leaves the room.

It doesn't take much time to clean up the chair and floor, just long enough to compose myself. Luckily, the cards were unscathed.

"Oh, it's on, Lee," Shawn promises when he returns in dry clothes. But a hint of amusement underlines the threat, lingering while his team proceeds to kick butt.

For once, he doesn't act like he hates me. I almost feel like we're on the same page, maybe even the same side. I practically float through the next two games despite Silas and I getting our asses handed to us. After they score the final point, I push back from the table, needing a bathroom break.

Knowing Shawn will take full advantage of me being gone to pull a prank, I wait to grab a new beer on my return. When I sit down and pick up my cards, I'm met with a handful of twos and threes — cards not used in this game. I laugh as I wait for Shawn to produce my real hand.

Five games later, we're tied up. We decide to play one last game before heading to bed, and Silas and I trounce them. Silas pulls me out of my chair to do a victory lap around the kitchen as he sings *We Are the Champions*. When he's done, I offer to clean up, then I hug Silas and Steven good night.

The song changes to *You'll Accomp'ny Me* by Bob Seger, and I turn to find Shawn handing me the empty popcorn bowls. I frown. "I didn't know you liked Bob Seger."

He smirks, enigmatic as always. "I do right now."

We finish cleaning as he quietly sings along. I grab the dishrag, spinning around only to plow into his solid chest. His fingers grip my forearms to steady me, though it has the opposite effect, and I'm lightheaded as I step away.

The big kitchen feels too small. We keep bumping into each other, no matter how I try to avoid him. I jump when his hand slides across my lower back as he scoots past. Each brush twists the rubber band of tension in me until I'm afraid it will snap.

I imagine that for a moment, wondering what it would look like. Would I yell in frustration? Or launch myself at him? The idea startles me, so I push it aside, feeling even more unsettled.

At last, the kitchen is spotless, which is good because I can't handle another second in here. The tension inside me has grown so taut that one more casual brush might shatter me. I set the dishrag down only to gape when Shawn opens his arms for a hug.

Like I gave his brothers.

Saying no would be rude, so I hold my breath as I shuffle into his embrace, wondering what alternate universe I've stepped into.

He wraps his arms around me and squeezes, picking me up off the floor. A thrill zips through me and I gasp. His familiar heady scent of sandalwood and balsam envelopes me, making my head spin even more.

When he sets me down, he is all playfulness as he ruffles my hair. "Night, Lee."

I shove him lightly and call over my shoulder. "Don't forget about my breakfast!" I head to bed, grateful I sound casual when I'm feeling anything but.

* * * *

The next morning, I'm up early enough to catch Sebastian before he leaves for his conference. It's a good thing too because when I ask if he has his phone charger, he sighs then tromps back upstairs. He gives me a hug before heading out.

His embraces are like warm hot chocolate — soothing and comforting. I picture Shawn's playful hug from last night. It was more like Vanilla Coke, sweeter than ordinary Coke, and too much of it would get someone all hyped up. Then I pull myself up short, realizing I'm comparing Shawn to Sebastian. I frown and shake my head.

Ten minutes later, Shawn appears, yawning. "Make it or go out?"

His deep voice is still thick with sleep. His hair sticks up every which way, begging me to tame it. A coating of morning stubble shadows his jaw. His tank top shows off his muscular arms, and I have to kick myself to get my thoughts in gear. He drums his fingers on the back of the couch, waiting for my answer.

"Ummm." I make a quick decision. "Out. Give me five minutes."

I dash to my room to throw on jeans, a T-shirt and hoodie then weave my hair into two braids. When I come back to the living room, he zips up his sweatshirt, shoves a baseball cap over his bedhead, then glances at me.

I shove my hands in my hoodie pocket. "Ready."

After hoisting his backpack over his shoulder, Shawn opens the door. I haven't even peeked outside, and I'm relieved to see the sun out and the sky clear. Early March in Michigan is always a crap shoot. A breeze makes things chilly, but I enjoy the brisk walk to Eat at Joe's.

The moment we step inside, we speak only Spanish to one another. It's tradition — great for practicing conversational skills and pronunciation, not to mention vocabulary. I always enjoy our breakfasts. It's the one time I can count on having fun with Shawn. Maybe because he hasn't learned enough Spanish to tease me.

I don't even need a menu, wanting the same thing I always get. It's called The Mess. A dish with potatoes, lots of veggies and diced ham, topped with scrambled eggs and cheese.

After we order, the waitress hurries back with our coffee. I put flavored creamer in mine, but Shawn takes his black. He slides me his latest Spanish paper while I sip my steaming java. He shifts in his seat as I read, and I meet his nervous gaze. He's adorable like this, a state I rarely get to see him in.

I'm pleasantly surprised to only find a few syntax errors. "*Buen trabajo.*" *Good job.*

His relief is evident as he slouches back against the booth. "*Gracias.*"

We conjugate irregular verbs until our food comes out, piping hot. I take a mouthful too soon, blowing as I chew, waving my hand in front of my mouth. Shawn laughs, sipping his coffee and taking his sweet time before his first bite.

"*¿Cuales son tus planes para Sábado y Domingo?*" he asks. *What are your plans for Saturday and Sunday?*

I shrug, the empty weekend looming before me. "*Tal vez Meg y yo tengamos una fiesta de pijamas.*" *Maybe Meg and I will have a sleepover.*

He bobs his eyebrows. "*¿Puedo venir?*" *Can I come?*

I groan, but I'm grinning. "*Lo siento, no llevo encage at fiestas de pijamas.*" *Sorry, I don't wear lace to sleepovers.*

A burst of laughter escapes him even as his eyebrows shoot up in surprise. My cheeks heat, but I cover it with a sip of my coffee.

"*Lee, si no lo supiera mejor, jiria que estas coquetando conmigo.*" *If I didn't know better, I'd think you're flirting with me.*

I duck my head. Is that what I was doing? Flirting? I stab at my food, shoving a bite in my mouth to keep from responding.

That's as far as he pushes it, thankfully. Except I don't have an answer for myself by the time breakfast is over. I don't know what to make of this side of Shawn. First the way he stared at me when I was topless, then helping me clean the kitchen and initiating a hug. Now, gentle teasing and banter?

Who is this man? And why does he suddenly not hate me?

After he pays our bill, we head out, switching back to English. "You're definitely improving," I say as we walk down the sidewalk.

"Was that a compliment?"

I shrug. "Well, you are."

And he doesn't wipe that smug smile off his face the entire way home.

Chapter Ten

Shawn

After breakfast, I pull my running gear on, itching to move. I can't help smiling—breakfast was fun today, more so than usual. Lee's audacious lace comment floored me, but it also gave me hope. Then she topped it by actually complimenting me.

This day couldn't get any better.

I hurry out the door, waving to Meg and Lee who sit on the couch as Meg gushes about her latest date. I hear the name Chad but don't pay it much attention, knowing how quickly she goes through guys.

I flip through my mental checklist for today as my strides eat up the pavement. I need to fix the things Lee pointed out in my Spanish paper. I have an assignment for Lit class—not the trope thing. Although I do want to read another couple chapters in Lee's book.

I started the one with the guy in the kilt last night, and to my surprise, it hooked me. I can't wait to read more. In the privacy of my bedroom, of course.

As I finish my loop, I slow to a cool down pace until I reach my front steps. I walk inside, mopping my forehead with the hem of my shirt. Leah and Meg are still on the couch, and Leah's eyes widen when she sees me.

Or more accurately, the bare strip of my torso.

I smirk and take my time, not minding in the least that she's checking me out. But she clears her throat, and a wicked smile crosses her face.

"Shawn," she says, pulling out her phone. "I've got a song for you."

I know what it is before the first notes start. *All Shook Up*, the same song she teased me with last night blasts through the air. I glare at her, but don't mean it. Inside I'm doing flips that she's teasing me so casually.

She laughs, a tinkling sound I revel in. I wish I could show her how I really feel, but it's too soon. So I keep up the act and growl, raising my middle finger as I head upstairs to shower. As I go through the motions of washing, I try to figure out how I can rope her into spending time with me this weekend. The days are counting down till Spring Break, and I need to keep up this momentum. I want her to be this comfortable with me all the time.

My brain isn't coming through for me though, and I yank on a comfy pair of gray sweatpants and a clean black tee, annoyed. I stalk into my room, noticing the book on my nightstand. Maybe I can get some ideas from it. Or at least let my brain mull over the situation while I'm distracted.

The bed bounces as I fall onto it. Two more chapters down, and the main characters are already kissing. I'm jealous of how fast things move in the fictional world.

Silas strolls by, whistling an unrecognizable tune. Before I can change my mind, I call his name. He backs up, popping into my room and raising his eyebrows in a silent *"what's up?"*

Shit. Now that he's here, I don't know if I can say it.

He bursts out laughing. "You really got yourself into a jam this time, doncha bro?"

I frown, wondering if he really knows what's going on.

He rests his back against the door frame, jerking his chin toward the stairway. "Yes, I noticed you chasing after Lee. What gives?"

I sag, relief and anxiety churning my stomach as I tell him the whole story.

"Personally?" he says when I finish. "I think you two would be perfect for each other. There's some obvious chemistry there." His approval eases my tension, but he blows me away when he continues, "What do you need from me?"

This is why I love my brothers. We always have each other's backs.

The new Marvel movie came out last weekend and it's not unusual for a group of us to go. Lee often drags Sebastian along, despite the fact that he hates movie theaters and superheroes. With him gone, I feel extra awkward asking Lee myself, so I mention the idea to Silas.

He lifts a shoulder. "I know Steven's busy tomorrow, but I'll go. Maybe I'll even bring a date and ditch you afterwards, you know, throw in some forced proximity."

I recognize the phrase and scrunch up my brow as I try to recall where I've heard it. "Isn't that a trope?"

His grin is full of mischief. "You're not the only one who reads smut."

The admission surprises me, and I shake my head as he saunters off, resuming his awful whistling. *I never would have thought...*

That evening, Silas asks Lee about going to the movies while I'm in earshot. Once she agrees, I casually throw out that I'd like to come. Neither one objects, and I feel like I won an Olympic gold medal.

My mind doesn't stop playing out how the outing could go. If Silas gets a girl to show up, maybe I can even pay for Lee, like a real date. I watch a slow-motion fantasy play out before me, my image slinging my arm around Leah, offering her our shared popcorn. Warmth spreads through my chest when she doesn't object.

The next day, the hours drag until it's time to leave. I make sure to wear a hoodie, in case she gets cold. I can picture it, my too big hoodie swallowing her, and an ache fills my chest. I push it aside as we all pile into my car. The ride is casual and comfortable, filled with laughing and teasing. As we walk inside the theater, a girl calls out Silas' name.

Silas' dates always make me feel...off. Every single one has something in common with Meg, despite the tension between them. And this girl is more like her than most. Short in stature, long dark hair that hangs to her waist, curves, heels and a bright smile.

"Who's that?" Lee asks.

Silas shrugs. "A girl from the coffee shop." Where he works part-time. He grins as the girl hurries over to fling her arms around him. "What are you doing here, Morgan?"

"Oh, I was supposed to meet some friends, but they bailed. What are you doing?" She bats her eyelashes innocently.

Lee's expression grows stonier when Silas invites Morgan to sit with us, and I try to lighten the mood by nudging her. "Hey, you've still got me." I hoped she wouldn't be too upset, that she'd at least give this a chance.

But she scoffs. "Shawn, I've never had you."

"Well, this is your big chance. A once in a lifetime shot to be my date to the newest Marvel movie."

Her forehead furrows as she studies me. "Yeah, right," she finally mutters, stepping away and shaking her head.

I shove my hands in my pockets, feeling a dark cloud move in above me as we wait our turn for the ticket counter. What was I thinking? On what planet would Leah ever consider going out with me? When Silas chuckles at something Morgan says then wraps his arm around her, envy stabs me. That casual touch, that easy air—neither will ever happen with me and Lee.

I pay for my ticket, knowing Leah will refuse if I offer to buy hers, but I decide to go down swinging. I tell her firmly, "I'm getting enough popcorn to share. No arguments." I'm not sure why it's so important, but I need this.

Her sigh is exasperated although she nods. Slightly mollified, I go fill my drink while she gets her ticket. It may not be a date, but at least she doesn't hate me so much that she refuses to share a popcorn. A small win, but I'll take it.

As we settle into our seats, Morgan ruins everything by leaning across Silas to ask Leah, "How long have you two been together?"

Leah shoots one glance at me then doubles over, letting out a belly laugh that echoes through the theater. She even slaps her thigh. The motion cements my bad mood, knowing our chances of being anything more are next to none. Silas shoots me a sympathetic look, but I grit my teeth, focusing on the screen.

What a shit show.

The dark cloud above me rumbles. Why did I ever think this would work? I can't believe Silas and Sebastian even encouraged me. This is stupid. I hold my popcorn in one hand, bouncing my leg as I look straight ahead.

"Hey." Lee nudges me. "What are you sulking about?"

I don't answer, leaning away as I fold my arms.

"At least share some of that popcorn you promised me."

Maybe if I ignore her, she'll go back to thinking I hate her and we can return to how we were. Lee continuing her journey to become her old self. Me not having my hopes crashed on the rocky shores of reality.

She snorts. "Oh, now you're not going to share? After that tantrum you threw? I guess I'd better go get my own."

I grit my teeth. When she stands, my hand flies out of its own accord to clamp over her wrist. I give a sharp tug, silently demanding she sit, then I thrust the bag of popcorn into her lap and cross my arms once more.

She pops a piece into her mouth, looking smug. "Thanks." Then she reaches into her purse and pulls out a box of Raisinets. "Want one?"

My eyelids lower halfway as I give her my driest glare. I hate raisins. Everything about them — with or without chocolate — makes me want to vomit.

"Just being polite."

I turn back toward the screen, ignoring the rustling from her direction.

"Maybe these are more your speed."

She sets a bag of plain M&Ms on top of where my arms meet. I blink at the offering, surprised by my favorite candy. I work my jaw back and forth as I consider what this means.

Maybe this isn't a date. But she remembered my favorite candy, agreed to share my popcorn and teased me about not liking raisins. It's a step in the right direction, and I can live with that.

The black cloud begins to dissipate, and I ease my arm out from under the candy, grabbing it as one corner of my mouth tips up. I straighten, risking a glance at her. She tosses a handful of popcorn into her mouth, casually chewing as if waiting.

For me.

A full smile spreads over my lips, and I shake my head at her smug smirk then reach toward the popcorn. "Give me some of that."

I bump her shoulder and hog the arm rest between us. She fights back for a second, giving up when I relinquish half of it. My hope buoys once more.

I add a quiet, "And thanks."

Her lips part then she swallows and her nonchalance returns. "Any time."

The movie is great. Lee and I have a running stream of snarky commentary the whole way through. She predicts the plot twist, and I throw a piece of popcorn at her when she's right. She picks it off her chest and eats it, making it hard to look away.

Morgan gets up as soon as the credits start, and Lee cries, "Wait! Don't leave!"

The words are almost an order, and Morgan leaps back into her seat. I try to stifle my laughter as Silas shoots us both a glare then calmly explains about the extra clips we always stay for. But after the first one is over, she tries to leave again.

"This one's not too bright, is she?" I whisper to Lee.

She snorts, and I try not to laugh as Silas gives me a dirty look before talking Morgan into sitting down again. Once the clips are done, we head to the lobby. I wait for Lee to get out of the bathroom, studying Silas as he pushes a piece of hair back behind Morgan's ear. Even her laugh is so similar to Meg's.

I wrinkle my nose.

"What's that look for?" Lee says, startling me.

"Oh, I…" I swipe my hand over my face. "Is it just me or does Morgan remind you of Meg?"

"Definitely," she says. "Most of his girls do. He really has a type."

We stare for another moment before I ask, "Do you know what happened between them?"

She lifts a shoulder. "Your guess is as good as mine. Meg tells me everything, except that. The topic of Silas is completely off limits with her."

Silas saunters over, his arm slung around Morgan's waist. "Well, I'm going home with Morgan. You two have fun." He waves, then guides her out the door.

I didn't think far enough ahead for this. "Um, home?" Could I sound any more lame? I want to smack my forehead, but I refrain, wishing I had a plan. Anything to prolong this time with Lee.

"Yeah, I've got some more reading to catch up on."

"Okay." It's hard not to deflate, and I get in my head on the ride, berating myself the whole way. I punch on the radio so I don't have to talk, focusing on being annoyed with myself.

I give her the world's most awkward wave when we get inside then hurry upstairs before I make a bigger fool of myself. The house is empty though. I blink at the realization that it's only me and Lee. Maybe I haven't lost my chance after all.

I scramble into sweatpants, grab the romance novel and head back downstairs to tap on her door. I can't help drinking her in when she opens it. The way her hair is casually tucked into a messy bun combined with her hoodie and soft plaid lounge pants has my dick twitching. I want to cuddle the shit out of her.

Her eyebrows shoot up.

"I was just…" I show her the book. "No one else is home, so don't feel like you have to hide out in here. I'm going to read on the couch." I shrug. "You know, if you want some company."

Her lips tip, and she nods. "I'd love that."

I settle in at one end of the couch as she emerges with her book, which looks decidedly less romantic than mine.

"*The Scarlet Letter*," she says, with a longing sigh geared toward the novel in my hands. "Which part are you at?"

My cheeks go hot as I describe the scene in the garden where their kiss went a little too far for what was proper, but her amusement makes it all worth it. Soon, she's engrossed in her book, lounging across the couch.

The air between us is comfortable now, not the least bit awkward. Exactly as I had hoped.

Chapter Eleven

Leah

The week leading up to Spring Break is a flurry of assignments, library shifts, and hanging with Meg. The morning of our departure dawns. Or doesn't, since Steven insists on leaving before the sun even thought of rising.

I'm not looking forward to fourteen hours in the SUV with three tall guys. Leg room will be a precious commodity. Steven sits in the driver's seat, Silas shotgun, and Shawn stands next to the car, drumming his fingers on the car roof. He seems particularly grumpy this morning.

Sebastian got up to see us off, and I linger in the driveway to say goodbye to him. "Good luck with your presentation. Let me know how it goes."

"Thanks. Text me when you make it to the condo, okay?" He pushes his glasses further up his nose.

"Let's go!" Shawn yells, punctuating his command by opening the door and gesturing for me to get in.

But I hesitate. A week of vacation stretches before me. Trey and Judy love to spoil us rotten, so I bet I'll get some free food out of the deal. Plus a free place to stay, warm weather, a beautiful beach. I should be over the moon.

Except I'm going on a trip without the security blanket of my two best friends.

I must look as uncertain as I feel because Sebastian pulls me into a hug, murmuring, "Shawn promised he'd be on his best behavior."

Shawn chooses that moment to lean through Steven's open window and lay on the horn until Steven shoves him away.

I glare at Shawn, then burrow back in Sebastian's arms, muttering, "If that's his best behavior…"

Sebastian squeezes me once more before he steps away. "You'll have a good time, plus you need this."

He's right. It's been so long since I've done anything for fun, and the beach is calling my name. With one last wave, I hitch up my courage and my backpack, glaring as I walk by Shawn before I climb into the backseat of the car.

"About time," he grumbles. After shutting my door harder than necessary, he hurries around to slide into the backseat next to me.

Steven doesn't even wait until I'm buckled before pulling out of the driveway. Silas has earbuds in, playing air guitar in the front seat with way too much energy for this early hour. I tuck my backpack between me and Shawn, wondering how I'll survive fourteen hours in this cramped space.

Especially with Shawn already grumping at me.

He glares again, and I stick my tongue out. He shakes his head, slipping in his own earbuds and turning toward the window. I follow suit, pushing play on a random playlist. As I lean my head on the glass, I watch the scenery roll by and let the music speed us along.

After one break, Silas talks Steven into letting him drive, and I get shotgun. Shawn promptly falls asleep in the back seat. His soft snores fill the car as I share a chuckle with Silas. At the next stop, we all take a minute to stretch before ambling into the gas station.

Shawn walks by my side, and I nudge him. "So, is snoring the latest form of meditation?"

He glares, but the corner of his mouth twitches before he stomps away. I grab Reese's Cups and a Coke, standing outside as long as possible before Steven demands I get in. I do, reluctantly, settling in behind Silas. The problem with Steven at the wheel is that he doesn't like to stop. It's all about making good time.

After another hour, my legs are cramping, and I'm dying to stretch out. That middle seat looks less and less appealing, making me thankful Sebastian didn't come. Talk about no leg room. I groan, shifting again.

Shawn glances over, his expression softening as I rub my knee. "I have an idea." He grabs his backpack from the middle of the seat, stashing it on the floor. Then he gestures for me to do the same.

I frown before I follow suit.

He pats his lap. "Feet up here." My hesitation must annoy him because he tugs on my pant leg until I comply, lifting both my calves to rest on his thighs. Then he swings his legs over, straightening them so his feet land in the space behind Silas, and our bodies form a big X.

It feels so good to stretch. I point my toes, flex my calves and let out a long, contented sigh as Shawn chuckles. I tilt my head. "Yeah, okay, good idea."

A stunning grin lights his face, but it disappears so fast, I wonder if it even happened. I fall asleep not long afterwards, waking up when the car stops. The harsh interior light has me blinking, and a sweatshirt falls to my lap as I sit up. I frown in confusion, glancing at Shawn.

He shrugs. "You looked cold, all curled up in a little ball."

Now that he mentions it, my knees are tucked up on the seat, wedged between us. I've been hogging all the space. My cheeks grow warm as I return his hoodie. "Thanks."

"No problem." His lips tilt up.

"We made good time," Steven says. "It's barely eight p.m."

I ignore his gloating as we all tromp up to the second-story condo together. Trey and Judy greet us with exuberant hellos and hugs. Trey grills the guys about traffic and routes while I wander across the living room to the open sliding glass door. The warm evening air wafts in, filtered by the screen that leads to the balcony. I shove it open and step onto the balcony. Judy follows.

We lean against the rail as I drink in the view. "It's beautiful. Thanks again for letting us stay here." The building is a couple blocks from the water but high enough that I can see the ocean sprawling before me. I bet sunrise here is gorgeous.

"Sebastian told me you guys split up," Judy says tentatively.

I'm not surprised she knows. They're all close to her.

"I wanted to see for myself that you're okay. I know how he can be. He didn't mess things up, did he?"

Guilt pricks me again, and I shake my head. "Oh no, not at all. He's been busier since he's presenting more, but we decided we're better off as friends."

I turn around, the hard iron biting into my back as I lean against it. "Actually, he was amazing," I say softly. "He helped me through some really difficult times and never pushed me beyond what I was comfortable with. I'm so lucky he's my best friend."

She rests her hand on my arm. "I can't tell you how happy I am to hear that."

Shawn moves, catching my attention as he turns his head away, though his torso is still angled toward the balcony. He's closest to us, and I bet with the way the breeze is blowing, my words carry to him.

I decide to take a chance. "You have some amazing sons. I'm thankful everyday—for all of them."

Shawn may be grumpy and he may hate me, but he's been there when I needed him. He glances our way, freezing when his gaze collides with mine. He ducks his head, this time turning his body completely. But not before I glimpse his smile.

Judy pats my arm. "I think they're the lucky ones."

My cheeks go hot, and it's my turn to duck my head.

"We want to take you guys to dinner before we leave." She pauses at the threshold. "We keep hearing about this place that has amazing burgers, but Trey wanted to wait until the boys were here to try it out."

"Burgers sound great."

The guys are excited too, though my eagerness dims when I have to climb back into the car. I text Sebastian and Meg on the way, letting them know we made it safely. We pull into the parking lot behind Trey and Judy, and I read the sign — *Mugs 'N Jugs*. Weird name.

Shawn holds the door open, all hint of grumpiness from this morning gone. The hostess greets us, and I blink at the uniform — a tight, short shirt with the logo on front and shorts that show a lot of skin. Silas focuses on one waitress in particular, a pretty lady with jet black hair and legs for days.

Judy steps in, blinking in surprise before looking at Trey, who asks, "You up for trying the food?"

She glances at me, and I shrug. It doesn't bother me, and of course, the guys seem enthralled. As the hostess leads the way, I think about the name again, clapping a hand over my mouth to stifle my laughter.

"What?" Shawn asks.

I nod to a waitress. "Mugs..." I point to my face. "And jugs." I waggle my eyebrows as understanding lights his face.

He snorts out a laugh as I take in the décor. The dark wooden floors reflect the artfully scattered lights dangling from the ceiling with their metallic lampshades. Rows of bare wooden tables sit between the blue vinyl booths that flank each wall. The hostess leads us to a six-person table where I'm stuck between Shawn and Silas, no elbow room in sight.

I order a raspberry ale, listening to Trey and Judy interrogate each of the guys in turn. My favorite part is watching them lose concentration in the middle of a thought as a waitress walks by or bends over. Only Shawn seems to be immune. He answers each of their questions with no problem, and none of the employees make him crane his neck.

Even though I know several of them are his type — tall, athletic and smiley.

Now that I think about it, I haven't seen Shawn with anyone in months. Since around the time Sebastian and I started dating. I know he's under a lot of pressure to graduate this year, but that's unusual for him.

"How's school going, Leah?" Judy asks, jarring me from my thoughts about Shawn's love life.

He nudges me when I don't answer right away. "Tell them about your anthropology class, about how well you did on that paper."

I'm surprised he remembered. "I'm considering pursuing anthropology further, actually." I find myself looking at Shawn. Again.

He nods encouragingly.

I clear my throat then explain the premise of my paper. "So, the day they hand the papers back to us, I space out, only half-listening for my name. I panic when I never hear it." I press my lips together, still annoyed at myself. "I frantically run up to the TA and I'm like, 'you didn't call my name, but I turned in my paper. I swear.' She heaved the longest sigh." Which I demonstrate. "Then she points to a list of four names on the chalkboard. 'Is your name on that list?' I nod, beginning to feel I'd missed something important. 'Then, if you'd been paying attention, you'd know that your paper was chosen for its excellence, and you're supposed to present it at our next class.'"

I smack my hand against my forehead. "I could have died." Everyone laughs, and I can't help joining in.

Judy says, "But that's great, having your paper chosen. What an honor."

I nod, still smiling as they move on. When Shawn grins at me, my stomach flips so I take a drink of my raspberry ale to distract myself. Our food arrives. My bacon burger is as delicious as it was hyped up to be and the sweet potato fries are perfection.

Shawn keeps stealing them from my basket, until I smack his hand. "Dude, seriously!"

"Dude?" He raises his eyebrows. "I guess we really are at the beach."

I lean closer to hiss, "I didn't think yelling jackass was appropriate."

He just chuckles. "They're good fries."

"You *have* fries." I nod toward his almost full basket.

"Yours are better." He turns to me as he says it, and we're suddenly close — too close.

I scramble away, knocking my beer right into Shawn's lap. "Shit!"

He stands the glass upright as I grab for the extra napkins, pressing them to the wetness spreading over Shawn's thighs. He sucks in a sharp breath, catching my wrist and gently moving my hand.

Through gritted teeth, he says, "I've got it. Thanks."

I gape at him, even more horrified than before. I just had my hand —

I drop my forehead into my palm, realizing the table is still a puddle when my elbow ends up sopping wet. Everyone moves at once, helping us mop, telling me it's okay, pushing our food out of the way. I scoot my chair back and flee to the bathroom.

Even after I take my time in the stall and wash my hands, my cheeks are still red. I sigh as I dry off, wiping the damp paper towel over my sticky elbow. If it had been Silas, we'd make dick jokes for days. Or Steven. He'd say something stiff and awkward, making me feel better because I wouldn't be the only one floundering.

But no, it had to be Shawn. For once in his life, maybe he'll just let it go.

I suck in several deep breaths then walk out the door only to run smack into the damn guy. I bounce off his chest, jerking away as if burned.

His gaze drifts over me. "I see you escaped unscathed."

"From the beer anyways. I think my cheeks might be permanently pink." I try for casual teasing but the embarrassment of it all crashes down on me. I bury my face in my hands, and my words come out muffled. "I'm so sorry, Shawn."

"I know, Lee." He bumps me with his elbow. "It's okay."

I peek at him, surprised to find his expression matches the sincerity of his tone. "You're not going to tease me about it forever?"

He shifts his weight, a mischievous smirk crossing his lips. "I'll at least try to wait till tomorrow."

I lower my hands and let out a relieved sigh.

"Good thing I'm not trying to get a date tonight." He gestures to the darkened front of his khaki shorts. "Everyone knows ladies love a man who can't hold his liquor."

The twist on the phrase makes me laugh, relaxing me further. I wave him off. "Just flash that ridiculous smile you're always throwing around. You'll have them swooning in no time."

He stops in his tracks, turning to me in surprise. "Was that a compliment?"

I decide to roll with it, patting his shoulder to cover up the fresh embarrassment hitting me as we walk toward the table. "Least I could do after dousing you."

"You've always gotta be difficult, don't you?"

"Me? *I'm* the difficult one?" The casual teasing puts me completely at ease, and I give it right back. "Who ate all my fries?" I sniff. "I take back my compliment. You deserved a beer in your lap."

"Whatever, but do me a favor and give me a warning if you plan to cop another feel." He pauses to smirk before adding, "Maybe not in front of my parents."

I scowl as my cheeks start burning again, but he just laughs.

When we sit back down, no one mentions the incident. Conversation flows normally, and Shawn's shorts are almost dry by the time his parents pay the tab. We all head outside, realizing when we reach the car that Silas isn't with us.

Shawn sighs. "I'll get him."

Probably picking up that waitress. I chuckle to myself then hug Trey and Judy in turn. "Thanks for dinner, you guys. And for letting me tag along."

Trey nods, but Judy pulls me in for another hug and says, "Of course, sweetie. You're welcome anytime."

Shawn finally returns, dragging Silas behind him. The guys say their goodbyes, and we wave as their parents drive away.

Once they're gone, Silas pulls out his phone. "I got her number, and there's a big beach party tonight not far from our place. Who's in?"

Steven grins, Shawn shrugs and I yawn. We stop by the store for drinks and snacks then head back to the condo. The more they chatter about this party, the less appealing it sounds. I'm worn out from traveling and sick of being with people. I want nothing more than to curl up with my book after taking a long, hot shower.

At the condo, the guys have already worked out room assignments, insisting I have my own room. Steven pulled the 'I'm oldest' card, so he gets a room to himself, leaving Silas and Shawn to share the one with the king-sized bed. While the guys get ready, I unpack before changing into lounge pants and an oversized T-shirt. Then I perch on the couch, delving into the story while I wait for them to leave.

"Wait," Shawn says. "Aren't you coming, Lee?"

"Naw. I'm tired and gross." His concerned expression has me holding up my book. "Honestly, I just want to read."

He pauses packing the cooler, frowning. "You sure you're okay by yourself? I could stay...if you want company."

Surprise hits me at the offer, but I wave him off. "I've got plenty of company right here, and they're much quieter than the three of you."

Silas sticks out his tongue while Steven rolls his eyes.

Shawn mutters, "Okay." He doesn't look at me again, and he shuts the cooler lid with more force than necessary.

I shrug it off as they head out. Relief crashes over me and I finally relax, trying to remember the last time I had a place to myself. Sure, I've had a few moments here and there, but living with five other people makes alone time pretty scarce.

Especially since the incident. I know I became a homebody afterward, and my friends made it their personal mission to not let me turn into a recluse. I see their worry any time I decline an invitation to go out, and I know they think I'm regressing. But sometimes, I simply want to be alone.

Like tonight.

My shower is heaven, unrushed and quiet without Meg barging in. Grabbing my book, I try lounging on the couch, thrilled with the idea of sprawling across it without anyone telling me to move over or turning on the TV. But it's the most uncomfortable sofa I've ever been on so I move to the recliner where I devour my novel, the cozy stillness punctuated by the crashing of waves carrying through the open slider.

By the time midnight rolls around, I'm ready for bed and the quiet is too much. At home, I always have someone to say goodnight to. I brush my teeth, knowing better than to message Sebastian, who is the opposite of a night owl. And Meg is with her family.

I settle for a quick group chat to Shawn, Silas and Steven, sending a simple goodnight. As I climb into bed, my phone buzzes and I snatch it up. It's Shawn.

Goodnight.

And a sleepy emoji with three Zs coming out of its mouth.

I'm surprised he texted, but I'm happy someone responded. Yes, they're adults. Yes, they're more than capable of holding their own, but it's nice to know they're alive. I roll over, easily drifting off, and sleep like a rock through the night.

Chapter Twelve

Shawn

My ringing phone jolts me awake. Disoriented, I try to figure out where I am. A living room, on a couch? Silas' snoring rumbles to me through the closed door of the condo. I sit up, groaning as the dots connect. He always snores after getting drunk, and I hadn't been able to sleep so I'd crashed out here.

The delicious smell of bacon and coffee hits me on my inhale, almost compensating for the stiffness in my back.

And neck.

And hip.

Damn, this couch is uncomfortable.

My persistent phone rings again, and I sigh when I see it's Sebastian. I answer with a gruff, "Hey."

Leah pokes her head around the corner of the kitchen, and the question of the mystery chef is solved.

I give her a quick wave, not bothering to put on a shirt as I cross to the slider and step onto the balcony.

"Did I wake you?" Sebastian asks.

"I'm on vacation," I say, exasperation coating my words. "It's nine a.m. on Spring Break, of course you woke me." I rub at my neck, trying to work out the lingering knot. "What's up?"

"Leah texted me you guys made it okay, but I wanted to check in. See if you were making any progress."

He and I had talked before we left. He'd been pleased with our movie outing and that I'd convinced her to read with me. He thought it showed real progress and made him comfortable enough with not tagging along. As long as I swore to look out for her.

Which I did.

Now it's time to see if she and I can make it through this week without any disasters, along with our baby steps toward being friends. If all that goes well, then maybe we can take another step toward becoming more.

"She stayed in last night." I explain about the party after dinner, how she'd bowed out.

"I was afraid of that."

So am I. This new place, new people, it's going to be overwhelming after being in her little bubble for so long.

"I'll make sure she gets out." If nothing else, I'll tick her off enough that she can't stay inside. Not exactly on par with being friends, but if that's the only way, I'll make it happen.

I change the subject. "How are you holding up? Making sure to eat?"

"Yeah. Leah left me that lasagna, and I've got lunch today with Professor Harrison, a last-minute run through before the conference."

"Good." We'd all been nervous about leaving him alone. "Just...don't screw this up."

He chuckles. "You either."

I pause, trying to picture him those words coming out of his mouth, and I burst out laughing.

"What?"

"You actually saying 'don't screw up'." I pull out my best over the top impression of him, arrogant with a hefty dosing of haughty. "A mistake now would have consequences most dire." And I can't help laughing more at my words.

"Jerk," he mutters. But the underlying amusement lets me know he doesn't really mind.

"Aww, I miss you too, Seb."

"Okay, okay, now let me talk to Leah."

I shove open the slider, shut it once more then stride to the kitchen where I offer the phone to Lee. "Sebastian wants to talk to you."

She yanks her gaze from my bare chest to my face, her cheeks tinging pink before she snatches the phone from my hand. Her tone is relaxed though when she says, "Hey, Sebastian!" She shuts off the burner beneath perfectly done scrambled eggs.

Bacon sits in a pan on the back of the stove, keeping warm, and the smell makes my mouth water. I pour myself a cup of coffee then lean back against the counter as I take a sip.

"No," she says sharply, glaring my way. "I didn't go out last night. I was tired after all that traveling, and I'd been cooped up in the car with your three giant brothers. Then we had dinner with your parents, so you can see why I wanted some peace and quiet."

Her clenched jaw lets me know I'm going to get it when she hangs up. I keep my expression carefully neutral, appearing as unruffled as possible. This is my time to throw down the gauntlet and make sure she doesn't hide for the rest of the trip.

"Sebastian." His name is clipped, like she cut him off. "I promise I will go out. I didn't come all the way to Myrtle Beach to sit in the apartment." She presses her lips together. "Fine." Then her expression softens, as does her tone. "You take care of yourself, too. I'll talk to you soon." And she hangs up.

She turns her stormy glare on me, and I set my coffee cup down just before she smacks my phone into my chest. I manage to catch it, wincing as she jabs a finger into my shoulder.

"What the hell were you thinking worrying Sebastian like that? As if he doesn't have enough going on with his upcoming presentation and fending for himself."

I lift a shoulder, enjoying how riled she is. "I promised him I'd look out for you. That includes updates."

She throws her hands in the air. "I don't need a babysitter."

Her beauty is even more forefront when she stands up to me. Her cheeks are flushed, her eyes flash and she vibrates with an energy that draws me in. Her hair is piled messily on top of her head, several strands hanging down to frame her face. Those perfect lips part as I step closer.

"Maybe not," I say quietly. "But I'm going to keep my promise. I'm not letting you be a recluse this trip."

"It was one night!" She's almost yelling, and I can't stop staring at her mouth.

"Good." My voice is low and husky. "Let's keep it that way."

Her breathing is ragged as she stands before me. I lean in, and she freezes. I focus on her lips once more, unable to fight the pull.

Steven's door opens, and he darts down the hall toward the bathroom. The noise startles Leah. She reminds me of a bird, leaping backward, arms flailing. I'm surprised she doesn't squawk. Then it registers what's behind her, and I act before I think. My hands fly out to grab her waist, pulling her toward me, away from the stove and the hot pans.

She goes rigid at my touch, her hands hovering in the air just above my bare chest. Her lips part, astonishment written all over her face. Her gaze drops to my pecs, and she lowers her hands ever so slowly as if she's fighting the urge to touch me. But my skin pulls her in, like a magnet too strong to resist.

The moment she touches me, heat flares through my entire body. Her breath hitches, and she spreads her fingers wide. I have to swallow, my mouth drier than overcooked bacon. I flex my hands on her hips, wanting her closer. Needing to devour her. I lean down, unable to help myself.

Steven clears his throat. "Am I interrupting?"

Leah shoves me away, and I stumble into the counter, hating the panic on her face. I answer for both of us, saying casually, "Nope. Lee made us all breakfast and I was thanking her."

She gapes for a second then anger darkens her face. "Yeah, it was definitely nothing." Her gaze flicks to my torso again, and her lips press together before she adds,

"And put on a damned shirt." She whirls around, stalking over to the cupboard to grab plates.

I frown, wondering what I did, but when I go to ask she glares.

"Shirt. Now."

Annoyed at her mood swing and frustrated with our interruption, I stomp toward the bathroom, snatching up my shirt on the way and dragging it over my head. I kick the bathroom door shut then lean against the sink and stare at my reflection as I try to quiet the tornado of emotions within me.

What the hell was that? And what was I thinking? The goal here is to be friends with Lee, not stick my tongue down her throat.

The image of her staring up at me with those luscious lips begging me to devour them has me gripping the counter tighter, trying to get myself under control. *Fuck me.*

But I know that's the last thing she needs, some guy forcing himself on her. Vance manipulated her into giving more than she was ready to, and I refuse to be like him.

No matter how the sparks fly between us.

I take a deep breath and let it out through my nose. Friends. That's my goal, first and foremost. We have to become friends before we can build up to anything more. And I need to prove to myself that being friends with her won't cause her pain. I know Sebastian thinks my fears are unfounded, but I can't help the doubt hovering in my mind.

I lean forward to turn on the cold water. Cupping my hand under the stream, I splash my face. Once. Twice. The shock of the cool liquid grounds me, and I feel better as I dry off.

Now I just have to keep my hands to myself.

When I return to the main area, Steven and Leah are chatting about the party last night. They each have a full plate and a steaming mug in front of them. Leah nods to the extra plates on the counter as I walk by. Evidently she's not too mad, since she still wants to feed me.

After I take my share of food and sit down, I jump into the conversation, describing how awesome the party was, complete with a DJ and a keg. I glance at Leah, then clear my throat. "We made plans to go to the beach today with some people we met last night. If that's okay with you."

Surprise flashes across her face. "Your friends won't mind if I tag along?"

"Well, they're kind of expecting you." She blinks, and a twinge of hurt twists in my gut. What did she think, that we'd make plans and not include her? That she was going to have to fend for herself? I set down my fork. "Lee, we're not leaving you high and dry. I meant it when I said I was going to look out for you."

She stares at her plate. "I'm just...shocked you mentioned me at all last night. You guys were having a good time, and it sounds like there were plenty of other people there."

My eyebrows shoot up, but before I can say anything, Steven pushes away from the table and picks up his empty plate. "I'm gonna go take a shower."

Once he's gone, I sigh. "You're one of us. I don't just mean on this trip, Lee. Always. You have to know that."

"Yeah, I mean...I do."

She shoves a forkful of eggs into her mouth, still avoiding looking at me. So I reach across the table and touch her hand. To my surprise, she doesn't jerk away and slowly lifts her chin until her tentative gaze meets mine.

"Then why wouldn't we bring you up? You're not some secret. You're part of our group, and whatever we do, you're included." When her silence stretches on, I pull back into my own space and resume eating, wondering if I said too much.

"Why you, Shawn?" Confusion knits her eyebrows together.

As much as I want to tell her everything, I know it's too soon. I don't want her running for the hills, so I settle for a partial truth. "Sebastian and I are close, so it's no surprise he asked me to watch out for you. I take my promises seriously, and I intend to do my best." I pause, bracing myself for what comes next. "But more than that, I want to fix this between us. I'd like to be friends."

"Friends?" Doubt fills the word, and I know I need to give her more.

"That day at the pool?" I begin hesitantly.

Her fork clatters to the table and her back goes ramrod straight.

Not exactly the best opening, but I continue. "When you kiss—"

"Yes, Shawn," she replies, each word tight. "I know what day you're referring to."

"I'm sorry, Lee." Her head whips up, her startled eyes shining as I swallow and try to find the words. "You...surprised me. I didn't mean to push you. I realized who was kissing me and I went to step back, to step out of your hold and..." I lift a shoulder. "You fell before I could grab you."

Her frown is deep as she searches my face.

"I don't hate you. Not then, and not now." I grip my fork tighter. "I'm sorry I let you think that." Silence fills the space between us, and I think that's all I'm going to get.

But then she reaches across the table to touch my arm. "Thank you, Shawn, for explaining. That…means a lot to me." She draws her lower lip in to nibble on it, searching me as if not sure where to go from here.

I know she feels this tension between us, but that's more than we need to cover now. Baby steps. She needs to trust me first.

So I lay my hand on top of hers and say, "Friends?"

Relief drops her shoulders, and she smiles so brightly I have to blink. "Friends."

Silas stumbles out of his room, taking the attention off me. Once he gets coffee in him, he begins his own tales of last night, mostly about the waitress Cherie and her many friends. I make sure to thank Lee for breakfast and help clean up, then we pack for the beach.

The weather is perfect—hot enough for a swim with a slight breeze to keep the humidity down. The sun blazes overhead in its full glory, not a cloud in sight, and the waves are high enough to be interesting. Much better than the gray, cold March in dreary Michigan.

Cherie calls Silas' name when we arrive, and he salutes us before rushing away. The woman Steven hung out with most of last night waves him over, but with all the people we met, I can't remember her name. Her tan skin is flawless and her dark hair turns bright red at the tips. I'm left alone with Lee.

Who rubs her foot on the back of her calf.

"Lee? You okay?"

She nibbles on her lip but quickly puts her foot flat on the ground. "It's just...new people means more unknown."

I know she hasn't branched out from her comfortable circle in a long time. "This isn't back home," I say softly. "The rumor mill here is a clean slate." I can't help my smirk. "Until we get a hold of it."

One corner of her mouth tips up, but she doesn't seem completely convinced.

"C'mon, Lee. I can be Velcro until you're sure." At her skeptical expression, I chuckle. "That's what friends do, right?"

She hitches up her beach bag then raises her chin. "Let's go."

We stake out a spot with the group, several people coming up to greet me. I make sure to introduce Leah, but she still hovers near me, not fully emerging from her shell.

Time for drastic measures.

"Look." I point toward the volleyball court where some of our friends are gathering, including Silas. It's the perfect icebreaker. "You gonna let me kick your ass?" I know she won't be able to resist the challenge.

"Hell no." She smirks then tosses her ponytail. "But I will kick yours."

Silas punches a fist in the air when we arrive, and he picks Lee first. They paired up a lot in high school as well as in our impromptu backyard games. They work well together, and I know they'll be hard to beat, which makes it all the more fun.

I head to the opposite team, tossing my shirt away. Leah's gaze slides over my torso, and I can't resist winking which makes her bristle, looking adorable as ever. I love throwing her off her game. She has on her jersey shorts and tank top, more clothes than the other women, but I don't give them a second glance.

Lee is more than enough for me.

It takes some time to get our synergy down, but we finally find our flow. I get to the net at the same time as Lee and crouch low, trying to stay ready, but she playfully sticks her tongue out at me. My mind immediately jumps to all the things she can do with that tongue.

I quickly refocus as Silas serves, and we return it. One of their players bumps it to Silas who sets it to Lee. Her form is perfect. It's mesmerizing watching her leap into the air with her arm outstretched, ready to smack the ball over the net.

Until I remember I'm supposed to be the one stopping her.

I leap up just in time, raising both hands above my head, palms close, fingers wide so I can block. But she spikes around me, the air from the ball whooshing past as it fans my fingers.

The ball slams into the sand seconds before Cherie does.

Leah lets out a triumphant, "Yes!" She punches the air then gives Silas a complicated high-five that has me shaking my head. She practically dances back to her position, and I hold my fist under the net, wanting to give her credit.

"Nice one."

Her answering smile makes me glad I'm wearing sunglasses.

Chapter Thirteen

Leah

Our team wins by a decent amount. I can't even express how big my ego is after making Shawn eat dirt several times.

"Rematch?" Silas asks Cherie.

"Oh, yeah. It's on."

I glance at Shawn, remembering his earlier challenge. "So, who kicked whose ass?"

"At least I get a second chance."

We take a quick break, and I head over to our cooler where I slug some water. I'm definitely too warm now, so I peel off my shirt, revealing my purple bikini underneath.

This suit was my favorite last year, so I'd eagerly packed it. But when I put it on this morning, the elastic wasn't the same. It felt worn out, and I'd had to tie it tighter than usual. It'll have to do for today.

Shawn glances at me and starts choking on his water.

"You okay there?" Silas slaps him on the back.

Red-faced from lack of air, Shawn nods. "Went down the wrong pipe." He smacks his chest a couple of times, looking anywhere but at me. "Ready?"

More than one head turns as we jog back to the court, all the girls drooling over the guys I'm with. One lady drives by, does a double take and nearly runs into a trash can.

I nudge Shawn. "You almost caused an accident."

He seems puzzled, and I gesture to his torso, deliberately roving my gaze over him. It's rare to see him blush, but he does when my meaning clicks. I can't help laughing.

"C'mon. Let's play." He stomps off, back to his grumpy self once more.

I sigh, wondering how I'm supposed to keep up with his yo-yo moods. It doesn't get any better when he screws up multiple times, growing even more annoyed with himself. They barely have five points when we win. He starts to storm away, but he stops on the edge of the court and turns back to me.

To keep his promise.

Two women rush toward us. One is fair-skinned with silky auburn hair, the other is dark-skinned with dark curls tight to her head, and they greet Cherie first with squeals and hugs. She pulls them to our side of the court as they ask about the game.

Cherie points to me. "This one was on fire." She turns to scowl at Silas. "No wonder you picked her first."

He chuckles, not looking the least bit sorry. "Eh, we grew up together. I'm the baby of the family and Lee's my age, so we were constantly lumped with each other." He nudges me. "Sometimes it works in our favor."

I can't help my grin.

The auburn-haired lady returns it. "Ah, we finally get to meet the infamous Leah. Glad to see you're living up to everyone's expectations. These guys don't shut up about you." She jerks her head toward Shawn. "Especially that one."

I turn to glance at him, but he ducks his head.

"I'm Vicki by the way, and this is Keisha."

Keisha gives me a warm smile. "It's nice to put a face with all the hype."

I'm reeling. The idea that these guys would actually talk me up when I wasn't there has me feeling unsteady. Shawn in particular. Maybe he meant what he said about being friends.

Cherie scrunches her nose as she surveys her sandy body then mine. "Well, I think at least two of us need a swim. You guys want to come?" Silas steps closer, but she shoves him away. "Not you. Girls only."

Vicki and Keisha laugh then link arms with me, while Cherie loops hers through Keisha's. And just like that, I have friends. Shawn gives me an acknowledging nod as we walk by, a proud smile tipping his lips. Warmth spreads through me. It didn't matter how grumpy he was, how upset he was over losing, he still took the time to make sure I was okay.

Just like he said he would.

The four of us race into the surf, squealing and laughing as the waves splash our sun-warmed bodies. The water is cool but refreshing, and once I'm out deep enough, I take a moment to wipe off the sand as best as I can.

It gets cool fast, so we all hurry back to shore where we dry off. I grab a raspberry ale and my phone before I follow the girls to a couple of lounge chairs while Cherie sprawls on her towel in front of us.

Keisha cracks open her hard seltzer and takes a sip. "All right, Leah. Spill." She and Vicki lean in. "Which brother are you with?"

"Oh." I feel my cheeks heating. "Um, none of them. They're family friends. Our parents are close, and we grew up together." I pause to take a bracing drink. "Actually I just broke up with Sebastian."

Identical frowns cross all their faces, and Vicki asks, "Who's Sebastian?"

I let out a little laugh. "Their other brother."

Keisha gasps. "There's *another* one?"

I nod, grabbing my phone and pulling up a pic of him. They pass my phone around, pretending to swoon and being generally ridiculous.

"He's hot," Vicki says, fanning herself.

Cherie scoffs. "Have you seen the rest of them? I'd be more surprised if he wasn't."

Keisha studies me. "So there's nothing going on with you and Shawn?"

I nearly spit out my drink. "Shawn?" I squeak. Images from this morning rise unbidden in my mind. Him walking around shirtless, leaning toward me with his intense gaze focused on my lips, his bare chest under my fingers. "No, I, um, actually just found out he doesn't hate me."

They all burst out laughing as I stare in confusion.

"Why in the world would you think that the man—" Vicki stops to jab her thumb in his direction. "Who can't keep his eyes off you, who almost got hit in the face with the volleyball because he was practically drooling over you in that bikini, hates you?"

Another memory pops into my mind, Shawn coming into my sitting room as I stood in front of the mirror in only my lacy bra. But I scoff at myself.

I like his body too, that doesn't mean there's anything else going on. Pushing all imaginative thoughts aside, I start from the beginning and catch them up on Shawn's all over the place reactions and mood swings.

Cherie stands up, brushing herself off. "If you think for one second that man isn't into you, you're on crack. He's fighting some hang up that's holding him back, but the sparks are definitely there." She scans the beach, lighting up when she sees Silas. "Speaking of men, I'm going to go get that one."

In Cherie's absence, I get to know Vicki and Keisha better. They're on Spring Break from Colorado and rented a van with a bunch of the others. Keisha is studying engineering, and I pipe in with my aspirations to become an anthropologist. Then I ask Vicki about her dreams.

"I'm going to open a salon with my sister. After I get my business degree, so I know what the hell I'm doing."

We all chuckle. The conversation shifts to this trip, and we begin exchanging stories of all that's happened so far. Vicki and Keisha play off each other so well, I can barely stop laughing. My cheeks hurt.

After another hilarious tale, I double over and when I sit up, my bikini top feels loose. I reach back to touch the strings, grimacing when I realize they're half undone. Stupid, round strings. I cinch them back up, nice and tight. Luckily the fabric is still damp and clinging to me so nothing would have happened.

Steven plays grill king when lunch rolls around, the woman with red-tipped hair hovering near him. I tag along with my new friends as we approach the food line. I ask them about the woman with Steven, but she's not part of their group.

We pile up our plates as we continue trading road trip stories. I'm finishing my food when Shawn jogs over.

"Lee, we need one more." He jerks his chin toward the volleyball court.

Now that my friends know he's fair game, I notice more than one chest sticking out further than before, and I stifle a laugh. "I just opened a beer, Shawn."

He turns his puppy eyes on me. "Pretty please."

Keisha turns to me, as if to ask how I can stand it, and the answer is, I can't. So I hand her my drink. "Keep it cold for me?"

She barely nods, her awe-filled gaze back on Shawn.

My chuckle can't be contained as he and I walk toward the court. "You've got quite the fan club."

"What?"

"You can't tell me you don't notice all the girls fawning all over you." I glance over my shoulder at my new friends. "Don't you see anything you like?"

He stops short and says firmly, "I know exactly what I want."

Then he strides away, leaving me gaping after him. We get to the edge of the court as I wonder about his statement, turning it over in my mind.

But he distracts me by grunting, "You're on my team this time."

I take up a position near the net. He moves to the back corner, as far from me as he can get. I dig my toes in, focusing as the other team serves. We volley back and forth, fast and furious. There are some serious saves, amazing spikes and fantastic blocks.

When they set to me again, I pull back like I'm going to spike. At the last second, I tap it over the person's outstretched hands instead. The ball falls to the sand behind him, no one else close enough to help.

Our team cheers, and everyone rushes over to high-five me. When Shawn grabs me in a one-armed hug with a huge smile on his face, my stomach flips. I find myself looking to him after each of my digs or blocks because I crave that dazzling grin, need to see those green eyes flash with approval.

It's addictive and confusing, to say the least.

One point away from winning, we're locked in another serious volley. The other team sets up for a beautiful spike, and Shawn misses the block. I manage a full-out dive, face-planting in the sand, but I get under it enough to pop the ball in the air. My teammate slams it back over for the win.

"That was some save." Shawn's hand appears in front of me. "Good game, even if you are a sand monster."

"Yeah, yeah."

I manage a sputtering chuckle, wincing at the grit in my mouth. I sit up and slide my fingers to grip his wrist. He hauls me to my feet. Then he sucks in a startled breath before smashing me to his chest.

"Your top," he growls.

As if I can't feel my bare breasts against his gritty chest. As if I can't feel his hand splayed across my back where my strings should be. I swallow as my cheeks flame, and I rest my head on his shoulder, wishing I could disappear. This is so much worse than the groping incident at the restaurant.

"Lee, it's okay," Shawn murmurs. "No one is paying any attention. If they glance this way, it just seems like I'm hugging you. Why don't you get yourself… situated, and you can tie your suit back up?"

Moisture pricks my eyes, and my throat is thick. I fight the tears of humiliation with a sniff.

"Hey, it's all right. I'm here, and I promise I'm not looking."

The full reality of my position crashes down on me. I'm partially naked against Shawn's chest, and heat rushes through me. My lips part as I gape at him. He firmly looks away from me, over my head, staring out at the ocean like he promised. The tension between us stretches to a breaking point, and I have to glance away.

Friends, we're just friends.

I pull myself together and quietly admit, "It's the second time this happened today. These stupid round strings won't stay put."

"Leah," he says my name like a gentle caress. "Get yourself decent then let me tie the knot. It won't come undone again." His eyes flash with anger on my behalf, never dropping below my face. "I'm sorry it happened at all."

Reaching between us, I adjust myself so I'm all the way covered and hold the suit firmly to my chest. "Okay."

Shawn fumbles for my strings then spins me around to tie them himself. He even redoes the top one. "I promise, this will hold."

"As long as you help me get it off later." My words are met with stunned silence, and it dawns on me what

I actually said. I start stammering, "I—I meant..." When I turn to face him, my attention catches below his waist.

Where he has a situation of his own.

When he sees me notice, his cheeks redden. It makes sense. I had my bare chest plastered against his, then I accidentally mentioned getting off. Shawn just saved me, the least I can do is help him.

"Walk with me." I don't give him the option of saying no. I grab his wrist and start moving, careful to stay in front of him.

We make it to the water where we both dive under as soon as possible. I break through the surface, shoving my hair out of my face as Shawn emerges. I can't help following the rivulets of water as they sluice down his sculpted torso. The tension between us is too much, so I wave before I split off from him, and we both go our separate ways.

I rinse away the sand as best I can, then gingerly tug at my top while my chest is under water. Relief courses through me when the knots don't so much as budge. Back at shore, I find my beer and curl up in my chair where I pretend to read my book as I replay the embarrassing scene over and over in my head.

Silas checks in. "You good? I saw you hugging Shawn..."

He would notice that. I quietly tell him what happened, and he blinks in shock then leans forward to check the knot himself.

"Solid. Good thing Shawn was right there. He always has the best reflexes."

I barely finish nodding before he darts off with a quick wave, and I think over his words, grateful for Shawn's quick reaction. His rescuing me is becoming a habit, as is me not thanking him. Guilt twists in my stomach, and I know a thank you is the least I can do.

My shoulders feel tight as I walk over to where he's chatting with a few guys near the fire they've had going all day. I could use a break from the afternoon sun. After I tap his shoulder, I jerk my chin, asking him to follow me under an umbrella where I settle onto the sheet in the shade. He sits nearby, staring at the water.

The air between us now holds an awkwardness that I hate. I don't know what to do with this tension since it's not our usual butting-heads type. This is *more*, and my stomach knots in its wake.

But I force the words out. "I never said thank you."

A muscle ticks in his jaw. "You shouldn't have to thank me. That shouldn't have happened, and I'm sorry I didn't see it before you got up."

"These strings suck, but your quick thinking made the situation a whole lot less embarrassing overall." I duck my head. "So, thank you." When he doesn't respond, I nudge him.

He scowls but mutters, "You're welcome." Then he takes off.

I watch him go, happy to be finished with that awkward conversation. Vicki and Keisha join me a few minutes later, and soon the shade is the place to be.

The afternoon melts into evening, the air turning chilly as the sun descends. We pick at the leftover food, munching our way through dinner. Eventually everyone gathers in clusters around the campfire. I forgot to bring my sweatshirt, so I chat with the girls, rubbing my arms as goosebumps prickle my skin.

"Two options." Shawn appears next to me. "You take my sweatshirt or—" He pauses, raising an eyebrow. "We cuddle."

I ignore his empty threat. That'll be the day. "Or we go back."

"Is that what you want?"

His assessment brings back his earlier words, that he won't let me be a recluse, and I raise my chin, refusing to be the first to call it a night. "Not yet."

"Good. I'm glad you're having fun." Poking my shoulder, he repeats, "Two options..."

"Sweatshirt," I say with a sigh.

He yanks the shirt over his head and tosses it at me. When I pull it on, it's still warm from his body heat and smells of him— sunscreen, balsam and sandalwood blending together.

"Thanks," I grunt, trying to hide the thrill zipping through my body as his scent wraps me in a soothing hug.

"You're welcome." He ruffles my hair then heads back to his friends.

I smooth my hair, both annoyed and relieved at the familiar gesture. Maybe we can get back to our normal selves. Then I realize Vicki and Keisha are gawking at me. "What?" I pull the too-long sleeves down to cover my fingers.

"Are you sure you were with the right brother?" Vicki says.

I frown. "Well obviously Sebastian wasn't right for me. That's why we broke up."

"Girl, that man is hot. I'm surprised you even need a sweatshirt after the way he looked at you." Keisha fans herself.

I study him across the way, the firelight dancing over his sharp profile as he talks to Steven. I know better than to let myself hope, and he's been quite clear about his intention to be my friend. "He's watching out for me because Sebastian asked him to."

"You keep telling yourself that." Vicki snorts.

Chapter Fourteen

Shawn

Steven corners me on my way back to the fire. "Okay, what gives?"

"What do you mean?"

He glares, crossing his arms and making himself as tall as possible. He's always done this, to try to intimidate others into telling him the truth. But I've still got two inches on him.

"With Lee." He sighs, softening. "You're into her, aren't you?"

I swipe a hand over my face, not answering.

"How long? Does Sebastian know?"

"Yeah, he knows." I scratch my neck, trying to figure out how much to say. "I don't know how long. Definitely since the night after the library." I fill him in, explaining how I want to be friends with Lee.

"Friends?" he scoffs, shaking his head. "Yeah, that's why you two practically set fire to the kitchen this morning."

"There was a fire in the kitchen?" Silas asks, taking a swig of beer as he joins us.

"Not quite," Steven says dryly. "But there might have been if I hadn't interrupted."

"Oh, were you and Lee making sparks again?"

I groan, not surprised they're ganging up on me.

"Bro," Silas says, clapping his free hand on my shoulder. "The whole world knows. Why do you think not one single guy has hit on her today?" He smugly raises his beer to his lips. "You've got 'touch her and die' written all over you."

"Fuck," I mutter.

Steven asks, "What's the big deal? You like her, you're trying to fix things with her. Good for you."

"I just…" Haltingly, I tell them my reservations about disaster striking every time we're together. Further confirmed by her loose strings today. I should have noticed earlier, before I hauled her to her feet. I've already blown it, on our first full day here.

Silas rolls his eyes. "None of those things were your fault. She's lucky you were there. Same with her strings earlier — you've got amazing reflexes."

"I wondered why you were hugging." Steven frowns then nods. "Good job there. And Silas is right, she's lucky you were there. Then *and* the other times."

Their confident reassurances have me doubting my logic. Maybe I need to cut myself some slack. Maybe they're right. Hell, even Sebastian told me I was being an idiot for blaming myself. I don't know if I can ignore all of them.

Steven grows even more serious as he says, "Don't forget, this is Leah we're talking about. *Our* Leah. You can't be playing at this. You have to know for sure."

The weight of what I'm pursuing presses on me, but I straighten my shoulders and say firmly, "I do."

Silas studies me, his expression similar to Steven's. "Good. Don't fuck this up."

"Noted." I try not to choke on the pressure as I explain further. "That's why we're starting with being friends. I don't want to push her into anything she doesn't want." The memory of Vance hangs in the air, a phantom still haunting all of us.

"Smart." Admiration lines Steven's voice. "You're already doing better than Vance."

The words bolster me further, then I turn the tables on him. "So, the woman with the red tips?" Silas leans forward as I say, "You hung out with her last night and today. Have you found your Spring Break fling?"

Steven hasn't dated much since high school. His best friend and love of his life left him for his other best friend. It didn't end on good terms, and he's been cautious about who he chooses to spend his time with ever since.

"Actually, I think I have."

We all share a grin.

"Does she have a name?" Silas asks.

Steven groans. "I don't remember it, and the friend she came with disappeared with some local. No one I've asked knows, so I've been calling her Red."

We both laugh at his predicament, then Cherie beckons Silas over and we go our separate ways. The evening flies by, and the temperature drops steadily. I huddle near the fire, wishing Lee had taken me up on my offer to snuggle.

I watch her as much as I can without being a creep. She seems at ease with Vicki and Keisha, her laughter floating over to me more than once. I'm grateful for that. If things were different, I'd be sitting with her. I'd settle behind her, pulling her back to my front and frame her with my legs. I wonder how she'd feel in my arms, melting against me as we shared body heat.

A bark of laughter from the guys nearby yanks me back to reality. I give Leah one last wistful look before I focus on the conversation. Eventually, the party winds down and we put the fire out before we gather up our stuff.

Silas leaves with Cherie, and I'm thrilled I'll have the bed for the night. That couch was awful. I'm still feeling the effects. We wander home, and Steven has the same woman with him. They walk in a wobbly line, wrapped in each other's arms and lost in their own little bubble. I wonder if he ever figured out her name.

Leah huddles in my huge hoodie. Her bare legs stretch from beneath it, the hem of her shorts peeking out with each step. A wave of possessiveness washes over me as she chatters away about her new friends and how much fun she had today.

I can't wait to tell Sebastian.

Lee goes right for the bathroom then to her room. Steven and his woman disappear too, so I claim the shower. It feels amazing to wash the sand and sunscreen away, but I'm tired so I make it quick. When I pad out in just my shorts, I notice a light in the kitchen above the stove. Lee is still in her bikini, rummaging through drawers as she mutters to herself.

"Lee?" I keep my voice quiet, trying not to startle her.

She yelps, jumping back with her hand on her chest. "You scared me."

"Sorry. What are you doing?" The light is dim, but I swear her cheeks flush. When I step around the corner, her foot drops to the floor and I frown. "Seriously, Lee, what's up?" She mumbles a response I can't understand. "What?"

Heaving a frustrated sigh, she blurts out, "You tied the knot too tight!" My breath catches but words keep tumbling from her, always honest to a fault when she's had plenty to drink. "I tried to yank it off." She even pulls on the band, but there's no give. "It won't budge. Damned old suit."

"What were you going to do, cut it off?" Her chin drops, and I know I'm right. "Come here, Lee-bug. I'll help you."

She shuffles toward me, nibbling on her lower lip. It makes my groin tighten. Then she presents her back to me, and I realize what I've volunteered to do. She must realize it too because she crosses her arms over her front. Her back is ramrod straight, and I brush her heated skin as I reach for the knot.

"Ready?" My voice cracks. *Slick, Wrighting. Show her just how cool you can be.*

She nods, and I go to work. It takes all my concentration to focus on undoing the knot instead of drooling over her almost bare back or the shapely curve of her backside. I don't need a repeat of the earlier situation. Definitely don't need to be spearing her in the ass. That thought nearly strangles me, and I will myself to calm down.

Once one string finally loosens, it's smooth sailing from there. The thudding of my heart is so loud, I'm surprised I don't wake Steven as I move on to the next knot. The top string is hidden by the curtain of her hair, so I sweep it over her left shoulder. My fingers graze her neck, and she shivers, sucking in a breath.

I grit my teeth, reciting the Pledge of Allegiance in my mind. Anything to distract me and my overeager cock, which doesn't have an ounce of manners. This knot doesn't take as long, and I drop the strings, stepping away.

"All set." My words are strangled.

"Thanks." Her tight answer reaches my ears just before she rushes away at a pace just below a run.

I pray to whoever is listening that she has a different suit for tomorrow as I crawl into bed then drift off to sleep. A dull thud and a muffled curse wakes me way too early. I crack an eyelid to find Silas hopping up and down on one foot with his face scrunched up.

"What are you doing?" I groan.

"Sorry." He drops his foot to the floor. "I'm taking Cherie out for breakfast before her shift and wanted to change quick, but I hit my shin. I'll come back after. Probably going to crash out again."

I wave him off, wanting nothing more than to go back to sleep. He takes the hint and keeps his noise to a quiet rustling as I roll over and drift off before he leaves. When I wake up next, the sun streams in through the open door. Annoyance flashes through me that he couldn't even take the time to shut it.

I take a moment to stretch, reveling in the refreshed feeling that comes from sleeping on a decent bed. I will never sleep on that fucking couch again. Swinging my legs over the edge, I stretch once more, but as soon as I stand, the need to piss hits me full force.

Hurrying to the bathroom, I groan when I hear the shower running. I peer down the hallway. Lee's door is shut, but Steven's is open. I cross my fingers hoping it's him. Or maybe Silas came back.

I tap on the door, gritting my teeth when Leah calls, "Who is it?"

Fuck my life.

I tentatively crack the door open. "Lee, I hate to do this to you but I have got to take a piss. I swear my eyes are yellow."

Silence. Then the shower curtain rustles as if she's confirming its shut. Meanwhile I'm going to make a puddle on the floor.

"All right. Just play some music?"

"I don't have my phone," I grit out.

"Use mine."

I fumble to put in the pass code she gives me then select the first thing I see that's loud. Shinedown blasts as I flip open the toilet. No wonder they call it relieving yourself.

When I finish and flush, I wash my hands then kill the music. "Thanks, Lee. Sorry about that." *But now that I'm here...* "What do you want to do today?"

"Seriously, Shawn?"

"What? It's not like I can see anything." Though saying that has images popping into my head, and I push them away. I really hadn't been trying—

"Out!" she says, reminding me of that day in her sitting room when she only wore that lacy blue bra.

I grapple to get my thoughts under control then ask, "Did you see Steven before you got in here?" I lean one shoulder against the door jamb, making myself comfy. She's not all the way riled yet. I haven't heard *that* tone.

She grumbles to herself. "No. Both bedroom doors were open, so I assumed you'd all left and I had the place to myself."

Her thoughts echo mine, and I grin. "Wanna hit the beach? Supposed to be another nice day."

The shower curtain moves, and her adorable face peeks out. "Can we talk about this *after* I'm dressed?"

"I thought it'd be nice to know what I should wear."

She practically growls, yanking the curtain shut once more. "Don't you have plans?"

"Yep. I'm your Velcro, remember?"

"That explains why you're still here."

I bark out laughter at her grumpy retort.

"Yeah," she says reluctantly. "I'd like to go to the beach again, if you don't mind."

"That's all I needed to know." I push open the door, then pause. "Oh, and Lee?"

She peeks out once more.

"Bring a sweatshirt this time, or else we really will be snuggling." I wink as she rolls her eyes, and I close the door behind me.

As I get dressed in swim trunks and a white T-shirt, I realize this is the first time on this trip that I've made plans with just her. My mind starts racing. Maybe I can take her to eat before we go to the beach. My parents gave us all money before they left. What better way to spend it? I think about our Spanish breakfasts, how comfortable things always were between us during those times, and I mull over how I can recreate that feeling between us.

Silas stumbles in and shucks off his shirt.

I say, "Hey," but he just grunts before flopping on the bed. "You gonna crash for a while?"

"Yeah. Cherie's working until four then she'll meet us at the beach. I'll be down sometime between now and then."

"'Kay." I grab a few things then head into the hallway.

Lee is curled up in the recliner, a book on her lap and her beach bag at her feet.

I fill her in about Silas' plans, then clear my throat. "I, um, thought we could maybe get a bite to eat before the beach."

"Sure. I haven't eaten yet."

We decide on a mom and pop shop that has all-day breakfast, then we start walking. It's another gorgeous sunny day, though the humidity is up so the air is on the sticky side. We both have a light sheen of sweat on our skin when we get to the restaurant.

The silence between us hasn't been awkward, but I miss her usual chatter. As I reach for the door, I say, "*¿Solamente en Español?*" *Only in Spanish?*

She stops, a crinkle forming in her forehead. "Why?"

"We always have fun at those breakfasts."

"Yeah..." She studies me thoughtfully. "We do." I open the door for her, but she says, "If we can do that in Spanish, we can definitely do it in English."

A challenge underlines her words, and I'm not sure if it's for her or me or both of us. She pauses at the threshold to glance over her shoulder with a smirk.

"But I reserve the right to change my mind if you start being too difficult."

I chuckle as I follow her in. The waitress leads us to a little booth in the cozy dining room. The place is fairly busy for a weekday. Wait staff bustles through the aisles with trays or coffee carafes. The majority of the tables are full and a low hum of conversation fills the air.

We sit across from each other, both ordering coffee when the waiter appears. She gets an omelet, I get eggs

Benedict. Then silence falls, and I resist the urge to twiddle my thumbs as I try to think of something to say.

"How'd it feel sleeping in a real bed last night?" She unfolds her napkin, slipping it into her lap.

"Amazing."

"I can't believe how uncomfortable that couch is. And that you slept on it!" She shakes her head. "You're a better person than me."

"Yeah, well, you haven't tried to sleep next to Silas when he's snoring." We share a laugh. Another pause stretches as we get our coffee then I ask, "Have you heard anything from Meg?"

She goes on about how Meg has been stuck on a family vacation in a run-down cabin in Tennessee where she's practically on top of her parents and siblings. Doesn't sound like a relaxing vacation to me.

When she's finished, she puts her hands on the table. "I'm going to find the restroom." And she pops to her feet without checking the aisle.

Where a server is barreling down with a full tray of food.

I grab her waist, pulling her onto my lap in time to avoid a collision. She yelps, gaping as the server flies by.

"Oh," she says, her cheeks turning pink.

"I thought you might prefer to eat your food rather than wear it." My words are teasing, but I can't quite find the smile to match. Not with her luscious ass perched on my thighs. Not with her hip against my stomach. Not with my hands on her waist.

"Yes, I would." Her wide eyes search mine as her fingers flex on my shoulder. Tension crackles between us until she lets out an exasperated sigh.

"What?"

"I just don't know what to do with you, Shawn."

My mind races as I think of all the things I want to do, but I hide it with a smirk. "At least I know I'm not boring you."

One corner of her mouth tips up. "No, you're not boring." She holds my gaze for another beat then pointedly peers both ways down the aisle. "All clear."

It takes a lot of willpower, but I release her and watch her hurry away. Her words echo in my head, but I still don't know for sure if she's ready. Or if she trusts me fully. It's getting harder to even function around without wanting to touch her all the time. It's difficult to keep my hands off her, the girl I love.

The strength of that word crashes into me. It's the first time I've thought it since Sebastian called me out. The first time I've allowed myself to label this pull to her. My fear has always been at the forefront, but not anymore. My brothers' reassurances wash over me, solidifying that all those instances weren't my fault. That my presence actually helped. I truly believe them, can see that Leah and I are good for each other.

Now I have to figure out how to convince her.

Chapter Fifteen

Leah

Brunch went surprisingly well, though Shawn became a bit more reticent after my near collision. He kept studying me. An unspoken question hung between us, but I ignored it, carrying on about how much fun I had yesterday.

Afterwards, we stop by the condo to grab the bag and cooler then walk in comfortable silence to the beach. One of the posters on the lampposts catches my attention.

"Oh, they have an aquarium!" I eagerly pull out my phone, typing in the website. "Wow, they're open late too."

"I didn't know you were a fish girl."

"Maybe I just want to see sea turtles." I frown at my words. "See sea turtles. What even is English?"

Shawn laughs and some of the tension dissipates as we walk the last block. I keep thinking about the aquarium. I know Vicki and Keisha are leaving the day after tomorrow, so we'll be here one more day than them. Maybe then I can go play tourist. Maybe I can even swim with the dolphins!

I drop the beach bag on an empty spot on the sand, and Shawn sets the cooler next to it then strips off his shirt. Sweaty from the humidity and the hot sun, I yank mine off too, more than ready to swim.

"Different suit," Shawn comments, glancing out at the ocean before his gaze darts back to me.

I nod. The navy-blue two-piece has a pullover, racerback top. It pushes my boobs together, making it seem like I have more cleavage, but I feel more secure. I shimmy out of my shorts, revealing my cute low-rise bottoms. "I didn't want a repeat of yesterday."

His focus lingers on me, jerking away when Keisha and Vicki holler my name. He shoves his hands in his pockets.

I wave at my friends, pointing at the ocean to let them know I'm swimming first. "You want to come for a dip?" I'm not sure why I feel the need to invite Shawn, but he's still standing there.

He hesitates. "Nah, I'm gonna go." He jerks his head in the direction of one of the bigger groups before walking off, kicking the sand as he goes.

A hint of disappointment ripples through me, and I wonder at his dejected stance, but I shake my head. I shove all thoughts of him aside as I plunge into the ocean. The water is refreshing, bordering on too cold. I don't stay long, hurrying back to shore. Shawn grabs a beer from the cooler as he watches me walk up. He moves to hand me my towel.

"Thanks." I bury my face in it, then flip it over my shoulders to wrap around my arms and stomach as I shiver. "I think the water's colder than yesterday."

He's staring at me, my chest in particular. Which is when I realize my nipples are showing, taut from the cold. He swallows, following my movement as I shift the towel to cover all of my torso.

An infuriating twinkle appears in his eyes. "Yep, looks like it's a tit bit nipply out there." With a wink, he leaves.

I gape after him, unable to believe he said that. Shaking my head, I let out a little laugh. I reach for a hard seltzer, making sure my towel stays in place as I head toward Vicki and Keisha who are sunbathing on a sheet on their stomachs. I lay next to them, eager for the sun to warm me.

We greet each other cheerily and chit chat about our mornings. No one has any plans for the rest of the day which suits me just fine. I'm contemplating rolling over when a shadow falls across me.

"You haven't sun screened yet." Shawn's deep voice is almost a growl.

I glare up, shielding my eyes from the sun. "What are you, the sunscreen police?"

He crouches next to me. "The last thing I need is to answer to Sebastian for you being lobster-red. Or, worse, getting sun poisoning. Let's go."

The only thing red is my face from being treated like a wayward toddler, but I push myself onto all fours then pop to my feet. I follow him to an umbrella where we sit in the shade. Growing up with the Wrightings, I'm used to them hovering over me, even more since the incident.

It's just usually not Shawn.

He thrusts a bottle of sunscreen in my lap, and I huff as I loop my hair into a messy bun.

"I can do your back if you want." His offer is tentative, like he's trying to make up for being a jerk.

When I see his sincerity, I nod. After I pour sunscreen into my hands, I start on my face and chest. He kneels behind me. Then his hands are on my shoulders, gentle and careful as he glides along my skin. I suck in a breath at his touch.

My stomach does a funny little flip, and tingles shoot down my spine. But I ignore the sensations, focusing on making sure sunscreen covers every bare inch of me.

Not on the way his fingers feel as they slide over my shoulders. Not on the way his hands dip under the edges of my straps. Not on the way my skin heats as he rubs in every bit of lotion, going lower and lower down my back.

Every muscle in me is tense when he finishes, and I can't help my sigh of relief. I end with my legs, glancing over to find him staring at me.

"What?"

"You missed some." He rests his fingers on my cheek as his thumb strokes my temple.

I close my eyes, unable to move.

"There." But he doesn't take his hand away.

My eyelids flutter open to find him still staring at me. His intensity sends a thrill shooting through me. It's too much, so I turn toward the waves, needing some space. Keisha and Vicki walk over, breaking the tension between us.

Vicki coils a piece of auburn hair around one finger, raking her gaze over Shawn. "Hey, we're going to get some ice cream. You guys want to come?"

Annoyance flashes through me, and I want to snap at her.

"Ice cream sounds great." Shawn stands, waiting for me to agree.

I'm beyond confused at my vicious reaction. Vicki is my friend. Why am I so annoyed with her? "I think I'll pass. I want to sit in the shade and read for a bit."

A shadow crosses Shawn's face and his smile dims, but Vicki links her arm through his. As they walk away, a bitter taste floods my mouth, and I clench my fists. I catch myself, forcing my fingers open while inhaling slow deep breaths.

Why am I being so possessive? Maybe I was closer to sun poisoning than I thought. I grab my book, find my drink and ignore the weird sensations. I open to my bookmarked page, choosing to lose myself in a different reality instead.

A while later, something cold hits my arm, and I squeal, jerking away. I scowl at Shawn, who grins and offers me a cup. I tuck my bookmark into my book before I reach for the container, peering inside to find mint chocolate chip ice cream. "My favorite!"

He sits beside me, resting his forearms on his propped-up knees. I study him, trying to figure out how he knows this about me.

He notices my puzzled expression. "It's my favorite too. You don't remember that day we all went to the park?"

I have no idea what he's talking about, so I shake my head then scoop a cool, creamy bite into my mouth.

"Our parents took us to that big wooden park in South Haven. You and Meg came, too. We stopped at Sherman's first to get ice cream, but my brothers teased me for wanting mint chocolate chip. They thought it was so boring." He looks out at the ocean.

I keep my focus on him as I take another bite of my delicious ice cream.

"I was upset. Then you stormed up to the counter, pushing past them, and said you wanted mint chocolate chip, too. Because it was the best. And anyone who said otherwise couldn't play on your swings anymore."

This doesn't ring any bells for me, but warmth spreads through my chest as I watch Shawn tell the story. His expression is soft, like he sees the memory playing in his head. I'm glad I did that for him. My swings were a big deal, back in the day.

"You must have been four or five, so I guess I'm not surprised you don't remember."

I slip another spoonful into my mouth, savoring the sharp jolt of the mint on my tongue. "Thank you. This is delicious." I lean over to bump him with my shoulder. "You can play on my swings anytime."

We both laugh.

Then I realize my other friends didn't come back with him. "What'd you do with Vicki and Keisha? I thought Vicki was going to permanently attach herself to you there for a minute." I can't help the bite that creeps into my voice.

A knowing grin spreads over his face. "Oh, that's right. Miss Leah doesn't like to share." He chuckles. "I forgot about that."

I duck my head. As an only child, sharing had been the bane of my existence — another reason my parents forced me to hang out with the guys so much. It was such an issue that they'd made up a little chant about me not sharing.

He nudges me. "Don't worry, Lee. I'm all yours."

My head shoots up. His words are way too serious, but I relax at the twinkle in his eye.

"The girls found other prey while we were getting ice cream."

He nods in the direction of a picnic table where Vicki and Keisha now sit with two new guys. A band of tension eases inside my chest, one I don't examine too closely, and Shawn doesn't stop grinning while I finish my ice cream.

I lick the spoon clean as he asks, "What's next?"

We decide to check in with the others and walk toward the picnic table as Silas and Cherie come up with ice cream of their own.

Keisha squeals as she and Vicki rush over to meet us. "You're just in time. There's this club a few blocks over, and these guys want to take us." She and Vicki exchange an excited glance. "They're locals! Wanna go?"

I freeze. The idea of a club, pulsating with music, full of strangers dancing around me has my chest tight and tension knotting my stomach. Silas looks at Cherie who nods eagerly. Shawn waits for my answer, but I can't speak. I turn to him, hoping he will hear my silent plea to save me.

He doesn't even hesitate, casually slinging his arm over my shoulders. "Sorry, I promised Lee we'd go to the aquarium tonight."

My lips part as I gape at him. A slow smile spreads over my face, and he grins back.

Delight fills me as I tell the others, "Yep, we're going to the aquarium." I realize how rude I sound, like no one else is invited. "I mean, you guys are welcome to come if you like."

Vicki and Keisha shake their heads then Vicki frowns. "An aquarium over a club?" She lifts her shoulder. "To each their own, I guess."

Relieved I don't have to explain myself further, I sag against Shawn. It feels natural, letting him support me like this. And that scares the crap out of me.

"You want to go get ready?" he asks in my ear, as the rest of the group makes plans to meet at the club in an hour.

I nod, stepping away so his arm falls back to his side. A flash of disappointment crosses his face, but he jerks his chin toward our stuff. Silas and Cherie walk back with us so he can grab some clothes then get ready at her place.

Before he takes off, I ask, "Has anyone heard from Steven?"

They both shake their heads, leaving me frowning. I gesture for Silas to go and Shawn to shower first, then I call Steven as I pick out my clothes.

He answers on the first ring. "Hey, Lee, what's up?" His words are a little slurred.

"Where are you?" I use my best no-nonsense voice.

"Lee," he whines.

"No, don't give me that." I don't want to pull the responsibility card, especially on him. *But seriously.* "You took the car, leaving us all stranded — no note, no checking in all damn day. Where are you?"

He sighs and goes quiet for several moments as the noise around him lessens. "You're right. I went with Red back to her condo, and it's been a huge pool party all day. Track me, if you want. I'm not sure of the address."

"You're staying there or taking a cab back to the condo, right?"

"Yes, ma'am." He sounds sincere, and I know he'll keep his word.

"Okay." Relief trickles through me as I pause. "Steven?"

"Yeah?"

"Be safe, okay?" I don't like worrying about him.

"Of course. I'm sorry, Lee-bug."

"Thanks." And I know he is. "Have fun." I hang up, sighing as I sit heavily on the bed.

Shawn comes out of the bathroom. A towel loops around his waist, and he looks better than anyone has a right to. He does a double take at my somber expression. "Everything all right?"

I straighten, nodding. "It's fine. Steven is partying at some condo with Red." Then I laugh. "I don't think even he knows her real name."

My breath catches when Shawn leans against the door frame—his right arm propping him up, his left hand gripping the towel. I swallow, trying to remember what I was saying. "He promised he'd either stay there or get a cab home." Speaking of… I grab my phone, pulling up the Find My app to see Steven. "He's not far." I hold my phone out to Shawn.

He walks over, taking it from my hand. His sandalwood-balsam scent crashes into me, catching me off-guard with its overpowering headiness. I blink, trying to center myself, and I fixate on the several droplets of water clinging to his bare chest. One quivers on his right pec, and I'm jealous of it. I want to reach out, to touch it.

When he nudges my arm, I jerk back, gulping in air. He places the phone in my hand, our fingers brushing again. Electricity jolts through me.

"Um." I leap to my feet, desperately needing an escape from him and the feelings threatening to burst to life inside of me. "I need a shower."

He blocks the door, and I have no way to get past him without touching the bare expanse of his smooth, chiseled chest.

Panic flutters, but I manage a simple, raw, "Please."

He lets out a breath, and his chin dips in the faintest of nods before he leaves the room. My knees almost buckle in relief, but I grab my clothes and race to the shower.

Under the soothing effects of the spray, I start to examine the fluttery feeling inside of me, the electricity, the desire. I haven't felt this way since…before. And I'm not ready for it, especially not with Shawn.

We've just begun to explore being friends and this attraction keeps shooting between us like a downed electrical wire, spraying sparks everywhere. I've hardly wrapped my head around the idea that he and I aren't enemies. That he doesn't hate me.

It's too new.

The memory of that day in the pool washes over me, how I'd opened myself up only to be humiliated. I know he didn't mean to push me in, but he didn't come after me either. And he only now apologized. Can I trust Shawn not to hurt me again? Shawn, the guy who teases me at every turn, who pushes my buttons and goads me into making everything a competition.

What if this is just a game to him?

Although another part of me chides myself for the thought, since Shawn has never been malicious one day in his life. And he's always been there when things went to shit. Like my bikini strings, the latest catastrophe he's helped me through. Warmth spreads through me as I sift through memories from the trip, remembering all the little moments he's kept his word.

Even when he's pissed or annoyed, he's waited for me. Stuck by me. Through awkward conversations and weird jealous moments.

I can depend on Shawn.

The realization takes me by surprise. He's nothing like Sebastian, who got so caught up in his tasks that he forgot me. And Shawn has never once pushed me into something I'm not ready for, the way Vance used to. Case in point, how Shawn stepped in, offering to take me to the aquarium when he saw my panic about the club.

I marvel at the change in my thinking toward him as I go through the motions of washing. Yeah, the attraction is too much right now. But each day I've felt a little more comfortable with him, and suddenly the idea of actually being friends doesn't feel quite so out of reach.

Friendship seems like a great place to start.

* * * *

Shawn

The moments between me and Lee are stacking up, like a Jenga tower. It's not a matter of if the blocks are going to fall, it's a matter of when.

I see how she responds to me, especially when I'm shirtless, like in her room a minute ago. I felt her lean into me when I slung my arm over her shoulders at the beach. She even relaxed for a few amazing seconds before she caught herself, and I find myself craving more of that.

I want to be her rock, the one she depends on. The way she'd turned her pleading gaze on me when her friends asked about the club…how she'd instinctively looked to me for help. I want that all the time. And I'm excited for this outing, just the two of us.

Reaching for my usual T-shirt, I hesitate. I know this isn't an official date, but it wouldn't hurt to dress a little better than normal. I grab a polo shirt instead then step into my nicest pair of jeans. I even take the time to check my hair, taming it some so it's not quite so out of control.

After I'm satisfied, I sprawl in the recliner, pulling up the aquarium on my phone while I wait for Leah. A few minutes later, she emerges, her hair pulled back in a sleek braid, and her skirt stops mid-thigh, showing off her tanned legs. The fitted V-neck shirt accentuates her chest, and it's an effort to keep from staring.

I have to swallow at my dry mouth before I can speak. "You look nice."

"Thanks." Her smile grows. "So do you."

"Our Uber should be here soon." I finish punching buttons on my phone before I stand up. "I checked out the aquarium. They have some well-rated dolphin and whale shows that could be fun. There is a swim with the dolphins event, but it requires reservations and it's all booked up for today."

Disappointment crosses her face, and I can hardly stand it. "But they have an exhibit where you can pet stingrays."

And the light is back. "Really?"

I can't help chuckling at her eagerness. She's practically bouncing on her toes. "Leave it to you to want to pet some slimy sea creature."

"Hey, it's not something I can do every day. Why not get excited about it?"

"Because…it's a slimy sea creature."

Her lips part, and her eyes widen. "Wait. You're not afraid of them, are you?"

"Afraid?" I scoff, even as my stomach clenches at the idea of touching one. "I wouldn't say afraid. But I have no desire to put my hands on anything that comes out of the ocean. I'll happily eat it, but pet it?" I wrinkle my nose. "No thanks."

My phone dings, saving me from further teasing. "Uber's here. Ready?"

She nods, and I open the door for her, following her down the stairs. I confirm he's my driver, then we both hop into the back where her unfailing grin lights the space.

"Shawn?"

"Yeah?"

"Thanks for thinking of this." She turns toward me, looking up through lowered lashes. "I kind of froze when they asked me about the club."

I nod. "Do you regret not going?"

She lifts a shoulder. "Sort of. I would like to hang out with Vicki and Keisha some more. And I love dancing." She sighs. "I wish I could stop being so scared all the time."

I reach over to rest my hand on hers. "Hey. You've been doing great stepping out of your comfort zone. You've made new friends, tried new things." I squeeze her hand, then tease, "Even hanging out with the likes of me." I give her hand a gentle squeeze. "I'm proud of you."

A faint blush tinges her cheeks. "Thanks, Shawn. I'm glad we're friends."

My heart leaps at the word as she squeezes my hand then moves to her own side of the car. It's another win, a step, and even though I wish it could be more, I take it. My happiness doesn't dim as I settle back into my seat and watch the scenery fly by.

I'm willing to be patient because she is worth the wait.

Chapter Sixteen

Leah

The aquarium is huge. The main entrance opens to a wide circular room with multiple hallways branching off. Every bit of space is welcoming, from the royal blue carpet to the geometric signs in bold colors pointing the way to each exhibit. We walk down a small flight of stairs as I gape, trying to take it all in.

"What do you want to do first?" Shawn asks.

The sound of splashing catches my attention, and the tank full of stingrays draws me to it. Several people are scattered about the edges, dipping their hands in the water. One little girl squeals as a sting ray glides right up to her.

I bounce on my toes then race to the side of the tank. The perimeter is lined with fake rocks of varying heights, so everyone has access. The petting area is actually very shallow and, as I get nearer, I realize the back of the tank is much deeper, a place where the rays can be antisocial if they want.

I rest one knee on a rock and lean down, holding my hand flat out. Several rays swim in a constant loop, gliding from one person to the next. I hold my breath as the first one approaches—a mammoth one. It swooshes right under my hand, and I ease my fingers onto its back.

"What's it feel like?" Shawn asks, making no move to come closer.

"Smooth, soft, a little slimy, but not in a gross way. Kind of squishy." Another swims up a little further out, and I lean over, anxious for another pet.

Shawn inhales sharply. "Geez, Leah, don't forget you're wearing a skirt."

I pull back, because I had forgotten. Then I realize what his statement means. "You were checking out my butt."

He glowers. "Kind of hard not to when you put it on display like that."

I laugh, a lightness spreading through me, and I can't stop grinning, especially when Shawn glares even more. "Oh, knock it off, you big grump." I pause, wavering on my next words, but I decide it's worth saying if it'll bring him back his cheerier self. "It's not like I don't sneak peeks at your amazing torso whenever I get the chance."

His frown disappears as he blinks, then a smug smile spreads over his face.

"Now, quit pouting and try this." I grab his hand before I can second-guess myself.

Electricity jolts through me the moment my fingers touch his. His wary expression doesn't show much confidence in me, but he allows me to pull him toward the tank. Where he stops. I tug again until he sighs and bends so both our hands touch the water.

"It's fun, I promise." I let go but stay close.

The big ray starts our way, and anticipation bubbles within me. Shawn's mouth is tight, his arm rigid with tension. I never thought Shawn would get freaked out over something like this. The ray swims up, and my fingers meet it.

Shawn hasn't moved, so I rest my hand over his, pressing down in a gentle motion. His eyes go wide. He swallows, then one of the ray's massive fins slips out of the water and crashes back down, splashing Shawn. I gasp, stepping back as my laughter slips out. His entire right arm is drenched, and the sleeve of his green polo shirt is now several shades darker than the rest.

"See?" I say with a sheepish grin. "Totally worth it."

He chuckles then frowns at my torso. "How are you still dry?"

"I obviously pet better than you do." I lift my chin. "He likes me best."

Shawn's eyebrows lift then, fast as lighting, he wraps his wet arm around my midsection and pulls my back flush against him. I squeal and squirm before I get away, but now my shirt is damp. He flicks his fingers at me as I survey the damage.

"Jerk." But I'm smiling and my heart is racing. It's just water after all. Another ray splashes nearby, making us both step back.

"Okay, what next?"

I turn in a random direction, Shawn's playful hug looping through my mind as we walk down a hall. It takes a few minutes for my butterflies to settle, but there is plenty to distract me. Every exhibit in the aquarium is fascinating, and we take our time wandering through the massive building.

But one stands out—a huge walkthrough tunnel with a massive tank on all sides of us. It feels like we're actually on the bottom of the ocean. I cringe as a shark swims toward us, its rows of teeth clearly visible.

Then I see my favorite thing in the whole aquarium. "Shawn, look." I grab his arm as I point, watching the sea turtle in complete awe. "It's beautiful." I freeze as it swims over us, and I crane my neck to follow its path.

I realize how close Shawn is when he exhales and the warm air caresses my neck. When he shifts slightly, my breast grazes his upper arm, making my breath hitch. I clear my throat, stepping away as my cheeks warm.

But he stays as relaxed as ever. "There's another one." Shawn points to a second turtle swimming our way. "Get over there, and I'll take your picture."

Soon we're both posing with various sea creatures, taking turns snapping photos of each other. My favorite is when a huge shark swoops by and Shawn flails his arms like he's terrified. I capture the moment, laughing the whole time.

A kind passerby offers to take a picture of us together, and Shawn doesn't hesitate to hand her his phone. When he casually slings his arm over my shoulders, every muscle in my body tenses at his touch. His warm hand cups my upper arm as he tugs me to his side. My heart might explode out of my chest if my pulse races any more. It's not until the lady encourages us to smile that I remember to do so.

But once it starts, my smile doesn't stop.

After managing to stay dry at the dolphin show, we decide we're ready for dinner so we exit by way of the gift shop. I make a quick trip to the restroom. When I come out, Shawn hands me a little paper bag.

"What's this?" I peek inside to see a silver chain with a sea turtle charm on it.

Shawn shrugs. "I thought you'd like it."

"I do!" I pull it out to examine it more closely. The details are exquisite, and I love the way the iridescent shell catches the light. "Put it on me?"

I hand him the necklace then gather my hair to one side. He lowers it over my head, setting the clasp into place. The brush of his fingers gives me goosebumps, and I freeze, needing a moment to brace against the dam inside me that wants to burst. *Just friends,* I remind myself, even though his touch feels more like a caress than a casual bump.

"Thank you," I whisper, turning around. I don't trust myself to hug him, but I wish I could.

"You're welcome."

We have dinner right on the beach, exchanging pictures and laughing over some of our more ridiculous ones. The air between us is fun and easy, just the way I like it. Eating fresh seafood on the shore of the ocean while the breeze caresses me…what could be better?

It's nearly ten p.m. by the time we get back, and we're the only ones home. Shawn shoves his hands in his pockets. "Want to watch TV? Or play a game?"

I purse my lips to one side as I think. "TV sounds nice. But I want comfy clothes first."

"Good plan."

We meet back in the living room a few minutes later, both of us in lounge pants and T-shirts. I wrinkle my nose at the couch, choosing instead to sit on the floor.

"You could have the chair."

I shake my head. "You take it. No biggie." He seems like he's going to protest so I lean forward, grabbing my ankles. "I want to stretch."

My excuse does the trick, and he flips through the channels while I stretch both legs in turn. It feels good after all the walking we've done. We find a game show where contestants are shown the first letter of the answer and have to fill in the rest. We compete to call out our guesses, the light competition giving me a heady rush.

Silas and Cherie come in as the second episode is wrapping up. He waves then raises his eyebrows at Shawn, who shakes his head.

When their door is closed, I say, "I'm sorry." I wouldn't wish that couch on my worst enemy.

He shrugs. "Eh. This chair is comfortable enough. I'll try it for tonight."

I wish him luck then we exchange a soft goodnight before I get ready for bed. Guilt pricks me, that I have my own room and he's relegated to the living room. I wish I could be brave enough to offer to share my bed, but I'm not. And I know Shawn would refuse if I offered to take the recliner.

Between that and my tangled feelings where Shawn is concerned, I'm simply restless. Sleep eludes me. When I do drift off, it's only a light slumber.

I wake up at a slight noise, bolting upright.

My mind races to Steven, and I hurry into the hall, but I don't see anyone. Water running echoes from the bathroom. Steven's door is shut, and I peek into his room. The grip of tension eases in my chest when I see him sleeping alone in his bed, safe and sound.

I pull his door shut, turning around to find Shawn right there, studying me. "What?" I keep my voice quiet.

"You can't help yourself, can you?"

I stare at him, not sure what he means.

He sighs, walking over as he searches my face. When he's close enough to make my heart pound, he brushes a stray piece of hair back from my forehead. "You always take care of us, always worry about us. It's what you do." He pauses, his lips tilting up. "That's why we love you, you know."

My heart skips a beat at the word love on his lips. Panic flutters in me, but I talk myself down. He said "we", as in *all* the brothers. "I love you guys, too."

He softens, going tender and squishy like a marshmallow. "I know, Lee. I see you." And he pulls me into a hug.

I stand there, rigid and weird, wondering if I'm still dreaming.

His lips brush my cheek as he whispers, "Goodnight," and heads for the chair.

I'm left gaping after him. My hand touches my cheek where the feel of his lips lingers. Did he do that on purpose? I shake my head as I walk back to my room. It had to be an accident—there's no way he'd kiss me. I almost laugh at the idea.

Back in bed, Shawn's words, "I see you," keep running through my head, followed by his hug and the accidental brush of his lips against my cheek. I toss and turn the rest of the night. Weird dreams wake me, but I only remember bits and pieces, like a pair of intense green eyes.

It's barely light out when I stumble from my room. I frown when I find Shawn on the couch again. Evidently the chair didn't work. I grab a glass of water, wishing it were coffee but not wanting to wake him with the noise of prepping it. I grab my book and head for the balcony.

The air feels heavier today, and it smells like rain. I sit in the plastic chair, my feet propped up on the metal railing as I watch the storm roll in from the ocean. The sky darkens, going from a beautiful, cheery blue to a serious, dull gray. Then suddenly, it's black. The wind starts as a playful, gentle breeze but grows into a fierce gale. It's all I can do to keep my book on the right page so I quit fighting.

I close my book and set it on my lap to watch the seething water as the huge waves crash against the shore. The sliding door opens. Shawn appears with two cups of coffee in his hand, and my hoodie draped over his arm. He offers me a mug then the sweatshirt.

"You're up early," he says over the wind.

I nod, sipping the coffee. "Thanks." I set the cup down and pull on my hoodie. The temperature has dropped quite a bit since I came out, but it's still so much warmer than Michigan.

"It's going to storm, huh?" He takes the other chair, leaning forward with his elbows on his knees.

"Yeah."

We sit, watching the ocean as the air grows heavier with impending rain. If someone stuck a pin in the clouds, I'm sure they would burst. I glance at Shawn. The growing tension between us feels similar, and I wonder what will happen when it breaks.

The sky lets loose, and Shawn yelps, jumping up to race for the door.

I stay, basking in the warm rain as I tuck my book under my chair. Then I tilt my head up and close my eyes. I've always loved rain, loved thunderstorms.

Watching them roll in is my favorite entertainment. I'll sit on the couch to watch lightning like a movie, and I sleep better in the rain than any other time.

"Leah, come on!" Shawn darts back out, grabs my coffee and my book then places them just inside. He steps in front of me and yanks me to my feet.

Then we're standing face to face in the pelting rain. Drops of it cling to his long eyelashes, framing those emerald eyes. His sandy hair plasters to his head, rain dripping down his nose. My gaze is drawn to his damp lips as his tongue darts out to lick the moisture off them.

Lightning splits the sky, followed by a huge rumble of thunder.

I gasp, this time letting Shawn haul me into the condo where he slams the slider shut and yanks his drenched shirt over his head. The shirt hits the floor with a wet plop. He stalks down the hall to the bathroom, returning with two bath towels. He hands me one before drying off with the other then takes his shirt to wring it out in the sink.

I hurry to my room to put on dry clothes. I hang my wet ones in the shower after twisting them a few times to get the excess water out. Then I rush to the living room, only to find Shawn in the recliner. My face falls before I can stop it.

"What?" he asks with a hint of exasperation.

I feel like an idiot, clasping my hands in front of me and twisting my fingers together. I glance out of the slider door. The spot he sits in has a perfect view of the storm.

He sighs then stands up, moving to the couch. "Happy?"

I beam, bouncing into the spot he just vacated. I twist around, curling up in the chair on my side with my hands under my chin. The sky streaks with purple lightning.

"You and your storms."

I turn back to find him watching me intently. "Yeah, and?" He doesn't say anything else, so I turn around to focus on the lightning.

A pinprick of guilt hits me that he's relegated to the couch *again*. Then he lets out a yawn.

"You could crash in my room. If you want."

He tilts his head, brows knitting together. "I didn't get much sleep. The chair doesn't go back far enough."

I give him an encouraging smile. "Go on then."

"If you're sure." At my nod, he stands. "Okay, I will. Thanks."

I turn back toward the slider, feeling warm from our exchange and exhilarated with the show. As I relax to the soothing cadence of rain, sleep beckons. I try to fight it but finally my eyes stay closed as my sleepless night catches up to me.

Chapter Seventeen

Shawn

It's not quite one when I finally get up, and Steven stumbles out of his room shortly after. Silas sits at the table, alone, playing on his phone. I frown, looking for Lee, but then I find her still curled up, facing the slider. She must've fallen asleep to the storm, and I can't help grinning at the adorable sight.

We talk in hushed tones, all of us starving. Since Cherie already left for work, Silas offers to grab Mexican food from a place up the road. We put in our orders, including one for Lee who gets the same thing from every Mexican restaurant—two tacos, a side of rice, hold the beans. Steven changes then goes along with him.

I sit at the table, still waking up. I can't believe I slept that long, but damn did it feel good to stretch out in an actual bed. Lee hasn't stirred when Silas comes back, then Steven slams the door, and I wince.

"Do you have to be so loud? She's still sleeping."

"No, I'm not," Leah mumbles, sitting up. She lets out a yawn, then stretches her arms wide, revealing a tantalizing glimpse of bare skin between her pants and top. "Something smells good." She hops off the chair, coming over to sit next to me at the table.

Steven teases. "Sorry, we didn't order any for Sleeping Beauty."

Her face falls, and I have to turn away from her devastated expression. I hurry to the kitchen to grab a beer, then pause to get one for Leah too. I twist the cap off a raspberry ale, relieved when Steven slides her the food.

She lights up like an amusement park at night. I set her ale in front of her and she turns that blinding smile on me, sending a thrill through my chest. I wonder if I'll ever get used to her looking at me like that.

"You guys are the best," she gushes, removing the lid from the tin foil container. "Seriously, the best."

Silas pops into his bedroom, and Lee watches the door expectantly after he re-emerges. He laughs. "Cherie had to work. She left ages ago."

"Oh." Lee frowns then glances at her phone. "How is it one already?"

With the afternoon stretching in front of us, I pull out my phone. According to the weather app, the rain has settled in with pop up storms continuing through the night.

"Anyone have plans?" Lee asks around a mouthful of food, carefully holding the taco over the pan as grease drips onto the dish.

We all shake our heads.

"It's Sebastian's big presentation day," she reminds us. "We'll have to check in later."

I'd lost track, and I'm glad she remembers.

"Wanna play some cards?" she asks.

We're all in, hurrying to finish our food then clear the table. Four games later, we've each won two, and this is our rubber match. Lee sits sideways, her toes on my chair, practically begging to stretch out. I nod at my lap. She hesitates, nibbling on her lip, and I've almost given up on the idea when she moves.

I tense as her calves come to rest on my thighs, then I relax, enjoying the feel of her weight. I have to shift to get comfortable. I don't want her to think she's too much, though, so I rest my hand on her shin, covered by clingy black yoga pants. She shivers when I glide my thumb up and down.

From my touch?

I do it again, just to see, and she has the same reaction. Steven deals our last card, and she stays overly focused on her hand. I try to hide my smugness at how I affect her.

It's hard to concentrate as Silas calls trump, and they eke out a point. I have to let go of Lee to adjust my cards after the next deal. A second later, I return my hand to the still-warm spot and resume my thumb gliding. It feels right, being connected to her like this. I wish it could be this way all the time.

My cards are crap, but Leah is so triumphant when she calls hearts alone. She lays down the second highest trump card, saying, "You either have it or you don't."

Steven is our only chance, and when he plays a lower card, I groan.

Lee beams and lays down the rest of her cards. "I guess that makes these good then." She and Silas jump up, double high-fiving and dancing around like they won the world cup.

We all exchange the obligatory good games, then Silas' phone dings.

"It's Cherie." Grinning, he darts off to answer.

"What happened with Red?" I ask Steven, taking a sip of my beer.

Lee sits back down. "Yeah, what's her name?"

"I texted her earlier today, but, um, I have no idea what her real name is."

Steven's not usually like that, and I have to laugh.

Silas comes back out. "You care if I use the car? I want to take Cherie to dinner."

No one has any objection so Steven grabs the keys, tossing them to Silas. We all say bye as he heads out of the door. Steven's phone dings, his face lighting up when he reads his text.

He rapid-fires back and forth, becoming more and more panicked. "She wants to go out again. I'm two days in. I can't just ask her name...I'll look like a complete dick. What do I do?"

I come up blank, and we both turn to Lee.

She lets out an exasperated sigh. "Invite her here, have her come up. Be busy. I'll introduce myself and get her name." She shrugs. "Simple."

"Holy shit, you're brilliant." He sends another text, then gives her a big hug. "Okay, I'm gonna go get ready. Lee-bug, you're the best."

I can't help staring at her, thinking of all the times she's taken care of us. How many problems she's solved. I remember her checking on Steven last night, and my insides turn to a gooey mess.

I just love her.

She grabs the cards and starts shuffling. "Rummy." Then she deals, not giving me a chance to protest.

Not that I would. I'll take any chance to spend more time with her. I've won my second hand when a knock sounds at the door. Steven is nowhere to be seen, which is perfect. Lee hurries to answer.

The petite woman stands in the doorway wearing a green sundress and tosses her red-tipped hair over her shoulder. "Hi, I'm meeting Steven."

"Oh, hi, yes. Come in." Lee moves aside, and the woman steps in. "I knew he had a date, but I have to say, I cannot for the life of me remember what he said your name was…?"

Her airy laugh annoys me. "That's okay, I'm Amaya."

"I'm Leah. We may have been introduced at the beach the other day, but I met so many people it's all a blur." They laugh again, and Lee nods to me. "That's his brother Shawn."

I wave, marveling at how well Leah's plan worked.

Steven appears, all dressed up in his button-down black shirt and khakis. "I thought I heard voices."

"I was getting reacquainted with Amaya here," she says smoothly.

A huge smile crosses his face. "Good, but I'm afraid I have to steal her away now." He gives his date a little bow. "Amaya, you look amazing." He offers her his arm before escorting her out of the door.

As soon as the door shuts, I start clapping. "That was something, Lee."

She dips low in an exaggerated curtsy. "Why thank you, kind sir." Her phone chimes with a text, and she grins as she reads it. "Sebastian nailed his talk. They're all going out to celebrate."

I wonder what celebrating for him would be like and try not to laugh at the awkward picture of a bunch of stuffy botanists mixing up dirt. "Awesome." As she texts him back, I pull out my phone. "Wanna get out of here for a while? There's a bowling alley not far."

It's still gray outside but not raining at the moment. I sense her hesitation, so I waggle my eyebrows. "They supposedly have the best pizza in town."

"Oh, well, in that case, we have to go."

We laugh, then I wait for her to actually decide. We had fun at the aquarium, just us, and I think she's enjoyed our time together. I know this is a little different because I'm asking her to deliberately spend time with me, so I give her plenty of space.

Finally, she nods. "Yeah, sure. Why not?" She glances at her yoga pants and tank top. "Give me a minute to change."

I grin like an idiot, bobbing my head. As she disappears, I punch a fist in the air, feeling like I won a battle. Leah agreed to go bowling with me. No strings attached. No coercion involved. Simply to hang out with me.

That's a huge win in my book.

A few minutes later, I emerge in jeans, tennis shoes, a Monty Python T-shirt and a zip-up hoodie. Lee returns wearing a similar outfit, minus the hoodie. Her *More Cowbell* shirt always makes me chuckle.

Her hair is pulled back in a messy bun, and she checks her phone as we walk toward the door. "Vicki and Keisha were supposed to go on a dolphin island boat ride today, but it got postponed due to the weather. A group backed out, and they have enough openings for us. Including Steven and Silas' girls."

She hands me her phone, and I skim the details. A four-hour excursion with dolphin and whale watching plus a stop halfway at a place called Shell Island. Each tourist gets to bring back a seashell of their choice.

The price seems reasonable and one glance at Lee tells me she's excited about the idea, so I shrug. "Fine by me."

She beams. "I'll text the others."

Her fingers fly across the screen as we keep going. She's not paying any attention and heads straight for a pole on the edge of the sidewalk. I clear my throat, but she doesn't even pause.

I have to act fast, so I grab her waist with both hands, pulling her to an abrupt stop. She sucks in a startled breath, looking first at my hands, then at the pole she nearly walked into. I laugh when she ducks her head.

She steps away from me, leaning against the pole as she finishes her text. "They're all in." Then she shoves her phone in her pocket. "Okay, I'm paying attention now."

We make it to the bowling alley with no further mishaps. It's a Wednesday night and not too busy. We order a pizza, determining it can't be the best in town, not with all that grease. Neither of us are spectacular bowlers, and we're pretty close in skill. Three games later, she beats me by a couple pins overall.

"That was fun. Good idea," she says, sitting down.

Her last syllable is muffled, and I watch her fight a yawn. It is almost midnight. I can't believe we were here that long. I guess that's the whole *time flies when having fun* thing.

We return our rented shoes, teasing each other about missed pins as we pull on our sneakers. Our jovial mood dissipates when I open the door to find it pouring outside. And Lee doesn't even have a hoodie. We stand beneath the overhang, staring into the rain.

"We could call a cab," I suggest.

She rolls her eyes. "It's a couple of blocks. We're not going to melt."

She starts to walk out, but I stop her. "Hang on." I sharply tug down the zipper on my hoodie and yank it off, then I pull her to my side in a determined move that leaves no room for argument. It's the best I can do.

I know she wants to protest, so I give her my best glare before I spread the shirt over us like a tarp and wait for her to grab a corner. With a sigh, she huddles under it, leaning in to my side. Heat flares between us, a stark contrast to the cold rain.

I fight the urge to sweep her in my arms, to kiss the lip she keeps nibbling. But resolve crosses her face as she sets her jaw and nods. She wants to go.

Moving makes it worse as we hurry down the sidewalk. She grazes and bumps me as she huddles closer, trying to avoid the rain. But its merciless onslaught soaks us before we make it one block. My shoes squish with each step.

I'm thankful when we finally climb the steps to the condo. She's shivering by the time we get inside, and I'm sure she's just as eager to get out of her wet things as I am. Then I turn and see that both my brothers' doors are shut.

Fuck. Of all the times to not have dry clothes.

I'm freezing, and I can only imagine how cold Leah is. I toe off my shoes then peel my shirt over my head, tossing it into the kitchen sink along with my zip-up. I keep a fist on the waist of my jeans to stop them from sagging down my hips as I shuffle toward the bathroom.

I toss a towel back to her, refusing to peek in case she's already stripping. I shut the bathroom door to give her privacy then towel off my hair and torso. A few moments later, a tap sounds on the bathroom door and I yank it open.

She inhales a sharp breath, her eyes locked on my chest. I grip the door jamb so I don't haul her into my arms and kiss that look right off her face. Her bra straps are visible above the towel that cinches around her torso. Her shapely legs are bare below it. I swallow at my dry mouth, then my gaze lands on the objects dangling from her fingers.

My boxers and a dry shirt.

"I managed to get these from your room."

I stare at the carpet as I mumble, "Oh, um, thanks." Out of the corner of my eye, I see her shiver, running her hand over her arm and wish she'd let me warm her.

"Shawn?" Her obvious hesitation has my head jerking up, and she searches my face, opening her mouth once then snapping it shut.

"What, Lee?" Worry creeps in. "What's wrong?"

"I just…" She tightens her grip on the towel, pulling it higher on her chest. "Why don't you sleep with me tonight?"

I clutch the door jamb to keep from falling over. "What?"

"The bed is big enough and we're both adults." She swallows then raises her chin. "Just give me a couple minutes to change."

And she spins on her heel, hurrying to her room while I gape after her. Still reeling, I shut the bathroom door, shucking off my drenched jeans and throwing them in the tub, followed by my equally wet boxers.

This is what Lee does, I remind myself. She fixes things. Me sleeping on the couch is a problem she wants to solve, nothing more.

I take my time drying off and wringing out my clothes. Then I brush my teeth. Twice.

Hoping it's been enough time, I pad down the hallway. I push on the open door and shuffle in awkwardly. This is a big step, and a huge test of my self-control. Lying next to her all night, not being able to touch her or hold her.

Leah is already under the covers, huddled into a little ball facing me.

"You sure about this?" I ask.

"Y-yes. Get in here."

I shut the door and sit on the edge of the bed for a moment to bolster myself then ease under the covers. My bare leg brushes her foot, which is like ice. "Shit, you're freezing. How are you still so cold?"

I don't even think before sliding my arm under her head and gathering her to me. To my surprise, she doesn't protest, and I have to keep from wincing when her cold limbs collide with my warmth. But she hums, the sound making my cock twitch. Gritting my teeth, I order it to calm down. She burrows against my chest, and I curl around her, unable to believe I actually have her in my arms.

Willingly. Happily. And she's not moving away.

Soon her breathing evens, a sure sign she is one hundred percent relaxed. I prop my cheek on her head, thrilled that for once, I get to take care of her.

Maybe the rain wasn't such a bad thing after all.

Sleep claims me before long, and a few hours later, I wake with a start. My arm is still wrapped around Leah, who squirms in my hold.

"No," she cries, pushing me away.

I sit up, clicking on the bedside light. Leah huddles in a ball next to me, whimpering, and I touch her shoulder as I say her name. So she knows she's safe. But she shoves me away with a terrified cry then leaps out of bed to cower against the wall.

She stands there, staring at me blankly, her whole body rigid with fear.

"Lee, hey, it's me. Shawn." Relief hits me when her shoulders drop, and she repeats my name.

Her knees give out, and she sinks down the wall, burying her face in her hands.

I'm by her side in an instant, wanting to comfort her. "Lee-bug, you're okay, you're safe." I reach for her, hoping she'll let me hold her, but she flinches away.

As if she's terrified of me.

The reaction guts me like a knife plunging into my stomach. She's scared — of me. "Must have been some dream," I try one last time, hoping she'll prove me wrong, but the seconds tick by in silence as she holds herself together.

Maybe she just needs space. "I'll get you some water," I say, standing.

It takes everything in me to walk away when all I want to do is scoop her into my arms until she knows she is safe. I wish I could do more, and frustration courses through me at my helplessness.

I shove the glass against the water dispenser with more force than necessary and it sprays onto the floor. Muttering my annoyance, I quickly mop it up then try again. Once the glass is full, I walk back, keeping my motions slow so I don't startle her.

The flash of fear on her tear-streaked face breaks my heart, but the recognition dawning in her eyes gives me hope. I hand her the glass, careful not to touch her. She takes a sip then swipes at her damp cheeks.

"Tell me about it?" Perhaps talking will help calm her down.

She grips the glass with both hands as another tremor shakes her. "It was Vance."

Her voice cracks on his name, and I have to bite back the rush of anger because he still affects her. I hate that his presence is in her life at all.

"I couldn't get away. And there were people surrounding us, taunting me." She shivers, almost spilling the water, and finally sets it on the table next to the bed before wrapping her arms around herself. "They kept pressing in and Vance wouldn't let me go. I woke up to—" She stops, sucking a deep breath then letting it out in a whoosh. "I didn't know it was you touching me."

I rear back, unable to hide my reaction. She flinches again at the sudden movement, her response slicing through me.

I did this—me, sleeping next to her. My presence triggered her nightmare and caused her pain. The realization sweeps any fragile hope of our budding friendship out from under me so I have nothing to stand on.

Carefully, I school my face into a neutral expression, closing in any hint of emotion. Getting to my feet, I offer the only words I can. "I'm so sorry, Lee. I shouldn't have shared your bed. It's obvious you weren't ready."

She says nothing, her silence confirming my guilt.

Striding across the room, I grab my phone from the nightstand then pause with my hand on the knob. "You know where I am if you need anything."

When the door shuts behind me, I sag against the wall, pummeled by my guilt and frustration at myself. I can't believe I let myself hope. I can't believe I let myself think everything would be fine. I knew this would happen. I told Sebastian that anytime we're together, disaster strikes.

And I was right.

It's three a.m., way too early to call Sebastian even though I desperately need to talk. He'll know what to do. He'll know what my next step should be.

I resign myself to the uncomfortable couch, lying on it with a sigh. But I deserve the couch after triggering Leah's nightmare. I count down the hours until dawn, knowing I'm exactly where I belong.

Chapter Eighteen

Leah

I watch Shawn walk out of my door and listen to it latch behind him. The memory of the nightmare hovers, but more than that—the fear. Of being unable to get away. Of the rage in Vance's eyes as he reared back to hit me. Of the people surrounding us, taunting me.

I let the emotions wash over me, knowing if I fight, their grasp will only choke me. I draw in shaky breaths, one after another as tears leak out. A big part of me is relieved that Shawn left. I don't have to worry about working up the courage to climb back into that queen-sized bed next to him. I don't have to worry about his touch triggering another nightmare or prolonging it.

At the same time, I'm disappointed. It felt really nice to be held, even if my subconscious twisted it around. And it was my choice to let him in—I had no idea it would trigger me. But I can't bring myself to run after him and beg him to come back. He's doing what he thinks is best, what he thinks I need.

I couldn't take his offer of comfort then, but now that he's gone, I want nothing more than to hear his deep voice. I glance at my phone, annoyed to see it's only three a.m. I need more sleep, so I curl up on my side and try.

Every time I close my eyes, I see Vance's menacing sneer and hear the crowd's jabs.

Eventually I succumb to exhaustion. The ding of my phone wakes me, and I wince at the dull ache in my head. Tossing and turning for hours will do that. I'm surprised when my phone shows it's already ten-thirty a.m., later than I expected.

I read a text from Vicki, inviting me and Keisha to a girls' brunch before the outing today. When I say I'd love to, she responds that she'll pick me up in forty-five minutes. First, I need to visit the bathroom.

A low voice forms my name when I come out, so I pad toward the living room to investigate. Shawn paces back and forth in front of the slider with his phone to his ear.

"If you'd have been here, Seb." He swipes a hand over his face. "I've never seen her so scared. Because of me." His voice is strangled as if the idea tortures him.

Pieces click together as I realize he's telling Sebastian about my dream. Anger and hurt swirl within me because the last thing I want is Sebastian worrying. I stomp into the living room. Shawn's eyes go wide as I march right up to him.

"You told Sebastian?" When he nods, I hold out my hand for the phone.

"Leah wants to talk to you." He passes it to me, full of trepidation.

I snatch it away and step onto the balcony before shutting the glass slider firmly behind me. "Sebastian?"

"Leah? Are you okay?"

The concern in his voice has me pinching the bridge of my nose. I would've told Sebastian eventually, after he could see me in one piece. A fresh wave of anger crashes over me as I turn to glare at Shawn. He frowns, shoving his hands in his pockets and walking away.

"I'm fine. It was a dream — nothing more." I gaze at the ocean. "I was confused when I woke up. That's all."

"Really? Shawn made it sound like you were barely holding it together."

His skepticism has me gritting my teeth. "I was shaken afterwards, of course, but I just needed a few minutes to calm down. Shawn blamed himself for the nightmare, and he left." My voice cracks on that last word, but I quickly clear my throat, hoping Sebastian didn't notice.

He goes quiet for several moments. "Do you think him sleeping next to you triggered your nightmare?"

"I don't know." My cheeks are warm, and I hesitate. "It is the first time I've slept next to anyone since..." I trail off, watching a swooping gull as it glides down to the water. "It's not his fault though," I say firmly. "Nightmares happen, and I've had a lot of... experiences this week that pushed my usual boundaries." Resting my hand on the sun-warmed metal railing, I let the heat ground me. "Last night was probably the straw that broke the camel's back."

More silence, but I expect nothing less from Sebastian. I know he'll mull over my words before responding, making sure he says what he means.

"That sounds reasonable." Relief tinges his voice. "Actually, it makes a lot of sense."

The tension eases in my gut, and I begin to relax. "Yeah, I think so, too." Now that I've proven I'm all right, we can move on. "So, tell me about your conference."

His voice is light and cheery as he describes how well he did. He butted heads with the professor's "spoiled" daughter, but otherwise had fun. My heart feels like it'll burst to hear him so happy.

"I'm so proud of you, Sebastian. Great job."

"Thanks." He pauses. "I'm proud of you too, Leah. It sounds like you've stepped out of your comfort zone a lot on this trip and look how good you're doing."

"Thanks." I can't help smiling at his praise. "Miss you."

"Miss you, too."

He has a meeting soon, so we say goodbye. I hang up and let out a whoosh of air as I glimpse Shawn in the kitchen. My anger returns in a flash at how he overstepped. He did it the day after we got here too, telling Sebastian how I stayed in when they all went out. I know they're close, but he can't keep worrying Sebastian.

Especially when I'm fine.

Shawn sits at the counter with his head in his hands when I storm inside and toss his phone in front of him. I stick my finger in his face. "You had no right." I turn to leave, but he grabs my wrist.

"Lee, wait."

I jerk away. "I have to get ready for brunch with Vicki and Keisha."

He follows me as I blaze down the hallway and shut the door in his face. His voice echoes through the wooden barrier as I change. "Why are you so pissed?"

I set my jaw and glare. If looks could start fires, that hollow piece of wood would be incinerated in seconds. "Really? You have no idea?" I finish buttoning my jean shorts, then tug on my cute tank top and yank open the door.

Shawn stumbles in, and I cross my arms over my chest. I glare, waiting for him to figure it out. When he stays silent, I throw up my hands, beyond exasperated. "Why do you keep worrying Sebastian over things I can handle? Sometimes I need space." I shake my head and stand in front of the mirror as I pull a brush through my hair.

"I stayed in one night, Shawn. One." Anger drips from my words, and I fight a wince as a stubborn tangle catches on the bristles. "I'm allowed to be alone. It doesn't make me a recluse."

"I know that. I...I was worried because this whole week would be filled with new people and new surroundings. I didn't want you to miss out."

"So you tattled on me?"

One corner of his mouth ticks up. "It worked, didn't it?"

I smack my brush on the dresser and begin sectioning my hair for a French braid, while I chafe at his words. "Yeah," I admit reluctantly, "it worked." I begin braiding from the crown of my head, working to keep the strands smooth and flat against my scalp.

"I didn't call Sebastian this morning to tattle on you." Sincerity laces the words along with a hint of pain. I meet his eyes briefly before he swipes a hand over his face. "I needed to talk to him. Seeing you last night, how scared you were..." A muscle ticks in his jaw. "I thought I'd give being friends a try, but obviously this isn't going to work."

Frustration rips through me as I snatch up my hair tie and bind the end of my braid, then I whirl around to poke him right in his perfect chest. He rears back in surprise as I say, "Knock it off. You're taking way too much credit here."

Confusion furrows his forehead, and I let my hands fall to my sides, exasperated. "Look, Shawn. I won't lie. This week has been tough. I've been pushed out of my comfort zone more times than I can count. But I've made new friends and had some awesome experiences." I manage a smile. "Like petting a stingray."

His mouth twitches, but he studies the floor again.

So I bridge the gap, laying my hand on his shoulder. "You helped me through all of that."

He startles, staring first at me then my hand before meeting my gaze once more.

"You've been there, every single time. It didn't matter if you had just lost a volleyball game or retied my strings or we'd had the world's most awkward conversation. You were there." I step away, needing distance for this next part.

"Until last night." I press my lips together, trying to reel in my hurt. "You left because I couldn't handle being touched. You ignored the fact that I had made the decision to let you into my bed, that I invited you there. And you left."

Pain pinches his face.

"You left me," I repeat, my voice breaking.

"Oh, Lee." He steps forward, pulling me to him. "I didn't want to. I thought I'd caused it, that I hurt you just by being there. I never thought you actually wanted me to stay."

"Idiot." I pinch his side through his shirt, grinning when he yelps. Then I rest my head against his chest, allowing his embrace to comfort me, his scent to wrap around me.

"I *had* to talk to Sebastian this morning," he says quietly. "I didn't mean to worry him, but he's my best friend. And I've never seen you so scared. You wouldn't let me anywhere near you." His swallow is audible. "I thought I broke you."

I lean back, peering up at his handsome face as I shake my head. "No, Shawn. You keep saving me. Every time I turn around, you're there and…" I trail off, a lump forming in my throat that I have to push past to say the next words. "And I'm starting to depend on you."

He freezes, blinking as if shocked by my declaration. My gaze drops to his lips as hope blossoms within my chest.

"You're important to me, Lee," he says, tenderly. "More than you know. I don't want anything to jeopardize our friendship."

It's like a cold bucket of water poured over my head as I crash back to reality. *Friends, right.* I nod, stepping backward, out of his touch. "Yeah, Shawn. Me too."

Thankfully a horn honks outside as my phone dings. "I've got to go." I force a smile and say, "I'll see you at the boat."

"Okay. See you then."

I hurry to stuff a couple more things in an oversized purse then brush past him, nearly running into Silas in the hallway.

He frowns. "You good, Lee?"

I keep walking, calling over my shoulder. "Just dandy. Vicki and Keisha are picking me up for lunch.

Later." I rush outside and down the steps to jump into the van.

They both greet me, and I force a cheery tone then slump in my seat as soon as we're on the road. In the volleyball game of life, someone set me up for a perfect spike that I full-on went for.

And missed.

"You okay?" Vicki asks, her hazel eyes finding mine in the rearview mirror.

I shake my head, my throat thick. "Shawn friend-zoned me."

They both gasp and Keisha turns around. "What happened?"

Gratitude swells in me that I have them for support, and I let out a long sigh. Then I explain everything.

* * * *

Shawn

Silas peeks his head into Leah's room, frowning when he sees me. "What's going on?"

I swipe my hand over my face. "I don't even know." I had thought we were really connecting, that things were going great. Then she'd iced me out.

"I'm gonna..." He jerks his thumb toward the bathroom. "You start the coffee, then we'll get to the bottom of this."

Woodenly, I go through the motions of starting the coffee pot. Silas slips onto one of the stools at the counter as Steven comes out of his room, yawning. He does a double take at our serious expressions.

"What's up?"

"That's what I'd like to know," Silas says.

I lean forward on the counter as Steven claims the other barstool and I fill them in on last night.

"Whoa, back up." Steven stares me down. "You shared Leah's bed?"

I can't tell if he's upset or amazed. "Um, yeah. She asked me to." He glares, and I glare back. "You try sleeping on that fucking couch. You two are with your girls every night in nice comfy beds, and I get stuck in the living room."

Guilt crosses both their faces and Steven backs off. I continue my story, leaving out the details of the dream and reassuring them that Leah is fine before I jump into my call with Sebastian.

Steven shakes his head. "You really blame yourself for everything, don't you?"

"It all lined up," I protest. "Don't worry, Lee set me straight. I blame my relapse on lack of sleep and it being the middle of the night."

Silas snorts when I tell him how Leah got in my face then he grows serious as I recap the rest. Confusion furrows his brow. "That's it? Then why did she seem all upset when she left?"

Steven's head jerks up. "She left?"

I nod. "She's having brunch with her friends and will meet us at the boat." To Silas, I shrug. "I don't know. One minute all this tension was crackling between us and she kept staring at my mouth like she wanted me to kiss her. Then the next, she'd pulled up all her walls and was forcing a smile."

My brothers exchange looks before Steven says, "Tell me *exactly* what you said before she shut down."

"Okay." I rack my brain. "It was something like 'You're important to me, more than you know' and, 'I don't want anything to jeopardize our friendship'." I shrug again, but their silence has me glancing from one to the other, alarm rising in me. "What?"

Silas runs his hand over his hair, stopping at the back of his neck as he exchanges a grimace with Steven. "You want to give him the shovel or should I?"

Evidently I dug myself a deep hole.

Steven studies me. "Think about it, Shawn. You don't want to jeopardize your *friendship*." When I still don't say anything, he sighs. "You labeled what you two are. You stuck her in the friend zone."

"What?" I push upright, beyond annoyed. "No, I didn't. I mean, we are friends, right now. She said that herself…"

"But you don't want *anything* to jeopardize that friendship," Silas says quietly. "And it sounds like Lee took that to include any sort of a romantic relationship."

I play back the conversation, watching her reaction in my mind. As soon as the word friendship was out of my mouth, she withdrew. "I…I meant…"

Fuck. I fold my arms on the counter and drop my head down as I marvel at my own stupidity for several moments. Then I lift my head to frown helplessly at my brothers. "What the hell do I do now?"

Silas comes around the counter to clap me on the shoulder. "First let's get some coffee, then we'll figure this out."

"I sure fucking hope so. I've come too far to let her go now."

"Don't worry, Shawn," Steven says. "We won't let that happen."

I take in their steady, reassuring expressions, and I finally allow myself to hope.

Chapter Nineteen

Leah

I finish explaining about Vance as we pull into the restaurant. Stunned silence reigns for a long moment then Vicki and Keisha talk over themselves, telling me how sorry they are I went through that. I manage a small smile, thanking them.

The time it takes to get inside and sit down allows me to compose myself once more. Keisha orders a mimosa, and we all follow suit.

After the waitress leaves, Vicki asks, "So, your nightmare was about Vance?"

I nod, filling them in on last night and my confrontation with Shawn this morning. I rip the paper band off my silverware bundle and twist it in my fingers. "The tension between us was so yummy. I actually thought he might kiss me."

Both Vicki and Kayla lean forward, listening intently from their side of the booth. My pause must be too much because Kayla says, "So, what happened?"

I jut my jaw to one side, steeling myself as I repeat the words. "He said, 'You're important to me, Lee, more than you know. I don't want anything to jeopardize our friendship.'"

Vicki pushes back against the cracked vinyl, slumping down. "Well that sucks."

But Keisha tilts her head, studying me. "I don't know."

"It seemed pretty clear to me," I mutter, then move my arms as our server sets down our mimosas and waters. We take turns placing orders, and I get scrambled eggs, sausage and something called a blintz that sounds delicious.

As soon as the server disappears, Keisha resumes her thinking position, drumming her nails on the lacquered tabletop. "Something doesn't add up. I've seen the way he is with you and I don't buy the whole friendship-only thing."

Vicki sits up, her forehead furrowing. "Yeah, me neither."

I chuckle at how fast she changed her mind, then oblige when they ask about my backstory with Shawn. I don't leave anything out—the pool, our enemy status, how things have gradually gotten better since the library incident.

"Damn, girl, you two have been through some shit," Keisha says, letting out a disbelieving laugh.

"Yeah, we have."

Vicki is all smiles. "But that changes everything!" She looks between us. "Don't you see?" At our blank stares, she huffs in exasperation. "Okay, keep up with me here. Shawn is trying to change your whole perspective on him."

She holds up her fingers, ticking one off with each reason she lists. "He tried to make that movie thing a date. He promised Sebastian he'd watch out for you this week. He's kept that promise, spending every possible moment with you, including some alone time," she says triumphantly. But I'm still frowning and her grin fades. "He just wants to be friends *first*!"

Understanding dawns on Keisha's face and she claps her hands together, beaming. "Yes! That's exactly it. He's been so focused on getting you to the friendship phase that he hasn't even let himself think beyond that." She reaches over to squeeze my wrist. "It wasn't a label or a box. He just thinks that's what you need right now."

Vicki melts, clasping her hands under her chin. "He doesn't want to push you like your ex did." She sighs. "Damn, those Wrightings are not only hot, they're beyond sweet."

I sag against my booth, trying to comprehend what they're saying. I replay the moment again, picturing Shawn's intense green eyes, how he leaned in. I didn't imagine the attraction there, and while I believe he meant every word, I also believe my friends are right. He wasn't limiting us...he was trying to reassure me.

The way he always does.

The little moments begin stacking up in my mind. How even when I thought he hated me, I could depend on him. The day of the pool, he waited to make sure I was okay before he left. He was the first thing I saw when I surfaced. The night with Vance, he'd been my safe haven, and again after the library. Not to mention myriad small actions in between. Times I was down and he nudged me out of a funk by teasing or annoying me. How I'd be content to stay in my little bubble, but he wouldn't let me.

Awe fills me at all he's done, and it's hard to wrap my head around. Even when we were enemies, he looked out for me.

No wonder I'm so attracted to him.

I swallow at the lump forming in my throat as I allow myself to consider having more with him. The idea feels right. I'm not ready to outright confront Shawn about his feelings, or throw myself at him. But I am willing to see how things unfold between us, to let them progress naturally.

A flicker of excitement sparks within me, twining with anticipation. I can't wait. Our food comes, jolting me out of my thoughts and I realize my friends are watching me. "I think you're right."

Big smiles sprawl over their faces.

"You guys are the best, you know that?" I hold up my mimosa. "To new friends and new beginnings."

Vicki raises hers. "To Spring Break and flings."

Keisha adds, "And to not being friend-zoned."

We all chorus, "Hear, hear," then clink our glasses together.

Chapter Twenty

Shawn

I survey the wide selection of beer, surprised at the amount of choices in this little store. My brothers are busy grabbing what they want. Their girls have gone back to their places to change and will meet us at the boat dock.

"What should we get Lee?" Steven says.

I don't answer right away, still debating. Leah doesn't usually drink until later in the afternoon, but we'll be on the boat for most of the day. Steven taps his foot as I think. "Let's get her rum and Coke." Then she can have the option.

I'm in a much better place than I was earlier. Steven and Silas helped me work through my options. I don't think she's quite ready for me to stake my claim yet, and the main thing is that we're heading in the right direction. I want to keep showing her that I can be there for her.

But I also can't deny the tension between us, which is why I'll be watching what I say much more carefully from now on. Maybe I can chalk it up to a fluke and my actions will speak louder than my idiotic words. Starting with an apology gift for overstepping with Sebastian.

I know exactly what to get her.

"You ready?" Silas asks once the rum and Coke are in the cart.

"Not quite." I head down the candy aisle, ignoring the confused expressions on my brothers' faces as they trail after me.

A while later, we pull up to the dock parking lot, and Leah waits for us on the sidewalk. Steven and Silas grab their cooler bags, racing over to talk to her. But I hang back, unsure of my plan now that I'm faced with executing it.

What if it doesn't work? What if I've ruined my chances and Leah will never see me as more than a friend? I shake my head, trying to get a hold of my spiraling thoughts as I walk to the back of the vehicle and lift the hatch.

A moment later, Leah's soft voice says, "Shawn?"

Still preoccupied, I grunt on instinct, but regret it immediately. Not the way to show friendliness or attraction. I bite back a sigh and turn toward her. "Hey, Lee."

"Hey." Her expression is easy and casual, not at all shuttered like this morning.

Hope rises in me, and I wonder if she understands. "So," I say, settling on the bumper next to her. "How was brunch?"

She smiles as she tells me about mimosas and something delicious called a blintz. I drag my cooler closer, but the bottom scrapes over the spare tire compartment and she flinches. It reminds me too much of this morning, and a bitter taste floods my mouth as a terrible thought occurs to me.

"Leah?" I ask, my voice strangled.

Her head whips up, concern all over her face.

"Are..." The words don't want to form, but I force them out. "Are you afraid of me?" When she doesn't answer right away, I jump into explaining. "You flinched just now and it reminded me of this morning. You flinched when I reached for you and—"

"Shawn." My name is an exhale, her forehead crinkling as she places a hand on my arm.

Electricity shoots up from where our skin meets, and a thrill jolts through me, a warm spread of reassurance following it. Because she closed the gap. She touched me, and my fear dissipates even before her next words register.

"I'm not afraid of you. I've *never* been afraid of you." She drops her hand and lets out a sigh. "Sometimes I'm so far in my head, I can't see the real person in front of me. Like last night, all I could see was Vance."

Understanding washes over me, and I remember the night after the library. It wasn't me that she was flinching away from. It was him.

She crosses her arms over her chest. "I told Vicki and Keisha about all that this morning."

"Really?" Surprised, I study the two women, chatting and laughing with their guys.

"Yeah." Her arms fall back to her sides. "Going over our history made me realize something."

"What?"

"I have a lot to thank you for." She shifts her weight. "Even when we were at odds, you were always nudging me out of my comfort zone and cheering me on whenever I made progress. You were always there when I needed you."

My throat is tight, and I swallow, trying to relieve the pressure. I don't even know how to respond. I've never felt so seen.

"Thank you, Shawn." She barrels into me, wrapping her arms around my torso.

Her emphatic hug catches me off-guard as my breath leaves me in a whoosh. She presses her cheek against my chest as I slide my hands over her back and give her a gentle squeeze.

"You're welcome, Lee-bug," I say huskily. "Anytime."

She steps away, clearing her throat before she glances at the cooler. "So did you guys get me anything? Or do I have to bum off everyone else?"

We still have plenty of time before the boat leaves, so I perch on the edge of the open hatchback and pat the spot beside me. "Of course we got you something." She settles in next to me as I continue, "You get rum and Coke, so you have the option of drinking or not."

Her smile lights up her whole face, and I can't help smiling in response. "But that's not all." I think of what I bought her, feeling like an idiot for going so overboard. "I, uh, wanted to apologize again for overstepping with Sebastian, so…here." I hold all the candy out toward her.

Her eyebrows jump up. "Trying to buy my forgiveness?"

"I wasn't sure which one said 'I'm sorry' the loudest."

She lets out a little laugh, spreading the assorted packages on her lap. "Shawn…what is all this?"

I point to the red bag of Skittles. "Your favorite when you were eight. You thought the red ones were the best, and you'd run around sticking out your tongue so we could all see what color it was."

Next I point at the shiny gold packaging of the Twix. "This was your favorite when you were thirteen or fourteen. You liked the peanut butter ones better, but I don't think they make those anymore. You'd always yell at me to get you one whenever we stopped for gas. A Coke and a Twix—the peanut butter kind." I smirk, remembering her hollering at me. "You never said please, but you always said thank you."

She blinks as the gold catches the light then whispers, "Thank you."

But I'm not done. "Once you started driving, I didn't see you as much. Although we did go to the movies a couple times, all of us. And for some unknown reason, you always get these." I gesture to the box of Raisinets, making a disgusted face.

Her indignant little laugh is adorable. "There's nothing wrong with chocolate-covered raisins. They're delicious."

I wrinkle my nose then point to the last candy. "But your favorite now? The one you grabbed on the way down here? The one you get in the checkout line at the grocery store, to treat yourself after shopping?"

She turns the Reese's Cup over in her hand, utterly silent, and I wonder if I really did go too overboard. Until she lifts her head and a sweet smile tilts her lips. "Thank you, Shawn. This is perfect."

All the tension in my body releases. A horn blows from the boat, signaling the start of boarding, so I nod to the cooler. "You can keep them in there if you want, so they don't melt."

"Melt? They won't get the chance. I'm going to eat them all, and you're going to help me." Despite her words, she tosses the candies back in the cooler then links her arm through mine.

I heft the cooler with my free hand, feeling lighter than a paper lantern drifting into the night sky. She keeps me close throughout the whole afternoon, and I seize every chance to share a casual touch with her. My hand at the small of her back as she steps on board, my arm behind her as I lean against the railing, my shoulder bumping hers as we tease.

I might even call it flirting.

Lee spots the first dolphin. She points, calling out to everyone as she bounces on her toes, unable to hide her delight. I soak up her energy. On the island, she deliberates the whole time over which shell to choose. Ultimately she narrows it down to two, but she can't decide.

I take one from her. "You get that one, I'll get this one. Then you can have both." What would I do with a shell anyway?

Her smile is worth it.

As the boat pulls into the harbor, she rests her hand on my arm. "How do you feel about going to that club tonight?"

"What?" I stare at her in surprise.

"I want to hang out with Vicki and Keisha more since they're leaving tomorrow. It sounds like fun." She pauses, glancing away before looking back at me. "But I don't want to go without you."

The admission almost knocks me over, reminding me how far we've come since the beginning of the week, and I hurry to agree. "Anything you want, Lee.

I'm up for it." She has no idea how much I mean those words.

She squeals, bouncing on her toes again before giving me a half hug. "Okay, I'll talk to the girls."

Once plans are made, we head back to the apartment. My sleepless nights are catching up to me, and I yawn.

Lee yawns too then grimaces. "I guess neither of us slept well last night."

We've got a couple hours yet before we need to get ready. "Maybe we should take a nap." When her startled gaze flies to mine, I realize how intimate that sounded. So much for watching my words. "Oh, I meant, um, separately." I jab my thumb toward my room, unoccupied for the moment. "I'll have to sleep on top of the covers, but…yeah."

Her cheeks are pink as she nods. "Right. Of course." She wipes her hands on the front of her shorts. "Yeah, I think I'll do that."

"'Kay. Night." I smack my forehead after she disappears. "Smooth, Shawn. Real smooth."

After a couple hours of sleep, I wake up completely re-energized. I take a quick shower and pull on my black jeans along with a fitted green mesh short-sleeved shirt. Then I go make two sandwiches, not wanting to be drinking on an empty stomach.

When I tap on Lee's door, she calls, "Come in." She sits up in bed, stretching sleepily.

My imagination goes into overdrive, picturing waking up next to her, seeing her all soft and sleep rumpled. Leaning in for a morning kiss which would lead to—

I jerk my mind back to the present. "I made you a sandwich. The shower's all yours, if you need one."

"Thanks." She takes a bite then nods toward the foot of the bed. "You can stay and eat if you want."

"Nah." I try to sound nonchalant though the idea of sharing a bed with her now would be playing with fire. "The crumbs," I say lamely, moving toward the door. "I've got some emails to catch up on anyway. Just, um, let me know when you're ready to go." And I hurry down the hall before I can make a bigger ass of myself.

I eat my sandwich at the table as I scroll through my phone. Not long later I hear the shower running, and I grit my teeth, focusing on my screen. It seems like forever before she comes out, but when she does, she takes my breath away.

Her gray leopard print sleeveless top has a higher neckline but it molds to her like a second skin, emphasizing her curves. The frayed hems of her black denim shorts are shorter than her usual style, showing off her long, sleek legs. Part of her hair is pulled back from her face while the rest hangs down, brushing the tops of her shoulders. And she's wearing just the right amount of makeup to make her big blue eyes stand out even more.

"Ready?" she asks, frowning when I'm unable to answer. "What?" She runs her hands down her shorts, smoothing them. "Don't I look okay?"

I sigh, unwilling to tell her how great her effect is on me. I rake a hand through my hair, deciding to deflect. "Leah, I'll be beating the guys off you with a stick tonight. Let's go."

Thinking of her being surrounded by guys has me bristling, and when she beams at the idea, it makes me even grumpier as we walk outside. We've crossed the parking lot when her phone rings. She lights up, mouthing Sebastian's name to me before she answers.

I half-listen to her side of the conversation.

"We're going to a club with our new friends. Too bad you're not here," she teases. "You'll be missing out on all my moves."

I try not to scoff. She's not the best dancer by any means, but she makes up for it with her exuberance.

Sebastian must have said something similar to my thoughts because she lets out an indignant, "Hey!" I laugh, and she shoots me a glare before changing the subject. "How're things at home?"

I study her carefully. A concerned frown crinkles her forehead, making worry well up in me.

"Sebastian?" That same worry laces her tone as she stops walking and demands, "What have you eaten today?"

I watch anxiously for her response. She is my barometer, telling me how concerned I need to be.

Her frown deepens and her free hand flies to her hip. "You put down whatever book you have open and go get food. Now." Her grip tightens on the phone as she chews on her lip.

My muscles are rigid as I wait, worry gripping my chest as I think of every possibility imaginable, each more gruesome than the last. The fact that he's talking is a good sign, I remind myself. But I can't shake the image of him tumbling down the stairs, laying there helplessly with no one coming to his rescue.

All because he forgot to eat.

Relief brightens her face, and she crumples onto a nearby bench. "Sebastian, you can't do this." She drops her head into hand. "Set an alarm on your phone or something. What if you'd passed out?"

Her voice breaks on the last word and I can see she's close to losing her composure, so I hold out my hand. I need to speak to my brother.

"Shawn wants to talk to you." She slaps the phone into my palm.

I take a few steps away and growl, "Sebastian."

"I know, I know," he interjects before I can say more. "I had breakfast this morning, I took my insulin and I'm eating now." The microwave beeps, punctuating his point. "I got caught up in my research with my roses. I want to see if I can increase pollen output to make a more sustainable flower for the bee population."

"Well, you won't be able to do that if you don't take care of yourself." It takes me a second to reel in my exasperation, then I say in a calmer tone, "Sebastian, we're not there to take you to the hospital..."

"I know. It was easier leading up to the conference. I was around other people who were eating so I remembered."

"Set alarms for tomorrow. Right now." Shuffling noises echo through the phone, and I know he's doing as I asked.

"Done."

Relief washes over me. "Good. I need to be able to tell Lee you're taken care of."

I glance at her. Panic hovers in the way she leans forward, huddled into herself. Her knuckles are pale where she grips the bench, and her unseeing stare goes right through me.

"She needs you to reassure her, Seb."

"Okay," he says softly.

I sit next to her and hold out the phone, but she shakes her head. "He's all right, Lee." I repeat everything he told me as I rub her back. "And he's set alarms for tomorrow, so it doesn't happen again."

She nods, then takes the phone. "Sebastian?" she asks, leaning against me.

The action startles me, and I wonder if it's intentional or involuntary, but I wrap my arm firmly around her shoulders. A thrill races through me at her proximity and trust. I push it aside though. She needs comfort now, not attraction. The phone is tucked against her left ear, which is closest to me, so I focus on Sebastian's responses.

"Leah, I didn't mean to worry you. You're supposed to be relaxing, getting a break." Sebastian stays quiet for a moment. "I'm sorry."

"It's okay, as long as you're eating now." She sniffs. "You're all set for tomorrow?"

"Yeah, I've got leftover lasagna. My favorite person left it for me."

Her mouth curls up, and she relaxes against me.

"Do me a favor, Lee-bug?" He never uses nicknames so it's no surprise when her smile widens as he says, "Have fun at the club. Dance your heart out, okay?"

"Okay, I promise."

"Good. I'm going to go eat dinner now."

She says a quiet, "Good night" and hangs up. But she doesn't immediately pull away from me. The moment stretches between us, her tucked into my side, then her chin drops to her chest and she sits up, guilt wafting off her in waves.

I tuck a finger under her chin, waiting for her to look at me. "Sebastian is a grown-ass man who can take care of himself—contrary to today's events."

"I know, it's just—"

I shake my head. "You deserve to be here. You deserve a break. Stop feeling guilty and punishing yourself. We're going to this club, and we're going to have fun."

She says a quiet okay then fondness crosses her face, and she chuckles. "He told me to dance my heart out."

"Well, then, let's go see about keeping your promise." I stand and offer her my hand, and I don't let go until we arrive at the club.

Chapter Twenty-One

Leah

Shawn doesn't let go until we walk into the club, and I flex my fingers, still tingling from his gentle grip. Butterflies linger from his touch though a hint of panic flutters. A sure sign I'm taking a new step.

I glance over, studying his handsome profile and imagining what those lips would feel like on mine when Keisha yells my name from the dance floor.

"Heyyyy!" Keisha rushes over. "Damn, girl, you look good."

Vicki is right behind her. "Yeah, you do. That shirt is gorgeous, let me feel."

They take turns touching my stomach, pulling on my shirt and oohing over the fabric. I silently plead with Shawn to rescue me, but he crosses his arms with a smirk. Glaring, I throw my hands in the air. "Okay, okay, it's a shirt. You guys go dance some more, I'm gonna get a drink."

It's enough of a distraction, and they sashay toward the floor.

I turn to Shawn. "Where's that stick you promised?"

"You're on your own with the girls. I only said I'd beat off the guys."

His words come out so wrong that I snort. "Wow, Shawn. All this time, and you never told me? I thought you'd be more likely to handle the girls, but if you want to beat off the guys…" I pat his chest with a cocky grin. "Have at it."

His cheeks turn bright red, and he starts stammering, but I'm already hurrying toward the bar. He sidles up to speak right in my ear. "That's not what I meant, and you know it."

I shrug, loving the proximity, loving the teasing. "I'm not judging." I order a Bahama Mama while Shawn gets a beer, still acting put out as he starts a tab.

The song ends and Vicki leads the way to the table they've claimed. Shawn seems ready to keep arguing, but I spot Silas and Cherie. I stand and wave them over as Silas tugs Cherie along.

One of my favorite songs comes on, and us girls head to the dance floor. The guys stay put, content to watch our drinks. We only dance for the one song, then I sit next to Shawn, who is deep in conversation with one of the guys. Our drinks go down easily, and I'm more than ready to dance again, but Shawn is still talking.

Silas seems as bored as me, listening to Cherie compare manicures with Keisha. I nudge him, jerking my chin to the floor, and he grins. We dance our way there, being silly and having fun. He pulls off the sprinkler and moves on to disco as I laugh.

Then Cherie appears, sliding up to him all sex on a stick, and I'm on my own. Silas shoots me an apologetic shrug before turning his full attention on his girl. A warm hand touches my shoulder, and I whirl around.

Shawn is right there, smirking. "Dancing with the wrong brother, aren't you?"

I fold my arms. "You were busy."

He sucks in a sharp breath. "Are you saying," he asks slowly, "that I'm the right brother?"

Panic trickles in, so I deflect again. "I promised Sebastian I'd dance my heart out." I raise my chin, challenging him. "So? Are we going to dance, or what?"

His emerald eyes radiate defiance as his voice dips, going low and husky. "Yeah, Lee, we're going to dance."

The air between us changes, thickening with tension as he grabs my waist, pulling me closer. Heat blooms within me, spiraling from his warm hands on my sides.

"My turn to feel this shirt everyone keeps raving about."

He pinches the fabric between his fingers, letting it pop back into place against my skin. My heart sounds like a freaking stampede as he slides his hand along my hip, up to my rib cage and back down, his gaze never leaving mine. Thankfully the music is loud enough to cover it.

I'm completely rigid as he leans in, his breath warming my neck. I have to swallow at my suddenly dry mouth.

"I thought you wanted to dance," he says.

Right. I reach out to place a hand on his big, broad shoulder, so firm under his silky short-sleeved shirt. I can't help rubbing my thumb over the dip in his defined muscle. Our hips sway to the beat, one of his legs positioned between mine. Despite the space lingering between us, I'm not used to being this close to him.

It's a new kind of torture.

Shawn's movements are fluid, mesmerizing even. Each muscle flows in time with the song — his hips, his shoulders, his lips. Talk about sex on a stick. My whole body feels flushed, my palms damp. A coil of desire winds ever lower through my abdomen. Larger cracks split through my barriers as want and desire bleed out, entrancing me with their heady spell. I lean forward as he does, brushing my chest against his.

It's too much and not enough at the same time. Shawn's molten green stare drills into me, his fingers press into my hip, and he drags me closer. His thigh brushes high inside mine, electricity jolting right to my core. I grip his shoulder tightly, carried away by the intoxicating sensations.

Then the song ends, crashing me back to reality. A wave of panic chokes me, fed by the headiness of my reaction to him combined with being on the brink of something I haven't had in so long. I blurt out, "I need some water."

I almost run for the bar, a churning mass of awakened desire mixing with the dread of reopening myself. It's been a long time since I had that strong of a response to someone. The panic still grips my chest as I go through my calming questions while I wait in the line.

Did I get hurt? *No.* Am I okay? *Yes.*

My racing heart begins to slow at the reassurances, so I keep going. Did I enjoy myself? I can still feel Shawn's thigh grazing mine, his fingers on my hips, and desire coiling low in my gut.

Hell, yes, I enjoyed myself.

The last of the icy grip melts away in the heat of the memory. I remind myself of my decision at breakfast, to let things between us unfold naturally. This was just the next step. I order two glasses of water and chug one, then take the other with me. Why do I have to freak out each time we move forward? I sigh, starting to feel down on myself.

But I pull the brake on that train of thought. No pity party. I'm making progress, even if I'm only inching forward. I survey the writhing mass of bodies pressing in on the dance floor then the crowded tables.

I'm here, aren't I? That's a win in my book.

As I sit down, I search the room for Shawn and find him talking with an older lady who nudges a younger one toward him. She's pretty, too. A stab of jealousy shoots through me, and I press my lips together.

He shakes his head then strides back toward our table, doing a double take when I glare. A smug grin tips his lips and he leans down, his delicious scent caressing me as he says in my ear, "Don't worry, Lee. I told her no." He pushes away, heading for the bar as I gape after him.

Vicki and Keisha exchange a knowing look, but I wave them off as Silas and Cherie sit down, entwined around each other. Shawn brings us both a drink, and the easy air between us is restored, staying comfortable for the rest of the evening. The drinks flow, the dancing is crazy and we shut down the club.

With teary hugs, I say goodbye to my new friends. We promise to stay in touch, and I thank them for everything. My throat is thick when they leave.

Silas and Cherie stumble home with us. I have to grab Shawn's arm more than once, as tipsy as I am. He finally wraps an arm around my waist, and I lean into him, not sure if the warmth spreading through me is from his touch or the alcohol.

As I brush my teeth, I mull over the idea of asking him to share my bed again. I've pushed myself a lot today…what if I have another nightmare? But the awful couch looms in my mind, and I can't let him suffer any more.

I march out to the living room where Shawn is settled on the sofa. I grab his wrist then tug.

He peers up at me, frowning. "What?"

"Come on. My bed is plenty big for both of us."

But he shakes me off. "It's fine, Lee. Go to sleep."

I put my hands on my hips. "No, it's not fine. You've barely slept this week."

Silence hangs between us as he studies me. "What if you have another nightmare?"

I drop his wrist, but hold his gaze. "Then give me my space until I recognize you again. And this time, don't leave." The plea in my words has me feeling vulnerable, but it does the trick.

One corner of his mouth ticks up. "If you're sure, Lee."

"I'm sure. Come on."

This time he lets me pull him to his feet, lets me lead him to my bed. Warmth spreads through my chest that he trusts my judgment. He's wearing shorts and a T-shirt again, his standard nighttime uniform.

As we climb in, I manage to joke, "I'm not even cold tonight, so I promise to stay on my side."

His exasperated smile is followed by a pointed, "Goodnight, Lee."

I whisper back, "'Night."

When we lie down, I curl up as close to my edge as possible, my back to him. His breathing evens out right away, and I envy that as my brain plays through all the events of today.

I linger on his sweet gesture of apology candy, and my lips tip up. I may not be completely ready for him yet, but I think I could be in the not-so-distant future.

I'll just have to keep putting one foot in front of the other, one step at a time.

But someday seems closer than it ever has before.

* * * *

When I wake up, my pillow is breathing. I open my eyes to find myself sprawled across Shawn's bare chest. His arm is wrapped around me, and I freeze, staring at him. His eyes fly open. Meeting my shocked gaze, he rears back, pulling away.

"Guess I got cold." I feign nonchalance as I sit up to stretch. My tank top rides higher on my abdomen.

Shawn stares at the exposed skin then shakes his head as if dazed. He quickly rolls over, only to fall out of bed. His messy hair appears first before he blinks at me.

"You okay?" I lean forward to check on him.

His gaze drifts down, and he lets out a strangled groan then leaps to his feet. "I'm gonna…" And he disappears into the hall, shutting my door behind him.

I need caffeine before I can process everything that just happened, so I wander to the main area where Steven and Silas sit on the couch. I don't see Shawn, but I hear the shower going. After I grab my mug of coffee, I decide I want fruit for breakfast and pick up a strawberry Pop-Tart.

Close enough.

I perch on a barstool, sipping my coffee and nibbling my Pop-Tart. Shawn joins us not long after, acting like he didn't run out of my bedroom a few short minutes before. So I follow his lead.

"What's on the docket for today?" Steven asks, wrapping both hands around his mug.

Silas doesn't even look up from his phone when he answers. "This is my last chance to hang out with Cherie, so I won't be seeing much of you guys. If you know what I mean."

Since we're leaving tomorrow, it doesn't take much imagination to figure it out. I try not to wrinkle my nose as I sip on my coffee. Shawn glances at me, but I shrug, not having a definite plan. We turn to Steven.

"I'm in the same boat as Silas. Me and Amaya were going to hang out."

Shawn asks, "Was there anything you wanted to do, Lee?"

I feel a little silly with my idea of a fun day so I shrug again.

"No, seriously. If you could do anything today, what would it be?"

Even Silas seems to be waiting for my answer.

I brace myself for teasing. "I want to play tourist." When Shawn doesn't react, I continue, my enthusiasm growing. "I want to get some souvenirs for Sebastian and Meg. Maybe something for me. I'd also like to play mini golf." It's one of my favorite things to do when I'm on vacation.

To my surprise, Shawn is smiling. "Sounds like fun."

I study him suspiciously. "What are *you* planning to do today?"

"No plans. Maybe I'll tag along with you—if that's okay. These guys would prefer I didn't join them, for obvious reasons."

Silas snorts and shakes his head while Steven glares.

But I feel the need to make sure Shawn is truly on board before I agree. I narrow my eyes and fold my arms. "Are you going to complain any time I drag you into a tourist trap? Or make fun of me the whole day for my shopping choices?"

His grin makes my knees wobble. "I can't promise I won't tease you, but I promise that I won't complain. It'll be fun."

"Okay. I'll finish eating, then we can go?"

He nods, and I hurry to finish my last couple bites so I can get ready.

I aim for cute, a swishy floral-print skirt with a bright blue top and strappy sandals. I pull my hair partially back, leaving a few pieces in front to frame my face. I debate wearing makeup, decide what the hell and put a bit on. It's my last day here and I want to look good for my pics.

At least that's what I tell myself.

When I come out, Shawn waits for me on the recliner with his phone in his hand. The other guys have disappeared, and their bedroom doors are shut again. It's definitely time to get out of here.

Shawn blinks at me. His throat bobs as he stares, taking long enough that I glance down to make sure I don't have a rip or something.

He flexes his fingers. "You look nice."

"Thanks." I still don't know how to wrap my head around Shawn saying sweet things.

To me.

On purpose.

I'm much more comfortable with his teasing. "Ready when you are."

We shop all morning, picking out souvenirs for ourselves and our friends. Lunch is right on the beach, a delicious meal on a boardwalk, and I linger over my food, wanting to soak up every ray of sun.

I'm excited to head to the mini golf course which is everything a beach town attraction should be. To start with, we're greeted by a pit full of alligators. The reptiles are only a foot or two long, but still.

A sign says we can feed them, and I beam at Shawn. "Should we?"

His smile is as wide as mine. "I'd be disappointed if we didn't!" Then he pauses. "You're not going to make me pet one, are you?"

I shake my head at the ridiculous notion, laughing when he wipes his brow in exaggerated relief. We take turns feeding the gators bits of hot dog with borrowed poles, and I insist on photos for posterity's sake. After our hot dog pieces are gone, we select our balls for mini golf. I pick purple, and Shawn chooses green. I take my time with each hole, enjoying the nuance of the place.

We get through number five before Shawn starts teasing. "I thought you said you were good at mini golf," he says, marking down my score. He's kicking my ass.

I scoff, peering down my nose haughtily. "I never said I was good—just that I wanted to play." We both laugh. "But I think I've given you enough of a head start."

My competitive streak rears its head, and I determine to focus on the game instead of my surroundings. I manage a two on the next hole and a three on one where we have to jump our balls over a stream. Shawn gets stuck when he has to time his shot with the mechanical alligator's opening and closing maw.

I lean in close to peer over his shoulder as he writes down his score, gloating that I'm gaining on him. We walk into the next hole together, a cave with a waterfall thundering through an opening. Water drips from the ceiling every so often, and the air is cooler inside but still thick. I line up for my shot when Shawn grunts.

He scrunches up his nose and his cheek is damp. He glares at the ceiling then yanks the hem of his shirt up to swipe it over his face. His rippling torso has my lips parting, and I itch to run my fingers over his smooth skin. He drops his shirt, focusing on me. I must be on the verge of drooling because he smirks.

"See something you like?"

Great. He needs a reason to be more cocky. "Just paying you back for checking me out at the aquarium."

He laughs. I ignore him as I line up, only to completely mess up my shot. The ball lands on the other side of a mound, directly opposite the hole. He grins wider, and I fume, knowing he credits himself with my mistake.

My annoyance only grows when his ball lands beside the hole. He walks over, swiftly knocking it in while I end up with a four. With only a few holes to go, I can't afford to be this distracted.

But two can play that game.

He goes first at the next hole since he's once more in the lead. I make sure I'm in his line of sight when I bend down to adjust my sandal. My skirt barely brushes mid-thigh, riding up almost to my panty line with my action.

"What are you doing?" he growls.

I stand up, smiling with all the innocence I can muster. "I had to fix my strap. It was rubbing."

"Well, are you finished?"

When I nod, he mutters to himself and lines up. I toy with the hem of my skirt, drawing attention to my leg. He shifts then grits his jaw and swings. Too hard. His ball bounces off one of the bricks, ricocheting back up the green to land neatly at his feet.

I try to stifle my giggle, but it spills out at his annoyed glare.

"You think that's funny?" His mouth twitches, lightening his gruff tone.

I put my hand on my hip and raise my chin. "At least *I* kept my shirt on," I retort, regretting the words when heat flares in his eyes.

He stalks toward me, dropping his club to the ground. I can't move, pinned by his intense stare.

"Are you trying to get my attention, Lee?" he asks, standing so close his nose almost brushes mine. "I assure you, you have it."

My stomach flips at his nearness, his sandalwood and balsam scent enveloping me. His lips are right there, hovering, and I wish I could feel them on mine.

"Lee…" His expression softens, my name a sweet caress.

I can't help leaning toward him. It's like he is the sun and I am an asteroid, drawn in by his gravity. I don't stand a chance.

His hand cups my cheek. His thumb grazes a path along my cheekbone. Anticipation coils within me, and I am wholly in this moment. There is only me, Shawn, and the tension crackling between us.

He shifts forward ever so slowly. At last, his lips brush mine, and my heart stops. My whole body freezes as he pulls back, only for my heart to restart at the same time a wave of panic crashes in. I turn away, bands of anxiety tightening in my chest as I struggle to draw air.

But he stays. His hand settles on my back, and he leans down so I can see him. "Breathe, Lee. With me." His movements are exaggerated as he puffs his cheeks to expel air then loudly sucks in.

I mimic him. Sweet air fills my lungs and I stagger to a nearby bench to collapse onto it. *Holy shit.*

"You okay?" he asks, standing near me. At my nod, he says, "Good. Cause I've got a game to win."

I gape, but he just winks, completely nonchalant. Not at all freaked out that the barest touch of his lips almost had me spiraling into a full-blown panic attack. Nope, he goes right back to normal, teasing Shawn.

I could kiss him, just for that.

Chapter Twenty-Two

Shawn

I do my best to pretend that Leah's almost-panic attack didn't gut me. I know she needs normalcy more than someone fawning over her right now, so I goad her, bringing her competitive streak back to life. And I can't be more proud when she actually beats me. I also can't help singing the Bob Seger song about the lady accompanying me, if only to keep my hopes up. Someday. Someday she'll be mine. Someday I'll kiss her and she won't fall to pieces.

Hopefully sooner than later.

We grab tacos from a food truck then pick up drinks before heading back to the condo. We have the apartment to ourselves, so we lounge on the balcony with our beer as we play cards. Cribbage is our game tonight. We play round after round until the sun sets and it grows dark.

More than once, her gaze dips to my mouth before jerking away. She liked the kiss.

The realization keeps a steady grin on my face.

Her words before the boat trip resurface, that she's never been afraid of me. Even though her reaction to our kiss hurt, I know I can't take her panic personally. It doesn't matter who kissed her, her response would have been the same. It doesn't matter who held her the night of her nightmare, she still would have flinched away.

But I'm glad it was me.

As we finish our last game, Silas and Steven return with their respective girls to disappear into their bedrooms. Luckily, I already have my stuff laid out on the arm of the couch. I won't ask Lee to share her bed. If she's up for it, she'll invite me, and if not, I'll wrestle with the couch.

She comes out of the bathroom, and I grab my clothes to take my turn, but she touches my arm. "You can bunk with me again. If you want."

Hope buoys me, tangling with relief. "You sure?"

She nods, a pretty blush staining her cheeks, but she doesn't duck her head. "Friends don't let friends sleep on uncomfortable couches."

"Thanks," I say tenderly.

The word 'friend' echoes within me, a building block in our foundation that I've worked hard to secure. She scurries off to her room, and I keep grinning to myself as I change into jersey shorts and a T-shirt then brush my teeth. *You'll Accomp'ny Me* plays in my head the whole time. Her door is slightly open, and I ease my way inside, anticipation flickering in my stomach.

The bedside lamp is on, and I feel her watching me as I shut the door then make my way to the bed. She faces me, curled on one side with a pillow clutched to her chest. A protective barrier, perhaps?

I click the light off, darkness swallowing us as I shuffle under the covers. I crave her touch, missing the way she wrapped around me last night in her sleep, so I shift closer, stretching my arm out against the pillow barrier. My fingers brush her knee, and she doesn't move away, even as her breath hitches.

"Goodnight, Lee." My fingertips caress her once more, as I itch to hold her. But I refrain, forcing my hand back into my space as I roll over so my back is to her. "I had fun today."

She doesn't respond before I fall asleep.

It's an uneventful night, at least. I wake up first, still on my side of the bed, and I sit up. Leah doesn't seem to have moved either. She looks so serene that I can't help smiling as a wave of tenderness envelopes me.

I ease into the hall where I shut the door behind me. Both my brothers' doors are closed, but no sounds reach me. Thankfully.

Replaying the trip in my mind, I start the coffee then pull out leftovers for breakfast. We're friends now, me and Lee. It's official. We've come further than I had hoped, sharing a kiss and even a bed. I can't wait to tell Sebastian.

When Lee stumbles into the kitchen, I pour her the first cup of coffee. Her grateful smile has desire stirring within me, but I rein it in, sitting at the table to eat while she heads for the balcony. Silas and Cherie emerge. I say a quick goodbye to Cherie, then they go out to talk to Lee while I take care of my plate before I begin the task of packing.

Twenty minutes later, I haul out my bags. Silas mopes at the kitchen counter while Steven says a prolonged goodbye with Amaya near their room.

Lee sets her last suitcase near the entryway, watching the farewell. "I bet you're glad you didn't do the fling thing. Kind of nice to have your heart intact, isn't it?"

Her words stab at me, and a wry smile twists my lips. *My heart intact, yeah, right.* We've made progress, but I'm nowhere near where I want to be. Leah is still out of reach.

She studies me with concern. "What, Shawn? What's that look for?"

She's not at all ready for the declaration of love that surges to the tip of my tongue. I bitterly swallow it then grab the keys off the counter and pick up her bag. "Leave it alone, Lee." I brush past her, down the steps to the parking lot.

But she rushes after me. "Are you okay?"

A long sigh escapes me, and I pause when I reach the asphalt. "You're not ready yet, but I'll tell you someday, okay? I promise." I stare at her, long and lingering, wishing it could be this moment. But it can't, and again I swallow down the words. "That's all I can give you right now." I turn around, striding toward the SUV.

The ride home is quiet as Silas and Steven deal with leaving their girls. Steven I'm not surprised about, but Silas? He's more of a one-night stand kind of guy so the fact that he stuck with Cherie all week...I guess they had quite a connection.

I keep getting in my own head over my final conversation with Lee. Frustration wells up within me. I want to make her mine, but my gut tells me to hold off. I just wish I knew for how much longer.

She's been quiet, too, and I wonder about her silence. Is it in response to ours? Maybe she's even thinking about me, and the thought has a bubble of hope rises in my chest.

An hour in, Lee sits straighter, a determined set to her jaw as she stares out of the window. I frown, wondering what she's up to.

She smirks as an Arby's sign comes into view. "Arby's, A."

Seriously? We used to play the alphabet game all the time as kids. Each of us tries to race through the alphabet, finding words starting with consecutive letters. First one to Z wins. But it's been years.

Silas groans. "Leah, really?"

I study her, trying to gauge how serious she is, but she arches an eyebrow. A Buick drives by and she smirks. "Buick, B."

Silas grips the handle above the door, spying an Audi coming up, and he claims it first. Steven taps the window with his fist as Lee relaxes against her seat, one corner of her mouth tipped up. Here she is rescuing us again. I can't look away from this beautiful woman who cares about us so much.

I see you, Lee. I see you.

But I blink the words away as a sign for the airport comes into view.

Hours later, Lee gives into exhaustion, curling up in the back seat. When I put in my earbuds and try to close my eyes, all I can see is her. All the brave moments she stepped out of her comfort zone. All the times she looked to me. All her smiles and laughs. All the bits of tension crackling between us.

It's not a bad way to pass the time.

The clock reads after midnight when we pull in, but she barely stirs as we climb out of the car. She yanks her hood over her face, hiding from the interior lights. I chuckle as I open her door.

Silas peers over my shoulder. "Should we wake her?"

"Nah," I say. "Let her sleep."

I bend down, scooping her up into my arms. I love the feel of her, and I pause as she inhales a sharp breath, hoping I don't trigger a panic attack. But she instantly relaxes and warmth blazes through me as she burrows into my chest.

As if she belongs there.

Chapter Twenty-Three

Leah

I wake up the next morning to the unnerving feeling of being watched. Someone perches on the edge of my bed, and I peer past my covers, relaxing when I see Meg. She squeals, pouncing on me.

I laugh, hugging her back. "Oh, I missed you."

We talk over each other as I lift up the covers so she can crawl in next to me. I have a lot to catch her up on. When a knock sounds at my door, I call, "Come in."

Shawn peers in then leans against my doorway. "We've got a full breakfast cooking, so come out when you're ready. We'll try to save you some." He pauses when I raise my eyebrows. "We heard her squeal, so we knew you were up."

Meg and I dissolve into laughter as he shuts the door. I try to fill her in as fast as possible, hitting the highlights.

She interrupts several times to ask, "*Shawn* did that?"

When I finish, I shift uneasily, nervous at what she thinks, but she just grins.

"Well, it sounds like you had a hell of a Spring Break."

I nod like an idiot.

Silence reigns between us as she stares at me, then she bursts out, "Seriously though, Shawn? Are you sure this isn't a Stepford Wives thing, and you were brainwashed or replaced?"

"No, Meg." Warmth buzzes through me, vibrating my chest at the very thought of him. "It's the real deal."

She studies me for a long moment before pulling me in for a hug. "I'm happy for you."

I embrace her tightly, relief unknotting my stomach.

When she steps back, she nods toward the door. "Let's go get some breakfast. I know someone's been missing you."

I light up at the thought of Sebastian. I missed him, too. We race into the kitchen, which is a hub of activity, and I call, "Sebastian!"

He whirls around with a huge smile on his face. The toast and knife go on the counter as I barrel up to fling my arms around his middle. He holds me tight, resting his chin on the top of my head. We rock back and forth for several moments then exchange grins before I let go.

"Anything I can do?"

The answer is a collective, "No!" so strong I take a step back.

I turn to Meg and laugh. "Guess I'll sit down, then."

Once the food is on the table and we're all gathered around, I feel complete. Happiness floods me to the point of bursting as I watch everyone chatting and teasing. These are my people, this is where I belong. It's good to be home.

* * * *

The next five days pass in a blur of settling back into my routine. I can't believe it's already Tuesday. Thoughts of our vacation bubble up as I sit at the empty table with my bowl of cereal. I really miss the sunshine. The sound of the surf plays in my head, and I picture Shawn shirtless on the beach. I definitely miss that.

As I eat, I remember each day, each of our interactions. His teasing, his pushing, his protecting. When I get to the end of the week, I linger on mini golf. Specifically that delicious kiss.

How he'd hovered there. The intense look in his green eyes and his husky tone. His thumb on my cheek.

"Whatcha thinking about?"

Shawn's voice breaks through my memories, and I jump, my hand flying to my chest. My cheeks are on fire as I stare at my mostly empty bowl of cereal.

"Ooh, blushing, must be something good." He nudges my shoulder before taking the seat next to me.

Sebastian is right behind him, a microwaved breakfast sandwich on his plate. "Leave her alone, Shawn." He sits on my other side. "She's got to get to class."

I smile gratefully at Sebastian. We had lunch yesterday before my Monday library shift, and it was good to catch up. I filled him in on Spring Break, leaving out the kiss. It felt weird, the idea of discussing that with him.

Sebastian told me in more detail about his last conference and how he has another one this weekend. His research is taking off, and he even applied for a grant to be able to spend some time in the university greenhouse over the summer. I'm happy for his career, but I'd hoped to spend more time with him this weekend.

I resist the urge to sigh as I shovel my last few bites into my mouth. Shawn's elbow bumps me, and I glance his way. But he just winks. The gesture stuns me for way too long, which only pisses me off.

I'm thankful for the walk to class and the chance to burn off some of my frustrated energy. Shawn's casual touch lingers in my mind. It's amped up since we've been back, and the tension in me coils tighter every day. I don't mind the contact or the teasing air between us.

But I also want more. I find myself replaying our kiss over and over, missing our closeness from the trip. Especially at night. My bed feels empty without him, but it's not like I can march up to Shawn and demand he come sleep with me. My cheeks burn just thinking about it.

That's not letting things unfold naturally.

Meg doesn't help, always gushing about Chad. They're still together, to everyone's surprise. And while I'm happy for her, I'm envious too because I feel stuck.

The day flies by, but Wednesday stretches into the longest day ever. One thing after another goes wrong. I forgot to print out my paper for English, and my cloud backup didn't save it, so I run home to get it in the cold drizzle. Which makes me late for anthropology. Where we have a pop quiz. I miss it, getting a zero for my grade.

After lunch, I drop my book for math in a mud puddle. Then my backpack slips off my chair in class, spilling its contents everywhere. To top everything off, my favorite pair of jeans rips as I pick up my stuff, leaving a gaping hole down the back of my thigh.

With my hoodie around my waist, I slouch in my chair, stewing until class is over. Then I hightail it home.

Throwing my backpack in my room, I grab comfy clothes, yelling to Meg, "I'm taking a shower." I step in, hoping to relax under the scathing spray.

Meg rushes in. "Grabbing some makeup. I'm late for study group."

It's not a big deal. We run in and out all the time, but she doesn't shut the damn door. She leaves it wide open, and she doesn't hear me call after her, my voice lost in the bustle of her rushing out of our suite.

Hopefully she closed *that* door.

It looks shut from here, but that stupid latch doesn't give me much confidence. I finish pouring the conditioner in my palm and set the bottle back in the caddy. Which is when Shawn pushes into the sitting room door, stopping stock still as our gazes lock through the clear shower curtain liner. He gapes at the full view he has of my wet, naked body.

I really meant to get a shower curtain after our last one ripped. It's on my list.

I don't even have the energy to be mad, not with how awful this day has been. All the fight drains out of me as I wrap my arms around myself.

"You have the worst timing." I manage to turn most of my body away, sagging against the shower wall.

"Not from where I'm standing." He simply leans against the door jamb, wearing his cocky grin.

I can't deal with him—his smirk, his teasing. Not on top of this horrible day. I drop my head in my hands, fighting tears. It takes everything in me to ask, "Shawn…please?" I try to keep my voice normal, but I still sound broken.

When I raise my eyes to meet his, his forehead furrows and his mouth tightens. He steps toward me, reaching out as if…to comfort me? Then he shakes his head, striding forward to push the bathroom door shut. I stare at the closed door, my arms still wrapped around myself.

I'm shaking inside and out, feeling completely raw. I finish washing, dry off then pull on my comfy clothes and step out of the bathroom. Where I find Shawn sitting on our couch with his forearms on his knees and his hands clasped together.

He shoots to his feet when I appear.

Exasperation hits me, pouring into my one word. "What?" What could possibly be so important that he can't just leave me alone?

"I—" He stops and rakes a hand through his hair. "I wanted to make sure you're okay." Those green eyes find mine, not leaving my face.

I blink, surprised when I don't see an ounce of teasing in him. The stark concern unnerves me. "Um, yeah. It's been one of those days."

"Do you want to talk?" He shifts from one foot to the other. "If not to me, then to Sebastian?"

I sigh. Thoughtful, but no. He's more work than I want right now. I shake my head, my damp hair slapping my face. I just want to break down on my bed.

Alone.

"Okay. Do you need anything else?" He steps closer. "How about a hug?"

I'm in his arms before I can refuse, his sandalwood-balsam scent crashing over me. I melt against him. I don't even hug him back, my arms hanging limply at my sides as I let him hold me. I didn't know I needed this.

His warm hand rubs my back as a chuckle rumbles through him. "You don't have to worry about me picturing you in your lacy blue bra anymore."

A small snort escapes me before I can stop it. I pinch his stomach through his shirt, then bring my forearms up to rest on his chest as I cuddle into him.

He chuckles again, his voice huskier than usual when he says, "If you ever need to even the playing field, just say the word. I'll let you know the next time I'm showering, and you can bust in on me."

His absurd words have my lips tipping up. I meet his amused gaze, shaking my head. "You're ridiculous."

"Yeah, but it got a smile out of you." He tilts his head. "You okay? For real?"

I step out of his arms and nod.

"Okay…holler if you need anything, all right?"

I watch him leave, surprised at how much better I feel. My bed still calls my name, but I no longer need to cry. Instead, I curl up with a book, putting it down every once in a while to replay the sweet moment. Warmth spreads through me each time, like my own personal sunbeam.

Half an hour later, a soft tapping sounds from my sitting room door. I pad over to open it. No one's there, but a small grocery sack lays on the floor. Curious, I peer inside, delighted to find Reese's Cups, a Coke, some chips and some cookies.

I send Shawn a text right away, telling him thank you. A beaming emoji is my reply, and it's enough.

Emerald eyes and a dazzling smile torment me both Wednesday and Thursday nights. I can't remember anything more specific, although a deep sense of longing lingers.

Friday morning, I sit in my bed, frustrated with my restless sleep and the lack of forward movement with Shawn. I remember my breakfast decision, how I want things to progress naturally.

Except they're not progressing, and I'm surprised at how much that bothers me.

I think back to before Spring Break, to before the night at the library. How we used to snark at each other, how angry he made me. His constant teasing and jabs. The way he pushed. But since the night at the library, we've changed.

I've gotten to know him. Where before he had walls up, keeping me at arm's length with his teasing and grumpiness, now I feel close to him. I want to know more, want to experience more. I feel safe with him. I always have, but this is on a deeper level.

I can depend on him.

Reviewing my time with Sebastian, I frown. I always thought of him as safe, steady and reliable. While he is my friend, being more with him took a toll on me. I never knew if I'd be remembered, never knew if our plans were important enough to follow through on.

Shawn has never once made me feel like that.

A tingle goes through me just thinking of him. I replay all the renewed feelings — the stomach flips and thrills, the full body tingles and electricity, the pulse of desire that never goes away. They scared me at first, but I've grown used to them, little by little. As if edging into the ocean one foot at a time.

I think again of the kiss at the golf course, Shawn's intense eyes as he leaned in, how soft his lips were when he pressed them to mine. My heart pounds, and I suck in a shaky breath, overwhelmed by how much I want to feel that again.

I'm ready.

The words fill me with relief as well as a hint of panic because I know this is what he's been waiting for. Me. Although the idea of talking to him has my stomach twisting, even as a thrill rushes through me. It's time for the next step.

The day is spent practicing what I'm going to say to Shawn. Though everything sounds stupid, I keep trying. After classes, I attempt to do homework, but I can't focus. An hour passes before I stretch and decide to grab a drink. As I'm walking by the front door, I hear Steven talking so I swing it open to investigate.

He almost falls in, his arms full of plastic cups and pop. "Hey!" He grins. "Thanks."

My eyebrows knit together as he saunters into the kitchen. I start to shut the door, but Silas walks up, his arms full just as full, with Shawn hurrying behind him. My glimpse of Shawn has all my nerves rushing back, except now isn't the time. I need to get to the bottom of this first.

I ask Steven, "What's going on?"

Silas walks by, frowning at Steven, then they say in unison, "You didn't tell her?" They glare at each other.

When Shawn steps over the threshold, they turn their glares on him. He balks. "What?"

Steven says, "You didn't tell Lee about the party tonight?"

"No." Shawn's gaze whips to me then back to his brother. "I thought Silas was going to."

Silas grunts. "I thought Steven was."

"Enough," I bite out, shutting the door and stalking into the kitchen. "Tell me now." They all fidget, not looking at me as I fold my arms and wait.

Shawn sighs. "It's not every night that Sebastian isn't here."

"Yeah." Silas nods. "We try to make sure we're not interrupting his need for peace and quiet most of the time, but we gotta have fun too."

It's Steven who finally addresses me. "You of all people understand how he is. We wanted to take advantage of him not being here and have a party."

I flinch at the word and wrap my arms around myself, remembering the last party we'd hosted with the fiasco that ensued. All thoughts of talking to Shawn disappear, taken over by memories as my chest tightens. A house full of people I don't know, Sebastian not here to hide away with me.

Shawn rests a hand on my shoulder, interrupting my spiraling thoughts. "We honestly thought we'd cleared it with you. We'd never do this without telling you, not on purpose."

I inhale his scent, feeling calmer with him near. Silas bobs his head, and I see the truth in their faces. I drop my arms, my chin falling, too.

"It's just...the last time we had a party here..." I automatically turn to Shawn, and I bite my lip.

"Shit." The word is little more than a whisper.

His arms fly around me, yanking me to his solid chest, and I bury my face in his shoulder, clinging to him. I hear the others leave, giving me the privacy I need.

"We weren't even thinking about that, Lee. We had such a good time hanging out during Spring Break, and we wanted more of that." His fingers flex on my back and his voice is tight as he says, "I'm so sorry."

I nod against his chest, my cheeks damp.

"If you want us to cancel, that's fine." He pauses. "But I promise no one here tonight will say anything mean, let alone lay a hand on you. You'll be safe. I'll stay with you the whole time, if that's what you need.

We only invited a few friends each, people we know well. It won't be a huge bash like that was."

Silence hangs between us as his words sink in, then he adds, "But it's completely up to you."

My heartbeat starts to return to normal, and I can breathe again.

The front door opens. A surprised gasp sounds behind us, and Meg's voice slices the air, "Now what have you done, Shawn?"

The surprised laugh that bursts out of me is half-snort. I push away, though my fingers don't want to leave Shawn's chest. I force my hands to swipe at my cheeks. "It's okay, Meg." I sniff.

She glares at him, even as she puts a protective arm around me.

"No, really, I'm fine." I say it to both of them, meeting his eyes and gratified to see him relax slightly. "The guys are having a party tonight, and I had a minor freak out since the last party here didn't go so well."

Meg's eyes grow huge.

"Shawn was being helpful." I glance at him again, smirking. "For once."

He glowers but his mouth twitches. "So, what do you say?"

I think it over, surprised to find I'm not panicking now that I've had time to adjust to the idea. Shawn's offer echoes in my mind. "I'm game, as long as one of you is with me the whole time." I frown. "Bathroom excluded for obvious reasons."

They both laugh, then Shawn nods, tilting his chin down and promises, "You don't have to worry about a thing."

I meet his gaze, warm, steady, intense, and desire rushes through me. I say huskily, "I know."

We stare at each other for a long moment, the air growing thick between us until he brushes past me and breaks the spell. I let out a huge breath.

Meg fans herself. "What was that?"

My lips tip up in a soft, wistful smile. "The beginning of something new."

Chapter Twenty-Four

Shawn

Lee disappears with Meg to their suite to get ready. Meg says the word boyfriend, making Lee squeal before they shut the door. I turn to find Silas glaring after them. He stomps away, taking his aggression out on shoving the furniture toward the edges of the room.

I meander to the kitchen where Steven fills a cooler with beer and I help. Next, I grab the pack of bottled water, planning to make a nonalcoholic cooler. But Meg waltzes in with Leah on her heels, and I nearly drop the pack.

Holy shit, Lee looks hot. Tight jeans cling to her legs, making them appear even longer. Her little tank top shows off her shoulders as well as several inches of her sleek midriff. Confidence exudes from her as she swings her ponytail and grins at me.

A far cry from when she learned about the party.

Tension I hadn't even noticed loosens in my chest, and I can't help giving her a wink.

Pink tinges her cheeks, but she ignores me to survey the mess of cups and packages. Her lips press together and her hands fly to her hips before she declares, "If we're going to have a party, we're going to do this right."

Soon the counter is a neatly organized array of opened packages of cups, markers to write names with, napkins, plates and bowls of snacks. She even labeled the coolers.

Then Steven's phone dings, making us all turn toward him, and a wide smile spreads over his face before he rushes out of the kitchen. We all hurry to the doorway to see what the fuss is about. When he flings open the door for Amaya to walk in, Lee and I gasp together.

"Did you know about this?" Lee asks me.

"I had no idea they were even still talking."

She shakes her head, but ducks under me to greet Amaya. I give her a small wave when Leah comes back, chuckling. "I guess we won't see much of him this weekend."

I move back into the kitchen to grab a drink as Lee explains to Meg who Amaya is. But she's interrupted when Meg's phone buzzes followed by a knock at the door.

Meg squeals, "He's here!"

Grabbing Lee's hand, she drags her to the other room. Curious, I follow, wondering just who 'he' is. Meg yanks open the door, ushering in a tall, athletic guy with close-cropped hair. He kisses Meg on the cheek as Lee shifts her weight, nibbling on her lower lip.

Then her right foot lifts, rubbing against her calf.

I'm by her side in an instant, leaning in to whisper, "You okay?"

She blinks at me in shock, but her foot eases to the floor. "I think so." She looks back at the guy. "I'll tell you in a few."

Meg stops short when she sees me, a brief frown crossing her face, but it quickly disappears. "Leah, this is Chad, my *boyfriend*." She smiles as she emphasizes the word. "Chad, this is my best friend, Leah." She glances at me. "And one of the Wrighting brothers, Shawn."

I stick close to Leah, waiting for her reaction.

But she seems at ease as she shakes Chad's hand. "Nice to meet you."

"Likewise," he says before shifting his attention to me. "Thanks for hosting."

I shake his hand as well. "Glad you could make it."

Meg tugs on her boyfriend's arm. "Come on, let's get you a drink." They head toward the kitchen, her elbow linked with his.

I don't budge, staring at Lee as I wait for an explanation.

She waves me off. "I was thinking that Chad isn't someone I know, that any of you know, and it freaked me out for a second." Then she pauses, frowning. "Wait, what gave me away?"

I smirk at her feet. "You did that calf rub thing you always do."

"I did?"

"And you're right, we don't know him. Meg needs to know he shouldn't stay over until you're okay with it." I study her, making sure she's truly comfortable.

"She never brings guys back here until I'm good with them. You know that." It's part of their agreement.

"Still might be worth mentioning, since the party's here tonight."

She rolls her eyes. "Fine."

"Good." My grin is smug. "Now, what are you drinking?"

I lead her to the kitchen where she decides on a rum and Coke, which I happily make before I grab my beer. It doesn't take long for the party to be in full swing. About twenty-five people show up, and Leah greets the rest of them by name. She begins to relax, the alcohol making her cheeks flushed. She dances, plays beer pong, and sings badly to the songs she knows.

I stay near her, only sipping my beer so I don't lose focus. A couple of times I tag Silas in, but otherwise I don't let her out of my sight. Even though I haven't seen any sign of unease since Chad's arrival.

Her cup is never empty for long, and soon her volume is permanently set to loud. Though it needs to be, if she wants to be heard above the music. After one exuberant dance with Meg, Lee waves her hand at her face, her flush more pronounced. Then she wanders to the back door and steps outside.

I let out a sigh, hurrying to grab two sweatshirts. That little tank top won't cut it against the chill of a March Michigan night. No matter how overheated she is. I rush out of the door, hoping to reach her before she goes to the tree house.

Luckily, she's just standing on the lawn, staring up at the night sky.

I yank my sweatshirt on. "You're supposed to stick with one of us, remember?"

She ignores me. A determined expression crosses her face as she tries to sit but misjudges the distance, falling the last few inches, which she finds hilarious.

Drunk Lee is adorable.

I chuckle and hand her the zip-up. "Here. It's still March."

Our fake spring is here, the teaser of warm weather that makes the grass green up and the trees start to bud. But I never trust it, especially this early. Michigan always has another trick up her sleeve. Leah fumbles with the sweatshirt until I unzip it for her, and she pokes her arms through, leaving the front open.

I sit, trying not to laugh at the state she's in. "Wow, I can't remember the last time you were this drunk."

"Yeah, it's been a while." She elbows me. "It's your guys' fault, making sure my cup stayed full." She blinks several times then sets her drink down and flops onto the grass. "Yep, I definitely blame you."

I finish off my own beer, leaning with my arms on my knees as I suck in the cold, refreshing air and relish the music being relegated to background noise.

She lets out a big sigh. "I'm really sick of your green eyes, you know. I can't even close mine without seeing them."

Shock hits me as I whip my head toward her. She studies my face for a long second before she turns to stare up at the sky. I don't even know what to say. But I stay quiet, hoping for more.

"You won't quit, even in my dreams." A hint of anger underlines her words, but her lips tip up.

The revelation hits me hard, like a firework exploding in my chest. She dreams about me. My heart pounds, and I'm at a loss. "Shit, Lee." I rake my hand over my face. "I forgot how honest you are when you're drunk."

I expect her cheeks to go pink or for her to duck her head or something, but she gives an awkward shrug.

"Better take advantage of it since I probably won't remember anyhow. The stupid world is already spinning."

"The world is always spinning," I tease.

She swats her hand toward me but misses, and I study her delicate fingers as they entwine with the grass, wondering if I should take her up on the offer. A free peek inside her head? Unfiltered, unvarnished?

I can't pass it up, and I lace my hands together. "You...really dream about me?"

"Yep." She bites out the word.

"Why does that make you mad?"

She flings up a hand, nearly smacking herself in the face, then laughs at herself. "I..." She sighs. "I'm not mad. I just don't know what to do with all these ridiculous feelings."

"Wait, what?" I frown. Does she not want to like me?

"That's why I picked Sebastian in the first place." She flops her head over to look at me. "He didn't make me feel the crazy things you do."

I gape, unable to fathom what she's telling me. I've seen her reactions to me, felt the tension crackle between us, but to hear her admit it... The words carve into me, each one a monument of how far we've come, and I feel like I've reached the peak of a mountain after climbing for days.

But she's not finished.

"I can't think when you're around. I don't know what I'm supposed to do with all this..." She gestures to her torso. "The stupid stomach flipping and tingling and jolts." She growls. "Whatever the hell it all means."

Pure elation shoots through my whole body, and my grin feels like it might crack my face. Never in my wildest dreams did I imagine she was this ready for me. That she was feeling all of that. *For me.*

I want to prove her words. My smile drops as I search her face which is so full of longing, then I shift closer.

She freezes, her forehead furrowing. "Wh-what are you doing?"

"Testing something." I stretch out beside her, propping my hand under my head. "Tell me how you're feeling." The distance between us is negligent but I'm careful not to touch her. Not yet.

"Um." She licks her lips as her gaze lingers on my mouth. "My heart is racing, and I'm breathing faster."

A thrill runs through me at her words. "Yeah?" I touch her cheek, turning her face toward me and bringing our lips even closer. "And now?"

"My stomach flipped." She sucks in a breath then whispers, "I like it when you touch me."

Damn, this woman is going to be the death of me. My groin tightens, but I would never take advantage of her, especially in this state. No matter how much I want to feel her in my arms again.

"I like touching you." I can't resist one more test, and I drop my hand to run a finger over her bare collarbone, relishing the smooth feel of her skin. "And now?"

"Everywhere you touch feels electric." Her thighs clench, then her hands form into fists. Desire wafts off her as she gazes up at me, and longing coats her voice when she says, "Shawn, kiss me, please."

An echo of that longing reverberates through me and I lean in, hovering above her mouth. I imagine it for a brief moment, claiming her the way I wanted to that day on the golf course. The way I've wanted to every second since.

But I stuff the feeling aside, picturing cold water flooding my veins to calm me down. I slowly shake my head. "I want you to remember it when I kiss you."

Her face falls, confusion muddling her eyes.

I don't want to hurt her, don't want to leave her confused and wanting. But I have to protect Lee at all costs, even from herself. She would hate herself—and me—tomorrow, so I force myself to stand up. To walk inside. To get Silas.

He's on the edge of the dance floor and steps away immediately when I touch his arm.

"I have to be done," I say, desperation coating my words. I glance at the slider once more, the glass barrier all that stands between me and the woman I love. "You'll watch out for her? Make sure she gets to bed?"

His forehead furrows. "Of course." When I don't move, his frown deepens. "You good, bro?"

"I will be."

It's enough to satisfy him, and I watch him make his way outside, the slider door shutting between us before I deadhead to my room. I shut my door hard.

Tomorrow, I promise myself. Tomorrow I'll make her mine.

Silas texts me when Meg puts her to bed, while I sit in my room, trying to ignore the thumping bass beneath me. It beats out Leah's name in different rhythms, thrumming through me as I try to decide what I'll say. I can't just blurt out that I love her. She may be ready for the next step, but saying that would be like pushing her into the pool all over again.

Eventually it quiets and I drift off to sleep. Tomorrow arrives, and excitement tears through me. I shower quickly, pull on jeans and a hoodie, then hurry downstairs.

But the house is silent.

The mini suite door is shut and the living room is empty, so I indulge my need to creep over to the door and listen. Nothing.

A large part of me wants to barrel in there, to see for myself that she's fine. But I'm sure she is, and I don't need to freak her out. I swipe my hand over my face, then force myself to the kitchen where I go through the motions of getting a bowl of cereal.

When I scroll through my phone, nothing keeps my attention. With each spoonful, my bowl gets emptier and time passes slower than I have ever felt. Every creak of the house has anticipation jumping inside me, but Lee never appears. Resigned, I rinse my bowl then set it in the sink with the other dishes.

But I pause. I must be in desperate need of a distraction because the next thing I know, I'm voluntarily washing the pile in the sink. It eats up a whole twenty minutes, then I dry my hands and sigh.

Even though they did a precursory clean up last night, the counter is still sticky. The coolers are full of water with a few cans or bottles floating inside. And the trash is overflowing. So I get to work, checking each task off the list. It's the least I can do since someone straightened up after the party, and I didn't help.

I check my phone when I'm finished. Eleven a.m.

Tension winds through me, and I feel like a rubber band stretched to the breaking point. Leah's door remains stubbornly closed. Heaving a sigh, I walk over to sprawl on one of the couches and flip through my options. I find a basketball game, but I pay it no attention. It's noise, filler, while my true focus is that damned door.

I toy with the idea of texting her, but ultimately reject it. She rarely sleeps this late, so she must need it. She'd been plenty drunk last night. I frown, hoping Meg or Silas made her drink water before she went to sleep. Or staged some painkillers and a water bottle on her nightstand.

Maybe I should check with them.

I toss my phone down before I can start a message, knowing I'm being ridiculous. A minute later, I shut off the TV and trudge upstairs. I step into my room, immediately on edge by the piles of clothes I've put off taking care of. I make quick work of them, then move on to my different drawers. By the time I'm done, everything in the dresser is folded in neat stacks and the drawers shut all the way.

Half an hour has passed. Now what?

I make my bed, organize my desk, then resort to cleaning the bathroom. It's twelve-thirty when I'm done and I can take no more. I go partway down the stairs, making sure I haven't missed her. But no. Her door is still closed.

That's it. I'm going for a run.

It takes me no time to change into my gear then I head outside. As soon as my muscles are warmed, I begin to push myself, needing an outlet for this restless energy that consumes me. My strides eat up the pavement, and all I can hear is my pounding footsteps.

My mind empties as the catharsis of the run takes over.

Chapter Twenty-Five

Leah

I am a complete slug today. It's almost one and I haven't even been out of bed yet. But my water is now gone, and my headache has ebbed to a slight pulse that I can ignore. I force myself upright, deciding a shower will do me good.

When I get out, I feel human once more. And hungry.

With my book tucked under my arm, I head for the kitchen. Meg's door hangs open, and I'd bet she went home with Chad. The house is quiet, unsettlingly so.

It's also really clean. I do a full spin, taking in the pristine kitchen. I wonder who had all that extra energy after the party last night, but I shrug it off to open the fridge. None of the leftovers look good and cooking is too much work. I grab a cold bottle of water then head to the pantry, emerging with a bag of chips.

Grease always helps.

The front door opens and Shawn saunters in, freezing when he sees me. His shirt is damp with sweat as is his forehead, and he's wearing his running gear. Doesn't take a genius to figure out where he's been.

I give him my usual smile, but he stares like I have two heads. "What?" I ask, self-consciously running my fingers through my hair.

He clears his throat, ducking his head. "Nothing. How long have you been up?"

Popping another chip in my mouth, I lift one shoulder and finish chewing before I answer. "A while. I didn't want to get out of bed."

His lips press together as he nods and shifts his weight. Why is he being so awkward? He clears his throat again then says, "How are you feeling?"

"Pretty good now." I nod to my chips. "Finally up to eating something."

His head bobs, then he sighs, jerking his thumb toward the stairs. "I'm uh, gonna go shower."

"'Kay." I toss another chip in my mouth and sit at the table to read. Soon my water is gone. Engrossed in my book, I move the bag of chips to the counter then walk over to refill it. The steam in this book is delicious.

I turn the next page, leaning against the counter as I take a sip of water then reach for a chip. I chew slowly as I soak up the words.

"Whatcha reading?" Shawn appears from nowhere, snatching the book from my fingers. Evidently he's back to his usual confident self, and his eyebrows shoot up as skims a few lines. "Ooh, hot stuff."

"Give me that!" I whirl on him, but he holds it high, out of reach. I jab him in the gut with my elbow, the pain bending him down so I can grab the book.

He groans, rubbing his stomach.

"Serves you right." I find my page and lean once more on the counter, needing to finish this scene.

Except Shawn lingers. Awareness creeps over me, making it impossible to focus on the typed words when I can feel him there, hovering.

Then he moves.

One of his hands rests on the counter near my elbow, and I slowly straighten. He's so close I can feel his body heat against my back, making my mouth go dry. His sandalwood-balsam scent envelopes me, underlined with his own essence, and desire flickers low in my belly.

His other hand frames me in, and I close my book, anticipation coiling within me as I set it on the counter. I tilt my head to glimpse his handsome face. His lips are right there. His hot breath brushes my cheek, and my stomach flips.

"Did Sebastian ever make you feel like this?"

"What?" The question takes me by surprise, and I try to turn around, but he doesn't let me, using his weight to pin me against the counter. A thrill zips through me. I know if I said the word, he'd let me go in a heartbeat.

But I stay quiet, loving the contact.

His chuckle reverberates through me, traveling all the way to my toes. It makes me squirm again.

"Keep going. I don't mind." His nose brushes my neck as he inhales, and the growing hardness against my ass robs me of coherent thought.

I go still, hyper aware of every place our bodies touch. My skin is on fire. "Shawn..."

His lips brush the shell of my ear as he whispers, "You were with the wrong brother."

"Wait, what?" I freeze, trying to process the words. "What do you mean?"

But he dodges the question. "I know you feel it. This tension between us, this attraction." He rocks his erection against me and I press my thighs together. "Did I make your stomach flip?"

The fact that he nailed my reaction has me on edge. "How do you know what I'm feeling?"

"You told me, last night."

Memories slam into me, bits and pieces coalescing into a bigger picture of me telling him the absolute truth. I feel raw and exposed with him knowing so much about me when he hasn't said so much as a syllable about how he feels. A flimsy excuse tumbles out. "Shawn, I was drunk."

He scoffs, "You're always the most honest when you're drunk."

"What about being friends?" I say, desperate for any sort of familiar ground.

His lips graze my cheek as his mouth moves. "Friends don't make you feel like this." A delicious thrill spirals in me as he kisses my cheek firmly — like he wants me to know it's no accident. Then he pushes off the counter and steps away. "I want more, Lee. Whenever you're ready."

I spin around, wanting that too, but now that the moment is here, I can't form the words. Panic flutters at the edges of my vision, the familiar response to any new step. I can only stare as he walks backward, our eyes locked the entire time. At the edge of the kitchen, he winks, turns on his heel and saunters off.

Determination courses through me as I suck in a bracing lungful of air. I want this. I want him.

And the panic can fuck off.

"Shawn," I call, rushing after him. Relief courses through me when he pauses on the landing. "Did we kiss last night?" I know Shawn would never take advantage of me like that, but I want to hear him say it.

A furrow appears in his forehead as he walks down the stairs, stopping at the bottom. "No. You asked me to, but I wanted you to remember it."

I can't look away from his lips, needing to taste him again. "If you kiss me now, I'll remember."

His green eyes darken, and he crosses the room in three quick strides to stand before me. His scent overwhelms me, and I lean in to inhale him. When I meet his gaze, hope etches into every inch of his face.

"Tell me what you want, Lee." His attention dips to my lips as he shifts closer. "Just a kiss?"

My stomach flips, but I shake my head. "I want you, Shawn. I'm ready for more." His breath hitches, and I give him a soft smile. "I had planned on telling you, but I couldn't find the words. Or the right time."

His throat bobs as he swallows, then he reaches up to cup my cheek, running his thumb next to my mouth. "Well, I guess I beat you to it." He leans in slowly, giving me plenty of time to change my mind.

But I won't.

I close the distance, touching my lips to his. Electricity shoots through me like the fiercest storm, and I reach up to cling to his broad shoulders so my knees don't buckle. His other hand slides to my waist, tugging me flush against him. It's like I've been eating off-brand chocolate my entire life and finally have a taste of Ghirardelli.

All the teasing, all the flirting, all led to this, and I know I'm exactly where I'm supposed to be.

Any remnant of my barriers is smashed to smithereens when he deepens the kiss, and I moan into him. I press against his chest, relishing the way the firmness feels. I want more, need more, but the panic I've held off pierces me.

I break away, and he lets me go. I take several steps back, staring at him from a safe distance as I suck in air. He doesn't move to touch me. Concern flashes over his face, but he keeps the space between us.

As if knowing I can't handle it right now.

When my breathing returns to normal and my heart slows once more, I hang my head. "I'm sorry." Why do all my broken parts have to be so visible?

He closes the distance, tucking a finger under my chin and tilting my face up. "You have nothing to be sorry for. You're opening a door that's been closed for a long time and having to face memories that are painful. There's no time frame here, we're going at your pace. However fast or slow that may be."

The affirmation that my reactions are valid, that my feelings are valid, washes over me, and my throat gets thick.

"I will never take your panic personally, Lee. I want to be with you every step of the way. Because one day, all of this will be nothing more than a memory and you'll be whole again."

The words fill me with hope. "I'd like that."

He crushes me to him. I wrap my arms around his waist as he rocks me back and forth. His embrace washes away every hint of panic, and I drink him in. The feel of his muscular back under my fingers. His defined chest against mine. His firm hands holding me tight. I relax into him.

Then my stomach growls, and he laughs. "Can we go somewhere and talk? Get you some real food?"

I nod, staring at his handsome face. "Yes, please. Those potato chips aren't cutting it. I'm starving." I step back, frowning at my comfy clothes. "How about I go change and we meet back out here?"

"Great. I'll change too."

Excitement bubbles in me as I pull on a long-sleeved navy-blue top and faded blue jeans. I hurry back to the living room as he comes downstairs. His sandy brown hair hangs down on his forehead, and I want to rake my fingers through it. His emerald eyes twinkle as he takes me in, that cocky smirk on his lips. He wears a knit long-sleeved shirt that clings to his lean form and dark blue jeans that hug his hips.

Yummy.

"Joe's?" he asks, and I nod.

I step outside, reveling in the sun's brightness, feeling as if she shines solely for us. Even if the breeze is a little chilly. We fall into step next to each other, a hint of awkwardness hanging between us.

I try to lighten things up. "So we've done the enemies thing and we can check being friends off the list. What's our next goal? Casual dating and see what happens?"

I shoot him a grin, but Shawn grabs my arm—a gentle but firm grip—halting me in my tracks as he steps in front of me. His piercing gaze makes my mouth go dry at the depth of emotion swirling there.

"There is nothing casual about what I feel for you, Leah." His voice is raw, and his words carry an intensity that makes me shiver. He drops his hold on my arm, but his eyes never leave mine. "I'm in love with you. Completely, utterly, with all my heart, in love with you."

My breath whooshes out of me as my lips part. *Love?*

"I've fought it since the day at the pool, if I'm being completely honest. I just didn't see it before." His fingers graze my cheek, and one corner of his mouth tips up. "When you moved in, you were so much trouble — this headstrong, beautiful girl with her string of guys. You killed me."

"Yeah, I remember just how dead you were, the endless rotation of girls you brought home."

He stays serious. "They all had one thing in common, the same reason none of them stuck around for any length of time." He gazes at me tenderly. "None of them were you."

I can only blink as his declaration hits me. Shawn loves me. I start walking again, needing to move.

"Say something?" He falls into step next to me.

"It's…hard to wrap my mind around."

He nods, and we both stay quiet until after we're in the restaurant. The hostess leads us to a corner booth. It's horseshoe shaped, so I slide partway in. He keeps scooting until he's next to me, and his knee brushes mine. My heart beats faster as my stomach flips.

We take a minute to look over the menu then put in our order. After the waitress leaves, Shawn studies me, still waiting for my reaction or acknowledgment.

"You're really in love with me?"

He laughs, reaching over to grab my hand. He laces our fingers together, resting them on top of his muscular thigh. "Yep. Head over heels."

"Why?" I blurt out, immediately wishing I could take it back.

His eyes soften. "Lee..." He strokes the back of my hand with his thumb. "You never give up. You've been through some hard things, but you keep fighting to move forward, to get back on your path. You love fiercely and are so protective of your people."

The string of compliments is too much, and I duck my head.

"You never back down from a challenge, and that tongue of yours can be so sharp."

I glance up, only to find more of that delicious heat in his gaze, and my cheeks warm.

"I can't wait to see what else you can do with it." His teasing wink tells me there's no pressure, that he's only flirting.

So I elbow him.

Our food comes, along with our drinks, and I'm happy for the distraction. He lets go of my hand so we can eat. My loaded waffle fries are messy but delicious, and Shawn dives into his burger with gusto, smiling at me with ketchup on the side of his mouth.

"You've got something." I tap my cheek. He shifts closer, and I raise my napkin up to wipe it off, studying his lips.

"Better?" At my nod, he leans in. "Good. Then I can do this without covering you in ketchup." And he touches his lips gently to mine.

My head spins as I pull away, both corners of my mouth tipped up. We eat for several moments in silence, me mulling over the past. There is one thing I've never figured out. "Why did you let me think you hated me?"

A sad smile crosses his lips. "It was a combination of things. That day at the pool...I really wasn't expecting you, Lee. You weren't the annoying little girl who challenged me at every turn. You were all grown up, and in that bikini no less."

Satisfaction shoots through me, that I affected him even then.

"I couldn't wrap my head around it. It felt…wrong to be attracted to you. Like, you'd always been more of a sibling then suddenly, you weren't."

"I can see how that could be weird." I'd never seen him through the same lens I viewed the others. Somehow he'd always been set apart in my mind, though I hadn't actually considered more with him until that day.

"So I didn't say anything. Then you moved in, and I tried distracting myself with other women." One corner of his mouth tips up. "But like I said before, they weren't you. I'm sure I would've figured it out eventually, but then came Vance." He stares past me, clenching his jaw before he speaks again. "I opened the door, I told you he was there, and I didn't prevent him from hitting you."

I gape at the guilt in his voice. "Shawn!"

That was certainly not his fault, could never be his fault. He stares at my cheekbone, and my gaze hits the table. The memory cracks between us, as sharp as Vance's knuckles against my cheek.

"When I saw you, that mark on your face." The toppings ooze out of his burger from how hard he grips it.

I lay a gentle hand on his arm, staring down pointedly. His eyes widen when he sees his deformed burger, then he sets his food on the plate and takes a deep breath. He wipes his hands on a napkin, avoiding my eyes. I want to help him, so I slide my fingers along his wrist until he drops the napkin to lace his fingers with mine.

Now he has something to hold on to.

Chapter Twenty-Six

Shawn

I try to smile, but it disappears in the face of that memory. I tighten my grip on her hand before I shake my head. "I've never felt anger like that in all my life." Silence hangs between us for a beat then I force myself to admit, "That confirmed to me I wasn't any good for you, Lee."

She gasps again.

"I know better now. It was another excuse to avoid my feelings." I lift a shoulder, pausing to figure out how to put my fear into words. "I convinced myself that every time I was supposed to look out for you, something disastrous happened."

She frowns, but lets me continue.

"Sebastian called me out on it, the night after the library." I can't help chuckling. "He called me a coward, actually. Said I was taking the easy way out by letting you think I hated you."

A crinkle appears in her forehead. "He and I were still dating then."

"Yeah, it was definitely weird coming from your boyfriend. But he said he loved you enough to be whatever you needed for him, and he knew you'd outgrow him eventually."

A hint of guilt flashes across her face. "I never meant to use him."

"He knows that." I let go of her hand to wrap my arm around her. "I have him to thank though, because we wouldn't be together now without him confronting me like that." I drop my arm, and she nibbles at her lip. The urge to kiss her rises in me, if only to stop her worrying, but she speaks before I can act.

"I couldn't have handled you then," she admits.

"I know." I study her for another moment, realizing how unsure she's feeling. I touch my knuckle to her cheek. "And you're wondering if you can handle me now."

She sucks in a startled breath, as if I read her mind then her eyes widen even more.

"What?" I ask, nervous about what she's putting together.

"You know me."

I frown. "Well, yeah."

She shakes her head. "No, I mean, I just realized how well you know me. Not only my favorite candies, but how far to push me, when you can tease me, when I need my space." She blinks at me, awe in her voice. "You really do love me."

My cheeks go warm at her words. "I do, Lee. I do love you."

"That day you saved me from my loose swimsuit strings…" She trails off, a smirk tipping her lips. "Did you get a hard-on because my boobs were plastered all over your bare chest? Or was it the getting off comment?"

A bark of laughter escapes me, and I shake my head. *This woman...* I never know what's going to come out of her mouth. But if she wants to play, I'm game.

I lean closer to whisper, "I was already having a tough time keeping it together with your gorgeous rack all over me. But that comment made my imagination take off like a shot." I give her a cocky grin.

Her chin juts into the air. "It was a wardrobe malfunction. Excuse me for my little slip of the tongue in the wake of that embarrassing moment."

"There was nothing little about what you were doing to me." I intently watch her reaction, hoping I haven't pushed too far.

She freezes, staring up at me with stark desire on her face then her gaze drifts to my lap. My cock stirs, between the memory of that day and her attention now. Her cheeks flame as she squirms in her seat.

I can't help chuckling at her reaction, how obviously turned on she is. I would love to take her somewhere to act on that longing, but I know we need baby steps here.

"I'm going to hit the bathroom," she says, jumping up and hurrying away.

Concern hits me as she races off, but I push it aside, knowing I've given her a lot to process. I've had weeks to come to terms with my feelings. I need to give her the space to do the same.

We're here, though. This point seemed so unreachable after Sebastian confronted me. But now she wants to be with me, and I feel like I could conquer the world. When she returns with an easy smile on her face, I relax completely. She sits down in the booth, bouncing her way to me. My eyes are glued to her chest as she moves.

She pouts when she settles next to me. "I hate this booth."

"I don't."

She elbows me, but there's no heat behind it. She picks up her Coke, and I take a chance, reaching over to rest my hand on her thigh. When she tenses, I arch an eyebrow, making sure she's okay with me touching her. Her answer is to shift her leg until it rests against mine.

Triumph soars through me, and I lift my drink. "To us, and a new beginning."

She taps her glass to mine. "Cheers."

As we finish our food and drinks, Leah grows quieter. When the waitress comes to clear our plates and asks if we want a refill, she doesn't respond, lost in her thoughts.

I nudge her gently and she startles, but I repeat the question, trying not to be alarmed. I see her struggling, though I don't quite know with what.

She finally answers, "I think I'm ready to go."

As we wait for the check, I caress Lee's thigh, trying to reassure her. But her muscles tighten under my fingers, so I pull away, giving her space as I pay for the meal. The moment I put my card back in my wallet, Lee races from the booth, striding toward the exit. I hurry after her, my concern amping up.

She shoves the door open hard enough that it bangs against the wall as she stumbles outside. She doubles over, resting her hands on her knees, and my chest tightens watching her pain. I rack my brain, trying to figure out what set her off, but I come up empty.

"Lee?" I bend down, putting my eyes at the same level as hers. "Can I do anything?"

Her breathing is shallow as she collapses onto the bench next to the building and drops her head into her hands.

"Can I hold you?"

She gives me the barest of nods, but I take it, swooping her into my arms. My tension eases some when she curls into me, soaking in my offered comfort. I hold her until she stops trembling.

When she begins to relax against me, I tentatively ask, "What happened?"

"I..." She sighs, pushing away to sit up. "I got in my head. You're stirring up a lot of feelings I haven't felt in a long time. It's overwhelming."

I try to tease. "Ah, yes, the stomach flipping, the heart racing, and the jolts."

But she doesn't smile like I expect, glaring instead. "Yeah, that stuff."

I study her for a long moment, deliberating what to say. "Lee, I can't say I wish I didn't make you feel that way, because that would be a lie. I'm glad I affect you. If it helps, you keep tripping me up, too."

Hope fills her gaze.

The idea of being vulnerable has tension gripping my gut, but I'll do it for her. "At the beach that first day, I could hardly focus on our second volleyball game because you played in that bathing suit." The memories have me shifting in my seat.

"You're beautiful." I swallow, trying to get my desire under control. "It's more than that, though. I know you're scared, but believe me when I say I'll never do anything to hurt you." I frown, needing to amend my previous statement. "I might be dumb and make mistakes, but I won't do anything on purpose."

"Thank you, Shawn. I know that. I trust you." Her fingers flex on my chest and she searches my face. "The last day of our trip, you had something to say but told me I wasn't ready to hear it yet."

I scoff. "You said that you understood why I chose not to have a fling, that it must be nice to have in my heart intact."

She presses her lips together as if annoyed at herself.

"Yeah, the irony was a little much." I drop one of my arms, keeping the other around her shoulders.

No longer hugging, we just sit comfortably against the bench. She leans in to my side, seeming calmer now. "It wasn't only the butterflies and stomach flipping," she says softly. "I pictured us walking together through campus. But my daydream...it turned into a nightmare, morphing into everyone calling me names." Her voice cracks on the last word.

"Oh, Lee." I pull her closer once more. "I'm sorry. I'm sorry you went through that and that you have such deep scars. I know it's a small town and a small campus, but I doubt very much people will care who you're dating."

"Even if I'm jumping from one brother to the other?"

Her words are so quiet, I nearly miss them, and the underlying doubt kills me. I pull away, leaning forward to rest my elbows on my thighs. "I can't control what people think or what they say, but they don't really matter to me." I glance over, hoping she'll understand. "The ones that do matter—Sebastian, Silas, Steven, Meg. They're all on board with us. So who cares what anyone else thinks?"

"All your brothers know?" Her cheeks tinge with pink.

"They'd have to be blind not to. I'm hopelessly in love with you, Lee, and I've been trying to get your attention for the past six weeks." She lets out a delighted laugh, and I pretend to grumble. "Sure, laugh it up. You're not the one who had their life threatened."

"What?"

I lift a shoulder, happy to see the light back in her face. "You know, the standard 'hurt her and I'll kill you'. I had to go through it three times." I frown. "Well, Sebastian's was more like 'if harm comes to her while under your care, you shall live to regret it', but I think that counts."

She's giggling helplessly now. "I wish I could've seen that."

I grunt. "Okay, next time my brothers threaten me, I'll be sure to record it."

"Thank you, Shawn."

I'm relieved things are comfortable between us once again. I trace her profile with my gaze, knowing what I want to ask next and hoping it won't set her off again. "So…should we make this official?"

"What did you have in mind?" She holds up her hand, studying her fingers. "I'm a size seven." At my blank stare, she grins. "You know, for my ring?"

Shock leaves me frozen, and relief crashes through me when she laughs. My shoulders sag, and I shake my head.

"You should've seen your face."

"Yeah, yeah." It's hard to hide my amusement though. She got me good. I lean toward her, propping my arm up behind her as our gazes collide once more. "Be my girlfriend, Lee?"

A dazzling smile spreads over her delicious mouth before she says, "Of course."

And we seal it with a kiss.

Chapter Twenty-Seven

Leah

It's been hard enough to wrap my head around being friends with Shawn, but now he's my boyfriend, and in love with me. My chest feels like it's been infused with champagne, all light and bubbly.

"What should we do next, Lee?" He arches an eyebrow.

It's almost five p.m., so we have plenty of time for whatever we want. I go over my options, loving the idea of doing something competitive. Shawn and I have always connected well over games.

"What about racquetball?"

He grins. "I haven't done that in forever."

Our parents used to be in a league while we were growing up and we'd spend hours at the court waiting for them. "Me either."

"That sounds fun." He nods decisively.

"Then maybe we could get pizza and watch a movie or hang out in my room." I hold my breath, unable to believe I suggested that. As much as the guys come and go from our space, we don't hang out there.

But I don't take it back.

I want this. I want to move forward, to start over again. With Shawn.

He goes still, knowing what I'm offering. "I appreciate that, Leah, more than you know. If that offer is still on the table after we're done, it sounds wonderful."

He's giving me an out. My throat gets thick with — relief? From being overwhelmed by his sweetness? I don't know, but I manage to keep it together. "All right then."

He smirks, mimicking me. "All right then."

My phone dings twice, and I pull it out, laughing at Sebastian's ranting text. "Sebastian should be home soon. Professor Harrison's daughter got into some trouble so they had to come back ahead of schedule. She's going to be permanently on his bad side."

Shawn just chuckles.

As I read my other message from Silas, my smile fades to a frown. "Amaya and Steven had some big fight. She left early." I show him the picture Silas attached of Steven looking all forlorn on the couch. "He must be devastated."

The need to take care of my friend engulfs me, and I nibble on my lip then I sigh. "Shawn?"

"What do you need?"

"Could we postpone racquetball? Maybe do movie night with your brothers instead? I think it would really help Steven." Worry courses through me. We've barely made things official and I'm already bailing on him to take care of his brother. I twist my fingers together, but Shawn covers my hands with his.

"Lee, remember how I said I love you?"

My cheeks go hot, and I nod, not looking at him. I'm not used to those words yet. *At all.*

"I love how you take care of my brothers. Asking you to ignore that would be denying a part of you, and I could never do that."

That night in Myrtle Beach flits through my head, when Shawn caught me poking my head in Steven's room to make sure he was safe. Shawn's words, *"I see you"* echo through me like a warm hug. "Thank you for seeing me. All of me."

His mouth tips up, then he pushes to his feet and holds out his hand, palm up. I step forward and slide my fingers into his, embracing the knowledge that I am his. As we walk home, warmth spreads through me at the rightness of our touch. A click echoes inside me — a missing piece falling into place, and I feel whole in a way I haven't been in a long, long time.

I order pizza on the way home. Even though we just ate, I'm sure the rest of them will be hungry soon. Then I give Sebastian a quick heads-up text and send Silas on a mission, one guaranteed to cheer Steven up. I disappear into my room to change into comfy clothes, then lounge on the couch as I wait for everyone else.

Steven doesn't move from his spot on the other end of the sofa. He stays glued to the game as he slumps in his seat. He seems broken.

Silas returns with his purchases, bee-lining for the kitchen. Sebastian isn't far behind. He gives a hurried greeting then disappears upstairs, all part of the plan. When the doorbell rings, Shawn grabs the pizza, then it's game on.

I stand up and nudge Steven with my foot.

"What?"

"We're kidnapping you."

He sags even more.

"You gonna get off the couch? Or are they moving it with you on it?" My hands go to my hips.

Steven frowns at Shawn and Silas poised at either end of the couch. He shakes his head, tucking his feet under him.

"Okay, don't say I didn't warn you. Carry on, boys." I signal the guys.

Shawn and Silas pick up the couch with Steven still on top. He yelps as they tip it and grips the arm, glaring at his brothers. Sebastian tosses sleeping bags and pillows over the stair railing where I arrange them. Once the floor disappears under the bedding, I grab Steven's wrist to yank him off the couch.

He doesn't budge. It's time for drastic measures, so I glance at Shawn, making sure he's ready. He nods. I grab the phone out of Steven's hands, tossing it to Shawn, who runs away. Steven leaps up, but Silas tackles him to the bedding-covered floor. Sebastian covers the stairs, in case Steven manages to get free.

I sit on Steven's chest, not moving when he groans. "Listen up. You've moped all day. Now you're stuck with us, and it's family movie night. Complete with pizza, root beer floats, and movie bingo."

The start of a smile plays on his lips.

"Guess what movie we're watching?"

He doesn't answer at first, but I keep staring until he does. "*Monty Python and the Holy Grail.*"

I jump up, holding my arms over my head in a victory pose. "We have a winner."

Silas hops off too, offering him a hand.

Steven gets to his feet, but his shoulders sag and a sigh escapes him. "I just…really liked her."

I wrap my arms around him, and he lets me, dropping his forehead to my shoulder.

"I know, and I am sorry it didn't work out. But now it's time to eat." I shove him toward the pizza. "I've got a prize for whoever wins bingo."

They clamor to know what it is, but I zip my lips. Affection surges through me as I watch them jostle for food. Steven argues with Sebastian over which goes in first, the ice cream or root beer—the same argument they have every time. My heart almost bursts with love for these idiots.

Arms loaded, we make our way to the living room, finding our spots. I'm sandwiched between Shawn and Steven while Silas and Sebastian sprawl in front of us. We have our bingo cards ready, ones I made ages ago with various characters or phrases from the movie. Sebastian presses play.

Each of us knows this film by heart. We holler out our favorite lines, laughing at the most ridiculous parts and our miserable accents. Silas gets the first bingo, so I run to my room, returning with the prize behind my back.

"For the dubious honor of collecting the first bingo, I present you with this." I drop a misshapen foil trophy in his outstretched hands.

He gasps and his mouth falls open. "How in the world do you still have this?"

I shrug. "I couldn't get rid of it."

Years ago, we commandeered a broken t-ball trophy for a new purpose—the bingo award for our movie nights, and traded it around. Somehow I ended up with it. I never could part with it. Watching them pass it around now, I'm so glad I kept it.

I settle back into my spot as Shawn tucks his arm around me. He looks down, making sure I'm okay, and in response, I lean into him, relishing the contact.

Steven sighs again, giving me his best puppy dog eyes then glancing at my hands. I fight a smile and lose, nodding. His grin is real as he flops a pillow next to me and lies down. I run my fingers through his hair, massaging his head.

The guys used to fight over who got to lay here, everyone loving my head massages. Except Sebastian. But Steven deserves it tonight.

We finish the movie that way, me cuddled against Shawn while I massage Steven's head. Afterwards, we all help put the living room back in order. It's not even eight yet. Silas suggests cards and Steven nods eagerly.

I try to gauge Shawn's reaction. I wouldn't mind being alone with him, but I can't deny Steven right now.

Sebastian yawns. "I'm worn out and think it'd be best if I get some sleep. Sorry, guys."

Steven hides his grin, and I know he's thinking about playing euchre, so we definitely can't bow out. I give Sebastian a hug, and we all chorus our goodnights to him then move to the kitchen to play cards. Two hours later, Steven and Shawn are declared the winners. Silas grumbles as he heads to bed, but Steven wraps me in a big bear hug.

"Thanks, Lee-bug. I didn't know I needed that."

"I know, and you're welcome." I hug him back, wrinkling my nose when he ruffles my hair.

He nods at his brother before heading upstairs, and I'm left alone with Shawn.

"Um, you ready to sleep or…?"

I wait, hope blossoming in me as he shoves his hands in his pockets. He rocks forward on his toes, and my lips tip up. I'm glad I'm not the only one feeling nervous.

"Or what, Shawn?"

"Movie, more games…" He trails off, glancing at the door to my suite. "I'm up for whatever."

I'm not ready for bed, either for sleep or anything more. I'd like to spend some time with just him though. It felt nice snuggling with him during the movie, maybe we could do more of that. "Is a movie okay?"

"Of course. Want popcorn?"

I am a little hungry. "Yes, please."

"You go pick something for us to watch."

I flick through my choices after settling in the middle of the couch, so Shawn has to sit by me. A basketball movie snags my attention. It's older and a romance, but maybe Shawn will enjoy the sports aspect of it.

He hands me the bowl of popcorn, easing next to me then slipping his arm behind me. "Good?"

I nod, leaning against his chest and feeling at home. "Is this okay?"

"Sure." He tosses a handful of popcorn into his mouth as I push play.

The movie is cute, but I begin to lose focus partway through, becoming more aware of Shawn. Our hips fit snugly together so I feel every time he shifts. His arm now drapes across my back with his hand on my hip. His chest rises and falls steadily, and I move with him. The popcorn is gone, the empty bowl on the coffee table, and I don't know what to do with my hands.

I reposition slightly, tucking my shoulder under his arm while my breasts press against his chest. Then I splay my fingers over his firm pecs, grinning when his breath hitches. I tilt my chin up to find his heated stare on me. "Hi."

A knowing smirk sprawls over his lips. "Hi. Want something?"

"Kiss me?"

"Anytime, Lee."

He lowers his lips to mine, my stomach flipping as electricity jolts straight to my core. I hum with pleasure, gripping his shirt in my fist and pulling him closer. He groans then slants his mouth, darting his tongue out to slide along the seam of my lips. I open for him, thrilling as our tongues dance together for the first time.

The kiss lasts a lifetime, but I never want it to end. The feel of his arms around me, his chest pressed to mine, his body at my fingertips...it's heaven.

And I want more.

"Shawn?" I pull back to ask, "Do you want to take this somewhere more...private?"

Tenderness fills his expression. "You set the pace here, Lee. Like I said, I'm up for whatever." He chuckles. "Though maybe a little more literally than before."

I suck in a breath at the obvious bulge in his fleece pants, my thighs dampening at the solid proof that I've turned him on. Hunger slices through me, for him. He is finally mine. I can touch him, kiss him, explore him to my heart's content, and I can't wait to get started.

Shutting off the TV, I bounce to my feet and tug him along behind me. "Come on."

He chuckles. "Easy, Lee. We've got all night."

I pull him into my suite then push him onto the couch in our sitting room. "Yeah, but I'm done waiting."

His eyes darken, desire flaring in them as he grabs my wrist. "Then come here."

Chapter Twenty-Eight

Shawn

Leah lets me guide her onto my lap, her lips parting as she straddles me. She hesitates before fully settling her weight on me, and my breath hitches when she does. My straining cock rests firmly against the heat of her apex.

It's all I can do not to blow my load all over my pajama pants.

She feels even better than I dreamed, and I tip my head back, groaning when she rocks her hips. "Fuck, Lee." But I will not be coming first.

Her thighs tighten against mine as she freezes. Her cheeks are pink. "Maybe not tonight."

The tremble in her voice bolsters my self-control, and I grimace. "Sorry. Bad choice of words. I only meant that you feel amazing." I gesture between us. "You, here, with me, all feels amazing."

Her fingers spread wide over my chest. "You do, too, Shawn."

Those gorgeous blue eyes linger on my lips, and I need to kiss her. I reach up, threading my fingers through her hair and tug her mouth to mine. Heat flares between us as she grips my shoulders. I slip my tongue between her parted lips, loving the way she tastes.

Then she pulls away, running her hands down my torso to tug at the hem of my sweatshirt. "Off."

"Yes, ma'am." And I pull it over my head in fluid motion, bare-chested beneath.

She drinks me in, determination settling on her face. She puts her hands on me, and a tremor rips through me at the touch. A slow smile spreads over her face. "You like that."

I nod helplessly.

She traces her fingers over my muscles, circling up to my shoulders, down my biceps then back across my pecs. Her gaze follows her movements, and she whispers, "I like it too."

The burning need to touch her, to explore her flares within me, and I grip her hips, slipping my thumb under the hem of her shirt. She stills when I touch bare skin.

"Can I?"

She moves first, taking off her hoodie. The flimsy shirt underneath does little to hide her pebbled nipples, and I nearly groan picturing them. I skate my hand up her side, over her shirt to cup her full breast. The weight of her in my palm has my cock straining even more, begging for release.

But I ignore it because Lee comes first.

Her lips crash onto mine as I cup and knead and squeeze her delicious breasts. She doesn't rock against me again, instead tearing her mouth from mine. Then she sucks in a big, trembling breath and I know she's overwhelmed.

I drop my hands, going still as I wait to see what she wants to do.

"I—" She cuts herself off, ducking her chin to hide her chagrined expression.

"You need to be done?"

She nods, still not looking at me.

"Lee." I grip her shoulder, rubbing it with my thumb. "Never hesitate to tell me what you need. I'll stop when you say stop. Go when you say go. You're in charge here, okay?"

Gratitude shines from her as she leans forward to sweetly brush her lips to mine before climbing off me. "You're the best, you know that?"

My rock-hard dick protests, but I ignore it, adjusting myself when she turns away. I stand, resting my hand on her hip and pulling her in for one more kiss. "Good night, Lee."

But she grabs my wrists. "Stay."

I frown, sure I misheard. "What?"

"Stay," she repeats. "Please? I've missed sleeping with you."

The idea of sleeping next to her is as appealing as it is torturous, but I can't deny her this request. "Sure." I also *need* to take care of myself first. One casual touch from her might have me exploding.

"Give me a minute?" I ask, jerking my head toward the door. "I'll brush my teeth, change and be back?"

She nods, and we exchange smiles before I hurry upstairs. In the safety of my room, I shuck my pants and grip my aching cock. I bite back my groan as I stroke myself, picturing Leah rocking her hips along my length. Her perfect breast in my hand. Her lips parted as desire coats her face.

For me.

The image is enough to send me over that edge and I come in my hand, pumping until I'm finished. I hurry to clean up, change into shorts, then brush my teeth before heading downstairs. Her lamp is on, but her eyes are closed as I crawl into bed. I turn off the light, settling on my back.

She rolls toward me, curling into my embrace with a contented sigh that makes my heart feel fuller than ever before. I drift off to sleep with a smile on my face and my love in my arms.

* * * *

The next morning, I wake up to a door opening and Leah still cuddled against me. I let out a surprised grunt when Meg launches herself onto the bed, talking a mile a minute about her date with Chad. I glare, waiting for her to notice that I'm not Leah, who is shaking beside me from trying to hold in her giggles.

I'm okay until Meg starts getting into steamier detail. When I turn frantically to Leah, laughter bursts from her. Meg's eyes widen as she stares at her friend across the bed. Then her gaze drops to mine.

I give her a wide grin. "Morning, Meg."

She recovers quickly. "My, what a deep voice you have, Leah. You should really get that checked out. You may be coming down with something."

I shake my head as Lee laughs harder. At last, she says, "You should have seen your face."

Meg glares. "You didn't put out the signal."

I interrupt. "Could you excuse us for a few minutes? I'd like to say good morning to Lee." When she doesn't move right away, I add, "I'm sure she'll tell you all about it."

Her face lights up, and she scampers from the room, shutting the door behind her. Lee grins shyly at me.

"Good morning," I say, letting my voice drop. "How'd you sleep?"

"Great." She ducks her head.

"Don't go disappearing on me now. I was hoping for a good morning kiss."

Her head lifts and the hope in her eyes has me tugging her into my arms. When our lips meet, she hums, bracing herself on my bare chest. I could get used to this…minus Meg's wake up call.

When I ease back, her smile matches mine as she brushes her hair behind her ear. "So what are you up to today?"

It's Sunday, and neither of us has to work. I glance at the door. "We should probably make this official and tell everyone. What do you think?" A hint of panic crosses her face, and I quickly joke, "Come on, you're not going to make me do the walk of shame alone, are you?"

She shakes her head, rising to my challenge. "Though maybe I should. Get you back for all the times you teased me."

"Were we keeping score?"

"You know how competitive I am." A wicked glint in her eye has me trying to decide if she's serious, but she laughs. "I'm kidding, Shawn."

A few minutes later, we walk into the main living room, hand in hand. Steven and Silas watch TV while Sebastian has his nose in a book and Meg scrolls on her phone. Steven looks up first, a slow smile spreading over his face as he nudges Silas and jerks his chin toward us.

A matching grin tips Silas' lips. "About time."

Sebastian and Meg beam when they see us. He actually sets aside his book and walks over to hug Lee. "I knew you'd come around eventually."

She sniffs. "You could've just told me."

"I knew you were smart enough to figure it out." He pauses. "When you were ready."

Lee lights up at the statement of trust, and I rub her back, sharing a knowing grin with Sebastian, who nods back.

Silas pretends to pout. "I didn't know you were doing the brother lottery, Lee. I would've bought a ticket."

She wrinkles her nose. "No, you wouldn't."

He laughs. "You're right. I'm happy for you two. Maybe Shawn will stop being such a grouch whenever you look at him wrong." I glare but he just laughs again.

Steven's expression now has a bittersweet edge to it, and I know he's thinking about Amaya. But the pain disappears as he looks at Lee. "I'm happy for you." Then he narrows his eyes at me. "If you hurt her…"

"I know, I know." We've already been through this, and I wrap my arm around her waist. "I'll take good care of her."

Sebastian chuckles. "Maybe I should make up conferences more often."

The room goes silent as his words register, and Lee says tightly, "What?"

His gaze darts around the room as he gulps. I frown, trying to make sense of what he said.

Lee pushes off me. "What did you mean by that, Sebastian?"

A trickle of fear winds through me. What did he do? Is he going to ruin everything? I just got Leah to be mine, but if Sebastian manipulated her... My stomach sinks.

He lets out a resigned sigh. "Leah, you and I were broken up, but you were stuck—"

"Tell me," she says through gritted teeth.

My mind races through the possibilities of what he will confess as tension grips my chest. If he lied about why he didn't go on Spring Break...

His fingers twist in front of him. "After we broke up, that week before Spring Break...there was no conference."

The weekend we went to the movies. I can handle that.

"Without me around, you could explore other options. You needed to spread your wings." Desperation laces every syllable as he pleads with her to understand.

But Leah's expression remains stony, and her fingers clench. Her muscles are rigid, reminding me of the moments after her nightmare when Vance still hovered in her mind. Is he haunting her now? My concern amps up with each second she stays silent.

She turns to me. "Did you know?" Her hurt and betrayal have me tongue tied, and she asks again with more force, "Did you know he lied to me?"

I shake my head, glancing at Sebastian for confirmation.

"He didn't know, Leah. It was all me."

Relief crashes into me when her shoulders sag though the hurt and betrayal don't ease as she turns back to Sebastian.

"You manipulated me."

The words are heartbreaking, the depth of pain in them making me ache. I reach for her but she steps away, shaking her head.

Her eyes grow wide and wild as her breathing becomes more ragged. Her gaze latches onto mine, desperation wafting from her. "I need to leave."

I nod. "Go. We'll be here when you're ready."

She lunges for the door, and I have to picture my feet encased in cement so I don't bolt after her. I wish I could exorcise Vance from her head forever. Erase all the scars he left behind.

But I'm not a magician.

I turn to Sebastian, and all my frustration coalesces into anger. He did this, with his meddling and lying. He hurt Leah. I grit my teeth and storm right up to Sebastian. "You will fix this. You *will* make this right. You—"

He holds up his hand to stop my tirade, defeat hanging his head. "I will, Shawn. I'm sorry."

It's enough to dampen my rage, and I give him a sharp nod. "Good."

I force myself to go upstairs to wait for Leah's return, but first I send her a text, telling her to let me know if she needs anything. Anything at all. Lying on my back on my bed, I rest my arms behind my head and stare at the ceiling.

Sebastian had better be able to fix this, because I don't know what I'll do if he can't.

Chapter Twenty-Nine

Leah

I race down the sidewalk, pausing as a vision of Vance swims in front of me. I keep moving and slowly his image dissipates. Each breath I expel pushes him further away.

But Sebastian replaces him. How he'd hugged me and said, *"I knew you were smart enough to figure it out. When you were ready."*

He'd been manipulating me the whole time.

A slimy feeling coats me as the remnants of my coercive relationship with Vance ooze over my skin. Sebastian, of all people. I never would have expected that from him.

At least Shawn didn't know. Yet the question lingers in my mind…how much of me turning to Shawn was actually *me*? And how much was Sebastian pushing me?

The thought drops in my stomach like a bowling ball. Shawn said Sebastian had talked to him after the library. Even before that, when Shawn had pressed me about my platonic relationship, Sebastian had seemed like he suspected more.

Did Sebastian plan our breakup? Did he purposefully avoid me, canceling our dates and forgetting me? The doubts slice through me, each one a knife straight to my heart.

My phone dings with a text message, and I pull it out. Shawn's offer to help is reassuring. At least one thing is real—he does love me. How I got here doesn't matter, at least in my relationship with Shawn. I know my feelings for him are true. Even if Sebastian manipulated the circumstances leading up to it, at least I have that.

My rush of energy dies suddenly, and I'm left feeling empty with a dull, pounding ache in my head. I turn around and trudge toward home.

Sebastian sits on the front steps, waiting. I come to a stop, trying to decide what I want to do. But I don't think I have a choice.

His eyes are laser focused on my every movement. If I run, he will hunt me down. I recognize the expression from when he starts pouring over his research. There's no stopping him when he gets to this point.

"What do you want, Sebastian?" I cross my arms and tap my foot.

"A chance to explain. After everything we've been through, I deserve that."

I let my arms drop to my sides, unable to deny him. "You hurt me."

He tilts his head, standing up to rest a gentle hand on my shoulder. "I know. I didn't mean to, and I'd like to make it right." I step away, and his face falls before he asks in soft tones, "Can we go get some coffee and talk? Please?"

I waffle for a moment, but I finally nod. I text Shawn where I'm going then fall into step with Sebastian. I start right in on my questions, needing to rip off the Band-Aid. "Did you stop hanging out with me, cancel our dates and forget me on purpose? To get me to break up with you?"

He falters, astonishment in his wide stare.

"The timing was so perfect, and I know you talked to Shawn after the library incident, when he realized his feelings." I search him, needing the answer. "Please, Sebastian, tell me the truth."

"No, Leah." His words are tortured, agony lacing his voice. "I would never treat you like that. Not on purpose." His lips press together before he says, "I hate that you would even think that of me."

"You lied once." I shrug, ignoring the stab in my gut from seeing him in pain. "I have no idea how far this manipulation goes. That's what I'm trying to figure out."

"I wasn't trying to manipulate you. At all." He shoves his glasses up his nose as we start walking again. "I knew by then that you and I were reaching the end of our relationship. Shawn and I talked. When he admitted his feelings, he immediately felt horrible since you and I were still dating. He didn't want me to break up with you because of him or he'd spend forever wondering if he'd done the right thing. We agreed the breakup had to come from you."

A bitter taste floods my mouth as my stomach clenches. I don't like that they talked about me and planned around my actions, but I let him continue.

"I'd just learned about the conference being the same time as Spring Break, so we talked about that as well. I thought if you still went, it might give you two an opportunity to spend more time together." His shoulders sag. "After we officially broke up, nothing felt different between us. You and I were still spending plenty of time together and I was ecstatic I hadn't lost my friend."

I can't help the bit of warmth that spreads through me at those words. I'd been thrilled not to lose him too.

"But I also wanted Shawn to have a chance. The conference over Spring Break had been a perfect excuse to duck out, so I made up another one for the weekend before. I thought having me gone would give you two a chance." He wrinkles his nose. "Plus that new superhero movie had just come out, and you know I hate those."

My lips part as I gape at him. He can't stand Marvel and going to the movies is the opposite of fun for him. Some of the pressure clamping my chest eases. Could it really be that simple?

"I'm sorry I didn't tell you sooner. I'm sorry I did it at all."

"I feel like a pawn in a chess game." I kick at a weed growing through the crack in the sidewalk.

"It was never like that, Leah." He sighs, pausing as if to find the right words. "I know you. If you'd made the wrong choice or hurt one of us — you never would have forgiven yourself. This way, it happened organically."

We reach the coffee shop, and he glances at me before he reaches for the handle. "It may seem like I interfered, but honestly, I tried not to. So did Shawn. We let opportunities present themselves and allowed you to do what you wanted in the moment."

I mull over the words as we wait in line. I understand what he means, but I'm not sure I'm ready to accept it yet.

At the table, I curve my hands around my warm French Vanilla latte. "I still feel like you were shoving me at Shawn every time I turned around." I twist the cup in my hands.

He frowns, leaning back in his chair. "Do you believe that you and I were going to break up soon — with or without Shawn in the picture?"

I pry the lid off my cup and blow while I think. Now that I know Sebastian didn't treat me badly on purpose, I can safely admit his behavior contributed to our break up.

That would have happened regardless of Shawn.

I think about Shawn's comment and Meg's hard questions. She would have found a way to ask those either way, and they set me on the path of breaking up with Sebastian.

"Maybe it wouldn't have happened when it did, but yes, I do think we would've broken up either way."

"Okay, good." He nods, leaning forward. "Now, how else did we interfere?"

I think about him lying about the conference and the events of that weekend. I still would've had breakfast with Shawn. Our movie wouldn't have changed, and Sebastian wouldn't have come. Though I'd have lost out on those quiet moments, reading with Shawn on the couch. My stomach clenches at the idea of missing that time.

But one interference does come to mind. "Shawn used you as an excuse to hang out with me on the trip, saying that you asked him to keep an eye on me."

Sebastian chuckles. "I did ask that, but only as my brother. I wanted to make sure you were safe, which I'd have done either way. Shawn may have taken it a bit further, but that's on him."

The pressure gripping my chest eases even more. Sebastian hadn't meddled nearly as much as I'd thought, but he'd still lied to me. "Okay, you're off the hook for butting in. I know you were doing what you thought was best, and I appreciate you and Shawn wanting things to work out the way they should." Vance's face swims before me, and I push it away. "That would be way too much like my ex."

"Leah," he says, reaching over to wrap his hand around my wrist. "I'm sorry I lied, and I'm sorry I hurt you." He squeezes me once then lets go. "Love you."

"I love you, too." Then I narrow my eyes at him. "But no more lies. And no more meddling!"

Relief shows in his smile. "So I shouldn't abandon botany to play matchmaker full-time?"

I shake my head, giggling at the absurd notion.

"In all seriousness, I am sorry for hurting you, but I'm not sorry you and Shawn are together. You two are my favorite people." He frowns. "Don't tell Steven and Silas, okay?"

I laugh as all my tension drops away.

"I want you both to be happy, and I think that you'll be happiest together. He really does love you." He arches an eyebrow, and I duck my head.

"Thanks, Sebastian. Apology accepted." I take a sip of coffee, thrilled to have my friend back. "So, what's new?"

He lights up. "I'm studying dogs right now. Did you know that their sense of smell is between ten thousand and a hundred thousand times better than ours? But they only have a sixth of our taste buds!"

That wasn't quite what I meant, but I can't help smiling at his eagerness. "I had no idea."

We finish our coffee and head home. Sebastian gives me a hug before we walk into the house. "Thanks for listening, Leah."

I squeeze him tighter. "Thanks for explaining."

We step inside, and I feel so much lighter than before. Silas and Steven glance up, concerned, but I smile, letting them know we're okay. Shawn is nowhere to be seen, so I pull out my phone to see a text that he went for a run.

Meg is also missing, so I head for our suite, wanting to talk to her properly. She's there, getting ready for an impromptu party Chad invited her to. I sit on her bed while she fusses with her hair.

"Did you work things out with Sebastian?" she asks.

I nod and fill her in.

Her relieved grin turns wicked as she glances at me in the mirror. "So, Shawn stayed over last night?" It's all the prodding I need to launch into the details, but she stops me with a gasp. "You had pizza and movie night without me?"

"Sorry, Meg. You were a little...occupied."

A smirk crosses her lips. "Yeah, I was." Then she huffs indignantly. "And it wasn't little."

We both laugh.

I finish catching her up on my new relationship status with Shawn, then she spends the rest of the time gushing about Chad. I'm so happy she found someone to settle down with. It's about time someone noticed how amazing she is.

I walk her out. As she leaves, Shawn jogs in, returning from a run. I assure him that I'm fine, that Sebastian and I are okay. Relief floods his face as he tugs me into a sweaty hug which I pull away from.

"You need a shower."

He laughs and kisses my cheek. "All right, but you owe me a hug."

"Fine," I say, my cheeks warm.

After he heads upstairs, I grab my novel and settle next to Sebastian on the couch. He gives me a soft smile before returning to his own book. Shawn comes down twenty minutes later, and we all spend the evening together, watching shows, playing games, stuffing our faces.

When it's time for bed, anticipation curls within me, and I turn to Shawn. "Meg's gone. Want to have another sleepover?"

His grin is huge. "You don't have to ask me twice. I'll grab my stuff."

I know it's only a few minutes, but the wait is agonizing. The moment he closes the door to our suite, I run to him. I tilt my head to give him better access as he trails kisses up my neck. Our lips find each other at the same time, and I sigh, clinging to his shoulders.

He grips my hips, pulling me close. I thread my fingers in his hair as a thrill zips through me. I press my chest against him, my breasts heavy and aching. My thighs clench as desire coils within me, pooling low in my abdomen. His thumbs slip under my shirt to graze my bare skin, and I gasp at his fiery touch. Evidence of his own arousal presses into me.

"Tell me if we're going too fast."

I shake my head. "More, Shawn. I want more."

His eyes drill into me, searching. He must find whatever he's looking for because his lips crash onto mine, and I stop thinking. His kisses burn right to my very center where a dull throbbing spreads lower between my thighs and higher to the taut tips of my breasts. My hips thrust to meet him, and he groans.

Adjusting himself, he walks me backward, pushing me firmly against the wall. When our tongues entwine, I can't help my moan. Our bodies are flush, no space between us, and one of his hands slides under my thigh, guiding my leg around his hip. His large hand cups my ass, pinning me to him. He rubs his hard length along my apex, creating a delicious friction through my yoga pants.

Then his other hand slides under my T-shirt. He pauses, searching my face for permission. I give him the slightest of nods and he moves slowly up. He sucks in a ragged breath when his fingers run over my lacy bra to cup my breast. He drags his gaze down, as if he can see me through my shirt.

"You and your lace," he growls. "I've dreamed about it."

He brushes his thumb over my nipple, and I can barely feel the fabric between us. I throw my head back with a moan, making him smirk.

"It haunts me." He rolls my lace-covered peak between his fingers as he rocks his hips, his erection grinding on my needy clit.

I gasp at the combined sensation, clinging to his shoulders.

"You like that?" His emerald eyes are hooded with desire as I nod. He does it again, thrusting against me. A wanton groan escapes me, and his smile turns cocky. "Hold on."

And he begins a rhythm that drives me wild. Between his skilled hand on my breast and his eager cock creating the most delicious friction, I move closer and closer to bliss. His mouth finds mine, our tongues entwining to the same pulsing beat.

When his thumb flicks my nipple once more, a jolt goes straight to my core. I careen over the edge, gasping his name as I shudder in his arms. He holds me until I go still, kissing me gently then guiding me to stand on my own two unsteady feet.

My wobbliness has him asking in concern, "Do you want to be done?"

I lean against the wall, staring up at those eyes—darker green than I've ever seen. Anticipation flutters through me. "No, I want more."

His lips find mine in a searing kiss. "I want to taste you, Lee." He rubs his thumb over my still-sensitive tip. "Here."

I gasp, but he's not finished yet. His hand leaves my breast, sliding down my ribs, between my legs, and I shudder when he touches my heated core.

"And here."

I close my eyes, reeling from the overwhelming tumult of desire. It wasn't what I thought he'd say, but the more I picture it, the wetter I become.

His lips brush my temple. "If it's too much, that's okay too."

"No, I want to." The flutters inside me aren't fear, but anticipation and desire as I take his hand and lead him to my bedroom. I bite my lip as I stand in front of my bed. *Okay, one or two might be butterflies.*

Shawn's expression is tender as he grips my sides, his thumbs caressing my hips. He tugs on the hem of my shirt. "Can this come off?"

My yes is barely audible, but I lift my arms as he pulls it over my head.

He doesn't move for a long moment, staring at me in complete awe. "You're so beautiful." He touches my cheek, trailing a finger down my neck, over my collarbone, between my breasts. He runs his finger along the band of my pants, then tugs. "How about these?" I grab his wrists, helping him push them down, and he chuckles at my eagerness.

Then I stand before him in my lacy bra and matching bikini underwear, not the least bit self-conscious. Not with the hungry way he drinks me in. As if he's been starving for weeks and a veritable buffet of his favorite foods stands before him. His lips part, his breathing ragged—all from looking at me.

I love it. I reach for him, sliding my hand over his abdomen as he closes his eyes at my touch. "Take off your shirt?"

He smirks, ripping it over his head one-handed before my lips finish the final word. And it's my turn to drink him in.

I'm mesmerized, my gaze tracing each and every divot of his carved muscles. From his rounded pecs to his washboard abs, with a sprinkling of hair to the vee that points like an arrow to the bulge in his gray sweatpants.

"Keep staring at me like that, and I'll forget what I'm supposed to be doing." His jaw clenches, his fingers curled into fists.

I lick my lips, and he shudders. His reaction to me, to just my eyes on him, is a heady feeling that I revel in.

"Please, Lee." His voice is a strained whisper, almost begging as he stays stock still, completely at my mercy. "Let me taste you."

I love that I'm in total control of one of the strongest men I know. I nod, and he pounces, tackling us both to the bed. He straddles one of my legs, his chest tight to mine with his arms framing my head. His mouth eagerly finds mine as his hard length digs into my hip. I arch against it, panting when he pulls away to trail kisses down my neck to my chest.

His hot breath hits my nipple through the lacy barrier of my bra before he takes it into his mouth. The suction makes me grab a handful of his hair, needing to ground myself. He shifts to lie alongside me.

My hips buck off the bed as he laves me, and he chuckles. His left hand slides down my stomach, skimming my side, my hip, my outer leg before dancing along my sensitive inner thigh. I squirm, wanting more. He traces the seam of my panties before stroking once down the center.

He lifts his head to lock his intense gaze with mine. "I can feel how wet you are." He crooks a finger, running it along the elastic edge and leaving a scorching trail of heat in its wake. His lips move to my other breast.

"Please," I beg, gripping the comforter to anchor myself. I'm not even sure what I'm asking for.

But he knows exactly what I need. He kisses his way down my stomach with lips so light they make me writhe. His finger continues sliding up and down the inner edge of the lace of my panties. His torso hovers over my thighs, nudging them to open further, and I have a second of hesitation.

"You okay, Lee?"

I pause before I answer, pushing aside the shadows of panic as I swallow then spread my legs for him. "I want your mouth on me."

Leaning in, he pulls aside the lacy covering. His tongue finds my sensitive bundle of nerves, running over and around it as desire pulses low in my belly like a flooded river crashing against a dam. I don't know how long I'll be able to hold out.

I moan as he picks up the pace. When he slides a finger inside me, I gasp, grabbing a fistful of his hair. I can't believe we're here together, like this. It's more amazing than I ever imagined.

When he sucks on my clit, it's too much, and fireworks explode within me. My hips keep moving as I ride his tongue. His finger continues sliding as the dam shatters, and I dive over that edge, fracturing into a million pieces. It takes several long moments to come back to Earth.

Chapter Thirty

Shawn

I can't look away from Leah as she comes. Her eyes closed, head tilted back, lips parted. She is breathtaking, and I brought her to this point. I don't move until she stops bucking, then I sit up, grinning ear to ear.

Her eyes flutter open, and she chuckles. "Yeah, Shawn, you did good."

The praise ripples through me, my smile growing impossibly wide and she laughs again. I need to hold her, scooting up alongside her to pull her into my arms. Her elbow brushes my rock-hard cock, and I bite back a groan as she freezes. But she doesn't shy away, instead her eyes dip to the tented front of my gray sweatpants.

I watch her, barely able to move in anticipation of what she'll do next.

She holds my gaze as she rests her hand on my chest then inches down my torso. I tense when her finger slides along the band of my sweatpants, and I ache to feel her hand wrap around me. She leans up to kiss me, her other hand shoving me down onto the mattress.

I love how she's taking control. Her breasts mold to my chest, soft and supple. She presses her thigh to my cock, making me buck.

Exactly like I made her do moments ago.

She grins against my lips. "Sucks, don't it?"

Her cocky attitude only turns me on more. She kisses me again, then shows me mercy, slipping her hand into my pants. I jerk at the brush of her fingers, nearly coming on the spot. She glides her thumb over my damp tip, slickening her grip as she wraps her hand around me while swallowing every one of my groans.

She eases into a perfect rhythm, her grip firm and movements fluid. I can't resist reaching up to cup her breast, loving the fullness of her in my palm. I splay my other hand across her bare back as my dick hardens even more.

I jerk my mouth away, murmuring her name. My breaths are heavy and ragged, then she stares at her hand wrapped around my cock. And that's all it takes. She watches in fascination as thick white ropes coat her hand and my stomach, a pleased grin on her lips.

When I'm done, she presses her mouth firmly to mine then bounds out of bed before I can say anything. I lie there, reveling in the feeling of release brought to me by the woman I love as my heart returns to a normal pace. Water runs in the bathroom, and she returns minutes later with a washcloth.

I clean up, then hit the bathroom. When I come back, I slip my arm under her head. She rolls right to me and I kiss her soundly, feeling beyond content.

I hope she's feeling the same. "You good?"

She nods, and her smile shows me just how relaxed she is. "You?"

Tenderness wells up within me as I brush away a piece of hair from her face. "Lee, I have you in my arms. How can I not be good?" I can't help glancing at that lacy bra still covering her chest. "And you're still wearing your lace, so yeah."

She wrinkles her nose. "Take a good look because I'm not sleeping in it."

My eyebrows shoot up at the insinuation, and my cock stirs. "Want me to help you take it off?" I tease.

Her cheeks turn pink as she shoves me away. "No." She pushes out of bed, snatching up some clothes then stomps to the bathroom.

I watch her go then roll over, sighing when my sweatpants ride up my calf. I hate sleeping in pants. Mulling over the idea, I decide to take a chance and shuck them off, leaving me in only my boxers. Leah comes back in a T-shirt and shorts, and I don't move as she scoots under the covers.

When her bare leg brushes mine, a soft gasp escapes her.

"Is this okay?" I whisper.

She nods then snuggles against my chest. Relief trickles through me, that I didn't push too far, that tonight was another success. Her breathing quickly evens, and I close my eyes, knowing I won't be far behind.

* * * *

The next morning is Monday, and we begin our week the same way we always do. Classes, work, assignments. Even though everything is different because Lee is officially my girlfriend.

The thought blindsides me at the oddest of moments, never failing to make me smile. It's not the only thing I have to be happy about though. I can't believe there's just a month to go then we'll both be graduating. I never thought I'd get here.

And I definitely wouldn't be this close without her help in Spanish.

We're both super busy with end of the year projects. The only time I get to see her are the evenings we stay home and hang out. Meg is home both Monday and Tuesday night, and Lee is uncomfortable with me sleeping over, so I don't. But I miss it, the way she curls into me, her soft smile when she wakes up and sees me, having that extra time with her.

Wednesday evening, we have the house to ourselves and we snuggle up to watch a movie. I toss another handful of popcorn in my mouth, munching away when Lee's phone dings.

She sits up as she reads the text and she beams. "Mom and Dad are back from Arizona."

Her parents spend most of the winter down there, and I know she misses them.

"They want to meet for dinner." She glances at me, her hesitation evident. "Wanna come?"

"Sure, if you want me to." Though my stomach twists at the thought, which is ridiculous because I know Bob and Mary. But I haven't met them as Lee's boyfriend…

She gasps and stops typing. "We should have Trey and Judy come too! It'll be one big catch-up session."

I sag against the couch.

"What? You haven't told them yet?"

I shrug, feeling sheepish. "I haven't talked to them. I'm not trying to keep it a secret or anything. I can text them right now but then I'm going to get the phone call from Mom demanding all the details and —" I sigh and swipe a hand over my face. "I don't know if I have the capacity for all that."

She laughs. "I completely understand." Her gaze drops to the couch. "I haven't told my parents yet either."

I chuckle even as worry pierces me.

I must not keep it off my face because she rests her hand on my thigh. "I was waiting until they got back." But a crinkle appears in her forehead. "I've been trying to figure out what to say...how to tell them I'm with a different Wrighting." She wrinkles her nose. "It feels weird to tell people that."

"Do you think they'll be upset?" I say, wondering if I have cause for even more concern.

"I don't see why they would be as long as I'm happy." She hurries to add, "Which I am!" Then she presses her lips together. "Do you think your parents will be upset about it?"

"No. Not in the least. They know you, Lee. It's not like you're going through each of us in turn, using us to add to the notches in your bedpost." I cup her cheek, gliding my thumb over her soft skin. "They'll be happy, especially when they see how perfect we are together."

Her delightful lips tilt up, and I lean in to brush mine against hers. "I think dinner will be a great time to tell them."

She nods then eases back to return to her text. "Me too. How does Friday sound?"

"I'll check with my parents, but it works for me."

It ends up working for everyone. When Friday comes, I work my usual shift at the rec center, coming home in time to get ready. Leah's knee bounces the whole way there, and we hold hands as we walk inside, facing our parents together.

They hardly bat an eye, going straight for hugs and congratulations. Not one single awkward moment pops up, and I relax as Leah does. By the end of the evening, she's pressed up against my side, her warm hand gliding along my thigh and making me think very inappropriate thoughts for our setting.

"Ready?" I ask her.

Desire shines in her gaze, and I have to reel in my reaction as I shift in my seat. Her mouth curves wickedly, as her hand climbs higher under the table. I swallow, and she chuckles then moves away.

"Yeah, let's go," she says in my ear.

I want nothing more than to kiss her senseless, but my dad announces that dinner is on him, starting an argument between him and Bob. I shake my head, hug my mom and Mary then wait as Lee embraces everyone. It doesn't seem like our parents will be leaving any time soon.

She glances at her phone before I help her put on her coat. "Meg won't be home tonight."

Anticipation coils within me, and I can't wait to get back, but Bob stands up, saying he'll walk us out. Tension grips my stomach at the serious look he shoots my way.

We barely make it outside before he asks, "So, Shawn, what are your intentions with my daughter?"

Nothing like being put on the spot.

Leah cries, "Dad!"

He doesn't budge, and I straighten my shoulders. "Well, sir, it may seem sudden for you, but the truth is, I'm in love with your daughter and have been for a while." I can't help smiling at her with all the tenderness I feel. "I only realized it myself a couple months ago, but I've been fighting it a lot longer than that out of respect for Sebastian."

She laces her fingers through mine, squeezing gently.

"But she chose me, sir, and I promise to try to be worthy of that choice. I'll take care of her. And we have Sebastian's full support."

Her smile shines on me then she beams at her dad.

"Sounds like you picked the right one, Leah." His words and small smile are begrudging, but I'll take them.

She leans into my side. "I couldn't agree more." She lets go of me to hug her dad once more. "Love you, Dad."

"Love you too, Lee-bug." He shakes my hand, says goodbye and heads back into the restaurant.

"Sorry about that," Leah says with a grimace. "Wasn't expecting him to give you the third degree."

We start walking back to the car. "You're worth it."

She ducks her head, but grips my hand. I pull her to a stop, unable to hold off kissing her a moment longer. I slide my free hand to her waist, loving her eagerness as she rises on her toes to meet me.

Our lips touch, electricity exploding within me as I groan. I yank my mouth away and touch my forehead to hers as I compose myself. "I need to get you home."

"Well, what are we waiting for?"

"Me to calm down enough that I can walk," I joke, mostly teasing.

Her laughter bounces across the parking lot, stopping short when a feminine voice calls her name. A group of four women Leah's age approach us. The way the sleek redheaded leader rakes her gaze down my body has me stepping closer to Lee. I want it known that I'm with my girl, and I'm happy here.

"Leah," she coos, glancing at me again. "Who's your friend?"

Leah seems smaller, as if she shrank into herself, so I answer, "Shawn Wrighting. Her boyfriend."

The blonde frowns. "Wrighting?" Her frown deepens as she studies me and asks Leah, "I thought your boyfriend's name was Sebastian."

"We broke up," Lee answers stiffly.

But the blonde presses on. "He was a Wrighting too, wasn't he?" Her lips form a little O. "Girl, are you double dipping? Brother sandwich?" She leans toward the redhead. "Talk about a snack!"

Leah protests, "It's not like that."

I bristle at their judgment then the redhead coughs out, "Slut."

Anger rips through me and I step forward, but Leah grabs my arm, shaking her head. When I open my mouth, she grits out, "Don't."

The redhead tosses her hair over her shoulder. "How many of you are there? Four, right?" At my angry nod, a sly smirk spreads across her face. "Halfway there, huh, Leah?" Chuckling, she walks away, the other women trailing after her.

Leah doesn't say a word, just rushes to the car and gets in, shutting the door hard behind her. I stare after her, then glance back at the group of women. It takes everything in my control not to run after them, to cut them down to the same small size Leah is feeling right now.

But I force myself to follow her to the car. Before I turn on the engine, I face her. "Who were they?"

Her jaw works side to side before she answers. "The redhead is Vivian. She's in my English class. She and her friends have seen me walking with Sebastian before and I know one has been out with Silas."

Silence hangs between us before I ask the questions burning a hole within me. "Why didn't you tell them off? Or at least let me defend you?"

She faces the window. "It wasn't worth it."

"Lee," I say softly, "you're worth it."

She shakes her head, the motion so minuscule I almost miss it. "Arguing only makes it worse."

I sigh, wishing she would look at me. Wishing we could go back to the easy moments of before. But she doesn't and we can't, so I drive us home in silence as she withdraws deeper into herself. I try to formulate a plan to bring her back, but nothing comes to mind.

I'm determined though, so even when she pops out of the car and rushes into the house without me, I haven't given up. I follow her inside, striding after her as she opens the door to her suite. Meg sits inside on the couch, tears sliding down her cheeks.

"Meg," Lee cries. "What happened?"

I stand there like an idiot, waiting.

"Chad—" Meg breaks off in a jagged sob.

Lee turns back to me, a mixture of relief and pain in her gaze. It's the first eye contact she's made since we left the restaurant, and my stomach twists.

"Goodnight, Shawn," she says, then shuts the door between us.

I glare for several moments at the wooden barrier as I try to get a handle on my frustration and hurt. I know Meg needs her, but I can't help wondering if that was an excuse. If she even would have talked to me if Meg hadn't been home.

When I turn around, all three of my brothers stare at me, and I hold up my hands. "I didn't do anything, I swear." The last thing I need is them kicking my ass. I hurry to explain, each of them growing more concerned as I finish my recap.

Sebastian pushes his glasses further up on his nose. "That is most unfortunate. She has been doing so well lately."

I sigh, sinking onto the couch next to him. "I know. Hopefully it's not too big of a set back." I glance once more at the door. "What happened with Meg?"

Silas snorts. "Some fight with her boyfriend."

Steven elbows him. "Then Silas made it worse by commenting on her red nose."

"I was just—"

"You were being a jerk," Steven says.

Silas folds his arms, slumps down the couch and mutters to himself.

"On that note," I say, standing. "I'm going upstairs."

The last thing I need is more drama. I spend the rest of the evening in my room, reading the other romance book Leah lent me. It's a cruel form of torture, watching them fall for each other when I can't be with my girl.

I manage to finish the book, setting it on my nightstand as I flop onto my bed with a sigh. I'd gotten my hopes up after the restaurant and had been excited about some quality time alone with Leah. I needed that.

Instead she was ambushed by those women. The memory plays in my mind and I hate how small she seemed. The fiery woman I love was nowhere to be found, her spark all but crushed out. I huff an annoyed breath then lean over to turn off the light. I gaze into the darkness, waiting for sleep to come. It finds me eventually, and I drift off into fitful dreams.

* * * *

The next morning, I wake up in a grumpy mood. I pull on my running clothes then trot downstairs. Leah and Meg are on the couch, and Lee pops up when she sees me.

"Hey," she says.

"Hey," I grunt.

"Can you come here for a second?"

I sigh, following her to the kitchen. I've been plagued all morning by restless tension and moving is the only way to fix that. But I can wait until after we talk. She hops onto the counter, stretching her arms toward me. When I step closer, she grabs my waist, tugging me in to stand between her legs.

"I'm sorry, Shawn. I know I shut you out last night, and I shouldn't have done that."

One of the anxious bands gripping my chest loosens, and I rest my hands on her thighs. "It's okay, Lee. Are...are you doing okay now?"

Her easy smile is a relief to see, and she nods. "Much better. Meg and I talked about a lot of things last night. It helped."

"Good." I mean it, too. Nightmares of my broken girlfriend haunted me all night, making me in desperate need of this reassurance that she's truly okay.

"Will you kiss me now?" She tips her face up.

I tease, "If you insist."

Our lips meet. I'm hesitant at first but she pulls me closer, slanting her mouth against mine.

She breaks away to say, "Meg's going to her parents' for the night."

"Good," I growl and kiss her again.

Only for Silas to interrupt us with a groan. "Kissing in the kitchen is so not allowed."

Every fiber of my being protests pulling away from her, but I do. I hold her stare though, seeing the echo of my longing reflected in her eyes. "Meg's still home?"

"Yeah, she hasn't left yet."

I rake a hand through my hair. "Then I'm definitely going for a run." I have to do something to combat this ache threatening to consume me. "Let me know when she's gone."

Heat flares in her gaze and her voice is husky as she says, "Believe me, I will."

Chapter Thirty-One

Leah

I stare after Shawn, loving to watch him leave. That ass won't quit. Then I make my way to our suite where Meg is hauling out her suitcase. I do a double take at her huge smile.

"Chad called! He apologized and is coming to dinner with my parents tonight."

I give her a big hug, excited that things have worked out for her. And even more excited that I'll have alone time with Shawn sooner than expected.

As Silas stomps through the living room and up the stairs, Meg's expression darkens. A pang hits my stomach. I love them both and hate seeing them always at odds.

"I wish you'd tell me what happened," I say, knowing her answer.

"Don't worry about it, Lee. It's in the past."

I don't push, we say goodbye, then she's gone. Steven already left for work, and Sebastian isn't here again — some botany event demonstrating new grafting techniques. Silas is holed up in his room, so I curl up on the couch with my book until Shawn returns with his damp hair clinging to his forehead, his shirt plastered to his torso. My mouth goes dry.

But he doesn't seem to notice, pointing to the stairs. "I'm gonna hit the shower."

I think about telling him that Meg left, but a wicked idea hits me, so I nod and watch him go. Shawn still owes me from the day Meg didn't latch the door. I wait until he's all the way upstairs before I tiptoe after him. Silas is the only one still home, and his door is shut.

I huddle against the wall in the stairwell as I hear Shawn come out of his room and the water in the bathroom turn on. I wait a solid minute, wanting to be sure he's all the way in, then I sneak inside.

They have a real shower curtain. We do too, now — I fixed that situation the next day. I clear my throat, and Shawn's head peeks out. He gapes when he sees me.

I smirk. "I believe you owe me."

He snaps his mouth shut, clearing his throat. "What exactly do you want here, Lee?" His voice is extra husky.

My lips part, his words opening several doors I'm not quite ready for. I slam them shut, blinking away delicious, wet images of us tangled together. "You got a pretty good show the other day. I think it's only fair you return the favor."

He nods, disappearing behind the shower curtain again. The end farthest from the spray opens in invitation. I inhale a sharp breath, my heart beating faster as I take slow steps toward the gap in the curtain.

Shawn is completely naked behind that flimsy barrier, and this is the first time I'll see him without a stitch of clothes. I've seen bits and pieces, but never all together.

I bite my lip as I gather my courage and peer in. My breath leaves me in a whoosh. He's so gorgeous. At least he has the means to put out the flames if I spontaneously combust.

The water slides over his upturned face and down his neck, sluicing off his impeccable abdomen. The vee directs me to his impressive cock standing at attention as if it knew I was coming. His thighs are tight and sculpted, like everything else. Then he turns around, giving me a view of his perfect back and ass.

I sag against the wall, needing some support. *Holy shit.* Images of all his beautiful parts float through my head as I close my eyes.

Then I'm stumbling forward as he yanks me into the shower with him. He catches me against his very wet, very naked body, and he laughs while I sputter, "You — you — "

He arches an eyebrow. I shove at his bare chest, but my hands slide off. He grabs my wrists, leaning forward to kiss me while dragging me further into the spray. His dick digs into me, then he freezes. I follow his gaze, my pale yellow T-shirt turning translucent under the spray. I don't have a bra on.

The bathroom door opens followed by the lid to the toilet banging against the top, and my jaw drops. I clamp my hands over my ears, burying my face in Shawn's chest. His shoulders shake with laughter.

"You run today? What's the weather like out there?" Silas asks before flushing.

Shawn waits for the noise to stop. "Bright, sunny spring day. Almost sixty already." His fingers splay across my back, his other thumb dipping under my shirt to graze my stomach.

"Nice. Thanks." The floor creaks near the doorway. "And don't think I don't know you're in there, Lee." He pulls the door shut behind him.

Shawn lets out his laughter with gusto as I drop my head into my hand, wishing I could disappear. This is gonna take some getting used to.

"What?" He barely holds back a laugh. "You think he couldn't hear us talking? Didn't think he'd notice a girl's voice?"

My cheeks go hot, and I pout, jutting out my lower lip. "I was stealthy."

His gaze drifts over my see-through shirt. "Uh huh. And what's the plan for getting back downstairs?"

"I wasn't planning on getting wet!" My words have my thoughts dropping between my legs, and I stammer even more. "That's not what I meant."

Shawn laughs, low and gravelly. An intensity settles in his eyes as he brushes his hand over my nipple jutting out against the soaked fabric. "So, how wet are you?"

I gulp as the motion sends a jolt straight to my core. "Wet enough." I add, "Meg left."

A growl escapes him. "I'd planned on taking care of this"—he presses his erection into my hip—"myself before you came in." He grips my ass, pulling me tight to him as he seeks the friction we both crave. "Maybe you want me to wait." A clear challenge flashes in his voice as he grinds on me again.

My thighs clench, need flooding me, and I look up at him through lowered lashes. "Have you washed yet?"

"No."

I give him my best coy smile, running my hands over his chest. "Well then, you'd better hurry up, because I'm getting impatient."

One corner of his mouth ticks up. Not taking his eyes off me, he reaches over my shoulder to grab the shampoo. When he lathers up his hair, I can't help digging my hands into the sudsy mass right along with him. Then he takes his time swiping the washcloth over every inch of his skin.

My fingers follow, trailing the suds in the places I'm brave enough to touch. I revel in the fact that he's torturing himself as well as me by prolonging this. I can't complain about a chance to touch him unhindered, although I practically pant with need when he rinses off, wet through and through.

He shuts off the water, stepping out at full attention. First he locks the door, then he tosses me a towel before grabbing one for himself. "Those wet clothes are going to make a big mess." That's all he says as he proceeds to dry off, leaving me to decide how much he sees.

I'm not confident enough to strip for him yet, so I whip the shower curtain closed. His chuckle sounds over my dripping clothes. My shorts slap against the floor, but it takes more effort to peel off my shirt. Finally I'm free. I wrap the towel around myself, still feeling way too exposed.

I wring out my clothes the best I can then open the shower curtain. Shawn waits for me, his matching towel sitting low on his hips. The bulge of his erection beckons, and I clutch the edges of my towel tighter.

He offers a hand to help me out of the tub then takes my wet clothes. "I'll go first to make sure the coast is clear. We can either duck into my room, and you can wear some of my things. Or we can make a run for your room."

I rake my gaze down his wet torso, then lower to his straining towel. I bite my lip. "My room."

His throat bobs. Opening the door, he peers into the hallway. When he beckons, I creep out after him, my heart racing. It's ridiculous. All the guys have seen me in a towel, a bikini, various stages of undress. Hell, Silas peed in front of me a few minutes ago. But something about this clandestine operation gives me a thrill, and I don't want to get caught.

I hurry downstairs after Shawn. The living room is empty, and we make a mad dash for my room. I lock my door behind me, flopping onto my bed. Shawn lands next to me.

We laugh, lying there, and awareness washes over me. My skin tingles as I remember I'm only in a towel.

So is he.

"I'm still wet," I whisper, loving how fast his head whips toward me, how dark his eyes are.

He licks his lips. "Can't let that go to waste." He pats his chest. "Come here."

I roll over, positioning my torso on top of his. My towel loosens but stays put for the most part.

"What do you want, Lee?"

The rough towel feels good against my sensitive parts, and I want to squirm. I want to feel his warm hands cup me, touch me. I want his mouth on me in multiple places. But I settle for, "I want you to kiss me."

He waits for me to come to him, tilting his chin as the familiar challenge dances in his gaze. It melts away any fear, giving me the confidence I need to scoot closer. The towel stays behind as my breasts spring free against his bare chest, and I hesitate, wondering if I should cover myself and keep the barrier between us.

But he sucks in an awe-filled breath, bolstering me. So I continue until my lips touch his, and I let out a contented sigh as we lie skin to skin for the first time. His hands rest on my bare shoulders, playing with my hair. We kiss until the fire in my belly, the ache between my legs and the desperation for him to touch me is too much to bear.

When I jerk my mouth away, he asks wickedly. "Now, what?"

Yanking my towel from between us, I guide my nipple to his mouth. Both of us groan with pleasure when he sucks it in. His other hand finds my opposite breast—kneading, rolling, flicking. I love every second of it, but I need more.

I whimper, and he pulls back to say huskily, "Just ask." He stares, waiting.

It unnerves me that he's making me do this, making me take control, but at the same time, I love it. He's pushing me just enough, like he always does. I trace his lips with my finger.

"I want your mouth on me." I guide his hands between my legs, and he sucks in a breath when he touches my heat. "Here."

"Leah, you weren't kidding." He brings up his fingers, glistening with my arousal, and sticks them in his mouth then hums with pleasure at my taste.

A jolt of desire goes straight through me at the sight. I wait for him to move, to roll me over like he did the other day, but he doesn't.

A mischievous grin tips his lips. "I think you're going to like this."

He tugs me until I'm kneeling then guides me higher and higher on the bed. Confusion courses through me, but I trust him, and I'm desperate enough to do as he bids. Once I'm near his face, he starts to lift one of my legs.

I realize what he's doing and I balk, shaking my head.

He meets my eyes. "Trust me. You get to be in total control, and it's a whole different angle." He rubs my thigh, gliding up to cup my ass. "If you hate it, roll off. No biggie."

I study him for a long moment, and he simply waits, sliding his hand down my leg. The idea of sitting on his face seems so dirty to me…

To hell with it.

With his help, I lift my leg up and over to straddle him. My gaze darts to his, but he's staring at my pussy, open and waiting for him. I feel exposed, vulnerable in this position, my muscles stiff and rigid as I wait.

Until he puts his mouth on me.

I immediately jerk forward, slamming my palm into the wall above his head. "Holy shit," I gasp, unable to contain my reaction.

He chuckles as I suck in a steadying breath, bracing myself for more. He moves to grip my thighs, holding me in place as he goes to work.

He fucks me with his tongue, delving deep and returning to swirl around my nub. The rhythm creates enough friction to have me panting before he dives back in. The fierce, endless cycle builds me toward a crescendo unlike anything I have ever felt. Then he takes that small bundle of nerves in his mouth and sucks.

I put my fist to my mouth as I scream out my release. Wave after wave crashes over me, but he doesn't stop until I go still. I roll onto the bed, trembling as he puts his arms around me.

"You're so beautiful when you come."

I burrow into his chest, needing the safety and shelter he offers after the rawness of what I just experienced. It takes several minutes for my breathing to return to normal and even longer for any energy to trickle back in. I finally lift my head to look at him.

He grins, completely cocky and full of himself.

I roll my eyes at his arrogance. "Yeah, I know. You told me so."

Chapter Thirty-Two

Shawn

The next week flies by, and bam, it's Easter. We go to Bob and Mary's for brunch then head to my parents' for dinner with the extended family. Leah wears a gorgeous green dress dotted with small white flowers. It stops right above her knees, and I can't keep my hand off her leg while I'm driving.

She bats me away again. "We're going to be around family, Shawn. I don't want to be all hot and bothered."

"Want me to find a back road somewhere, so we can take care of that first?"

Her lips part, but then she glares. "No, I just want you to keep your hands to yourself."

I pretend to pout, but I move my hand back to my own space. I want her in a good mood because I have something important to ask her. I clear my throat. "So, I have a question."

"What's up?"

"Well, this coming Friday is a party for one of my friends. Do you remember Dean?"

Her face scrunches up as she thinks then shakes her head.

"He's leaving right after graduation, moving to Seattle, and we're having a going away party for him." I pause to take a bolstering breath before I blurt out my request. "I'd like you to come. I want you to meet my friends, plus it'll be a fun time."

My hope dims as she looks away, her fingers bunched in the hem of her dress. "I don't know, Shawn."

"Hey, I know this would be out of your comfort zone, but I thought maybe it was time for that. I can do my usual Velcro act. You won't be able to move an inch without me right there."

"I'll think about it." She studies me. "I guess I made it through the last one without any mishaps." One corner of her mouth tips up. "Well, other than spilling my guts to you."

I reach over to rest my hand on hers, giving it a squeeze. "And see how well that turned out."

Both corners of her mouth turn up this time. "I *will* think about it."

"Thank you." It's enough for now, and we pull into my parents' driveway where I find a place to park. Then I hurry to open her door, doing a double take at the pinched expression on her face. "You okay?"

She lifts a shoulder. "It's only, the last time I was here was Christmas...with Sebastian."

I resist the urge to swipe my hand over my face. This wouldn't even be an issue if my parents had just kept their mouths shut about Leah dating him. But Mom was so excited that she'd announced it to everyone and now we have to deal with the repercussions. I made sure to tell her to keep Leah out of the spotlight this time around. I'm not going to stay away from her but we also don't need any shouting from the rooftops.

I don't show any of my annoyance, instead I give her my best smile and say, "Well, you're my girlfriend now. My family already loves you. My parents already approve. It'll be fine."

When I offer her my hand, she takes it, relaxing slightly. Mom greets us at the door in her apron, kissing our cheeks before bustling into the kitchen. And it's chaos from there. We go through the line of family scattered throughout the dining room and kitchen. Kids run back and forth, laughing and shouting until Mom shoos them away.

Leah seems fine through dinner. We sit with my aunt and uncle who regale us with the antics of their grandkids, the loud ones running around. Once we're stuffed, Leah heads toward the living room, and I offer to grab us some drinks.

I come back with a seltzer for her, beer for me, then sit on the couch next to her. After I hand her the drink, I sling my arm on the couch behind her, but she stays stiff and doesn't lean back.

Sebastian comes in, pouting as he sits on her other side. "Mom took my book."

It's hard not to laugh at his glowering expression, and I glance at Leah, thinking she'll join in my amusement. But she is rigid between us.

Before I can say anything, two cousins close to our age walk by. They stare at Leah, looking from her to me to Sebastian, then they shake their heads before leaning in. I can't make out their whispers but giggles pierce the air as they walk around the corner.

"Excuse me," Leah says, her voice tight as she shoves her unopened drink at me then takes off.

Sebastian turns to me with guilt on his face, but I shake my head. "Don't worry. It wasn't you." When he nods, I hurry after her.

I have a pretty good guess where she'll end up. Her favorite spot is outside—her thinking seat. Past the pool to the edge of the yard, I see her already nestled in the old maple tree with a split trunk. When I approach, she seems deep in thought as she stares at the grass.

"Hey." I keep my voice quiet, not wanting to startle her, "you okay?"

She gasps and nearly falls backward off the low tree branch, catching herself just in time. "I'm…" She trails off, shrugging instead.

I crouch to rest a hand on her knee. "Talk to me, Lee. What happened?"

She swallows. "I feel like your entire family is judging me. The way your cousins looked at us…the whispers." She shudders. "I hate it."

I study her for a long moment, feeling a hint of frustration. I love this woman, everything about her, and I don't know what more to do to prove it. Will it ever be enough? Will I ever be enough?

"I don't know what to tell you, Lee. I can't make everyone *poof*" —I flick my fingers open like performing a magic trick—"stop staring. I can tell you that I want to be with you, and I'm willing to put up with some gossip if I get to be your boyfriend." I tilt my head before adding, "As far as Sebastian goes, nothing rattles him."

"What about in the future?"

I suck in a breath at the implication even as she backpedals.

"I mean, *if* we're still together and Sebastian brings someone home…"

"Sebastian can handle that. He'll have to be up front with whoever it is, and I'm more than willing to explain my side if it'll help." I glide my thumb up the side of her knee, unable to hide my pleased smile. "You're really worrying about the future, huh?"

She ducks her head. "Maybe."

"Glad I'm not the only one."

My quiet admission has her chin whipping up, shock on her face.

"I love you, Leah, remember?" I stand. "What do you say we head home? One last walkthrough with our heads held high to show we're not ashamed?"

I offer her my hand, and I can feel her deliberation. As if she's deciding about more than this moment. At last, she slips her fingers into mine and stands up to kiss my cheek.

Relief flows through me as she offers a quiet, "Thank you."

I squeeze her hand. "No problem."

Then we walk back to the house to face everyone. Together.

By the time we get home, she seems back to her normal self and we spend the evening watching a movie before we part ways, since Meg is back. I offer to let her sleep in my room but Silas' room butts right up to mine and she doesn't want him to hear anything. Just talking about staying in my room has rubbing her foot on her calf. I know her suite is her safe space, and I want this to be at her pace…but I miss her when we're not together.

Wednesday is our next free night, and I offer to take her out for dinner.

On the walk over to Eat at Joe's, I try to sound casual as I ask, "Have you thought any more about the party this weekend?"

I know I'm pushing harder than she's comfortable with but this is important to me. I have friends I'd really like her to meet. Plus I'm desperate to show her that our relationship can survive outside our quiet little bubble. The biggest reason of all though, is that the more we get out there, the more news will spread.

And the sooner the gossip will die.

She hangs her head, my stomach sinking as she says, "I'm sorry, Shawn. I don't think I can do it yet. The party at our house was one thing since I knew everyone, and I had all you guys to watch out for me." She lifts one shoulder in a half-shrug. "This is just too much."

I shove aside the crashing disappointment, keeping my expression light. She obviously feels bad about her decision, and I don't want to make it worse. I reach over to rub her shoulders. "That's okay, Lee. Maybe next time."

I leave it at that as we head into the restaurant.

Chapter Thirty-Three

Leah

The night of the party is here before I know it. We grab a quick dinner before Shawn leaves, and to his credit, he never pushes or pleads for me to change my mind.

But I still feel guilty.

He's done so much for me. Nudging me out of my comfort zone over the past month. Never wavering in his love and support. So patient with our physical relationship.

Sebastian sits with me on the couch, not even peering up from his book as he says, "Did you know that some penguins propose to each other with a rock?"

I don't answer, annoyed at the interruption of my wallowing.

He turns another page. "I bet it takes a lot of courage, choosing that perfect rock and showing it to their ideal penguin."

I huff out a sigh. "You think I should go to the party."

His hazel eyes finally find mine. "I think *you* think you should go to the party. You're not exactly being subtle in your brooding." He smirks when I gape. "Makes it hard to read."

I grab the nearest pillow and throw it at him.

He chuckles, tossing it back. "What are you so worried about, Leah?"

I wrap my arms around the pillow, hugging it to my chest. "It's scary. All those people I don't know."

"Technically you have met some of them, even if it has been a while."

That's true. Shawn brought various friends here for parties over the years. Some even attended our last party, so they're not all complete strangers.

"What if I get there and it's too much? What if I freak out?" The tightness in my chest and the anxious twisting in my gut say it's not out of the question.

"Then Shawn brings you back. You know he would never force you to stay."

Sebastian's calm, logical responses tip the scale, slowly but surely. Only one worry remains — I'd hate to make Shawn go home early.

As if sensing my hesitation, Sebastian offers, "What if I drive you over? I'll hang out until you're settled so Shawn doesn't have to leave, but you don't feel obligated to stay."

I blink in surprise. "You hate parties."

"I'll survive," he says in his driest tone then stares at me. "Well, are you going to get ready or not?"

"Yes!" I fling my arms around Sebastian, almost knocking the book from his hands. "Thank you." I press a kiss to his cheek. "You're the best friend ever."

Fifteen minutes later, I emerge in a corset-style white top and a black swishy mini skirt paired with cute ankle boots. Nervous energy makes it hard to stand still as Sebastian triple checks his pockets — phone, wallet, insulin, ChapStick. It's a whole process with this guy, but at least he remembered it all himself for once. Finally, we head out.

My knee bounces in the car, and I find myself nibbling on my nails more than once, endlessly yanking my finger out of my mouth. Ten minutes later, we arrive, and I've never been more grateful because it means an end to Sebastian's 'helpful' distraction — a barrage of penguin facts.

The two-story house has a wide porch crowded with people. Cars line the street, and music thumps from inside. Sebastian sighs, gripping the steering wheel for an extra beat before taking the keys out of the ignition.

I send Shawn a quick text letting him know I'm here, then I touch Sebastian's tense arm. "Thank you again for doing this."

He nods, and together we walk toward the house. Despite how closely he sticks to me, my chest tightens more with every step. The inside is packed, the music overpowering, and I fight the urge to spin on my heel and run in the opposite direction.

I don't see Shawn anywhere, and I glance at Sebastian who shakes his head. We wind our way through the house to the back porch where I find immediate relief from the noise. I scan the groups scattered around, thrilled to see Shawn near the campfire with a guy I vaguely recognize. I tug on Sebastian's sleeve, and we share a grin.

Shawn is angled away from me, so I take advantage and sneak up behind him then tap his broad shoulder.

I can't help admiring his muscular back in his fitted long-sleeved shirt and the way those jeans cling to his ass. He turns around, beaming as he registers me.

"Lee!" He swoops me into an embrace so tight I can hardly breathe.

I laugh, hugging him back.

"What are you doing here?" His gaze lands on Sebastian, and his eyebrows shoot up. "With Sebastian?"

"I texted you. I guess you didn't hear it over all the noise." I shrug. "Sebastian was kind enough to give me a ride when I decided to be brave and support my boyfriend."

Shawn's expression turns tender. "Lee, you didn't have to come."

"But I know it's important to you, and you're always doing things for me. I wanted to do something for you for a change."

He brushes his lips against mine. "I think you do plenty, but thank you. And I'm proud of you." He turns to Sebastian. "Thank you, too. I know this isn't your scene."

Sebastian nods. "I'll stay for a few, make sure she's all right." He jerks his head toward the house. "I'm going to go find a water."

Shawn's gaze drifts back to me, sliding over my outfit. "You look amazing. You might freeze, but you look amazing."

I laugh. "Good thing I brought my scarf." His forehead crinkles until I loop his arm over my shoulders. I tilt my chin up. "Matches my outfit perfectly, don't you think?"

He kisses me soundly enough to make my toes curl. "I'm so glad you're here. Let me introduce you."

Shawn's friends are all as nice and easygoing as he is, with the same teasing sense of humor. Never once am I uncomfortable and, despite the number of people, the panic never shows up.

We work our way to the kitchen so I can get a drink. A gorgeous girl dressed head to toe in black with fishnet stockings, shorts and clunky, black army boots storms by. The stud in her nose moves as her nostrils flare, and she tosses her electric purple hair.

I manage to step out of the way, then continue into the kitchen where Sebastian grits his teeth as he snatches up a bottle of water. I walk over then nod toward the door she just exited. "Friend of yours?"

He grunts, ripping the cap off the water and tipping the bottle to his lips. "Professor Harrison's daughter, Calliope."

Ah, the one who made them leave their conference early. That explains the animosity. I've never seen Sebastian quite so worked up, and it strikes me as funny that someone who just reaches his chest can get under his skin that thoroughly.

"I think I'm good," I say, trying to give him a distraction. It's not penguin facts but maybe it'll work. "You can head out if you want."

His lips are set into a determined line. "I'll stay a little longer. Make sure *she* doesn't cause any trouble."

My eyebrows jump up, and I exchange a surprised look with Shawn. He shrugs then slings an arm around my shoulders. "Suit yourself. We'll be around if you need anything."

I wave once more to Sebastian before we grab a seltzer for me and refill Shawn's cup from the keg. Shawn introduces me to the rest of his friends and we take our time talking to everyone. When my drink is gone, I drag him to the dance floor. The sultry beat echoes through my body like an extra pulse, thrumming up desire as Shawn grips my hips and hauls my back flush to his front.

"I can't get over how hot you look tonight." His lips brush my cheek, then he kisses his way down my neck.

I grind on him, not the least bit self-conscious. We're the most sober people dancing, everyone else lost in a haze of lust and alcohol. One of his hands splays across my stomach, tracing the laces of my corset as he thrusts against me with his growing hardness. I want to do so many things with him, none appropriate for the dance floor.

Boldness bolsters me. I spin around to face him, straddling one of his muscular legs and clutching his shoulders. "How well do you know the house?"

He blinks and asks, "Lee, what are you suggesting?"

Pressing my chest to his, I bat my eyes, keeping my words low and tantalizing. "That we take this somewhere more private."

His throat bobs as he swallows, then he grabs my hand and leads me down a hallway. He turns to look at me more than once as if reassuring himself that yes, this is happening, and yes, I want to do this. I bite my lip, and he quickens his pace.

At the end of the hall, he peers into a room, opens the door wider and pulls me in. He locks the door after us. We're in a small study with a desk and a leather wing-back chair near a window. His arms circle me from behind, his hot mouth on my neck, and I moan when he grinds along my ass.

His fingers slide up to dip inside the top of my corset, my nipples pebbling at his searing touch. His other hand yanks up my skirt, caressing my heat. One finger glides over my slick folds as I moan his name. He must be more turned on than I thought, as eager as he is.

I tip my head back, my cheek brushing his. "So you like this top, huh?"

"I like all of it. I can barely keep my hands off you, obviously. You're trying to kill me, Lee." He punctuates his statement with another thrust, his hardness even more evident now.

I wriggle out of his grasp as he groans. Running my hands up his chest, I grin. "I think I can help with that." My fingers drift lower to hover at the clasp of his jeans. I dip a finger into his waistband.

His breath hitches. "Lee?"

The button comes undone easily, then I pull his fly down. I palm him through his boxers. His blazing heat scorches me, and I lick my lips as I stare up into his disbelieving gaze. He seems frozen in place. I drop to my knees, setting him free from his boxers as I run my fingers over his length, his skin soft as velvet. Air whistles as he sucks in through his teeth.

One of his hands darts out to grip my shoulder to steady himself, as if leaning against the wall isn't enough to hold him up. I run my tongue along the underside of his magnificent cock, slipping through the seam at the tip. He hums, his fingers tightening on my shoulder.

I love how undone he is. I take him fully into my mouth, hollowing my cheeks and using my tongue to apply just the right amount of pressure. His hips move in time with my rhythm as I slip back and forth over the hardened length of him. The salty pre-cum hits my tongue as he thrusts harder.

"Lee, I'm going to—"

But I cut him off as I grip him to me, reveling as he groans and shudders in my mouth. I swallow down every drop, licking my lips when I pull away to let his boxers cover him once more.

He tugs me to my feet where his mouth crashes onto mine. "God, I love you, Leah. You surprise the hell out of me every time I turn around."

I wrap my arms around his neck and grind against his thigh, hoping he'll get the hint.

He chuckles. "Don't worry. I'll take good care of you." He trades places with me, so my back is now to the wall.

Watching this powerful man drop to his knees before me is one of the most breathtaking sights I've ever witnessed. My skirt is hitched up to my waist. My panties disappear into his pocket, and he drapes one of my legs over his shoulder.

Need amps up in me, seeing his lips part as he stares at me. I know I must be dripping. I've been beyond ready for him since the dance floor and watching him come did nothing to tamp down the desire now raging within me. The first flick of his tongue is pure torture as he drags it up my seam. I grit my teeth to keep from crying out.

The next lick is the same, as if he's savoring every drop, and I'm having none of it. "Shawn," I whimper, writhing in his grip.

"Patience."

I shake my head. "No, now," I demand, feeling brazen as I thread my fingers into his hair and pull his face tighter to my heat.

His chuckles reverberate through me, his lips grazing my pussy as he murmurs, "Okay, Lee. I've got you," And he devours me with all the passion I'm craving.

I lean against the wall as he relentlessly drives his tongue into my center, electric jolts pulsing through me. His fingers set an equally demanding pace, curling up just right to stroke that trigger deep inside. The pressure builds within me, and I forget to be quiet. Forget about anything but Shawn and his tongue and his fingers as I ride his face, seeking that delicious high.

Then I'm there, clenching around him, gripping his hair as I bite out his name. My knees wobble as he lowers my leg to the floor and stands. When I can speak again, he kisses me once more.

"Was that what you needed?" He smirks, all cocky attitude.

"Yes. Took you long enough." I can't stop grinning. "Now, I *need* my panties back."

He reaches into his pocket, pulling them out with a smug grin. "Nah, I think they'll make a good souvenir."

"Wait, what?"

And he shoves them back into his pocket, laughing. Those green eyes twinkle as he waits for me to challenge him. If I press, I know he'll give them to me.

But I'm feeling confident as hell, so I toss my hair, straighten my skirt and raise my chin. "Fine. Let's go party."

We stop in the kitchen for a drink then hit the dance floor again. Satiated and buzzed on bliss, our dancing is calmer but still steamy. I doubt I'll ever get enough of Shawn.

My cup is empty before I know it, and Shawn walks with me to get a refill. One of his friends stops us, pulling him into conversation, and I gesture that I'm going to get my drink. He gives me an encouraging nod then turns back to his friend. It doesn't take me long to mix up a vodka tonic.

"Leah."

My name in that unexpected voice sends chills down my spine. I turn slowly, forcing myself to breathe in then out. Maybe I'm wrong.

But I'm not. I swallow at my desert-dry mouth as I stare at Vance. "What do you want?"

"I thought that was you." He saunters closer, but I move to keep the island between us, and he laughs. "Still playing hard to get."

My heart races, and my palms are damp as panic flutters on the outskirts of my vision.

"Pretty ballsy, coming in here with one guy and disappearing with another." His grin is sharp enough to cut. "I even heard that they're brothers." He raises an eyebrow as whispers ignite around us like fire in a dry, grassy field. "Maybe you need a third to round things out?"

"N-no," I stammer. *Slut. Whore.*

The words aren't imagined this time as I look around the kitchen. Each little group is staring at me, some with hands covering their mouths as they giggle with one another.

"What's the matter, Leah?" Vance's dark gaze bores into me. "Don't like an audience? I'd be happy to go somewhere more private."

I grip my cup tighter and the plastic crinkles loudly, reminding me of its fragility. It sounds a lot like my confidence. Anger seethes within me—that he's once again here, ruining a good night. "Why don't you go fuck yourself, Vance? At least that way you'd get some action. Maybe it would be enough to keep your pathetic nose out of my business."

He goes rigid, his eyes coating with an icy glare. "*What* did you say?"

I hold onto my fury, letting it bolster me. "I said, maybe if you weren't so hung up on me, you could find something better to do than being the campus gossip queen. It's getting old."

His nostrils flare as he steps toward me, his fingers clenched into fists. "Listen here, you little —"

"No, Vance. You listen, for once in your life. You are a coward who can't face the truth and hides behind the lies he spreads to make himself look better. *You* cheated on *me*, jackass." I don't even think as I toss my drink in his face.

My bravado flees at the swarm of anger wafting off him, as if I just threw a rock at a wasp's nest and got a bullseye.

Shit.

He closes the distance between us and raises his left hand like he's going to backhand me. But before he can swing, a familiar voice cuts the air.

"You lay one hand on her and you won't be able to walk right for the rest of your life." Shawn storms in, stepping in front of me as the color drains from Vance's face. "Oh good, you remember me, asshole."

Sebastian appears, standing next to his brother to form a wall between me and Vance. My knees buckle as bile rises in my throat. I barely catch myself on the counter.

"Leah?"

Meg's voice washes over me, cutting through the hum of whispers and murmurs that buzz too loudly in my head.

"What are you doing here?" I focus on her, my vision blurring as sweat dampens my forehead.

"Chad is friends with Dean. You were awesome taking on Vance like that."

I sway dizzily, but she catches me.

"Lee, it's okay." Her voice fades in and out as she turns to Shawn. She murmurs something then slips my arm over her shoulder.

Chad comes in on the other side, and they guide me out of the house. Away from the noise. Away from the stares. Away from the attention that I am once again the unwelcome center of. They take me home.

Where it's safe.

Chapter Thirty-Four

Shawn

Now that I know Leah is taken care of, I can focus on the asshole before me. Sebastian's jaw clenches, and I know we're on the same page. Vance will never mess with Lee again.

But a loud murmur sounds behind us, drawing the attention of the crowd. I glance back when Sebastian gasps, frowning as Calliope weaves her way in, her black shirt in her hand, her black bra on complete display. What is wrong with this girl?

She points at Vance. "You...you were supposed to be my date." The words are slurred.

It hasn't even been an hour since she stormed out of the kitchen. How much did she drink to get this trashed? She stumbles toward us, nearly falling, but Sebastian catches her.

His frown deepens as he studies her. "Something's wrong," he tells me.

"Vancey," she says, flopping her head to peer around Sebastian. "Make me another drink?"

White-hot rage courses through me, and I grab the front of Vance's shirt, lifting him onto his toes. "What did you give her?"

He stammers out, "N-nothing."

"I'm calling nine-one-one," Sebastian says as Calliope collapses in his arms. He lowers her to the floor. "Hang on, Calliope."

"Ish Callie…" she mumbles, her eyes closing.

He frantically dials, and I refocus on Vance. "Tell me what you did."

His gulp echoes through the silence of the room. "Roofie."

"You just saved yourself a broken nose." I lower him to the ground, but don't let go as Sebastian connects to the operator. He explains what's happening as Vance struggles in my grasp. I glare at the creep. "You're not going anywhere." I call to Sebastian, "Make sure they send a police officer, too. I've got the guy who did it."

The word 'police' spreads like wildfire through the house and people immediately disperse. This party is over.

Sebastian hangs up with the operator only to dial again. "Hi, Professor Harrison?"

I tune out the rest of the conversation as I study Callie. Sebastian covered her with her shirt, so she wasn't giving everyone a show. She seems so young. Too young.

A sinking feeling weighs my stomach as Sebastian hangs up and I ask, "How old is Callie?"

He frowns. "Nineteen."

"Shit."

The color drains from Dean's face.

"You should leave," I say.

But he straightens his shoulders. "Nah, man. It's my house, and someone should be held responsible."

"I'll talk to my dad. He's friends with a judge, and I'll make sure he knows the whole story." I turn my menacing glare back on Vance. "Every last little detail."

Sebastian follows the ambulance that rushes Callie to the hospital. I stay and speak to the two officers who take my statement then cuff Vance. They give Dean a ticket for serving minors, but don't take him in. By the time they leave, my adrenaline is fading fast.

I get an Uber, wondering how Leah is doing. Meg texted me when they got home, saying she was okay. I'm so very proud of my girlfriend. Not only did she stand up to Vance, she stood up for herself. I came in during the middle of her retort, amazed at the confidence she exuded.

But then the panic set in. I'm so thankful Meg and Chad showed up when they did, and because of their arrival, I was able to get Vance where he belongs. In jail.

I hurry into the house where Meg and Chad are on the couch, watching TV.

Meg sits up. "What took so long? Is everything okay?"

I fill them in on Callie and Vance, swiping a hand over my face as exhaustion hits me. I just want to crawl into bed with Lee, hold her in my arms and see for myself that she's in one piece. I jab my thumb toward the suite. "I'm gonna go crash."

"Wait," Meg says, not meeting my eyes. "Leah...wants to be alone."

"What?"

She glances up, her expression full of empathy and concern. "I'm sorry, Shawn. She barely spoke to me other than to say she wanted you to let her be for tonight." Her shoulders sag. "I don't know what happened. She was so brave, standing up to Vance, then she lost it."

I stare at the suite door, more than frustrated at the barrier keeping me from my love. I could easily waltz in there and ignore her wishes. I could tear it off the hinges and throw it across the room.

But that's not who I am.

The huge weight on my chest makes it hard to move. Somehow I manage to nod. "Okay. Well, then, good night."

I feel Meg watching me as I trudge to the stairs, and I check my phone once more, hoping for at least a message from Lee. But the screen remains empty, and I am left wanting. Again. I still shoot her a text, telling her I love her and I'm proud of her.

Despite Leah's rejection and my worry, the exhaustion pulls me into a solid sleep, so deep I don't even dream. The next morning, I keep one eye glued to her door, waiting for her to come out of her room. The minutes tick by as nothing happens and I busy myself with whatever mundane tasks I can to keep occupied. When the latch clicks, I hold my breath, but Meg emerges alone.

I stare behind her, waiting, but she shakes her head and says, "Her door's still closed."

My heart sinks, and I decide to give her until noon. The restless feeling gnawing at me spurs me to go for a run, but my usual outlet does nothing to clear my head as my worry for Lee circles. How far is she going to withdraw this time? Can we ever overcome this? Will she be all right?

And the biggest, most looming fear — are we going to be okay?

When I return, it's after eleven thirty and the door is still shut. My phone is still blank. I fight the helpless feeling, refocusing on taking a shower.

Once I'm clean and dressed, I return downstairs. Meg glances up from her space on the couch. Steven and Silas are awake, their voices echoing from the kitchen. Guilt hits me when I realize I haven't seen or even thought about Sebastian. I wonder what happened with Callie last night.

But Lee is my priority.

"I'm going in," I tell Meg, who nods, worry evident in her pressed-together lips.

I ease open the sitting room door, and see Leah's is still shut. I picture a keep out sign in my mind, then shove the image away. We're a team. I need to remind her that I'm on her side. Always.

She doesn't answer my quiet tap on the door, so I do it again. When silence greets me, I try the doorknob, almost surprised when it turns in my hand. I step into the darkness, waiting for my eyes to adjust to the dim light filtering in from the gray day.

Leah is a mere lump on her bed, blending in with the covers.

I perch on the edge of the mattress, touching her back. "Leah…"

"Go away," she whispers, her voice raw.

"Tell me what happened, Lee-bug." She sniffs but doesn't answer and I add a heartfelt, "Please."

"I'm no good, Shawn. Why would you ever want to be with a slut like me?"

"What?" I can't believe what I'm hearing. "Why would you say that?"

She doesn't roll over, just lifts a shoulder. "It's what everyone thinks when they see us together. It's what everyone whispered, not just last night, but every day after I broke up with Vance. Now they see me bouncing from brother to brother, and I'm exactly what they thought." Her voice is thick with tears, and I rub her back, trying to figure out what to say.

"Leah..." I want to fix this, but I don't know how. "I don't know what more I can do. I love you, Lee. Unconditionally. Irrevocably. Forever." I pause, as I realize that this isn't up to me. I've done everything I can to show her my love, to support her. But this last part?

It has to come from her.

"Nothing anyone says or does can change my feelings for you, but I can't make you see your worth. And I can't make you not care about what everyone else thinks. If you want to be with me, there are going to be some rough patches. Like this one."

I move to wrap my hand around her shoulder, giving her a gentle squeeze. It's time to push her. "We can get through them, together. If you let me in."

It's my usual challenge, and I wait, hoping she'll rise to meet it as I silently beg her to see that we're worth it. That we can win this, only I can't do it alone. Though defeat creeps over me when she doesn't respond, I refuse to give up on us. This might not be a battle I win right now, but I will not surrender. I will retreat, give her space to figure out what she needs, but I'm not waving that white flag unless she asks me to.

I force myself to stand, then lean over and kiss her temple. "I love you, Leah. All of you. Your past, present, and if you'll let me, your future. We're worth fighting for, but you have to be willing to fight too."

Then I leave.

* * * *

It's Sunday before Leah emerges from her room, and only because Meg forces her to. We're all worried about her, but Lee doesn't say a word, eating her can of soup with all the feeling of a robot before going back to her cave.

I've never felt so helpless.

"What more can I do?" I ask Meg.

"Nothing. Leah's got to fight her own battle this time. We've done all we can."

I'm pacing in my room upstairs as a rumble of thunder shakes the house. I stop to glance out my window, and of course, I think of Leah. This is the first thunderstorm we've had since that day in Myrtle Beach.

I smile, remembering how she tipped her head up to embrace the rain instead of running from it. The way the water droplets clung to her lashes and that heated moment when all I wanted to do was kiss her senseless. A wave of longing crashes over me as lightning flashes against the gray sky.

This vantage point gives me a perfect view of the storm rolling in, and an idea hits me. I may not be able to fix this for Leah, but I can get started on a project for when she comes back. Because I have to believe that — she *will* come back to me.

And I'll be ready.

Chapter Thirty-Five

Leah

I make it through the week, but I'm not sure how. The minutes all blend together, me on automatic pilot as I go from class to work to home where I tumble into bed. The others give me my space as I try to sort out what I'm dealing with.

Mostly I'm tired. As if my burst of confidence with Vance sucked the life out of me and all that remains is a shell.

I'm tired of dealing with the whispers and the second-glances. I'm tired of the names and judgy looks. I'm tired of not being able to live my life the way I want.

And I'm just too tired to change any of it.

Meg hovers, making sure I eat and shower. I wish I could come out of my fog long enough to thank her for it, but it's safe here. So I stay huddled within, waiting for my energy to return.

Friday night, Meg startles me by banging into my room, all dressed up. She sits hard on the bed and gives me her fiercest no-nonsense glare. "Leah, people are shitty."

I frown, pushing to a sitting position.

She rests a hand on my covered knee. "I've been there. Been called every name in the book—serial-dater, easy, whore, slut..." Her mouth tips up. "But I don't care what they think. I live my life the way I want to, because it's my life. The people that count—you, the Wrightings, my family—they love me exactly the way I am, and as long as I have that, it doesn't matter what anyone else says."

I can't speak as I try to process what she's saying.

"When are you going to let Vance stop ruining your future? You've got a good thing going with Shawn, but you've got to own your choices."

The words resonate within me, bouncing through my mind like a bullet ricocheting in an empty dumpster.

"We love you, Leah. Every scar, every fear, and the huge amount of good in you." She gives me a bolstering nudge. "That's what is truly important."

She leaves, coming back with a sandwich, a bottle of water, and an apple. "I'm going out tonight. If you need something, the guys are here. Especially Shawn." She pauses, her expression full of warmth. "Love you, Lee."

I swallow at the lump in my throat and manage to answer. "Love you too, Meg." My voice croaks as I add, "And thanks, for everything."

Her smile is huge before she hurries out of my room, shutting my door behind her.

I lie there for a long time, thinking about all the times I've run away because of what someone said. But they're only words. Their power is decided by me. I can choose what I let hurt me or what I let slide off my back.

Being with Shawn is the best choice I've ever made. He sees me, he helps me, he makes me better. Why would I ever be ashamed of that?

I don't have an answer.

I grab one of my books and eat my sandwich, letting my mind work in the background as I lose myself in my story. When I go brush my teeth, I let the party replay in my mind. Not the part with Vance, but my moments with Shawn. I'd gone there to support my boyfriend, and I'd ended up shutting him out.

Again.

That thought pummels my gut. He tried so hard to reach me, but I put my walls up so high, he never had the chance. What if one day those walls stay up? What if I let those opinions take over, ruling my life, like a bramble patch that grows until no one can get through the thorns?

Meg's words replay in my head. *We love you, Leah. That's what truly matters.* Followed by Shawn's words. *We're worth fighting for, but you have to fight too.* Time and again, their love has burst through my walls and pulled me back from the abyss. But I can't keep hiding.

I have to fight, too, and I can do that, knowing my boyfriend and friends will be there to support me every step of the way. For the first time this week, sleep is not an escape, and I'm excited to see what tomorrow will bring.

Tonight, though, it's enough to hope.

My night overflows with memory filled dreams, all the moments Shawn and Meg and the others have loved me. Only this time, I let their love start binding me back together. Piece by piece.

When morning comes, I feel renewed. The drain on my energy is gone, my fog has lifted, and one thing is crystal clear. Shawn is my choice, and I will defend that choice whenever necessary. Now all I have to do is tell him.

I get up, going out to the sitting room, surprised to find Meg on our couch.

"Leah!" She beams, leaping to her feet and wrapping me in a hug.

I hug her back. "Oh, Meg. I love you. Thanks for saying all that. You're completely right, you know?" Her smile stretches ear to ear and I can't help grinning back. "All I want to do is talk to Shawn. I need to fix this."

She steps back. "Yes, you do, but he's occupied right now." When I open my mouth to protest, she shakes her head. "Nope. Shawn has a surprise for you this afternoon, so you're going to have to wait."

"What?" I stare at her in confusion. "I haven't spoken to him all week. Have barely left my room. Why would he have a surprise for me?"

"Because he has faith in you."

The words are like the sun landing in my chest as warmth rockets through me. He never gave up on me, not once. I don't deserve him, but I'm sure as hell going to keep him.

"So Shawn is going to be occupied for a while yet, but that's okay because…" Her eyebrows knit together. "Sebastian needs you."

"What?" Worry springs to life.

"He went through some serious shit this weekend, and he needs to talk to someone about it."

I nod. "Okay. Just…" I take a moment to pivot, reordering my thoughts from making up with Shawn to helping Sebastian. The ache for Shawn doesn't dim, but I will help my friend. "Let me shower, then I'll take him out for brunch."

"Good." Relief shines in her face, and she steps forward to give me another hug. "Oh, Leah, it's so nice to have you back."

I lean into her. "It's good to be back." I pause before I reach my room, turning back to say, "Meg? Thanks again."

After a quick shower, I trot into the living room which is empty except for Sebastian, who has his nose in a book. But he's not on the couch. He sits on the bottom step, as if guarding the stairs. Several big thumps sound above my head, and I frown, wondering what's going on up there.

"Hey, Sebastian," I say, ambling over and assessing him.

He appears the same at first glance but when I study him closely, he seems tired, as if carrying a weight that is too heavy for him alone.

Another thud sounds, and I frown up the stairway. "Seriously, are they having a wrestling match?"

He lets out a little snort, closing his book. "Sorry. Upstairs is off limits and what they're doing is top secret."

My curiosity is piqued, but I don't argue. "Fine. Since you're not participating in whatever that is, let's go get some food."

He frowns, tilting his head as he looks me over. "You're back."

"I am."

Relief crosses his face, and he stands to give me a huge hug. "I've missed you, Lee."

My nickname warms me as I squeeze him tight. "I've missed you too." Pulling back, I assess him once more and guilt hits me that I haven't been there for him. "Sounds like we've got some catching up to do. What do you say?"

He nods. "I'll text Shawn."

Ten minutes later, we're walking toward Eat at Joe's, and I say, "So, fill me in."

"I got that grant I wanted to study my roses over the summer. Four months in the greenhouse." He grins ear to ear.

"Congratulations!" I reach over to squeeze his arm. "I'm so proud of you." And I mean it, although that doesn't sound like something I should be worried about. I let him chatter on with his plans until we're seated at the table. "Is there anything else?"

A flash of uncertainty crosses his face as our waiter appears to take our orders. I order a muffin and Sebastian gets his usual Western-style omelet.

"You don't want to tell me?" I ask, trying to understand his reluctance.

"No, it's not that." He pauses, staring at the table. "I don't want to upset you... We just got you back."

"Oh, Sebastian." I reach over to rest my hand on his. "Tell me. I'm not going anywhere." *Not ever again.* "From now on, I'm letting any hurtful words roll off me." I can't resist throwing out one of the million facts he's told me over the years. "Like a duck in a rainstorm."

"You do listen!"

"I try." We both chuckle then I tighten my grip briefly before pulling away. "And I'd like to listen now."

So he tells me what happened after I left the party. I gape, shocked that Vance would stoop that low, proud of how Sebastian handled the situation, floored at my boyfriend's self-control for not beating Vance to a pulp. "Is Calliope okay?"

He nods. "Vance gave her too much, and they had to pump her stomach. But she's home now. Went home the next morning." He glowers. "I'm furious at Vance for taking advantage of her like that, but I'm even more furious she was out in the first place. She's only nineteen!"

The waiter brings us our coffee and water while he sucks in a calming breath, his jaw set. "Do you know what she said when she woke up in the hospital?" He shakes his head. "She yelled at me for calling her dad. She could have died, and *that's* what she was worried about?"

"I'm glad you were there for her, and I know you did the right thing, even if she can't see it."

I hide my smile at how much she's gotten under his skin. I think back to how Shawn used to make me furious, and I marvel at how far we've come. His words of love from last week echo in my mind.

Love. He loves me, and for the first time, I truly believe it. He loves every single part, and as that reality sinks in, a weight lifts off me. I feel like a mote of dust riding a sunbeam and basking in the weightless warmth. I sigh as I revel in my contentment, even though I wish I could see Shawn.

Sebastian blinks, then his forehead crinkles. Our food comes, but Sebastian still studies me.

I wait for our waiter to disappear before I ask, "What?"

"You seem happier," Sebastian says. "I mean, not just since I saw you this morning, but now. Something is…different."

I shrug then peel the paper off my muffin. "I am. Really happy." I meet his assessing stare once more. "I have you and Shawn and Meg to thank for that."

He smiles again. "You're welcome. Just looking out for you."

Tears prick my eyes as the reality of how loved I am crashes over me. "Thank you."

We sip on our coffee, enjoying our food, chatting when we feel like it. My spirits rise more with every minute. I can't wait to see Shawn, and I wonder what the surprise could possibly be. But Sebastian glances at his phone, shaking his head when I ask if we can go home.

Despite the impatience dancing in me, I begrudge him a trip to the bookstore. When at last we're done, I ask, "*Now* can we go home?"

I'm thrilled when he finally says, "Yes."

Meg meets me in the living room. "Hey, guys. Good job Sebastian, you're right on time."

She drags me to my room, shushing me whenever I try to ask questions as she digs through my closet. At last, she settles on a black swingy skirt with a patterned sleeveless top. Its neckline is pretty low.

My frown doesn't deter her. "Put it on." She pauses in the doorway. "Wear something cute and lacy underneath."

As she shuts the door, I stare bewildered at the outfit, then I shrug and follow directions. Five minutes later, I'm dressed, and I step into the sitting room. "How's this?"

Meg shoots up off the couch, pursing her lips before she smiles. "Perfect."

Next she tackles my hair, which we leave down with a little bit of scrunching help. Then we move on to makeup, and she studies me as I finish my mascara.

"What?" I peer at the mirror, making sure I didn't royally mess up.

"I don't know. You look different." Then she gasps, her hand flying to her mouth.

Now I'm really concerned. "Seriously, what?"

Meg stands up, peering over my shoulder at my reflection in the mirror. "Your spark is back, Lee."

I start to blow her off, but I glance at myself and see that something *is* different. Sebastian commented on it too. My smile seems brighter, my eyes glow with a happiness that a bad day can't touch. I turn toward her.

"Shawn loves me." I lift my shoulders. "I finally get it. You guys are the ones that matter. You all love me so much, and I'm done letting everyone dictate how I'm supposed to feel. Shawn and I deserve to be together, and I will fight anyone who says otherwise." I swallow at the thickness in my throat. "You weren't the only one who talked to me, Meg. He did too, and I realized you're both right. Why would I ever be ashamed of the man I love?"

It slips out, and Meg's mouth forms a huge O.

My heart stops as my words sink in, and I say, "I love Shawn."

She puts an arm around me and rests her head on my shoulder. "He brought you back."

The declaration settles in me, stirring up my longing for him until I can hardly stand the ache.

Her phone dings, and she grins. "Let's go." She grabs my hand, leading me into the living room.

Shawn sits on the couch, reading the newest romance book I'd lent him. A huge surge of affection washes over me as I drink him in.

"She's all yours." Meg pulls me in for one last hug. "Have fun."

I return her hug, then watch her skip her way out of the door.

Shawn looks delicious in a pair of dark blue jeans and a short-sleeved white button-down shirt. The top two buttons are undone. I study him, taken aback again by how lucky I am. Not only because he's so handsome, but because of everything he is.

It's almost dizzying how much I love him. I roll the word in my head again. Then I lose myself in his emerald eyes, familiar and intoxicating, I inhale his comforting sandalwood-balsam scent and I realize how true it is.

I love this man.

He lights up, walking toward me. "You're back. Meg told me, but I didn't quite believe it until I saw you for myself."

I duck my head, brushing a piece of hair behind my ear. "I am." Then I raise my chin. "For good."

His dazzling smile grows even wider.

The stillness of the house unnerves me, and I glance around the room again. Has it gotten darker? "Where is everyone?"

He takes my hand. "It's just us."

"Oh." I stare at him, brimming with all the things I need to say. "Shawn, I—"

But he shakes his head letting me know he's only getting started. "Let me show you something first." He leads me upstairs to the landing where the ladder to the attic stretches down. When I glance at him, he nods encouragingly.

I climb into the attic, gasping at the transformation. The short-ceilinged, narrow space is covered with pillows and blankets. Battery operated candles flicker on several surfaces. A cooler sits next to an end table laden with snacks.

But what I like most is the view. We're higher than most of the rooftops here, so I can see for miles.

"This is so cool." I clamber onto the pile of sleeping bags, crawling over to lie on my stomach and stare out of the window. I hug a pillow to my chest as I kick my bare feet in the air behind me.

Shawn trails a finger up my shin. "You like it?"

I nod, glancing back with a frown. "Is today special? Did I forget something?"

"No, you didn't forget anything, but look out there, at the sky. Notice anything?"

I bite my lip as I study the clouds, swinging my feet back and forth. "The clouds are gray."

He nods, cocking his head. It all comes together in my mind, and I start to shoot upright. Shawn's hand zips out to grab my head, pulling me to him instead of letting me whack it on the short, angled ceiling.

I glance up from where I'm mushed against his chest. "Um, thank you. I got a little excited there." His laughter rumbles through me as I push off him.

"I'll say."

"Is it supposed to storm?" I ask, letting my eagerness show, though I'm careful not to bounce too high.

His grin is huge. "Yep."

"And we get to watch it from here?" My excitement ramps up even more. When he nods, I throw my arms around him. "Thank you, thank you, thank you!" I press my lips to his.

He cradles me, dipping me down until we're both lying on the blankets, him on top of me. I grip his hair, pulling him closer. Thrills run through me, excited by his nearness, by the thought of what is to come.

But first...

I pull back and say, "About this past week." I search his eyes, guilt hitting me at the hint of pain shining through. "I'm sorry, Shawn. I'm sorry I shut you out, that I let my fear and insecurities get the best of me." His gaze softens as I reach up to cup his cheek. "You're right. We are worth fighting for, and I'm ready to do that. I choose you, and I stand by that choice, no matter what anyone else thinks."

Unhindered joy brims in his eyes before he captures my lips with his. That effervescence bubbles between us, heady and giddy as I arch into him. He pours every ounce of love into his kiss, and I'm breathless when he breaks it off.

I can't help teasing, "That's why you sent everyone away, isn't it? You want me."

"I don't think it's a secret that I want you." He smirks, raising his eyebrows. "I just didn't think you'd want all my brothers right below us, listening to whatever we end up doing here. If we end up doing anything." He shrugs. "Plus there's the whole bathroom issue. We'd have to get dressed any time one of us wants to run downstairs, and raise and lower the ladder. It seemed easier to kick everyone out."

The entire gesture is beyond sweet, more thoughtful than anything anyone has ever done for me.

"Lee." He touches my bare shoulder, rubbing his thumb over my skin. "I hope you know I meant it when

I said whatever, whenever. I'm having fun, and I hope you are too. I'm just thrilled to have you in my life. We don't have to do anything today other than watch the storm and have a good time."

I scrunch up my nose. "Stop being so great. Seriously, you're giving me inadequacy issues over here." He lets out a soft laugh, and I lean into him. "All kidding aside, you're amazing, Shawn. This whole thing is absolutely perfect."

Rain starts falling, a soft pitter patter as it hits the glass, and I watch it trickle down the panes. "So, if we aren't getting naked, what's your backup plan?"

He grins. "I'm so very glad you asked."

Chapter Thirty-Six

Shawn

I can't be more thrilled that my surprise is going so well. I'd had my doubts when Meg told me she thought she had gotten through to Lee last night, and still didn't quite believe it when she confirmed this morning. A big part of me was afraid to hope.

But then I'd watched from the landing as Lee sauntered into the living room, the light back in her eyes, a radiant energy wafting from her, and my relief nearly made me collapse.

Our time here has only proved that Lee is her normal self, and the weight that's held me down all week lifts more by the minute. I crawl toward the end table, gesturing to the spread of food. "And there's more in the cooler."

She wrinkles her nose. "I just had a muffin with Sebastian."

"Well then." Undeterred, I pull out the cribbage board and deck of cards. "Cribbage, anyone?" She laughs, the familiar sound sending an ache through me. How did I go a full week without hearing it?

"How romantic."

I can't help teasing, giving her my best schmoozy smile. "I know how to charm the ladies."

"Yeah? Well, let's see if you know how to play cards."

Lee wins the first game, but keeps getting distracted, anxiously glancing out of the window as the sky darkens. As the energy builds in the air, I kick her butt in the second and the wind picks up partway through the third.

Then I hear it—the faint rumble of thunder. She jerks upright, stopping right before she hits her head. I can't help chuckling as I put the cards away.

"Ready for food?"

She nods, not turning away from the window. I shift the pillows so we can lean on the wall while watching the storm, then bring a tray with finger foods and our favorite drinks. One click turns out the lights, leaving only the candles glowing. The flickering dimness makes the shadows grow and the atmosphere even cozier.

I settle beside her, our shoulders touching. She gasps when purple lightning streaks the sky, illuminating the room for several seconds. Her foot moves back and forth as if charged with energy from the storm while her smile never dims.

We eat our fill, the symphony of the storm our background music. I put the empty tray on the nightstand, then lie once more beside her, lifting an arm. She sidles up to me, tracing the line of buttons on my shirt with one finger as I splay my hand over her hip.

I missed her. I missed this. And I grip her tighter, never wanting to let go.

"This must have been some project, cleaning all this up."

I glance around, picturing how dusty it had been with all the piles of junk. "The guys helped. We've been working on it all week."

"All week? But I was…"

"I know." I brush my knuckle over her cheek. "I didn't know when it would storm next, but I wanted to be ready for when you came back. My brothers all helped." It had been torture not knowing, but it gave me something to cling to. "We all believed in you."

She frowns, as if stunned. When will she understand how important she is? Not only to me, but to all of us.

"Lee…you know how you changed our plans to throw a whole pizza party with a movie and bingo because Steven was upset? That's how they all feel about you. We all love you."

"I get it now," she says. "Thank you."

A streak of lightning brightens the room as I stare at her. "I love you." Thunder crashes, and I look out at the storm.

She whispers back, "I love you, too."

A jolt goes through me at the words, that maybe she'll mean them just for me someday. But I know she loves us, and I gently kiss her hand. "I know you do, Lee." Her lips twitch, making me feel like I missed something.

"No, Shawn. I love you."

The smile drops from my face, unable to comprehend what I'm hearing. "What?"

"I love *you*, Shawn." She doesn't waver as I search her gorgeous blue eyes.

I suck in a gulp of air when I see the truth of that love in their depths, and I freeze. The moment is too fragile. I'm afraid one wrong move will shatter it and send me crashing back to reality.

But she starts talking. "I think I've wanted you for even longer than you've wanted me." She ducks her head. "That day I kissed you at the pool, I couldn't believe I found the courage to do it, but it felt so right." A small grin tips her lips. "Even the animosity between us didn't stop me watching you, wanting you."

I have to swallow at the thickness in my throat.

"That night, when Vance..." She stops, blinking and clearing her throat. "The moment I saw you, I knew I was going to be okay."

I think my heart might burst with love for her. All my dreams are coming true because of this woman, and happiness crashes into me in an overwhelming flood.

"I love the way you tease and push me. You challenge me at every turn, and it makes me better." She cups my cheek, then eases over to straddle me. "I'm sorry it took me so long to be ready for you. I'm sorry I've shut you out. I've been scared of what you could do with my heart if I gave it to you. Which is silly, because you've had it all along."

My own heart answers by thundering right beneath her palm. Maybe I should pinch myself. But no, if this is a dream I never want to wake up.

Her shoulders inch up as her gaze darts around the room before settling once more on me. "Say something?"

My lips part as I try to form how to say what I feel. "I'm so far beyond words right now, Lee. You've made me so happy." I cradle her face in my hands. Flashes of lightning flicker around us, illuminating her beauty. She is the single most entrancing thing on the planet. "I never dreamed I could be this lucky."

"Me either." She leans forward, brushing her lips against mine. "Make love to me, Shawn?"

I let out a surprised breath. "Are you sure?"

She nods, her gaze hungry and wanting as she slides her hands down my chest. Her hips rock against my growing length. "I want this. I need you, all of you. Please."

"Of course." Awe engulfs me as I run my hands down her back.

"I have an IUD, so if you don't want to use anything..."

I let out a bark of disbelieving laughter, shaking my head. Her questioning look has me explaining, "I must be in some alternate reality — all my dreams coming true in one night." I lean forward, stopping right before I touch my lips to hers. "Whatever you say, Lee."

The purple lightning flashes across the sky, igniting the fire between us. Her fingers thread through my hair, and our lips crash together as the thunder rolls, echoing through the room. Hunger consumes me, and I want to make her mine in every sense of the word.

I break away to yank off her shirt as she fumbles with my buttons. I unclasp her bra, thrilled at the unhindered view of her breasts. She shoves my shirt off, sighing into my mouth as she leans forward, no barriers between our torsos.

"I love looking at you," I murmur, reaching up to cup her breast before taking it into my mouth.

She moans, tipping her head back and rocking against me. My cock hardens even more. She reaches down to undo my fly as she moves off me. I help her shove my jeans and boxers off in one motion, groaning when she grips my length in her soft hand. I will never tire of her touch. She pumps me once, and I guide her onto her back, covering her body with mine.

Her hand slides up and down my cock as I worship her breasts until I can take no more. My groan is tortured as I rip myself out of her reach to trail kisses down her stomach to the waistband of her skirt. I slip my fingers under the elastic, and she lifts her hips as I take it off with her panties.

I trace a finger up her creamy thighs and over her soft abdomen. "So beautiful."

"You're not so bad yourself."

I kiss my way up her thigh to settle my face between her legs, and she doesn't say another word after I put my mouth on her. She only moans loudly, gripping my hair as she writhes under my tongue.

I can't help chuckling. "See? Aren't you glad I sent everyone away?"

But I don't let her answer before I delve back in, picking up the pace. I ease one finger inside, then another. Her inner walls clench around me, and I lap her up, devouring her delicious nectar as I keep up the rhythm. Her breaths come in faster, shorter pants and her fingers tighten their grip, holding me in place.

Then she tumbles over, calling my name, which has never sounded sweeter. She gasps, and I pump until she stops quivering. I stare at her, loving the flush of pleasure that tinges her skin.

I did that. I brought her to that peak of bliss.

Sitting up, I position my cock to rest at the entrance of her gorgeous pussy. She reaches for me, kissing me senseless before she bucks her hips, telling me it's time. My tip presses against her, then I slide in.

I let out a delighted groan. "So wet, so ready."

She only nods, waiting to welcome me fully. Once I'm buried to the hilt inside her, I gaze deep into her eyes, double checking she's all right.

"I love you," she whispers, shifting enough to make me groan with the effort of sitting still.

I brush my lips against hers. "I love you."

Then I start to move. I know it's been a while for her, and it's been a while for me. But it feels different. We read each other perfectly. I know just what she wants and she moves with me so well. We start off slow, our gazes locking together, steady and unwavering, as we join in every possible way.

Our bond strengthens with each thrust. All the rocky steps that led us here, to this very moment, have all been worth it.

I slip a hand under her shoulder, then I pick up the pace. Her breath hitches as I caress her cheek. Every moment with this woman has been earned, and I will continue earning each one for as long as she'll have me.

She rocks her hips to meet my thrusts. Her cheeks flush, and her lips part as we both climb toward that peak. I tighten my grip on her, plunging in harder, faster. I never want to let her go. My name is a whisper on her lips, and I nearly explode on the spot when I feel her first flutters around me. I hold her closer, keeping pace as my very breath disappears.

She gasps and goes rigid beneath me. I let go, pouring myself into her as she clings to me like I'm her anchor in the storm. I lean forward to rest my cheek against hers, savoring the few long moments of being so in tune. We stay that way, riding out the last few tremors while thunder booms around us.

I finally pull out, rolling onto my back and slipping my arm beneath her.

She curls in to my side, splaying her fingers wide over my pecs. "I didn't think it was possible to enjoy storms more than I already did."

Her sweet words make my chest feel like it will explode, and I press a kiss to her knuckles.

"You make everything better, Shawn. I know it took a while to get here, but it's definitely worth it." She squeezes my hand. "I'm glad it's you."

I sigh as I let go of her hand to wrap my arms around her once more, feeling more content than I ever have as lightning blazes across the sky. "I wouldn't want it any other way."

Epilogue

Leah

The front door slams open, and I look up, startled from my spot on the couch as Sebastian storms in. Even when his feathers are ruffled, he rarely shows it to this degree, and concern races through me as I set my book aside. A shiny blue package with a silver bow is tucked under his arm, and he pauses as he notices me.

My eyebrows are high, my eyes wide as I ask, "You okay?"

He glowers then tosses me the package. "Here. You'll enjoy these a lot more than I will."

I peel back the partially opened paper to find a box of chocolates, and I frown, glancing up at him for an explanation.

He sags against the wall, letting out a long breath. "Calliope's 'thank you' gift." He even air quotes it, another rarity. "I'm sure Professor Harrison made her do it. It was delivered with all the sincerity of a politician trying to get elected."

Sure it's a thoughtless gift for a diabetic, which I assume she knows since he works so closely with her father. But I don't quite get why it's bothering him this much. I frown, studying him. He hasn't been himself since taking her to the hospital, and that word has the pieces clicking in my mind.

Sebastian's condition has landed him in the hospital more than once, usually for forgetting to eat. But I can remember two times growing up where he was admitted, and it was beyond scary. I can just imagine how calling the ambulance for his boss' daughter, rushing her in for care and watching her fight for her life would be traumatic in its own right. I'm sure it brought up memories he'd rather keep buried.

Then she repays him with something he won't even enjoy and an insincere thank you.

I set the box aside and cross the room to stand in front of him. "Hug?"

He eyes me for a moment before nodding and stepping into my embrace. I wrap my arms around his midsection, pressing my cheek to his chest even as he stands rigid and unmoving. After several seconds, the breath whooshes from him and he holds me back as he relaxes. I don't let go until he does, knowing he will signal me when he's done.

It's a longer hug than I expected, but when he does step back, he gives me a small smile. "Thanks, Leah."

I beam back at him. "Of course."

"I'm going to..." He jabs a thumb at the stairs and trudges away.

If Shawn and I weren't going out for dinner with friends... "Sebastian?" I call, grateful when he pauses and turns back to look at me. "Shawn and I won't be out late. Maybe family game night after?"

He just lifts a shoulder and resumes his course, his disinterest making me more determined to cheer him up. Even if I know that what I have in mind will make the others grumble. Shawn hurries down the stairs, frowning as he pauses at the landing to look back at his brother.

"What's eating him?" Shawn asks as I close the distance to meet him at the bottom of the stairs.

I quickly explain. "But I have a plan!" When I tell him my brilliant idea, he groans, just as I predicted.

"C'mon, Lee. Anything but that."

I'm not taking no for an answer, and if I can convince Shawn, he can help me talk the others into it. I run my hand up his chest as I bat my eyelashes. "You can stay in my room tonight."

Interest sparks in his eyes.

I lean in, whispering, "And I'll be on top."

We've had fun exploring over the past couple weeks, and I learned his favorite position is me riding him while he has full access to my body. It's never been my preference, until Shawn. Plus it's a great bargaining chip.

Heat flares between us, and he glances at the clock on the wall then back to me. "You want to play, Lee?"

The familiar challenge in his voice has my thighs clenching and my panties going damp with anticipation. I nod.

His grin is feral, and he jerks his chin at my suite. "You make me come in the next fifteen minutes and be on top tonight, and I'll convince everyone else to be on board with your little plan."

I love the idea of adding stakes to our game, and desire coils within me. I trail my fingers down his taut abdomen, running along the waist of his jeans. "And if it takes more than fifteen minutes?" I don't plan on losing, but I need to know the consequences.

"We have some fun before dinner, you're still on top tonight, but *you* have to get everyone to agree to your plan."

"Deal." I tilt my chin, humming when he seals our bargain with a toe-curling kiss, then I lead him into the bedroom.

I'm still not comfortable staying in his room, with the thin walls that abut his brothers', but I'm getting used to having him here, with or without Meg. She sleeps with a fan and there's a whole bathroom between us. I try to keep my noises to a minimum when she's home, but sometimes, I forget. She hasn't complained yet, so I don't think she's heard.

I shut my bedroom door behind us, then push him back onto the bed. "Fifteen minutes starts now."

Ten minutes later we emerge, both wearing satisfied grins. I knew he wouldn't be able to resist me touching myself while I went down on him. On our way outside, he pulls me in for a searing kiss.

"I'm gonna have a difficult time getting through dinner with that scene in my head," he says. "You're so fucking hot, Lee."

I just smile sweetly up at him. "And you have some convincing to do, Shawn. Better get on that."

He grimaces, but pulls out his phone as we fall into step. I make sure he isn't in danger of running into anything while we walk.

"Done." He slips his phone back into his pocket then laces his fingers through mine.

We're meeting his friends at a little Mexican restaurant several blocks away. I've been trying to do more outside of my usual circle, and I adore the people he hangs out with. Many of them were at Dean's party, but no one has anything negative to say about it. All they remember is me telling off some jackass and throwing my drink in his face.

I get several compliments on my fitted tee that has a shiny butterfly emblazoned on the front. Conversation flows steadily, and I'm at ease the entire time. I'm finishing my last taco when Shawn bristles beside me. I look up to see Vivian, the redhead from my English class, stalking over with a smirk.

"Hello," she purrs, standing next to me. Her green gaze lands on Shawn. "Still with him? I'd have thought you'd moved on by now." She scans the table. "Are any of the other brothers here?"

Shawn's eyes bore into me, and I know he's worried that I'll do my usual run and hide number, but I have no need. The familiar panic is miles away, not a hint of fear or shame in sight. I meant what I said about making my choice and standing by it. I set down my taco, wipe my hand on my napkin, and reach back to grip Shawn's tense thigh.

"Vivian?" I say, keeping my smile sweet despite the steel lining my tone. "We're trying to have a nice dinner here, with our friends. Surely you have better things to do than bother me about my love life. But, since it seems to be so vitally important to you, yes, I'm still with Shawn. I love him, and I'm not going anywhere."

His muscles relax in my grip, and I glance back to exchange a reassuring grin with him.

Vivian blinks and sputters for a moment before I look pointedly at my food. "I'd like to finish eating before it gets cold. Any more of my personal business you need to know, or can I get on with it?"

She narrows her eyes and huffs out a breath before tossing her hair and stalking away without another word.

Shawn chuckles, sliding his arm around my shoulders to pull me closer. He kisses my temple. "My little spitfire is back."

I roll my eyes, needing to get out of the spotlight sooner than later. "I meant what I said. I really do want to finish eating before it gets cold."

He laughs again, raising his hands in surrender. "Don't let me stop you."

We wind down with no further interruptions, and after we've paid, Shawn and I begin our walk home.

He tugs me to a stop after a block, turning me to face him. "Lee, I'm so proud of you. Standing up to her like that."

I smile, sliding my hands up his chest. "I couldn't have done it without you. Love you, Shawn."

"Love you too."

We kiss right there on the sidewalk, tongues tangling for everyone to see. And I don't mind one bit.

As we approach our house, Shawn raises an eyebrow. "You're sure you want to do this?"

"Yep." Although my confidence falters. "Are they in?"

He hasn't told me yet if he was successful convincing them, but he just grins. "The moment I told them you requested their presence, all grumbling stopped." I glare as he laughs. "No, really."

He shows me his phone, and my smile grows at the group message of everyone complaining how they hate playing that game with Sebastian. He always wins. But as soon as Shawn says that I'm organizing it to cheer Sebastian up, they're all in.

My throat is thick as I turn my smile on Shawn. "Have I told you lately how great your family is?"

At home, I have everyone start setting up while I grab Sebastian. I tap on his door, alarmed when I step in and it's already dark. "You're sleeping? So early?"

He sighs and the bed creaks as he sits up. "No, I was just…thinking."

I flick on the light. "You've been thinking a lot lately and in my professional opinion, it's time to get you out of your head for a bit." I hold out my hand.

His gaze dips to his desk, which is emptier than usual. "I can't even find an animal right now that holds my interest, Leah." His sorrowful eyes find mine. "What's wrong with me?"

I drop my hand, going to sit next to him instead. "Nothing is wrong with you, Sebastian." I explain my theory and his lips part as he listens. "I think you just have a lot to work through with all this."

He nods. "You could be right. It does make sense."

"But," I say, standing once more, "it'll still do you good to take a break from processing, and I know just the thing." Again, I offer my hand, relieved when he takes it this time.

He lets me lead him downstairs, into the kitchen where everyone sits around the table. Two empty chairs wait for us, and I take the one next to Shawn.

Sebastian stammers as he sees the game laid out on the table, all the parts ready and his favorite blue piece waiting at his seat. He presses his lips together as I sit, staring at each of us in turn before locking eyes with me.

"But you hate Trivial Pursuit," he says.

I lift a shoulder. "Sometimes it's not the game, it's who you play it with." I pat the seat next to me. "Come on. We're all prepared to team up against you. Maybe we can actually beat you this way."

A slow smile tips his lips. "I should get one person. You know, to help me with the entertainment category."

We argue over teams, finally deciding that Meg and Sebastian will take on the rest of us. As much grumbling as they all did, we have fun, laughing and teasing when we get an answer wrong, cheering when we get it right.

During a break, Sebastian leans over, nodding at my shirt. "I'm not sure that butterflies count as animals, but they are a species I have yet to study."

The words fill me with hope, and I grin. "I have a butterfly fact for you." His eyes widen as I say, "They taste with their feet."

His brow furrows. "That settles it then. I'll go to the store tomorrow."

I lean back in my chair, thrilled that all is right in our world once more. Shawn's warm hand runs over my shoulders as he dangles his arm behind my chair. I glance up to find him staring at me with an intensity that takes my breath away.

The words he said to me that night on Spring Break echo between us. *I see you.*

And I know I am exactly where I belong.

Want to see more from this author? Here's a taster for you to enjoy!

Wrighting the Wrongs: The Wrong Idea
Maren Jenner

Excerpt

Sebastian

Months of research have culminated in this moment. I position the blank paper in front of me on the desk, aligning my pencil parallel to the sleek edge of the sheet. Fixing my eyes on the empty page, I focus on the problem in my mind.

Excitement fills me as my brain begins piecing the information together. The equation starts forming in halting bits, and I let my hand hover over the pencil, ready to snatch it up the moment the formula coalesces. A few more seconds and —

A knock sounds on my office door…my open office door. I swear I closed it. My frustration at the interruption turns to full blown annoyance when I see Calliope Harrison in my doorway. Since I'm Professor Harrison's TA and she's his daughter, our paths cross much more often than I'd like, especially when I'm working here on campus in the botany department.

"Yes?" I growl with more heat than usual as the remnants of my equation slip away. *She couldn't have waited one more minute?*

But no, Calliope will not be ignored. It goes beyond her electric purple hair, her brilliant blue eyes, and the shiny stud in her left nostril. She garners attention wherever she is, with her magnetic smile and infectious laugh. People are drawn to her, as if she is the light on a dark night and they are all moths.

Being pulled in, even when they don't want to be.

The images make me more annoyed, especially when she hovers over the threshold of my doorway, wasting more of my time. "Well?"

Still she hesitates, rubbing her index finger over her thumbnail as a flash of uncertainty crosses her face. Then I blink and her usual confidence is restored. She saunters in, one hand behind her back as she shoots me an impish smirk.

"Here."

When she tosses a package on my desk, my blank page floats to one side in the sudden draft of air, and I grit my teeth. Then my pencil rolls off my desk, landing in the trash can with a plunk. She's only been here two seconds and already my office is in chaos. I draw in a deep breath through my nose in an attempt to stay calm.

"What is this?" I try to sound civil, looking at the rectangle wrapped in shiny blue paper complete with a silver bow on top. It's obviously a gift of some sort, though why Calliope would ever give me a present is beyond my reasoning. We aren't anywhere close to being friends—we hardly tolerate one another.

"Dad said I should get you something. You know, for saving my life." There's a bitter edge to her tone, and her lips pucker slightly as if the words left a sour taste in her mouth.

Images assault me, flashes from that night. I'd only gone to the party to support my best friend, Leah, but I'd stayed because Calliope was there. She may be in college, but she was only nineteen and shouldn't have been at a party in the first place. As her father's TA, I felt responsible, like I needed to look out for her.

Chaos broke out after Calliope strutted into the kitchen, shirtless and slurring her words. Her date confessed to giving her Rohypnol, and I'd called nine-one-one as she passed out. It was terrifying. She'd looked so pale and fragile lying there on the tile.

I followed the ambulance to the hospital, not wanting her to wake up alone. The handful of times I've been rushed to the ER due to my hypoglycemia still haunt me, and I only got through it because of my family. Professor Harrison met me there, moments before the doctor came out to tell us Calliope was stable and waking up.

Her father made me come back with him, so she could thank me personally. But when she opened those brilliant eyes, even bluer against her paper white skin, she saw her dad first. Then me. And hatred blazed to life.

"You called my dad?"

I cut off the memory, rubbing my temple as I try to shut out the accusing words that echo in my mind.

"It's chocolate."

I blink, looking up again. I'd forgotten she was still here.

She nods to the package and repeats, "It's chocolate. I mean, everyone likes chocolate, right?"

The sharp smell of astringent lingers in my nostrils from the memory, and the very idea of throwing my blood sugar out of balance in the slightest has my stomach rolling. I nudge the box to the edge of my desk.

"Um, thank you." That is what one should say after given a gift, no matter how thoughtless it is.

She stares down at me, as if waiting for more, but I don't have time to babysit. If I concentrate hard enough, I might still be able to salvage that equation. I lean over to find my pencil.

"You're not even going to open it?" Anger flashes in her eyes, and her hands curl into fists.

I'm surprised she doesn't stomp her foot in typical spoiled brat behavior. "No." I find the pencil and sit upright, repositioning my paper before setting the writing utensil back in its proper spot. "You've already told me what it is, and I've thanked you. I have work to do."

A frustrated noise erupts from her, a cross between a snort and a growl. "You're such a jackass, you know that? I come here to thank you and you ignore the present then dismiss me like I'm wasting your time."

I stare back, unnerved by her tantrum. "If we're discussing bad decorum, I could point out that you interrupted my train of thought, disrupted my workspace and are now scolding me because *I'm* the one being rude." I push back from my desk and walk over to the door.

She merely gapes at me, her pert little mouth hanging open like a fish.

"As far as displays of gratitude go, your track record is less than stellar, if we're counting how you yelled at me after saving your life." I pause, pushing my glasses up my nose. "How about we both agree to stop wasting time? You can find someone else upon which to bestow your thanks, someone who might appreciate your particular manner of showing it."

She glares for a long moment, her face turning an odd shade of red that almost compliments her hair. "You...!"

I wait, but when she says nothing more, I glance at the open doorway, hoping she will finally take the hint. I don't know how much more blatant I can be.

She lets out sound just shy of a scream as she actually does stomp her foot. She storms toward me, stopping just outside my office to growl and glare at me once more before huffing off.

I can't help watching her go, a little tornado of fury rushing down the hall. Amusement twitches my lips until she disappears, then I close the door. Any hint of glee disappears when I repeat the process of trying to summon the equation.

Nothing happens. It doesn't help that every time I move the stupid, shiny package catches the light and draws my attention. Maybe I *should* have opened it.

Is she going to tell Professor Harrison I was rude? I try to push the thoughts aside, to concentrate on the formula I need, but a pair of glaring blue eyes swim in my mind when I close my eyelids.

She really does ruin everything.

* * * *

The next morning, I wake with a start, bolting upright and wincing immediately at the ache in my rock-hard erection from the sudden movement. *How inconvenient.* A quick glance at the clock shows I have twenty minutes before my alarm is scheduled to go off.

Morning wood, as they call it, is not uncommon for me. Biologically speaking, I'd be more worried if it didn't happen. But most mornings I lie here, ciphering on one problem or another until the blood flows elsewhere and I can begin my day without the mess that sort of release brings.

Today is not one of those days.

This is no mere morning blood flow issue that a simple distraction will solve, and I resign myself to having to take care of it. I make sure my box of tissues is positioned within reach then spit on my palm, preferring the natural feel of saliva over the slimy texture of lotion. Shoving my boxers down, I grit my teeth as I position myself to finish this as quickly as possible.

I'm not physically attracted to many people, so my material for stimulation is limited. Several summers ago, I had a casual relationship with the secretary where I interned for my dad. She was older, petite, with an easy smile and a comforting air that made exploring with her fun.

I settle on a memory of her sitting astride me as I begin to stroke myself and close my eyes. If I try hard enough, I can remember the feel of her thighs gripping me and her heat as she rode me. I grow harder still.

"Sebastian," the feminine voice calls, but to my horror, it's not the secretary.

A phantom Calliope bounces on me, her black lacy bra barely covering her taut nipples. I try to yank my hand away, cringing as she whispers my name again, and I force my eyes open.

But I'm already coming.

Hot liquid spills over my fingers, jetting onto my stomach as my body betrays me. *Fuck*. This is exactly the sort of complication I don't need.

* * * *

Callie
Three weeks later

I step outside into the glorious sunshine and suck in the fresh May air. Spring is in full swing as I walk across Southwestern Michigan University's campus, Smoo to us students, feeling freer than the songbirds singing in the trees. I'm officially done with my second year here, my twentieth birthday was this week, and my friends want to take me out to celebrate. They're even trying to bring a guy from their English class they've been raving about.

Now I just have to convince Dad to let me go.

His office is on the other side of campus from my last class, in the botany department. Professor Harrison to most, my dad is revered as the expert on all things plants. Parenting, on the other hand, he gets a little overzealous with. I know he loves me. I just wish he'd loosen the reins a bit.

With Dad as a tenured professor, I get free tuition, a perk I can't ignore and one Dad lords over me every chance he gets. My studies must be my topmost priority and since he's responsible for my tuition, he's decided he has full say in every aspect of my life. Where I live — at home, with him. Where I work — I can't. And how much I can go and do.

This phase of my life is supposed to be about spreading my wings, finding out who I am, but instead I'm stuck in the nest with my overbearing dad.

I step into the botany building, frowning as my eyes adjust to the dim light. I ease down the hallway, tiptoeing when I see Sebastian's door is open. The last thing I want to do is talk to my dad's arrogant, know-it-all assistant. Hurrying past the door, I glimpse him hunched over his desk, and I breathe a sigh of relief when he doesn't seem to notice me.

Dad's office is also open, so I waltz in, greeting him with a smile. He holds up a finger, pointing to the phone cradled between his shoulder and ear. I wander around the small office as he finishes his conversation. I always love looking at the photos in here because they remind me of happier times.

Me and him in the greenhouse, him standing behind me with his hands cupped under mine as I help him transplant a rose. Our smiles are identical. Another one has us with Mom before she died, standing in front of the newest greenhouse as my dad cut the ribbon at the opening ceremony. She looks so proud of him. Always his biggest fan.

A lump forms in my throat as I move away from Mom, grateful when I hear Dad hang up.

"Callie, done with school?" he asks, like I'm twelve.

But I nod. "Yep. Last day, check." I make a flourish with my hand, emphasizing my words.

"Wonderful, and now what are you up to?"

I rub the pad of my index finger over my thumbnail then catch myself. "Well, Jess and Lyssa were hoping to take me out to dinner. We haven't been out yet for my birthday and we can celebrate the end of another year, too. If you don't mind. They promised to have me back before curfew."

I don't know any other twenty year olds whose curfew is midnight, but fighting that rule is a losing battle. One I don't have the strength for at the moment.

He laces his fingers together over his stomach and leans back in his swivel chair. "I suppose you have been on decent behavior since the incident that landed you in the hospital."

I grit my teeth at his favorite bargaining chip of late, as if it were my fault some asshole roofied me. But I keep my tone sweet as I say, "And you know Jess and Lyssa." I leave the other guy out of it, not wanting to add any hiccups to the process.

His index finger taps his other hand as he thinks. "If you let me know where you end up, and promise no drinking, you can go."

It takes a lot not to punch my fist in the air. Instead, I beam and nod. "I'll text you as soon as we know where we're going. And no drinking, I promise."

"Very well. Have fun."

"Thanks, Dad. I will."

I rush away to find Jess, who hovers outside a greenhouse with her nose pressed to the glass. She just graduated, was accepted into the Master's program and Professor Maia handpicked her for TA. Most of my friends are in the botany department, since this is where I hang out. Luckily, there are some pretty cool people here and not all of them have sticks up their asses like Sebastian.

I poke her in the side, startling her enough that she yelps then laughs when she sees me. "Hey!"

We exchange a quick hug before I turn to the greenhouse to see what's so fascinating. "What are we watching?"

"My bees," she squeals. For her thesis, she did a whole study on one hive, and she's obsessed with her babies, as she calls them. "They're pollinating away. Just look at them."

Lyssa, Jess' girlfriend, groans as she joins us. "Not the bees again," She'll graduate next year, but has been testing several different projects to determine which will be her thesis.

"Hey, you!" Jess gives Lyssa a huge hug and a kiss. "It's official. I'm dating a senior. How's it feel to only have one year to go?"

Lyssa purses her lips and puffs her cheeks as she blows out a breath. "Scary."

I squeeze her shoulder. "You've got this."

Jess nods, then looks at me. "So, we going out?"

"Yep!"

All three of us squeal and jump up and down in true giddy fashion before Lyssa fumbles for her phone. "Okay, I'll text Silas."

An hour later, we're sprawled at Jess' apartment as we finish getting ready. After leaving campus, we stopped by my house to grab a few things, then came back here. I found a cute, tight miniskirt with a peasant blouse that shows off my shoulders. As I put the finishing touches on my makeup, I lean back to do a final once-over in the mirror.

It's only five, but I want to make the most of my freedom, so we're going out early. Silas offered to drive, even after he was informed of my curfew. He sounds like a great guy. Easy going, laidback. Not every guy is okay with my dad's demands.

Lyssa's phone chimes and she gives me a knowing smile. "He's here," she says in a singsong voice.

We hurry outside as excitement pulses through me. A man leans on the side of a sleek black SUV, and I know by his devastating smile that it must be Silas. He matches the girls' description perfectly. Tall—he has a good six inches on my five-foot-seven height. Curly, dark hair and amber eyes that twinkle along with his perfect white smile. He is the definition of handsome.

I can't help smiling back. But there's not a hint of a pull or a stomach flip or any sparks as we introduce ourselves and shake hands. Disappointment ripples through me, and I brush it off. We can still have fun.

We eat at a local Mexican restaurant, and I text my dad when we arrive. The food is great. Conversation flows steadily with Silas involved. He's hilarious and chatty, but I'm obviously not his type either, since he keeps eyeing our curvy, dark-haired waitress.

After dinner, we go line dancing. Dancing is a passion of mine, so I'm right at home, tearing up the floor for song after song with whoever will stay out with me. Silas has one drink, but switches to root beer afterwards. I stick with water, wishing I could celebrate like Jess and Lyssa, who enjoy their whiskey sours with obvious abandon.

At ten, we take a break, and Lyssa howls with laughter at Silas' story about a date he went on with a girl from English class. She darts forward, clutching her stomach with one hand and her full drink in the other.

It sloshes over the side, drenching my arm as I yelp. She immediately sobers, apologizing over and over. I dab it with napkins Silas hands me, but the damage is done. I push away from the table and hurry to the bathroom, annoyance swirling with a hint of panic. If Dad smells alcohol on me...

I don't think twice, yanking off my shirt and running the sleeve under the tap. Then I grab some paper towels and wipe my arm. It takes a while to dry, but I think I smell better. The worry won't leave me, though. It hovers in the back of my mind, taking over my thoughts.

My friends have to keep pulling me back into the conversation or snapping their fingers to get my attention. Finally, they leave me to my quiet. We pay our bill and leave in plenty of time, so if nothing else, I'll be home before curfew.

I try to relax in the front seat, letting the others chat around me as I stare out of the window. We're ten minutes from home when the SUV stutters then makes a funny noise. Silas steers us into a nearby strip mall parking lot, barely reaching the parking space before the car dies.

"What just happened?" I ask, panic rising in me.

"I...I don't know. It sounds like we ran out of gas, but the gauge showed we still have a quarter tank." He frowns then adds, "I'm sorry, Callie. Let me call one of my brothers. I'm sure someone can run us up some gas."

I nod, drumming my fingers on the door. Any other person could calmly text their parent and explain. I mean, running out of gas isn't my fault, right? We're not far from home. Dad could even come get me.

But I can hear the disappointment now. It isn't my fault, yet he'll blame me. For bringing him out of the house, for interrupting, for missing curfew. Nothing can ever just work for me. Tears prick my eyes, but I blink them away, refusing to cry. It wouldn't help anything.

Silas pokes his head back in. "All taken care of. My brother will be here in no time, so don't worry. We'll get you home."

The minutes pass, each one eating away at me like the hole I'm sure to rub through my nail. I keep flexing my fingers, pushing them apart, only to realize I'm rubbing again.

At last, headlights flash behind us, and I watch anxiously in the mirror as Silas gets out to greet his brother. The man appears, silhouetted by the lights — a lean, shapely form, taller than Silas by a couple inches. The low pitch of his voice reaches me, and I'm intrigued. Especially when I see the outline of glasses as he turns his head.

My mouth goes dry. A taller, leaner, glasses-wearing version of Silas? That would be my own personal type of crack. Intrigued, anticipation coils within me as he steps into the swath of streetlight.

Fuck.

Sebastian's hazel eyes meet mine in the mirror, and his jaw is set. The remnants of desire still tumble within me, like a dryer turning off. Reality crashes in.

Sebastian hates me — thinks I'm a spoiled brat who exists only to get attention. And I hate him just as much, the arrogant know-it-all, so deep in my dad's pocket he has Dad's asshole memorized.

This night couldn't get any worse.

About the Author

Maren Jenner lives in Michigan with her supportive husband and spunky daughter. She loves writing, and when she's not working on her next book, she's got her nose in a different one. Her summers are spent on any lake she can visit, but the beaches of Lake Michigan are her favorite.

She's been writing for as long as she can remember, and it's always been her dream to become a full time author. None of this would be possible without the love and support of her family and friends, and of course, her amazing readers!

Maren loves to hear from readers. You can find her contact information, website details and author profile page at https://www.firstforromance.com

Home of Erotic Romance

Sign up for our newsletter and find out about all our romance book releases, eBook sales and promotions, sneak peeks and FREE romance books!

www.ingramcontent.com/pod-product-compliance
Lightning Source LLC
Chambersburg PA
CBHW020508020726
47493CB00001B/231